I0712608

LIZARD
PEOPLE
DEATH VALLEY UNDERGROUND

BY THE SAME AUTHOR

Pedro's Pickles and the American Dream

_Nowhere Bound: A Spud's Reflections on Climbing
and Caving—and Other Useless Toils_

DAVID A. EK

First Edition

Minor elements of this story first appeared in the author's essay, "Into the Void, and We Shall Follow," published by *Weber: The Contemporary West* (2021, 37(2):90-97).

This book is a work of fiction. Any references to historical events, real people, real Lizard People, real organizations, or real places are used fictitiously. Other names, characters, places, and events are products of the author's imagination, and any resemblance to actual events or places or persons, living or dead, is entirely coincidental.

Published by:
Badwater Books
Catlett, Virginia

Editing: David Aretha
Cover Art and Design: Creative Publishing Book Design
Interior Design: Delaney-Designs

ISBN Paperback: 979-8-9876517-2-8
ISBN eBook: 979-8-9876517-3-5

Printed in the United States of America.

This book is dedicated to
my wife Cristina
for her consistent support and encouragement,
even throughout lizardly times.

Chapter 1

Death Valley's empty landscapes are full: full of broken dreams, broken promises, and broken spirits. They're filled with sorrow, loss, and not-so-simple suffering.

Only in the deep expanse do we find cold ironies, be it Romeo's assumption that Juliet had already fallen or DNA coding that tricks a moth toward its own fateful pyre. The Death Valley empty mountain wilderness is filled with subterranean portals and energy vortexes—darkest voids that become the inner workings of lost souls—for what's on the other side of a black hole if not the discarded cosmic detritus of what aliens consider normal existence? No, the Death Valley wilds are not dry and empty after all. Its inhabitants filled them with thirsting creatures desperate to consume—something, anything…and everything.

Chapter 2

Pavement is a curse in these parts. It lets in the pale, pathetic, and pampered. It lets in tourists—it lets in trouble. To Paddy, life here was not about comfort, skin moisturizers, sunglasses, sunblock, or parasols. Here he didn't block or hide from elements; they melded and fused into a distinct oddity and became one—kindred spirits.

Off in the distance, Paddy silently watched a dusted sedan get closer and closer. "It's probably a foreign make," he said softly so as not to disturb either the pleasant smell of the creosote bush after the recent cleansing rain or his commanding view of vultures searching for hidden thermals. *Too late.* He knew better than most that a mood once broken rarely returns as sweet. Instead, Paddy's attention turned to dust and the intruding.

The road led to nowhere other than Paddy's reclusive home. "I guess we're gonna have another visitor," he spat toward his close friend—the nearby shade-providing and sweet-smelling screwbean mesquite. As the dust cloud got closer, *Ahh, I see, it is a foreign make after all.* Such were Paddy's silent musings as he receded into the shade, the only shade, outside his falling-down trailer, far from the outskirts of Barstow, California.

Paddy had known of the upcoming intruder for the last five minutes—he saw the dust plumes comingle with the dust-devils fed by the afternoon's heat. While fully suspicious of the sedan's intentions, he didn't begrudge the dust-devils. *Everybody's gotta eat,* he surmised from the comforts of his mesquite shade. *Besides, it's wasting comfort to spend time frettin' over what fool reason a foreign sedan is coming here, off pavement, onto my road and my washboards,*

Paddy fumed. *For the sole purpose of invading my personal space—no less.* In a land where private means private, Paddy liked his privacy perhaps more than most.

I guess I'll have to make that hole even bigger, Paddy cursed as he watched the sedan thread its way through the last rut that he thought had guarded access to his trailer and his privacy. After the car stopped, it sat motionless long enough for most of the dust it dragged along to settle and coat nearby sage and saltbrush.

Paddy remained silent as a pale and wispy city-bred woman got out of her freshly dusted rented Toyota Camry. Paddy guessed her real car, *likely a Prius*, waited for her somewhere back East. He also guessed her business card read bean counter, ivory-towered academic, or perhaps a Greenpeace peacenik. Regardless, Paddy couldn't figure out why this pretty but pasty-faced woman ended up at his encampment. As she walked the remaining distance, Paddy scrutinized the intruder even further.

To Paddy, she showed a hint of middle age-ness, an experience born under shelter—certainly not from anywhere from the Mojave. He would have noticed, since skin here was sun-dried and wind-wiped and took the form of arroyos, washes, recesses, and crannies. Paddy always figured skin reflected the place and time of origin. For this reason, Paddy guessed she had a suburban home—a place where gentle light reflected from closely cropped lawns or lightly fallen snow as seen from the coziness of a sunroom. Paddy, again, regretted not digging the rut deeper. *Wishin', would've, should've* didn't change the fact that the pasty-faced woman approached Paddy intending to speak.

"Are you Patrick Darwin?" Pasty said to Paddy from underneath his screwbean mesquite.

"What brings you here, and what do yuh want? If you're sellin' anything, I'm not buyin'—for sure."

"I am most assuredly not selling anything, Mr. Darwin, but in that parlance, you may say I am buying, and I hope you would seriously consider selling."

"Whatcha just say? I'm selling? What am I selling? Do you want to buy my mouse-infested trailer? If so, then one hundred dollars—it's yours. The thing I'm not selling is my shade or patience. Again, what do you want?"

"My name is Katherine Emerson," she said while looking directly into Paddy's eyes.

"I'm sorry, ma'am, I don't want t' be rude, but I'm really not interested in anythin' you be sellin', so why don't yuh just go back to Boston and—"

"Wait," Katherine interrupted. "How do you know I am from Boston?"

"Please, now," Paddy scoffed. "With the *Ahw you Paughtric Dahwin* and other haughty enunciation, I recognize a Boston accent anywhere."

"You, surely, are not from Boston—are you?" Katherine stumbled as a javelina caught out in the cold.

"Please, me from Boston," Paddy laughed. "No, I'm not from B-a-u-g-h-s-t-i-n, but I've served with some that had been…. But since you're here, yuh might as well spit it out, Boston lady—why you're here, so you can be on your way.

"Thank you, Mister Darwin. I will be brief. My dear Uncle Sid is the only family I have left. I am afraid something terrible has happened to him. It has been over four months since I last heard from him. That is so uncharacteristic of Uncle Sid."

"That's common in these parts. He's probably laying up in a brothel or laying low in the mountains. I wouldn't worry 'bout it, but what does this have to do with me? He ain't here if that's what you're thinking."

"That is what Sheriff John Smithers said when I called his office, but Uncle Sid would not do that to me. We are proper people. Being his only niece, he wrote me often, but he stopped four months ago." Katherine briefly paused and scanned the surrounding hillside before once again turning to Paddy. "The last I knew, he planned to interview people living in the remote Panamint Range. No matter how many times I called the sheriff, he did not take my concern seriously."

"That's John for you."

"Since the sheriff didn't take my uncle's disappearance seriously, I got on the next available flight from Boston to look for him myself. However, once I saw the Death Valley mountains for the first time, I realized that I'm ill-prepared to search such rugged mountains."

"So, you came to see if I would help?"

"Yes, sir."

"Why me? How'd you ever heard of me or find me? This ain't no place on the way to anywhere."

"I asked around to see who knew the mountains best, and your name came up twice."

"You don't say?"

"Do you know the Panamint Range?"

"I guess'n I know the Panamints just as good as the next, but I know it for me, and I don't care to know them for you or any of your New York kin fool enough to crawl off and die or be eaten by a lion."

"My Uncle Sid is no fool, and he is not from New York; he is from a Midwestern university, and he had been staying in the Southwest for quite some time now. I suspect my Uncle Sid could get about well enough without getting himself hurt. He is certainly no fool, Mr. Darwin."

"Wait. You're not talking about Sid Emerson? I heard about that old coot! As far as I'm concerned, Sid Emerson's the biggest fool around, chasing after Lizard People and the like. I'll tell you what, if you give me a little cash, I'll check out each 'n every one of the area's brothels. If I see your uncle, I'd send him your way—how's that?"

"You are a most disgusting animal, Mr. Darwin. My dear Uncle Sid would certainly not step foot in brothels or any other seedy place where you likely spend your slovenly days and nights. My Uncle Sid is a bred and distinguished man of integrity."

"Meant nothin' by it, ma'am."

"I will pay you two hundred dollars a day if you search for him, ask around, and follow the clues. How many days do you think it will take to search the Panamint Range, Mr. Darwin?"

"Days? More like years—or never. At least more days than I got, ma'am. The Panamints is a big, lonely range, and if someone don't wanna be found, nobody ain't gonna find them, no matter how many days, months, or years they spend. This here, ma'am, is the place people go when they don't want to be found. If you get my drift."

"Nonetheless, I suppose in a few weeks we could make a good show of it, do you not agree, Mr. Darwin? Do we have a deal?"

"I'm not a detective, tracker, or bounty hunter. I just wanna be left alone. He ain't here, and I'm not interested in checking anywhere else. Best if you'd go elsewhere to look for fools. I've had enough dealings with fools to last a lifetime without going out lookin' for 'em."

"I do not know what you did or have done to get yourself in such a sorry condition, as I see now before me, Mr. Darwin. Where I come from, good people do not abandon and give up on helping other good people. From what I have been told, you served in the military—as had my Uncle Sid. Military people have a creed, do they not? You do not leave fellow service members behind. People outside of the military also do not leave people behind—at least good people do not. Good people also do not take no for an answer."

"If you stay long in these parts, ma'am, I suggest that you get used to it."

"From what I see, Mr. Darwin, taking a few days or weeks will not interfere much with your idleness. How can you just turn your back on someone in need?" she scolded as she stepped into Paddy's face and looked him close-up, directly in the eyes. "You, sir, are no gentleman."

"You got that right," Paddy chuckled. "I'm no gentleman. Never been one, and will not die one," Paddy said as he attempted to recede further under the screwbean mesquite—or anyplace to escape Katherine's unwavering stare. After Paddy scanned the horizon looking if the thermal-riding vultures were missing anyone, he turned again to Katherine, and whimpered, "I do like your spunk, ma'am. It's honorable and nice-and-right of a person to fight for their family. You said your uncle served in the military?"

"Yes, sir. He fought for his country overseas."

For what seemed like ages to Katherine, Paddy stared at his screwbean mesquite, then only later, lifted his eyes to scan the vulture-less horizon stretching toward Barstow. Throughout the whole process, Paddy repeatedly wiped his palms on his stained khaki shirt, as if he could rid himself of the whole ordeal as easily as he had the grease from his morning breakfast. While still looking at who-knows-what distant object or recessed memory, without turning toward Katherine, Paddy began muttering something that only brought from Katherine a blank stare. Sensing he was mumbling, Paddy repeated, "I suppose it wouldn't hurt to ask around here or there. I must say, I could use the money. You said two hundred dollars a day?"

"Yes, I did, Mr. Darwin. Do you require more?"

"Give me a moment. I'm thinkin'."

While Paddy paced back and forth in and out of the shade, Katherine's mind wandered to the last few days. When she first arrived, she had no idea where to start looking for her uncle. She began asking random strangers at gas stations, bars, grocery stores, and anywhere people gathered. Most avoided her as they would a tax collector. The first week passed without a single new lead or clue—and she had no idea what to do next. However, her legwork must have paid off since her next lead came to her. An old man at the gas station suggested she talk with a guy named "Torgerson," but when Katherine asked around for this man, she received nothing but confusion and silence. It seemed to Katherine that either this Torgerson guy was also missing or there were things about him that no one wanted to talk about.

Katherine gave up trying to locate the mysterious Torgerson guy. Her search for help changed for the better when she met Rocky in Ballarat. Katherine soon learned that Ballarat, the little ghost town located below the immense gravel deposits on the Panamint Range's western slopes, held many secrets. While many people in the Death Valley region knew Rocky, even more knew he liked to talk. He apparently enjoyed talking to Katherine, because after the moment they met, Rocky kept "jawin'" to Katherine—all the while spitting tobacco wads onto the ground, on any creosote bush he met, and even the lone passing tarantula. His "jawin'" was so cracked and guttural that Katherine could hardly understand.

"Are you'd de lady lookin' for Sid Emerson?"

"Yes. Do you know him?"

"I don't know'd him a-tall, but I'd heard a-him. Mostly, I'd heard stories."

"Would any of these stories provide clues to where he may be now?"

"I dunna know. I'd not be as yong as I were fifty-er years a-go. Mem-ry ain't as sharp no more. Sorry lady. Youd might wanna talk to Papa—he not only know'd everyone in these parts, but'rn he remembers."

"Where can I find this Papa character?" asked Katherine.

"Suppose up yonder at Ryan."

"Ryan? Where, or who, is Ryan?"

"Ya, Ryan. Papa's up at Ryan."

Nearly everyone in the Panamint Range knew Patrick Wall, but both friends and enemies called him "Papa." As Rocky often said, "Papa's a grizzled ol' prune who used t' live ta hard life of a hard rock miner. Next, he lived another life as'n ornery cuss." During Rocky's time on earth, Papa lived out his third, and probably last, life in Ryan.

Ryan, the historic mining town, sat on the speckled alluvial fan high above Death Valley's extensive borax fields. It was once the home to U.S. Borax and the 20 Mule Team Borax Company. The town also provided the setting for many *Death Valley Days* TV shows hosted by the actor and future president Ronald Reagan. Later, Ryan transitioned into emptiness—except for Papa, the historic town's full-time resident caretaker.

A local historical society now owns Ryan. It had been paying Papa to restore and preserve what an old borax mining camp used to look like. Papa fixed broken things and kept equipment and buildings running. He also gave lively interpretation programs and a semblance of mine camp experiences to children of all ages.

Although being more rough-edged than anyone she's ever met, Katherine took to Papa upon just one look at his wide grin and friendly greeting. Katherine figured Ryan must not get many visitors, since Papa gave her an especially attentive borax mining history lesson.

Papa sent her to Paddy. He told Katherine, "There ain't no better person to he'p you find your uncle than Paddy. If your uncle's out there in the Panamints, Paddy's your best bet in finding him." This is the reason she waited patiently for Paddy to answer back. Nothing in Paddy's expression or mannerisms indicated to Katherine whether he was going to help her find her uncle Sid, or not. The only motion from Paddy that she detected was his frequent wiping of his palms as he looked toward the distant hills.

"Shit," he muttered, as he turned to Katherine and said, "Sure, why not. I'll help you find your fool uncle." Later, Paddy never told a soul the reason he accepted the Boston lady's job offer. Papa figured he must have been tired of being alone. Maybe Paddy felt a kinship with both Sid and Katherine Emerson since rumors had it that Paddy had experienced his share of loss—somewhere in his shadowy past. But Papa knew better than most, that there is something about the Panamints that gripped lost souls. Whatever his reason, Paddy told Katherine to come back the following morning at seven so they could begin—with what, he had no idea, but he told himself that he would likely regret it.

"That's pretty early," said Katherine. "Are you available later?"

"Sun's hot later. Do you want to find your uncle, or do you want to shrivel your pasty skin in the midday sun? Your choice. I'm already shriveled as shriveled can be."

"I'll be here at seven."

CHAPTER 3

As Paddy watched the Camry's diminishing plume in the slanted rays of late afternoon, he fell into a reflective mood. *Will she truly want to know what happened to him? She should learn there are some things best left alone.* Still, he pondered, *There's something about the Boston lady that I like.* He abruptly put an end to such thoughts. *Paddy, you fool, those are dangerous waters you swore you'd never...*

Paddy must have been pondering long since when he looked up, the sun's lingering edge had touched the horizon. Welcoming relief would soon be everywhere, and Jupiter would cast its ancient light across Paddy's beautiful desert. The shadowy slits from catclaw stalks already stood in stark contrast with the opal-tinted sky. *Whoever called Montana Big Sky Country clearly hadn't been to Death Valley.* The evening star found its way through remnant heat waves radiating into the early night, which combined, offered Paddy a shimmer to the already perfect scene. The shadow dance took him back to deeply buried but fond memories. Paddy didn't move—he only looked, listened, and remembered.

Something woke Paddy—and it wasn't the warm desert air. It certainly wasn't the moon-shadowed screwbean mesquite looming over him. He found himself awake on his lawn chair and out in the open air at two-thirty in the morning. Paddy smiled at the comfortable warmth and welcoming view. As he stood, raspy mesquite leaves clawed his cheek and drew blood. Upon seeing new stains comingling with old on his ripped khaki shirt, with an even bigger grin, *Good, I'm back in my desert.* After a long stretch, Paddy took one last glance at the Milky Way as he climbed the broken steps leading into his falling-down trailer.

Although he liked some people, Paddy always had been a loner. Although he had been living in the same trailer for a long time, Paddy formed only a few lasting connections. He well knew that people that search for things, especially comfort, rarely find what they seek. So, after a troubled childhood, a troubled war, and even more troubling family emergencies, he found himself no longer searching. So, if a person's only goal was giving up, there was no better place to find it than within the confines of Paddy's broken-down trailer.

To Paddy, being alone meant he didn't have to answer questions or dredge up the past, could live without judgment. Holed up in his Barstow trailer, he didn't expect anything of himself, and no one expected things of him.

What have I gotten myself into? Paddy fretted as he dreamt of permanently losing the sweet smell of creosote bush by grimy urban dust brought forth by an approaching Camry. The disturbance and muddling of his once peaceful desert thoughts woke him up early and kept him awake.

The following morning, Paddy sat waiting on his bench looking at nothing—for nothing moved. He pondered even less. Paddy assumed Katherine would arrive late, since most city folk do. *Desert folk disappoint too*, he thought, *but that's another matter*. On this matter, Katherine surprised Paddy by being five minutes early.

"Good morning, Mr. Darwin."

"Call me Paddy."

"Okay, Paddy, where do we begin?"

"First things first. I have ground rules that must be stated or else I'm gone. For one, I travel and work alone, and I *don't* take orders from nobody, includin' you. I do things my way, or I don't do 'em at all—is that a deal?"

"Yes, Mr. Dar—Paddy. Thank you. So how do we begin?"

"Well, tell me everything you know about Sid Emerson. Why did he come here?"

"My Uncle Sid grew up in Michigan's Upper Peninsula. He spent his entire teenage years hunting, fishing, and walking in the woods. When not in school, every morning he left without telling anyone to only return late in the evening. His parents trusted him to stay out of trouble and anything that would bring shame to the family, so they let him wander the woods alone."

"How many brothers or sisters?"

"Only one. A brother, my father—but they always had an uneasy relationship. They had completely different outlooks on life and never saw eye-to-eye about anything."

"Tell me more what he did during his wandering days."

"When not in the woods, he would hole up in the library. He read every book the stacks had on ancient forest legends, mysteries, and as he liked to call them, 'freaks of nature.' That is all I knew about Uncle Sid as a child—other than through stories. Talking about stories, he could have been a professional storyteller. Later, when he used to visit us, I was just a child, he told us story after story, and I just loved them. I just sat there without moving a muscle—not even a church sermon could keep me so still. I had no idea how many were true, but it did not matter."

"What kind of stories?" Paddy interjected. "Any specifics?"

"I cannot remember any one, or any specifics. His stories were on everything, and nothing—mostly life in general. Uncle Sid found humor in the most peculiar situations, and he had a knack for bringing the story to life, as if I had been there all along."

"As a child, did you ever visit him? And when he came to visit you, how long did he stay?"

"We never went there. He always came to us. Uncle Sid did not visit often, but I treasured each one. He brightened my otherwise lonely childhood. Uncle Sid grew larger than life, and I loved him dearly. He was by far my favorite relative."

"What did he do for a living?"

"Patience, Paddy, I will get to that in due time."

"Yes, ma'am."

"Please, call me Katherine."

"Yes, ma'am—Katherine."

"He used to tell me his love of mysteries and spooky tales came from his childhood visits to the Mystery Zone, near St. Ignace, Michigan. As he retold the story many times, to his adolescent mind, the place defied logic, physics, forces of nature, and human understanding. The Mystery Zone held a special place in his heart, and he begged his parents to take him often. Later, as an older teenager, he grew sour on the place, thinking it too commercial."

"So, why the change of heart?"

"The mysteries lost their allure because he discovered logical explanations for each illusion. For instance, you learned that buildings set at off-kilter angles can mess with a person's sense of reference."

"Then he wanted to prove 'em wrong?"

"Perhaps, but deep down, I think he wanted to prove them right. I think he wanted to believe. He thought real unexplained mysteries awaited him out there to explore—he just needed to find them. Uncle Sid had a lifelong passion for learning, a treasured gift he received from his father."

"What did his father do?"

"He held a highly acclaimed science position in a local chemical lab, but his heart belonged to natural sciences—especially biology. As such, his father filled young Uncle Sid's mind with the wonders of the world around them; even things that other people would see as ordinary. But not to Uncle Sid or his father. They had an insatiable appetite to pursue quests—to get answers to why things are the way they are. Some people find satisfaction in the status quo and stillness—but not Uncle Sid's father."

"Sounds like your Uncle Sid's father was a good dad."

"Yes, indeed. How about you?" Katherine asked Paddy. "Were you close to your dad?"

"Me? My dad? You're supposed to be telling me about your uncle. This isn't about me or my past."

"Sorry," apologized Katherine. "I did not mean to pry."

Paddy's eyes dug deep into his eye sockets, as he said with a wagging finger, "Let's get something straight. My past is my business. Got it?" Suddenly, as if turning a corner, his softness and tone returned as quickly as it vanished. "Do you want something to drink, or eat? Beer?"

"Beer at this hour, certainly not. No, thank you!"

Paddy motioned for Katherine to pause what she had on her lips, as he scurried to the fridge. To Katherine, it looked more like a dumpster than a modern icebox, but to Paddy, it kept the beer cold. For a full minute, he rummaged through the dumpster and eventually returned with a Bud. He popped it open and began the first of several gulps. "Please go on. You told me about your uncle's dad. How about college? Did Sid Emerson go to college? Wait, you said he served in the military—"

Seeing Paddy's foot and hand twitches growing stronger, Katherine picked up the pace. "Yes, he went to college *and* served in the military. The Army drafted him in 1971. He went to college only after he came back from Vietnam—"

"Back East," Paddy interrupted.

"If you mean where he went to college, no. He used money from the GI Bill to go to college in South Dakota. But I know very little about his university days, and even less about his military service. However, I do know that his time overseas affected him deeply, but never, and I repeat, never, did he talk about Vietnam."

"I can relate."

Katherine had a fleeting notion to ask about Paddy's military service but decided otherwise.

"Did he see heavy combat?" asked Paddy.

"I believe so, but as I said, he never talked about it. When he came back, he had a hollowed-out face—with prominent cheekbones. He looked ghastly. He acted differently too. He had changed—and he knew it."

"I know a little about that myself."

"When the war ended," Katherine added, "Uncle Sid spent the rest of his service time in California, but I never knew what he did there. When the Army discharged him, he moved to the Black Hills and enrolled in college. He earned a bachelor's degree in geology from the South Dakota School of Mines and Technology. He does not talk much about this part of his life either."

"Some guys just like to keep private matters private—that's all. There's nothin' wrong with that."

Ignoring Paddy's opening, Katherine continued summarizing her uncle's past. "I heard stories that after he graduated, he had many setbacks and his life became complicated, but I never fully knew what happened. Whatever they were, they interrupted all his plans. Sadly, he never had a career in science. I think he regretted not following his heart."

"Why didn't he? Go into science?"

"No one knows. After graduating, he did not even look for a job. He just roamed the West. I think he tried to expunge inner demons and memories."

"That never works. Believe me."

"He seemed dark and lonely—from the few letters from that time. I do not think he worked everything out in his head. He told me in a later letter that he just ran out of money, but I think he grew tired of wandering, and he saw it got him nowhere."

"There's nothin' wrong with wandering," countered Paddy.

"Are you referring to the famous J.R.R. Tolkien quote, 'Not all that wander are lost'?"

"I wasn't specially referrin' to that quote, but it's true, nonetheless," Paddy said with quivering voice. "Many folks I know are equally lost whether they wander or not," Paddy said as his legs began shaking to some unknown beat. "Say, it's hot in here. What do you say we step outside and under the shade? It's just scraggly mesquite shade, but it's better than in here."

While sitting on wobbly chairs under mesquite shade next to his makeshift table, Paddy pointed to the Mojave skyline and said, with a deep breath, "Don't you just love it?" Ever since his eyes caught the skyline, Katherine could see Paddy's shoulders stood erect and his legs became as still as the sun's slow arc across the far distant horizon.

Katherine couldn't size up the stranger that sat across the table from her, but she surmised almost the instant she saw him look at whatever he looked at that he would much prefer wandering aimlessly in the mountains, alone, than listening to her go on and on about her uncle, but something in her Boston gut told her that he was the one to help her.

"What did your Uncle Sid do next?" Paddy asked as he interrupted Katherine's reflections.

"He eventually returned to Rapid City and took a job in the university library. I think if he had conducted original research, some of his old spark would have returned—something to do that was closer to his real passion. Reading science books written by others and helping researchers find relevant published studies kept him content, but I do not think it gave him happiness."

"Life's long," Paddy interjected. "You gotta be happy in doing the things you do."

"I agree," Katherine added. "However, for whatever reason, Uncle Sid stayed with the university library for the rest of his career. He retired early, not because he had enough money, but he itched to continue his Western travels and explore odd mysteries all his own— those he only read about while working in the library. He wanted to study real mysterious places, not like the commercial sites like the Mystery Zone."

"I thought he hated the place and thought it a hoax?"

"He didn't want to specifically study the physics behind the Mystery Zone. Instead, he wanted to study the fascination, obsession, and fanaticism of the true believers—believers of the deep mysteries far removed from the commercial Mystery Zone."

"So, was your uncle a true believer in supernatural forces?"

"I don't think so, at least not at first. A few of his colleagues at the South Dakota School of Mines and Technology told me it was only a scientific curiosity. I think he wanted to rekindle that feeling he'd had as a young teenager when he remained transfixed at the sight and spectacle of the Mystery Zone.

"I think he understood the mystery and allure of such places but could not comprehend it turning into an obsession where someone would lose all touch with reality," Katherine explained. "He devoted much space in his letters to this topic. He claimed he sought the foundational core of raw humanity, as he called it—the underlying truth and frailties of the human condition."

"So, he's one of those?" Paddy sneered.

"I am not sure I know what you mean by that," Katherine countered, "but he said he sought, and I paraphrase, the place where normal people keep hidden below their surface façade. He said he sought the outliers—people whose veneer had been worn thin by the struggles of normal existence. He sought societal outcasts," Katherine said before pausing. "He sought lost souls…. This is what brought him to Death Valley."

"Sounds like he came to the right place," Paddy chimed in, as he got up to get himself another beer.

"According to some of his letters, he was especially interested to discover the reason that armed with the same information, some people are pulled down dark pathways, while at the same time their neighbor may have a normal existence with normal beliefs."

"Well, he had his work cut out for him, here," Paddy added. "Did he come directly here from South Dakota?" He downed the last of his beers.

"No, not directly. First, he wandered for two years, maybe more. He left South Dakota for the high plains of Alberta, Montana, and Wyoming. From there, he wandered to the Southwest to spend time with the Navajo. Only then did he come to Death Valley."

"Is that it? Did he mention anywhere in Death Valley or the Panamints? Did he say who he met?"

"He just mentioned one name," Katherine answered. "Here, I will let you read the message he sent me—I printed it out."

> *Dear Kati,*
>
> *I pulled into Death Valley the other day. The place is as dry as a bone, but it's amazing how much life there is here—I guess a person has to know where to look. The land is bigger and more dramatic than I ever anticipated.*
>
> *In my last note, I wrote about the alien Lizard People conspiracy. Many people here believe Lizard People are working to enslave humanity. There's even a guy that goes by the name 'Lizard Len.' I plan to interview him soon. From what I've heard, he's over the top. I think this place will be great for my research. I'll let you know how things go.*
>
> *Take care.*
> *Love,*
> *Uncle Sid*

"So, he's heard of Lizard Len," Paddy said while thumbing the letter as if he was having trouble expelling something.

"Apparently so," replied Katherine. "Do you know Lizard Len?"

"Everyone around here has heard of him. I don't know the guy, but I've seen his face around, here and there," responded Paddy. "I avoid people like that. Do you know if your uncle ever met with Lizard Len, or anyone else?"

"As far as Lizard Len—no, I don't know. As far as if my uncle met with others, I believe if we find that out, we may find my Uncle Sid. Can we meet up with this Lizard Len guy?"

"I suppose so," replied Paddy, "but it is not like I'm a-gunna like it. The guy's a loon."

"One thing more about the messages," Katherine added, "as his stay progressed, his tone changed. As you just read, when he first arrived, he sought these people out for research—he was objective. Later, I sensed he was growing closer to the fringes. He said something about there's more truth out there than he ever before thought possible. Increasingly, he accepted their truths as a legitimate form of reality."

"As I thought, he became a true believer?"

"What are you talking about—you thought? You said he was likely holed up in a brothel—which is it?" chided Katherine.

"Well, I don't share all my thoughts, now do I?"

"Yes, I noticed," Katherine quipped. "Anyway, I began worrying about him when he stopped sending me messages. That is when I called the sheriff, but he did not help at all. Shortly later, I came here to find him myself. I am afraid he is in trouble."

"Okay, okay. I heard enough. I think I have a sense of who he was—"

"Who he *is*, you mean," interrupted Katherine.

"Yes, who he is. Regardless, this will help. If'n it's all right with you, I'll begin my search this evening. I'll head out to popular local watering holes where I can usually find the inebriated."

"My Uncle Sid is not a heavy drinker," countered Katherine.

"Yes, but those that may have seen him likely are. Besides, this is just as good a place to start as any other."

CHAPTER 4

In the same place where Paddy and Katherine began their search for Sid Emerson, a desperate search of an entirely different kind took place just a few years earlier. Like many Panamint searches, this one never strayed far from rumored mineral riches. This desperate search, like many others since, also never strayed far from a Torgerson.

"Gold, silver, and all that glitters hold a special power over your father," Bonnie often told her son Billy, despite him being too young to understand. "This is a universal and timeless truth about human nature and human obsession," she would say. "So, please, Billy, don't grow up to be like your father." Bonnie knew all too well that when it came to her husband, Bud Torgerson, vortex currents flowed only in one direction—like the Hotel California kind, where you can check in but can *never* check out. In the case with the Panamint Torgersons, Bud never checked out.

For months at a time, Bud left behind his wife Bonnie and son Billy as he explored desert lands far from pavement. Bonnie Torgerson saw with clear eyes and a sound mind how it affected their family, but she couldn't do anything about it. No one could. Billy was too young to comprehend the spell the land had upon a soul, and too young to understand his father.

Bud Torgerson prayed to his glittering waters so often, he ended up jumping in with unswerving fervor and faith with both feet—and it consumed body and soul. However, deep down, Bud knew his legs would never again touch bottom and that life's currents only presented him two options—sink or swim. Such is the nature of currents in Death Valley's baptismal waters. Bud convinced himself that each new vein would be *the* vein that would set him free. He kept telling himself he did it for Bonnie and Billy, but that was simply the fever talking.

Bonnie knew where her husband's veins ran. They became oxygenated from somewhere deep beyond the vortex—within the wide expanse between the Grapevine and Funeral Mountains' ancient folded and warped limestones and the Panamint's speckled granites and monzonites. Upheaved mountains held countless twists, turns, recesses, and convolutions—the perfect place for mysteries to lodge and fester. The perfect place to get lost.

The Grapevines were Bud's favorite. The jumbled, folded, faulted, and rugged mountain mass occupied the lonely deserts surrounding Death Valley—the continent's hottest and driest wilderness furnace this side of Dante's Inferno.

Heat, aridity, and isolation infused and connected veins, rock, body, and soul in unfathomable ways. The mineral and arsenic-laden amalgam surged through veins as fatefully as cancer through a cell wall. The Panamints and Grapevines called to Bud, and Bud obeyed. Throughout all his toils, he found neither peace nor gold in the rough and isolated ranges. However, since his addiction took hold, it became the closest to solace that he had ever known.

Bud came generations too late for the infamous Leadfield hoax. Reaching its zenith in the mid-1920s, the town originated from a scam and unscrupulous swindling intended for the inflicted. Bud would have fit in well in those heady times. Americans had gold fever and whenever such ailments existed, there would always be snake-oil salesmen around to exploit the unwary.

In the case of the Leadfield hoax and Titus Canyon boom, landowners advertised an abundance of lead ore ripe for the taking, a short distance from a nonexistent steamboat landing on a nonexistent Death Valley river. Facts didn't matter then anymore than they do now to Bud. The poor and desperate moved fast, eager to get in early before the price ballooned and they missed their chance. Laggards and those wanting to validate claims got left behind. The few that visited before investing were taken in by landowners that had scattered high-grade ore across the surface to dupe the overly eager.

Centered on this vortex, investors constructed homes, a post office, and a stamp mill. They strung electric wire and erected a tent city. Men, with their life savings sunk into the venture, soon found the little lead ore that truly existed was low-grade, limited in extent, and valueless. The fever broke—and all else along with it. Residents left town as fast as they entered.

When Bud Torgerson first visited the shattered townsite, only a few sheet metal buildings and splintered wooden beams remained. The historic site became a popular tourist attraction, but where most visitors saw fraud, disappointment, broken promises, and misery, Bud saw hope and potential. He convinced himself, without any basis, proof, or expertise, that the scam blinded the Leadville miners to the area's *true* potential. Bud heard the mountains call solely to him, "While there's no lead in Leadville, there *is* silver." Bud's faith in the voice became deep and unwavering.

Bud spent much of what should have been his better years searching for the elusive silver vein that he knew had to be there if he only dug deeper or over the next folded ridge or scarp. He searched distant horizons throughout the Grapevine and Panamint Mountains. He kept telling Bonnie they would soon have all the money they ever needed or wanted. She never fully believed he would ever find what he sought, but she loved him dearly, so she put up with plenty. She received little to nothing in return—that is until a baby boy came along. Bonnie adored her son Billy. Bud was too often far afield looking to strike it rich to know Billy. In his own way, Bud loved his son. He just never took the time to be around. In Bud's mind, this all would change—one day. One day. Maybe tomorrow, he would say.

Days turned to weeks and months turned to years. When Billy turned fifteen, the Torgersons found their lot in life hadn't changed, despite the passing of twenty years. Although Bud's faith never dimmed, his energy and enthusiasm faded with age, faded with excursion, and faded with bodily stresses. Only then did Bud begin to understand the true nature of what he had lost. Despite his growing awareness, Bud's faith and devotion to gold and silver's healing powers never faltered. Bonnie held no such allusions. The Panamints to her only meant hard work, misery, and the wasting away of what was once a good man.

Once again, Bonnie brought up, like she had dozens of times before, "Please, Bud, let's leave this place. It'll be the death of us. I don't see any future here. Please."

"Bonnie, don't you think I know'd that? That's why I'm doing this. It's for you and Billy," he would say. "Once I find it, we'll be set for life, and we can git out of this place. I'm close, Bonnie, I know'd it. Jest one more year—at the most, Bonnie. I promise. You'd see. We'd be set for life!"

Always the same story, she told herself. *Year after year after too many long years.* Bonnie grew tired of talk and of "someday...any day...soon." Bonnie viewed their home a prison sentence.

Maybe Bonnie's warnings and pleas to not grow up to be like his father paid off. By his fifteenth birthday, Billy finally understood both the landscape and his father. During the few times they interacted, Billy smiled only to maintain appearances. Happiness didn't live in the Torgerson household. Pretenses had become rote.

During the following winter, a biting snowstorm descended on the higher Mojave Desert. Bonnie didn't know why she fretted about, since the ground froze no worse than it had before—and she endured those without an issue. She wondered if the curious lack of night light made the difference. On this night, no moonlight and few stars penetrated the void. Bonnie searched through her old cedar chest looking for an extra blanket to warm her chilled bones. She had just splayed out the blanket across her shivering stiffness when a man burst through the doorway, breaking the Mojave silence as Billy let out a scream. The man's slipstream knocked Bonnie's East Coast knickknacks off her memory shelf. Billy's scream had barely subsided before the man lunged. Billy fell silent. Bonnie just stood and stared at the calamity. Her stare only broke when she called out, "Bud, is that you?"

"Yeah, darling. Who else?" Bud answered.

"What are you doing? All this stumbling, whooping, and hollering. Do you have a fever?" she screamed. "Are you drunk, again—good God, Bud, not in front of your son."

With his eyes only on Bonnie, Bud said nothing as he drew in closer, stepping on Bonnie's favorite knickknack in the process. Even the grinding of porcelain into the wooden plank floor proved not enough of a distraction to divert his attention. Oblivious to the destruction in his wake, he burst, "I found it, Bonnie! By God, I finally found it!"

"Found what, your whiskey bottles? I already threw them out."

"No, dear, I found silver. Silver. The *real* thing, and lots of it. We're rich. After all these years, I found it."

The next morning began cold and clear as had the previous, and just as dark. Bonnie woke not fully comprehending what had just happened. *Bud always said this day would come and their lives would be different. I just never believed him.* Bonnie had no idea what to do next. Planning for it happening had never occurred to her.

She still didn't know the location of Bud's silver vein— presumably somewhere in the Panamints. She only knew their life would soon be different—and that Bud had already left. He rushed off in the cold pre-dawn. He wanted to place a proper and legal stake and claim to his silver vein. He had worked too long and too hard not to ensure he recorded and filed all legal claims of ownership. Based on Bud's estimate, it was high-quality silver ore. He planned to bring back a few samples to the assayer's office.

Before Bud left, he packed one week's food and provisions. Under Death Valley's bright, star-filled morning, he left the doorway as fast as he came in—as fast as he had passed through thousands of times before. However, to Bonnie and Billy, this time felt different—only later would they find out why.

Bonnie constantly worried about Billy. *Whatever happens, it will be hard on Billy*, she fretted. But she could do no more to help their son until Bud came back with the assessor report.

Time went by slowly as they waited three days, five days, seven days, and on into the tenth. Fear welled in Bonnie with an intensity that she had never felt before. She sensed something must have gone wrong. It may have been her pacing, her tightly drawn face, or her frequent peering out the window, but her nervousness added to Billy's. "Mom, shouldn't Dad have been back by now?"

"Soon, Billy. Soon."

Three months later, a friend and fellow miner came by Sheriff John Smithers' office to deliver the news. He found Bud's badly broken body under tons of rubble inside a collapsed mine excavation. According to the miner, Bud's final resting place lay within a nondescript, worthless mine in a forgotten canyon. He had finally found his elusive peace. The miners removed enough rubble to pull out and identify the body, but they left him leaning against a rock next to his nondescript prospecting pit.

Word quickly spread of both Bud's death and that he had found a rich silver vein. Nature abhors a vacuum, and soon this grim vortex drew people in by the hundreds—all searching for Bud's silver and all pestering poor Bonnie and Billy to divulge the secret location. It became too much for Bonnie to take. She wouldn't let them do this to her Billy. Bonnie wanted nothing more to do with lust, voids, vortexes, the Panamints and the Grapevines, or empty promises. Bonnie gathered their few belongings and she and Billy moved to a small one-room apartment in Los Angeles. She planned never to return.

CHAPTER 5

Long before Katherine and Paddy met, and long before Bud Torgerson's desert demise, an unknown force stirred within Sid Emerson. It prompted a reassessment and willingness to let winds and fate guide his new path. Fresh from retirement, Sid left to find the *real* Sid Emerson.

Leaving his staid and normal existence behind, Sid sought not just to reside *on* earth, or pass *through*, but to get into it and truly *know* the earth and its people. At least that was the story he told his few friends. He remembered well the joy he once had discovering life's grand mysteries, unexplained phenomena, and the quirky non-conventional. For his new life, he longed to study beliefs that transcended the logical and rational—those that bordered on faith and blind devotion. Sid began to realize that beliefs rarely rely upon scientific rigor or evidence-based logical reasoning. Instead, they reside deep within the realm of faith and gut-level feelings—not unlike the definition of pornography: you recognize it when you see or experience it. However, not everyone shared Sid's faith. An old friend of his mocked Sid's plans by saying, "You're just having a midlife crisis. Why don't you buy a Harley, have an affair with someone younger—you know, like everyone else?"

"It is not a midlife crisis," he cried out, but I do want to feel young again." In the new Sid's mind, normal people seek the center and the predictable. He believed his new destiny lay somewhere among the vortexes and fringes—the mysterious place where the Earth's energy currents converge.

For some reason, Sid believed his convergence zone resided in a distant corner of the Great Plains, the place where the shortgrass prairie begins—and ends—with all infinity between. The Great Plains drew the retired Sid in as surely as nostrils collect desert dust. From his readings and instinct, he believed the origins of humanity's greatest mysteries and long-held secrets originated on the Great Plains. To family and friends, the lonely plains seemed an odd place to search for historic wisdom, since prairie expanse and prairie winds don't favor collecting anything, least of all anything tangible. However, Sid embraced his odd side. He liked the shade cast by lone prairie trees. He liked prairie smells. He liked the prairie's eternal timelessness—the crossroads of so many different cultures that passed through, but only a few tangible signs left behind. "You can't get any more mysterious than that," Sid said as he headed into the unknown.

As is often the case with prairie wanderings, the winds cast Sid about, from Moose Jaw to Medicine Hat, Funk to Fergus Falls, Williston to Wakita, Biddle to Buffalo, and all points and peneplains in between. Bedraggled and magical landscapes spoke to Sid in ways no other roamed lands had. He moved throughout the borderlands: the boundary between the U.S. and Canada, between the Great Plains' shortgrass prairie and the first trace of the Rocky Mountain's grand arc. It became the borderland between Sid's past and Sid's uncertain future. He knew not who or what called, but he aimed to find out. Sid envisioned it would be easy to get lost in such places—this notion was not unwelcomed.

He imagined there had been many people and cultures that already succumbed to open landscapes and their vestige inner voices. His initial wanderings had little direction or known purpose. Unlike the Mystery Zone of his youth, some Great Plains vortexes appeared as mere physical or metaphysical anomalies, while others appeared to have stronger and deeper spiritual leanings—if only he could unlock their mystery. For the first time in decades, Sid felt young.

Even as a teenager back in Michigan, Sid knew spiritual vortexes were rotating masses of energy that reportedly disrupted normal space and physics. However, as an adult investigator, he knew he needed to delve deeper. Deeper than teenage library books and deeper than commercial trappings. The new-agers of the day viewed vortexes as portals to other dimensions and a path to a balanced Earth. If true, Sid needed proof. But to do so, he believed he needed total immersion—the threshold beyond the world of rational thought and convention. As Sid fully knew, faith is a much more compelling force than mere logic.

From his teenage readings, Sid knew of the reported vortexes at Egypt's Great Pyramids and Great Britain's Stonehenge. He had not the money or inclination to visit Egypt or the Wiltshire plains. Fortunately for him and his budget, many spiritual vortexes dotted the American West.

The West also had commercial vortexes. At one in Oregon, paying customers could experience strange phenomena, including spatial distortion, and the sights of objects appeared to grow or shrink in size and proportion. While visiting this site, Sid knew that slanting floors, out-of-proportion building and room profiles, and optical illusions could explain all observed mysteries, so, he said, "Where is the mystery in that?"

It is not that he begrudged commercial exploitation. The Mystery Zone first attracted him to true mysterious forces. Sid believed that commercial sites expose a wider audience to Earth-bound mysteries—people who wouldn't have known of them otherwise. Sid liked the idea that there were accessible mysteries for people from all walks of life. "Everyone seeking the truth needs to start somewhere," Sid once wrote Katherine as he contemplated real vortexes in far-off Western wilds. What interested him most were the few vague reports of vortexes and strange Earth forces located on high escarpments within the wild northern Great Plains.

Sid also shared details of his progress with Katherine—not just facts and discoveries, or his latest journey, but everything. In one text, written early in his wanderings, Sid wrote, "Dear Kati, I am truly happy here. It's been too long. To be perfectly honest, until now, my visits with you as a teenager were the happiest times in my life. Times in the Great Plains looking for age-old mysteries are as joyful as were my visits with you years ago. Wish I could share more. You'll be in my heart, dear Kati."

Sid also shared research specifics, such as, "Within Great Plains vortexes, the people I interviewed reported feeling weighted down and unable to move when passing through real vortexes."

Joyous that he was once again experiencing joy, Katherine wrote back, "Have you ever experienced a real vortex yourself?"

"Only mild and casual experiences," Sid replied. "Not like what others had felt and experienced." Later, in the same message, Sid explained, "Some reported seeing swaying and glowing green lights coming right out from black ghostly apparitions dancing around the vortex's late-night light display. Imagine that! Still in other interviews, nighttime witnesses reported feeling weightiness, but only after the green lights had darkened and the figures faded away. No, my dear Kati, I never felt such an intense vortex experience before, but I hope I do—soon."

Even though Sid had amassed copious notes on vortexes and interviewed dozens of committed devotees, he still didn't know how or why they worked. However, with all that data, it became inescapable to him that vortexes must be real and cannot be easily dismissed. Unlike at commercial sites, there were no wizards behind hidden curtains within real vortexes.

Sid's growing vortex beliefs brought him to a crossroads. He believed he needed to choose research topics: Did he want to seek the answers on how vortexes work, or did he want to explore why some people wholly believed in these Earthly forces while others dismissed them when faced with the same evidence and observation?

He wrote to Katherine that the more he thought about it, his interest lay in the vortex faithful. "Kati, I want to explore the forces that drive *some* people incrementally into life-changing obsessive levels, while others can walk by without missing a step. This will become my new mission." With that renewed focus, Sid's instincts told him to delve even deeper into the northern Great Plains.

Native Americans have occupied the Great Plains well beyond oral traditions can recall—well beyond where stories, legends, and religion converge. Therefore, Sid's refocused wanderings led him straight to the heart of the Apsáalooke people—Crow Agency, Montana. Perhaps a bit too naïve, but Sid hoped a little of the Crow's prairie wisdom would rub off on him.

Regardless of the futility of the effort, Sid wandered the Crow Reservation seeking answers, seeking questions. He once read that an obscure spiritual vortex was located somewhere on Crow land. Sid had no idea if this meant within the current Crow Reservation, the reservation before the U.S. government shrunk it to steal the tribe's valuable natural resources, or within ancestral Crow land. "It could be anywhere," he wrote Katherine. This unknowing led Sid back to aimlessly wandering looking for a clue or sign.

Sid stopped the first person he saw walking by. "Hello, my name is Sid. I'm collecting data on…" The man just walked away, attempting to hide a growing grin.

Sid tried this a few more times, each with the same response. No one spoke with him, as if he had the plague. *Who can blame them?* he thought, since from the Crow's perspective, a total stranger just tried to pry into their culture's deepest and most personal secrets.

Sid sat on a roadside derelict pickup shell to rethink his strategy. He figured he needed credibility. *Why would they divulge their ancient knowledge and wisdom to a stranger?* he thought. What would compel them to give up their long-held secrets? He knew further attempts would probably not work, but he felt he still needed to try.

For hours, Sid wandered the dusty alleys, randomly skewed trailers, and aborted dreams of Crow Agency. The muddled town seemed to hold nothing of any permanence—at least to Sid's eyes. There were people and happenings that silently passed by; however, the town's stillness revealed to Sid neither a clue nor a sign.

The hot and dusty day drove the visibly idle youth to loiter in Crow Agency's ample shade. Sid's impression was that the idle youth loitered in the same spot regardless of the weather. Their lack of purpose was as obvious to him as wind-blown grit lodged in gums that no spit could ever expel. The idled teenagers interrupted their loitering long enough to momentarily glance at Sid, and then without interruption, return to their idleness. Sid dismissed them just as quickly, since loitering teenagers seemed the least likely to reveal the Apsáalooke people's historic secret—even if they knew themselves.

Suddenly he realized how naïve he had been to even think the Crow would open up and embrace him on his midlife mission. He chastised himself by muttering, "Did I think that just by strolling into town and asking a few questions the tribe would open up and answer deeply held secrets? Even if they knew, was I worthy enough, because, after all, what am I to the Crow?" He left the teenagers to continue loitering on their own, lost in their own world and indifferent to Sid and his quest.

Sid wandered elsewhere, hoping someone or something would blindly call to him. Nothing called. In this lonely silence stood only gas stations, BIA offices, a police station, a school, and a resident Foursquare Church. By the looks of it, Sid believed the Foursquare Church had seen thousands of people come and go, just not today. Perhaps that was why the Foursquare Church appeared to be so popular here, he thought. Residents may have recognized the need for spiritual divine healing, since clearly, there had been some backsliding. He couldn't vouch for the sinful part, but from his introduction, Crow Agency seemed to have down pat the economic depravity and hopelessness part.

Sid envisioned a long line of the lonely, idle, and lost, all slowly heading for the Foursquare Church, and all seeking atonement. Those most favored, if worthy, might find truth and redemption by speaking in tongues, as if conversing in some ancient alien language. Sid shook his head and shuddered to rid his mind of pointless musings. He intuitively knew there could be no salvation or atonement for these people any more than there could be for him, at least not today, so he wandered elsewhere to become idle himself.

As Sid walked away, he looked up and saw a sign—an actual sign in the church's front parking lot. The letterboard type sign typical of church billboards held the message—glaring right at Sid: "All lost souls. Come join us this Sunday, the guest sermon will be by the minister from Fort Smith." Sid interpreted the rest of the letterboard to be a sign directed solely to Sid: "There's a time to search and a time to give up as lost; A time to keep and a time to throw away—Ecclesiastes 3:6."

This got Sid thinking: There were too few people in Crow Agency to find anyone to talk about the Crow spiritual vortex. Fort Smith was bigger, and more traditional. Sid thought someone there might speak with him and provide answers, because, *Why else would the sign speak to me?* he told himself as he stood in awe at the Foursquare Church sign. Sid realized he had spent too much time being idle, and too much aimless wandering. At that moment—that specific moment, a higher presence spoke to him, through the Foursquare Church sign, that he needed to be more active. Sid knew the time of waiting for someone to come by was gone. Instead, his renewed self would seek out the experienced—interview tribal elders, not idle youth. Sid thought the Foursquare Church sign directed him to Fort Smith. Without any further hesitation, he got into his Jeep Cherokee and pointed it southwest toward the slated sky brooding over the Bighorn River and away from the forgettable hamlet of Crow Agency.

CHAPTER 6

More than two years after Sid's Fort Smith Medicine Wheel challenges, and long before he even heard the name "Sid Emerson," Paddy had challenges all his own.

Well, Paddy, you fool—you're committin' an act that gets many people killed in Death Valley, Paddy said to himself as he left his vehicle and struck out on foot to look for help. He knew the risks better than most, but he'd been waiting next to his broken-down Bronco for three days—he had little water and less patience left. *It may be weeks before the next rig goes up White Top Mountain.* Paddy knew very well that around big remote deserts, such as Death Valley, survival often depends on a vehicle. A simple car breakdown can turn a pleasant day's drive into an epic struggle for survival.

Before Paddy made that decision, he first traversed a few miles to a small natural spring he once found years earlier. He used the last of his water to get to this small spring. When he arrived, Paddy found only a moist mud patch. Trying to hold back his growing panic, he dug into the moist sand knowing that water could not be far below. His hole grew to only a foot deep before seeping water began filling the hole. Paddy let the mud settle out as much as his patience allowed before he lifted a handful of the wondrous nectar to his parched lips—and then promptly spat it out. "Salty. Too salty," he cursed as he forcefully tossed the dirt back into the hole. He sat next to the former spring and mulled over his options: *I can walk seven miles or so downhill into Hidden Valley and another three miles to Teakettle Junction.* Paddy believed this would provide him with a greater chance to hitch a ride than if he remained on White Top Mountain.

Paddy considered the drawbacks. *If no one comes, I'll be in an even hotter and drier place than White Top*, he fretted. He knew his best option involved the one with the greatest chance of getting water—no matter how far the walk or how long the wait. *I need water, and I need it soon. Damn, Paddy, you found yourself stranded in one of the driest places this side of the Owlsheads*, he said to himself as he stood and turned east. Just then, on a whim, he started heading down Dry Bone Canyon, hoping to later connect with a hiker coming up for the day. If not, then he'd have to go further downhill and across the blistering alluvial fan under full sun. *If I must cross the alluvial fan, at least I will be on pavement—and there's always people drivin' the pavement to either Scotty's Castle or Furnace Creek*, Paddy said to himself as he faced into the rising heat waves rising out of Death Valley's lowlands and took his next step.

A flat tire, of all things, is how he got into this predicament. Death Valley roads are hard on tires. This is why Paddy, like many experienced desert wilderness drivers, always carried two spares. However, this precaution helped Paddy little when in need of a third spare.

As Paddy stumbled down Dry Bone Canyon, his mind wandered to many things, including how he wished for a full moon so he could travel in the coolness of night. "Well, if you call a 105-degree night *cool*," he muttered as he continued his descent under the heat of the searing sun. His mind also stumbled upon the appropriateness of the canyon's name—Dry Bone. *I wished I had a dry bone to suck on now. Better yet, a wet one*, he lusted. To take his mind off salivating over dry bones, Paddy forced his thoughts to why he took the job in the first place. *I could be in the shade under my screwbean mesquite right now, sipping a beer. What do I know about investigating? So, now I'm left asbestos-mouthed, tinder-dry, on foot, and heading deeper into the furnace.*

Paddy had endured many other desperate walks, not only here, but in the Paktika Province, Haiti, and Somalia. When he thought about these deployments, they all became a blur. His many stumbles in Dry Bone Canyon didn't help jar his memory. *Whatever it takes,* he said to himself—*anything to distract my mind.*

With a determination borne of experience, Paddy forced his mind onto other thoughts. He thought of Katherine. He had no idea where to start searching for her uncle. *Clearly not on White Top Mountain.* He wondered how he'd allowed himself to get roped into such nonsense. *Damn, Paddy, did I get stuck in Dry Bone without any water only for money?* He dismissed that thought, since money had never been that important to Paddy. If dehydration had not dimmed his reasoning, he may have stumbled upon the notion that he accepted the job out of a guilty conscience—to at least be there for someone, like Katherine, since he wasn't there for Jen and Rachel. However, even with a dehydrating mind, Paddy had enough discipline to force his mind from ever traversing into that dark wilderness.

Since returning from the war, Paddy never held a steady job other than an occasional construction project. Everything reminded him of Jen and Rachel. He found himself increasingly jobless and living day by day on a cash basis—or barter and trade. This had left him nearly penniless when Katherine first stirred Paddy's dust. *There are limited construction jobs these days,* he thought as he began accepting the notion that he *had* taken the job purely for the money. *How could I stoop so low?* Paddy chastised himself as he continued his downhill stumbles. He considered his thoughts were just dehydration and heat exhaustion talking. However, despite the desiccating wind, he couldn't escape the notion that he charged a fee for investigating when *I know nothing about investigating. Now, I'm charging a fee for my stumblin' and foolishness?*

Paddy must have stumbled further than he thought because he already leveled out onto the alluvial fan's white expanse. *Well, Paddy, I'm not as helpless or lost as you thought. I do know the Panamints.* As if trying to convince himself, *Maybe I can help the Boston lady after all.*

He began his search for Sid Emerson a few days earlier by asking several long-term Panamint residents who were living off the grid and had a habit of knowing who lived nearby and who crept around suspiciously. This search brought Paddy back to old friends and acquaintances. A *pendejo* friend he hadn't spoken with in years said he heard a rumor someone may be squatting on White Top's northern or western flanks.

Upon second thoughts, Paddy's mind wandered to the notion, *Why would anyone hole up on White Top? There ain't enough water for the day, let alone an encampment lasting weeks or months. Only a fool would come up here lookin'.*

Paddy figured thinking of the investigation was better than focusing on water, or how to get back with spare tires. A passing thought had him wondering how a *real* investigator would search for a missing person. *If I'm gonna find Sid Emerson, I'll have to do it my way,* he confessed. *If Sid Emerson didn't want to be found, he's not likely gonna be,* he caught himself thinking the moment a strong up-canyon gust almost knocked him over. *If the sun doesn't get you, the wind will,* he cursed. As he resumed his stumbling, he could feel the wind vaporizing his every cell and pore. *I got to get out of the sun and wind.*

To keep his mind off the countless draws, arroyos, and cliff bands he skirted, and his many trips, falls, and bleedings he endured, Paddy focused on how he would search for Sid. *There're so many isolated areas where a person can get lost in, even on White Top Mountain.* Knowing people around there are accustomed to not butting into other people's business or divulging secrets, he didn't think asking around for the whereabouts of Sid would work. *That'll just send him deeper into the mountains.*

Paddy knew he would have to search likely places. He might never get a glimpse of the man, but it's harder to hide signs of a person's encampment. If there was anything he knew about this country, any encampment, no matter how secret, will be close to water. White Top Mountain, and most of the Cottonwoods, have too few dependable springs. The best water is in the Panamints and the lower Grapevine

Mountains. *The tow-slope Grapevine springs are too visible to people passing by, so that leaves the Panamints,* he surmised. *When I get out of here, I need to search known springs in the Panamints. If Sid is out there, I may have a chance of findin' his signs.*

Surprise Canyon was the first Panamint site that came to Paddy's far too withering mind. In Surprise Canyon, water runs everywhere, and year-round—not that common around Death Valley. The problem with Surprise, Paddy figured, were the crowds. For the last several years, crowds went up Surprise Canyon just to see an actual Death Valley stream—and to hike to the historic Panamint City ghost town.

Back in its mining prime, in the 1870s, a road led to the rough mountain town. The road remained passable on and off again, between floods and laborious road repairs, long after the silver bust and the town had gone belly-up. Paddy remembered well when he first arrived that 4x4s could drive all the way. The rattles and jolts would nearly shear your rig in two, but you could still drive it. That was before a severe wash-out, just a dozen or so years back, took out whole sections.

From that time on, only the most dedicated 4x4 drivers made it. In places, drivers needed to winch their rig up vertical rock. Surprise Canyon served as a test piece for serious canyon drivers. Paddy had been many things, but a fool on Death Valley 4x4 roads, didn't count among them.

No one drives it anymore—not since a cooperative agreement between the two land managers, the Bureau of Land Management and the National Park Service, fell through and a permanent driving closure took effect. Since then, the lush vegetation along the perennial stream came roaring back with a vengeance. *I would like to attack Surprise Canyon's water with a vengeance. I'm thirsty enough,* Paddy said to himself as he contemplated where Sid might be hiding.

These mental exercises kept his mind off his swelling tongue and cracking lips. They also helped narrow Paddy's search area. He only now needed to look in a wild and rough landscape the size of Connecticut. This didn't make him feel any better, nor did his lustings for Surprise Canyon's water. However, Paddy soon found he had just crossed the salt flat. He had only the short climb up to the roadbed.

"I made it, damn you!" Paddy screamed into the rising heat waves. "Woo-dang, I made it!" His lucky streak ran strong this day since his thumb and weary condition caught the attention of a passing driver after only a ten-minute wait. His soon-to-be ride slowed down, backed up, rolled down the window, and called to Paddy.

"What's up, Paddy? What the hell are you doing out here, of all places?"

Lots of people around Death Valley had met Rodney Horrovick, but few, if any, liked him. Rodney loved only two things, ORV riding and being mad at the world—and all its inhabitants. He had been the most outspoken critic of the park and of BLM closing Surprise Canyon to ORV use—and that never endeared him to some. Paddy never understood the reason for Rodney's hatred, but for a ride, he couldn't be picky.

"Hello, Rodney. Thanks for the ride. Are you headin' to Shoshone?"

"No, I ain't taking you to no Shoshone—I'm no damn taxi," Rodney snarled. "But I can take you into Beatty. What'cha doing on foot out here? That's crazy. But you've always been a crazy sons-of-bitch."

"How I got here, long story, but I could sure use some water. Got any?" As Rodney rummaged through piles of trash on the floorboard where he thought he left a spare water bottle, Paddy continued answering Rodney's questions. "I'm helping a lady find her missing uncle. As for being a crazy son-of-a-bitch, I'd admit that. After all, I'm ridin' with you, aren't I?"

"Oh, you must be talkin' about that East Coast lady that's been sniffin' around looking for Sid Emerson," Rodney said as he handed Paddy the sun-warmed and dust-kissed bottle that had been bouncing around on his floorboard for a week. "I heard about that, but I didn't know'd you be stupid enough to get involved. You know he's a nut case who believes in Lizard People, aliens, and all that crap?"

"Not sure if that's true, but besides, it has nothin' to do with finding him," Paddy snapped. "Why? Do you know anything about what happened to Sid Emerson?" Paddy asked between his sipping and savoring of Rodney's bilge water.

"Nah, I stay away from people like that; it's people like the Manson followers and the looneys and loners, like you, that's ruinin' the place. As far as I'm concerned, Sid Emerson can stay lost. No skin off my sorry ass if you know what I mean."

"Yes, we all know about your sorry ass." After a moment of reflection, Paddy added, "…but thanks for the ride, anyway."

Rodney Horrovick continued his tirade on Manson followers, Lizard People, and people like Sid Emerson who came searching for idiots and their crazy followers, but Paddy had long ago stopped listening. Instead, his thoughts shifted to how he would get back to White Top Mountain with spares. *It'll probably take days*, he silently cursed as Rodney continued droning away on Lizard People and aliens from the Draco constellation.

Paddy never put much stock in Lizard People legends, but he knew plenty of people who did. He also knew if he wanted to find Sid, he had to retrace his footsteps—and delve into the Lizard People legend. That meant mixing with the true believers. A grimace washed over Paddy's face with the thought he'd have to talk to Lizard Len. *Well, Paddy, if you're gonna find her uncle, you need to track down all potential leads—even if that means Lizard Len*, Paddy thought as they continued racing down the road. *I would rather talk to Rodney Horrovick than to Lizard Len*, Paddy thought upon more grimacing. Upon this last grimace, Rodney pulled his Jeep next to the Beatty Library. After thanking Rodney for the ride, Paddy headed straight to water, where he soaked it in as fast as his dehydrated body could absorb.

Paddy walked into the Nye County Sheriff's Office to use their phone. He had no cell phone, and even if he had, the area had only a weak cell phone signal—at best. He called Katherine and asked for a ride. While he waited, he thought back on his conversation the other day with the sheriff—the one across the California line. Paddy had stopped by to see if he could get Sheriff John Smithers to open an investigation into Sid's disappearance. He knew Katherine had already tried, but since Paddy knew John, he figured he could convince the sheriff to change his mind.

John and Paddy had known each other for a long time. Although neither would admit it, they both had things in common. Neither had many close friends. For Paddy, it was because he had turned into a loner. John had few friends because of his reputation as a police officer—not good enough to gain admirers, but not bad enough to be on the take or to miss the obvious. John had little passion for police work—he put in his time, but no more. Being a police officer always had been a personal barrier for John, while Paddy's whole life after being discharged had been a barrier.

As Paddy sat on the Nye County Sheriff's Office's bench waiting for his ride, he reflected on his conversation the other day with Sheriff John Smithers. The sheriff had seemed distracted, even uninterested. Little did Paddy know, but John had been increasingly concerned with Paddy turning into a driftless loner—almost a recluse. While Paddy kept up his spiel, John inwardly reflected, *Afghanistan changed Paddy.* Some rumors claim the death of Paddy's wife and kid had changed him, but John always figured the war had—maybe both. *The death of a guy's wife and only child while he's overseas fighting a senseless war must be hard on a guy*, John mused, as Paddy kept droning on and on. *Maybe it's a good thing Katherine Emerson hired him to find her uncle. Paddy will never find him, but the search will humor Ms. Emerson, and Paddy's talking and caring*

about something other than his grief may be enough to bring Paddy back to the human race—maybe. Sheriff John Smithers knew all too well the area already had too many loners, misfits, and people with complicated backstories.

Regarding Ms. Emerson, John thought a search for Sid Emerson would be a fool's errand and only lead to heartbreak and disappointment. *Sid, like so many others of his kind, is alive and simply doesn't want to be found. If so, it's not my job or duty to find Sid Emerson simply to organize a family reunion.*

During Paddy's attempt to convince John to change his mind on a Sid Emerson investigation, John's mind drifted increasingly to Sid's fate. He thought, maybe Sid is dead, lying face down in a remote canyon, baked, desiccated, and shriveled in a hole—or lying broken in an unknown mine shaft. John sorely wanted to shake some sense into Paddy and Katherine—and stop what he thought was a pointless search.

Tired of the conversation, John interrupted, "I will not devote staff time to look for Sid Emerson or call out the volunteer search-and-rescue team. If you and Ms. Emerson want to look, you're free to look and ask around, but without a lead, where would you even begin looking?"

John knew all too well a person has little chance of finding a body on purpose. Every couple of weeks, John and his deputies recovered bodies, but in known locations. *I'm not going to call out search teams to search in every nook and cranny of the Panamints, Cottonwoods, Last Chance, Greenwater, Black, Saline, and Funeral Mountains and all the canyons, arroyos, and mines within my county—I'm just not gonna do it,* John fumed. *Oh, I forgot the Owlshead Mountains,* John murmured. *How could I forget about the Owlsheads?*

By the end of Paddy's talk with John, Paddy clearly knew he had wasted his and John's time. Paddy had gotten no further in convincing the sheriff to help than had Katherine. *So much for my power of persuasion,* Paddy muttered to himself as he walked out of the office.

John's refusal to help, the other day when they last spoke, was fresh on Paddy's mind when Katherine and her rental Camry pulled up to the Beatty Sherriff's Office and motioned for Paddy to get inside.

❧

"What happened to you? I hadn't heard from you in a few days." The worried strains showed in her tone, as Katherine scolded him while opening the Camry's door to a bedraggled Paddy.

"Long story—maybe later," Paddy quipped, as he climbed aboard the welcomed ride.

As Katherine drove Paddy back to his Barstow trailer, he seemed quieter than normal. *What is it that haunts him and keeps his distance?* Katherine wondered. *He seems a nice and caring man, but I don't know anything about the real Patrick Darwin—not for my lack of trying.*

The silence inside the Bronco contrasted with the wind's wail and shrieks outside. If Katherine had her choice, she would rather fight a blast-furnace-style Death Valley wind than Paddy's painful Bronco silence. Katherine wanted to talk but searched for the right words. Paddy shifted in his seat under the dread that she found her words and would begin exploring them. *Silence is golden* may be a quaint platitude for some, but to Paddy, it formed his entire comfortable safe zone.

Although she was paying him to search for her uncle, Katherine didn't even know where Paddy went every day. He told her little. She knew he searched long and hard, but she only wished he would open up and talk more.

❧

As Paddy and Katherine sped and bounced along the washboarded and dusty road, they were both in their own private worlds. Paddy wondered why he took the job. He certainly could use the money, but he was not any more hard-pressed than he had been dozens if not hundreds of times before. *So, why now?*

She is likeable, Paddy reflected. *If she hadn't been, I would never have taken the job. I am not that desperate for a job that I would spend so much time with just anyone.* Paddy never liked city people, especially East Coast city people, but Katherine appeared to have a strength of character that set her apart. If Paddy had been honest with himself, he may have realized that he had taken the job because his ranger training taught him never to leave anyone behind. Clearly, everyone involved had left Sid Emerson behind—if by his own choosing, Paddy had yet to determine.

Paddy would likely have dismissed such thoughts, since there were hard-luck stories all around the area, and all of us, in one form or another, have been left behind. Paddy would think there is nothing special in that. We have all been left behind by someone, just like his unit left him behind during Operation Mountain Viper. There may have been more reasons that he took the job than he cared to think about, but Paddy remained undecided whether he regretted the decision or not.

Within the same bouncing Bronco, and along the same dusty road, Katherine's mind, equally alone, considered and weighed the silent, and clearly uncomfortable, man who sat next to her. She knew nothing about Paddy other than what Papa had told her. She needed someone who knew the area and people, but beyond that, Katherine needed someone she could trust. *I do trust him. What is it about the man that garners my instant acceptance, that he is trustworthy?* At first, Katherine treated their arrangement as purely contractual. However, after so many days in such a lonely country, Katherine began to think that she also needed a friend.

As Paddy remained silent on the long drive to Barstow, Katherine thought more and more about Paddy's search. *Where does he go every day?* she frequently asked, but Paddy typically evaded an answer—not in any obvious way, but in the end, still not divulging a thing. Although she originally agreed for him to search alone, she increasingly began dropping hints and suggestions that she would like to tag along and help. However, Paddy always found ways to cut her off and disappear without a word. Although she couldn't explain it, somehow she trusted him. She convinced herself that a warm and kind heart lay somewhere under his secretive and cold exterior. He knew this as well. This was why he forced himself to make sure *that* side of him never surfaced.

CHAPTER 7

Functional. Rice cakes and bologna… came to Sid's mind when he first rode into Fort Smith, Montana, *…no wine, berry cobbler, or even turkey stuffing. Functional.* An unremarkable impression of an unremarkable town—functional. Sid Emerson wanted functional. He wanted answers to his many questions—answers that he failed to get in Crow Agency earlier the same day.

Where did everyone go? Sid wondered as he scanned the nearly deserted streets. *Are they all at home? In a Foursquare church? Or avoiding the stranger who had come looking to expose their secrets?* Sid only saw one person in the desolate scene, so he remained fixed in his observation post—he simply watched. *Where are all the loiterers—like there had been in Crow Agency?*

Fort Smith's one lonely street dweller remained under Sid's eyes for a long time, since the man tottered on shaking legs that moved only with enough forward motion to keep the guy from falling on his sun- and wind-weathered face. Tired of watching the man's struggles, Sid approached and struck up a conversation.

"Hello, my name is Sid Emerson. Do you have a minute to answer a few questions?" The old man continued his slow tottering in silence. Raising his volume, Sid repeated, "Hello, I'm Sid. May I ask a few questions?"

"I heard you the first time. I didn't answer 'cause I don't know you, and you don't know me. So, that's that."

"Yes, we don't know each other, but my questions won't take long at all. If you need a lift, I'll drive you to where you're going."

"I don't need a ride. I just need to be left alone. But I can tell you won't do that until you ask your question. So be off with it. What do you want to know?"

"I'm here looking for a mystery spot reported somewhere on the nearby reservation. Do you know anything about its location?"

"I don't know nothin' 'bout no mystery spot." After a long pause and imperceptible forward movement, the tottering man turned to Sid. "Even if I knew about your mystery spot, I'd likely not tell you." After a short pause, and an even shorter forward motion, the lone man added without prompting, "But there is a medicine wheel nearby—does that count?"

"Yes, yes," Sid said as he lurched forward, almost knocking the old man down. "Medicine wheel. Yes. Please tell me about the medicine wheel."

"I don't know nothin' about it—no more than I know about you." After a few more wobbly motions, and seeing that Sid didn't leave, the old man said, "If you go to yonder gas station," as his shaking arm motioned down the street, "ask for Cornell. He may tell you something—if he's so inclined. He don't mind talking with strangers. Me, I just want to be left alone."

Sid did as the old man suggested and walked over to the gas station and approached a uniformed man pumping gas. "I'm looking for Cornell. Is he inside?"

"No. Cornell ain't inside. Why do you want to know?"

"I came to ask a few questions. Do you know when he'll be back?"

"What kind of questions? Maybe I can help."

"Down the street, an old man said Cornell may have some information on a nearby medicine wheel."

"Why didn't you start out with asking about the medicine wheel?" the station attendant exclaimed. "Sure, I'd be happy to talk about the medicine wheel. I'm Cornell. If you want to talk, let's step inside."

Glad for a distraction on such a slow day, Cornell invited Sid to sit at a small table next to the motor oil display. "I don't get many people come askin' about the medicine wheel. On a day like this, I'd talk about anything, but I always love talking about my medicine wheel."

"*Your* medicine wheel?" Sid asked.

"Sure. Can't say I know much about medicine wheels in general, but I know a bit about the Fort Smith Medicine Wheel." Standing stiff-shouldered and wearing a big grin, "Yeah, it's mine. I'm related to the person that built it."

"Aren't medicine wheels supposed to be ancient—hundreds or thousands of years old? How do you know if you're related or not?" Sid asked as Cornell settled into his chair crowded next to the oil cans.

"Suppose most medicine wheels are ancient, but this one's not. My grandmother's grandfather built it—at least that is what my uncle always told me."

"What is his name—the one who built it? When did he build it, and why?"

"Whoa—such a flood of questions. Slow down. Also, let's move the talk to the back office. I best not have this conversation in front of the window. My boss may drive by. I don't want him to think I'm goofing off by jawing."

Once at the office table, surrounded by seedy posters and out-of-date calendars, Cornell opened up and his words began flowing like tailwater below a dam. "According to my uncle, Scarface built the Fort Smith Medicine Wheel. He built it only a few years after the Battle of the Greasy Grass. Have you ever heard of the Battle of the Greasy Grass?"

"Sure," Sid replied. They used to call it the Battle of the Little Bighorn."

"Yeah," Cornell added. "That's the one where we Crow fought and died defending *your* people, including *your* General Custer."

The gas station back office became awash with conversation. Sid probed for answers, but Cornell talked just out of enjoyment of hearing his own voice—and to break up the day in the job he hated. Conversations overflowed, but in the end, Sid had no further insight into the real reason ancient civilizations built medicine wheels. Sid came no closer to knowing if they had ceremonial or religious value, were symbolic, or had practical or personal use or meaning.

"Maybe Scarface built the wheel as a monument to the Apsáalooke that died fighting *your* battle and *your* war," Cornell offered in obvious amusement. After several more random speculations, Cornell leaned back in his chair, chuckled, and suggested, "Maybe Scarface was bored. I can't imagine Fort Smith any more interesting then than it is now."

Cornell's conversation wandered into incoherent babbling. Sid began tuning out and thinking about the idle youth in Crow Agency. He envisioned a bored youth saying to equally bored friends, "Hey, guys! I'm bored. Enough of our idleness—let's build a ginormous medicine wheel." Upon further reflection, Sid imagined that scenario would *never* happen. If given the choice, idle youth would always choose to remain idle.

Cornell declined Sid's offer to take him to the wheel, saying, "I can't, buddy. I would love to, but the tribe don't allow any non-Crow to visit the Fort Smith Medicine Wheel, and I would get into trouble if I took you—"

"Why?" asked Sid.

"The tribe closed access after one of you guys vandalized my wheel a few years back."

"What do you mean by 'you guys'? I had nothing to do with it," implored Sid.

"You guys are all the same to me," said Cornell dismissively.

Cornell returned to his droning. Sid listened for another sixteen minutes but began to tune out after realizing that he was not getting any new insight into ancient Crow customs. Cornell only stopped his droning when a customer came to the counter to pay for his gas and to buy a soda. As Cornell rang up the sale, Sid walked to his truck to try his luck elsewhere.

During his short walk, Sid's mind wandered into a deep philosophical and reflective mood. He wondered if fate led him here from Michigan's Mystery Spot. *Perhaps, somehow, they were all meant to converge*, he pondered. *Perhaps this is my destiny—to tie them all together. That would be some feat. I would be a respected researcher the world over*, he mulled, over and over.

To Sid, mystery shrouds and permeates Great Plains medicine wheels. Most pre-dated the arrival of modern Plains tribes. To think clearly on the matter, Sid reviewed his basic understanding of medicine wheels. He told himself, *If I am ever to figure out Earth's mysteries, I must examine every shred of evidence. If I keep repeating what I know over and over, one day something will click, and it all will suddenly make sense.*

Some researchers claim medicine wheels date back six thousand years, Sid reminded himself. As this theory goes, as modern-day Native American tribes wandered into the Great Plains, each adapted their own stories and practices that made sense of the mysterious ancestral stone alters that they stumbled upon. No tribe doubted their strong medicine, but Sid imagined that they had even less information than he had to explain their origin, so the tribe could only speculate on their purpose or meaning.

Most medicine wheels were circular, built of small and medium-sized stones—and had diameters ranging from twenty to two hundred feet, Sid reminded himself. The classic medicine wheel consists of individual rocks aligned in a pattern resembling an old-style wagon wheel with an outer circle that connects to the interior radiating "spokes" that converge in the center.

Sid's medicine wheel thoughts soon drifted to the first recorded, and the most famous, medicine wheel. This grand and holy structure sits in the Bighorn Mountains, near the summit of Medicine Mountain. As Sid reminded himself, the name "medicine wheel" owes its name to this site, since early explorers found a wheel-shaped rock alignment high on Medicine Mountain. Consequently, early settlers called it "The Medicine Wheel." Later, when other explorers came upon similar structures in other locations, the name "medicine wheel" stuck.

Sid believed modern Native cultures knew more about medicine wheel origins than they let on. This presented Sid with a dilemma. If they knew of their meaning, but kept silent for hundreds of years, they wouldn't likely break their deeply held secret to him. *Besides,* Sid thought, *if medicine wheels have spiritual or religious meanings, then the truth would probably not make any sense to anyone who can't transcend rational Western thought. Like religion, such matters require cultural context and for people simply to believe in faith. This would be a fine research topic, if I had the time.* A lot swirled through Sid's head as he struck out for Wyoming's Bighorn Medicine Wheel. He knew he needed to experience this ancient wheel for himself.

To get there, Sid backtracked along the Bighorn River, cut over to Lodge Grass by way of Rotten Grass Creek and the Good Luck Road, drove up the Little Bighorn River, then went up the long and winding Medicine Wheel Highway that led him deep into the Bighorn Mountain's high country and to the small trailhead whose path thread its way up to the world's most famous of its 138-known medicine wheels.

Many questions passed through Sid's cluttered mind as he pulled off the main paved highway and began the drive up the narrow one-way gravel road. For a millennium, bright minds and the curious alike were unable to unlock the medicine wheel's secrets, so, Sid wondered, what chance did he have? Sid stressed over this dilemma as he continued the drive toward Medicine Mountain.

On the long drive, Sid went over many of the more common origin theories about the Bighorn Medicine Wheel. Many people have speculated that the wheel's spokes align with celestial objects as if the wheel served as an astronomical observatory. These people claim that on the summer solstice, the wheel's spokes pointed to Thuban, the brightest star in the constellation Draco.

Thuban is not just any star. The star held a special place in both early cultures and mythology. Sid read all about the theories while he worked in the university library. It was during these studies that

Sid first learned that the star closest to pointing north has changed with time. Back five thousand years ago, at the time when ancient Egyptians built the pyramids, and the mysterious creators first constructed Bighorn Medicine Wheel, Thuban, not Polaris, served as Earth's North Star.

While in the university's library, Sid read about many legends surrounding Thuban, including from the ancient Egyptians. Some scholars claimed they found more than one connection between the Bighorn Medicine Wheel and the great Egyptian pyramid Djoser. This was just one of the many research papers Sid read that convinced him that he needed to step out of the library into the real world of the Northern Great Plains.

While Sid had considered the Egyptian pyramid and Bighorn Medicine Wheel connection theory before, he mulled it over again as he pointed his SUV up the steep road that led closer to the fabled wheel. Sid saw many critical and logical flaws in the theory. For one, it hung on the belief that one of the wheel's spokes pointed to Thuban five thousand years ago. But with twenty-eight spokes, all radiating at different angles, there would be a spoke pointing to anything you wanted. Any spoke would naturally point to at least one star, no matter the day, season, year, or millennia. In Sid's mind, if a person traced any star's historic alignment over thousands of years, the number of spoke-star alignments would become infinite, only bounded by imagination, determination, and faith. Despite his logic misgivings, Sid believed the spoke alignments must have meant something. He simply didn't know what. At least not yet, he kept telling himself.

Sid also knew that the Egyptian pyramid connection stood on equally shaky ground. Many archeologists and astronomers claim the ancient Egyptian pyramids' outer corners pointed to Thuban at the time of construction. Besides the exterior angles, many researchers claim certain pyramid portals, doorways, and interior passages all pointed toward the sacred Thuban. However, Sid's logical mind debunked all such theories and conjectures.

Sid also intellectually knew that "ceremonial" was the go-to explanation for any unknown object built by early cultures. To Sid's way of thinking, this trite explanation only served to deflect from having to say: we don't know. *Besides,* Sid thought, *how can one truly quantify and articulate a purpose for the esoteric? Did Leonardo da Vinci paint* The Last Supper *for religious, spiritual, or ceremonial purposes?* Sid asked himself the clearly rhetorical question: *He may have painted it on commission for money? Perhaps he did not know himself. Maybe, like Cornell claimed, Scarface built the Fort Smith Medicine Wheel out of boredom.*

Sid considered the possibility that there wasn't a single purpose for medicine wheels. If medicine wheels were built or added to and altered for thousands of years by a variety of cultures, there may be as many reasons for their construction as there are medicine wheels. In addition, later cultures that moved into the region may have adopted or co-opted existing medicine wheels into their own culture, and adapted, maintained, and even modified them over generations for wholly different reasons than their original purpose. Sid considered the possibility that we may never know: The answer may have been lost to the land and wind of the mysterious Northern Great Plains.

CHAPTER 8

The following morning, as Paddy busied himself to go back to White Top Mountain to pick up his broken-down Bronco, Katherine didn't look forward to waiting by herself. Not anymore. She needed to be busy too. Curious about the Panamints, and the lure they have over so many people, including her uncle, she couldn't wait to visit them firsthand. Up until that day, she had only seen them from the distance on both the Panamint Valley and Death Valley sides. From valley bottoms, they didn't look that enticing, other than as an impasse or impediment. Without telling Paddy of her intention, she climbed in her Camry and drove to investigate the Panamints on her own.

From the map, the Hunter Mountain area looked accessible to a rented Toyota. From Barstow, the first leg traversed through salt flats, brush flats, and rocky flats: She went through Ridgecrest and Trona, passed the turnoff for Ballarat, and drove north on Panamint Valley Road. She passed Panamint Springs and turned at Lee Flat. The road continued through Joshua tree forests as it ascended to South Pass—and then over to Hunter Mountain. Camrys aren't built for rough roads, but it eventually got her to her destination.

Hunter Mountain has no distinct summit, only a series of forested nubbins on a broad, elevated plateau deep within pinyon-juniper country. More than one world separated this land from the fans and flats down lower. She stepped outside near an old cabin next to a large fence exclosure, and then paused to marvel at the scenery. In a small way, an exceedingly small way, she could envision the place could grow on a person—but not to the point of wanting to get lost in them.

Around the next corner, she came upon a pickup next to a small water tank. She didn't know it at the time, but the truck belonged to the owner of the last remaining cattlemen who still held a grazing lease within the greater Death Valley region. There used to be several, but they all left for greener pastures or were chased off by park rangers after Congress expanded the park. She stopped the Camry and got out.

From the lonely tank and lone pickup, Katherine saw no one in sight, only pinyon, junipers, meadows, butterflies, and cattle. Far in the distance, over a mile and a half lower in elevation, shone the shimmering heat of the Badwater Basin—the lowest spot in North America. It looked hot down there, despite the coolness of Hunter Mountain fresh air. *I never smelled air like this in Boston*, Katherine remarked as she walked into the forests with her eyes darting back and forth in childlike excitement.

She didn't walk far before she came upon a man lying on his back working on a waterline leading to or from the tank. She introduced herself and asked for his name. He continued in silence as he banged on the water line while cursing in a special Panamint sort of way. She called out again.

"I heard you the first time. Folks around here don't usually snoop into other people's business or ask about names or personal stuff," the man snorted.

"I am sorry to intrude. I am not from around here."

"I could never have guessed."

"I am not meaning to pry, but what are you doing?"

"If you really must know, I'm repairing this leaking water line. If I don't fix it, my cattle will die of thirst, so you can see, this is more important to me than socializing with a lady up from Los Angeles for the day."

"I'm not from Los Angeles. I come from Boston."

"So, Boston lady, what do you *really* want? I'm busy. After I fix this waterline, I need to go round up a lost bull that disappeared around the draw, over yonder," waving his wrench in a way that meant something only to him. "After that, I need to repair the hole in the fence she got out of—that damn fence the Park Service forced me to put up, for whatever reason, around *my* meadow."

"Your meadow?" Katherine inquired. "I thought this is park land."

"My family's been leasing this land for a generation before the Park Service came around," the man said with a grunt. "So, sure, it's my meadow. But now the Park Service tells me the meadow is home of a rare butterfly. I've never seen this damned butterfly, but my cattle get onery at times and they push their way into the fenced meadow. Each time, the Park Service says I need to make things right again. By the way I figure it, it hadn't been right in years."

This man had too many immediate practical needs to think about Katherine's missing uncle, Lizard People, or Earth's mysterious forces. As far as he was concerned, no mysterious force broke his cattle fence or compelled the park staff to report that his bull was running amok across the butterfly meadow. He had far fewer mysteries in his life than Sid had in his. He preferred it that way. He also preferred it when the park called, rather than having them "damn bureaucrats come and attempt to herd my cattle or mess with my fences. A bull is worth a lot of money, and if the parkies attempt to help, they only make things worse," he grumbled as he fumbled with the water line, wrapping his knuckles in the process. The rancher was grateful that the park called this time. While racing toward Hunter Mountain, he almost reached the meadow when he came upon the water line leaking precious water. Not long after that, the Boston lady interrupted him with a world of questions.

"Well, Boston lady, I must repair this waterline before my cattle dehydrate and die of thirst. After that, I have other things I need to do. So, as you can see, I'm too busy to pay you the proper greeting and introduction. I'm not trying to be rude, but that's just the way things are."

"I do not want to intrude or get in your way; I just have a quick question or two for you—if you do not mind. I just came from South Pass—."

"I know where you came from. I saw your dust nearly ten minutes ago. I'm just glad the parkies hadn't come to herd my cattle or look over my shoulder while I mend the fence. Instead, I now have a Boston lady looking over my shoulder."

"Again, I'm sorry to intrude and to be looking over your shoulder. I am Katherine Emerson. I am looking for my uncle, Sid Emerson. Do you know, or have you seen him? He is missing."

As John finished his repairs, he looked up at Katherine. "Well, Boston lady, I never heard of your Sid Emerson, and I know nothing of his whereabouts. Sorry." With that, he got in his pickup and sped up the road, leaving Katherine to watch his dust plumes rise high into the air and slowly drift away as Katherine stood alone with her thoughts and unanswered questions.

Buoyed by the dwindling dust, Katherine breathed in deep the fresh mountain air. Safe in her isolation, she put her guard down enough to wander alone into the trailless forest to see what made the Panamints so special.

From the water tank, she passed a high point that looked far down to the meadow, where she could see the rancher chasing after a bull that looked as if he had no intention of being herded, corralled, chased away, or to leave *his* lush meadow. Katherine sat to watch the comic chase.

She stayed on this promontory long after the rancher herded the bull out of the meadow and made the necessary fence repairs. She lost track of the time—simply smelling the scented air, taking in the lonely isolation, and attempting to comprehend the fact that Boston lies on the same planet, but somewhere beyond the distant curvature in normal space. As her conscience mind slowly began taking over, Katherine turned to face away from the meadow and the once lazily grazing bull. Within this new scene, the dark green pinyon and juniper foreground stood apart from the jagged cluster of orange lichen-stained boulders that dominated the middle-distance. *The place is quite lovely*, she silently mused. Suddenly, she froze.

Ahead, in the next clearing, appeared to be a dead body—a dead human. Katherine recoiled and wanted to run, but after a moment of thought, she regained her composure. *I need to report this to the sheriff.* Katherine discovered her first Panamint lesson—the entire region had hopeless cell phone reception. *Should I drive down to report it in person? That will take hours. Shouldn't I first check the man's condition?* Curiosity and the desire to help overcame fear, as she crept closer. As she drew near, fear again stabbed its hot tendrils through her already surging blood, pulse, and heaving lungs. *Is this Uncle Sid?*

She kept repeating to herself, *It is not Uncle Sid. It is not Uncle Sid*—more out of trying to convince herself than believing it. *My Uncle Sid is alive, so this is not him—it cannot. This dead man cannot be...*

Maybe the guy is not dead, she thought. *If not, why is his face to the ground? Do I really want to know? If he is alive, is he a deranged monster? A Manson fanatic? Paddy warned me not to travel alone up here.* For both fear and safety, she began creeping back to her car—in case he awoke. Too late. As soon as she began slinking off, the dead man, still face to the dirt, spoke.

"This genus should *not* be here. Its closest relative is over two hundred miles away," the dead man said in a muffled sort of way— perhaps the best he could do with his face still planted firmly in the dirt. Katherine could tell this voice was not her uncle's.

Katherine scanned the clearing to see who the dead man was speaking to. No one. This realization made her skin crawl. *Either this strange man will lurch at me any second, or else someone else remains hidden nearby.* Before the dead man uttered his next words, Katherine frantically considered her options. *I am far from home, far from Paddy, and far my car. If I run, the dead man will catch me long before I can reach the car.* Katherine's eyes darted around looking for other choices. *Maybe the dead man spent too many years alone in the desert. Is this what Uncle Sid will be like if I find him— when I find him?*

Katherine's darting eyes and frightful thoughts still searched for other options when the dead man, still with his head in the dirt, talked again. This time he mumbled to himself, in Latin, something about the *Myrmecocystus* genera, how this one shouldn't be here. It took Katherine minutes to realize the strange dead man was talking to her about ants.

During this whole "conversation," the dead man's head and eyes remained fixed on his ants. Occasionally, he pulled out a small magnifying glass and held it within two inches of the ground, still fixated on minute ants. For someone so still, his tone was animated. The realization that he probably wasn't an ax murderer didn't calm Katherine's nerves much, since she figured he must be "touched."

Eventually, internationally respected ant expert Ron Telling told Katherine his story about how he'd arrived on Hunter Mountain. He had been on an extended ant expedition in the deep jungles of Borneo. As soon as he arrived state-side, on a whim, Dr. Telling had the urge to dry out for a few days before heading home to Los Angeles. Apparently, for the last twenty years, Death Valley and his beloved Panamints were his "go-to" drying out place.

After becoming acquainted, Katherine opened the floodgate of questions about the whereabouts of Sid Emerson.

Turning to Katherine, he held an ant up close to her face and said, "Here is that *Myrmecocystus*. This little bugger is not supposed to be here. Isn't it strange?"

"I would not know. But about Sid Emerson, have you seen or heard of him?"

"The closest *Myrmecocystus* is a long way from here. I wonder how he got here." After a long pause with him continuing to stare at his ant, Katherine didn't know whether to repeat herself or walk away. Perhaps sensing her impatience, dismissively, Ron muttered, "I really don't pay much attention to people: It takes my attention off ants—earth's *only* fascinating creature. People, they rarely interest me."

Sensing further conversation would be pointless, Katherine left Hunter Mountain to Dr. Ron Telling and his rare and out-of-place ants.

CHAPTER 9

Far removed in place and time from Katherine's scare on the lonely Hunter Mountain, Sid found only empty spaces as he pulled his Jeep Cherokee into the Bighorn Medicine Wheel parking lot. Normally packed on weekends, Sid liked that he visited on a Tuesday. He had no knowledge that others were nearby—those that came on foot, from places and approaches unknown to most. It didn't take Sid long to gather his things and begin the walk up the trail that led to one of the world's greatest mysteries.

The coolness of the hour gave a freshness to the air that prompted Sid to breathe deep and smooth, in ways he hadn't in a long time. Others enjoyed the experience too, for despite the early hours, the nearby blooming lupines, phlox, columbine, and stonecrop brought out colorful butterflies *en masse*. The iridescent Melissa blues and black and orange flag-like Milbert's tortoiseshells gorged on flowing nectar as Sid began his journey toward the wheel. Despite his destiny unfolding, time had no meaning—not on this brisk, color-filled day. Ascending higher onto Medicine Mountain's shoulder, without knowing, he passed a faint trail leading to faraway places—a trail used for thousands of years, a trail known and used by only a few. Sid remained on the scarred, defaced, and official trail, once a gravel road.

Native peoples have been visiting the wheel for longer than even they can remember. A few tribal members take the paths—sometimes without notice. Sid noticed the many small rock offerings scattered on prominent cliff edges, but didn't appreciate their significance. Some had been there for generations, but one had been there for only three hours.

Nearby, and a few days previously, a young Blackfoot methodically erected the temporary structure with a sharp eye to ensure the right piece went in the proper place. Using boughs and sticks he brought up from lower in the valley, his small oval-shaped hut began taking form. The young Blackfoot found the place by following dreamy images. In his dream, he saw the place where five great holy men became so wise the Great Spirit borne them again onto the earth. They stood now on the edge of the cleft as five stone watchers searched the heavens for the Sky People's eventual return. Once convinced he found the spot seen in his dreams, the young Blackfoot placed the finalizing touches on his little shelter. From that point on, he eagerly anticipated the arrival of strong medicine.

Once completed, and loaded with supplies, he entered its tight entryway on the east side. The young Blackfoot began the ceremony by providing the Creator a word of thanks—specific words he practiced for days. He then lit sweetgrass and let its aroma fill and purify the air.

At 2 a.m. on the third day, just when Thuban's dim light began filtering through gaps in the hut, a rush of clarity suddenly flowed through the young Blackfoot—he heard from the Creator. As the young man received his message, out of respect, he offered tobacco smoke, sweetgrass, and sage. The time was right, the offerings sufficient, and the young Blackfoot pure enough in mind and spirit that he began a conversation with the Creator. He let the energy flow back and forth for four days. Afterward, he emerged from the now opened east door and left a renewed person with a clear sense of purpose and worldly understanding.

The young Blackfoot carefully deconstructed his miniature hut and ceremoniously returned the component parts to the forest floor lower in the valley. To mark the specific location of events, before leaving, the young man constructed and commemorated a small pile of stones next to the five spiritual watchmen standing guard overlooking the Great Plains that stretched into the near and far distance. Sid passed these ceremonial stones just a few hours later.

When Sid walked by, he didn't communicate with the stones, but he somehow sensed their ceremonial importance and significance. Instead, he sat on the edge of the escarpment and gazed at the expansive prairie in the distance and at the five stone pillars on the cleft's edge. Sid soaked in whatever energy he could get from such a short visit, then he continued the last few steps to the Bighorn Medicine Wheel—the mysterious object he came all the way to see and experience.

The wheel showed its age. Buffeted for thousands of years by the convergence of sand-laden prairie and mountain winds, the rocks looked as if the low-lying alpine scrub were swallowing them in place. Sid gazed along spokes to see with his own eyes their mysterious cosmic alignments. Sid scoffed at the claim that ancient aliens built the spokes as a guide to point home—if they ever needed to return. To find a home on a distant planet in the Draco constellation, an intergalactic traveler would need a better guide that a line of rocks on a Wyoming alpine escarpment. Instead, at the end of each spoke, Sid saw only the deep blue expanse of time and space. Since the sun shone in all its glory, Sid could only imagine the star-filled view if seen on a clear night on a summer solstice.

Despite the wheel's spiritual power, the physical presence evoked a power all its own. A narrow trail and a low fence circled the wheel's eighty-foot outer perimeter. As Sid contemplated wheel alignments and deeper meanings, a visitor whom Sid hadn't noticed approached from behind.

The lone visitor seemed to ignore Sid's presence. Without looking up or passing a word, the man began a slow clockwise circle around the wheel. After every few steps he stopped, reached into a drawstring-topped bag, and pulled out a small handful of darkened powder. He then, as if feeding a newborn, sprinkled a little powder at each spoke in his clockwise journey. Upon each ceremonial offering, the wind carried the powder high into the juniper-scented air as he softly spoke words or incantations inaudible to anyone but himself.

Sid desperately wanted to listen, hear, ask, and understand, but decided it would be too intrusive. Despite the man's total absorption, Sid offered a respectful "Hello" as he approached from upwind.

Without looking up, the old man reached for another pinch from his little pouch and began spreading more powder to the wind over the wheel. Only afterwards did he offer Sid a warm "Hello" in return.

Sid didn't want to intrude on such a solemn occasion, but after several false starts, he sheepishly said, "Excuse the interruption—do you mind if I ask a few questions?"

"Please go ahead."

"What are you spreading?"

"It's tobacco. I offer tobacco as a gift and a prayer."

"Do you live nearby?" asked Sid.

"No," the man replied. "I came here after a business trip to offer a prayer for my safe journey back to Wisconsin."

"So, you knew about the wheel."

"Of course. I've known of its existence my whole life. For as long as I've known about the stars, I've known about the medicine wheel and its power."

"Are you Blackfoot?" asked Sid.

"My mother is Ojibwe, but my father is Blackfoot. He taught me about the sacred wheel and how important it is to connect my present with my past, and the mind with the spirit. Where better way to do this than at this powerful spiritual place?" the old man said solemnly. "Are you here to pray too?"

"No, only to listen, watch, and learn," Sid answered.

Sid filled the man's ears with questions about the wheel, his ceremony, and as many other ancient questions that Sid thought the old man would tolerate. The old man answered Sid's questions, including the proper way to offer tobacco gifts—one pinch at a time, along with special and sincere words of thanks.

While the man answered Sid's questions, he seemed guarded

on any topic approaching personal or ceremonial. Sid didn't push the old man into any intrusive or uncomfortable conversation, so he eventually left the old man in peace. Afterward, Sid stood in the distance and watched the Ojibwe continue his ceremony, prayers, and circular preparations for his return to Wisconsin. Once the Ojibwe left a few minutes later, Sid had the wheel all to himself.

Slowly, Sid circled the wheel in a clockwise direction, just as the Ojibwe instructed, attempting to feel a connection—to feel anything. Sid repeated the circles, exactly as the man said, and in proper alignment with the natural movement of the stars, sun, and planets.

To breathe the experience in and let the wheel's energy course through his body, Sid closed his eyes and let his mind wander back five thousand years, back to the time the ancient Egyptians built the pyramids, and the Northern Great Plains people built the medicine wheel. In his mind, Sid envisioned Thuban's light shining down on craftsmen and holy men as they toiled to construct the perfect astrological marker while providing ceremonial offerings to their cosmic gods. Deeply immersed in his imagery, Sid envisioned constructing the wheel to heavenly perfection would have been the highest calling. Surely, only the best, brightest, and most pure holy men participated.

As Sid gazed at the remnant ceremonial perfection, he tried to imagine if any spokes aligned with celestial objects. If it did, it would likely have been on the most culturally significant day—the summer solstice. The scientific and objective parts of Sid's brain remained skeptical of any true cosmic alignment, but on this day, he tried to think as a true believer. Besides, Sid considered the notion that there's more to the world, and this wheel, than what our limited minds and limited experiences can possibly know or explain. While having such deep thoughts while standing alone at the Bighorn Medicine Wheel on the escarpment edge, with what seemed like the world at his feet, Sid felt a fresh invigoration, almost religious, in its depth and intensity. Suddenly, a warm sensation coursed through his body and radiated into the thin atmosphere: the faith that fundamental truths lying somewhere out there may yet be attainable.

As the afternoon sun waned, a coolness crept upon Medicine Mountain and its chill returned Sid to his present-day reality. As he begun to turn, he heard a noise. Two people slowly came into sight from beyond the crest—a frail old guy hobbling along with the assistance of a spry younger man. As soon as they arrived at the wheel, the old man pulled out a tobacco pouch and began spreading offerings in a clockwise direction as he limped alone while circling the wheel. The younger man seemed uninterested. Instead, he approached Sid and struck up a conversation.

The older man wanted to pay respect to the medicine wheel, but his advanced years prevented going alone. He asked his grandson to come along and help, and to learn. The grandson told Sid that the old man deeply believed in the old ways, traditions, and their Athapascan culture, but he himself "couldn't care less." However, he loved and respected his grandfather, so he agreed to help him pray at the medicine wheel.

As the grandson relayed to Sid, from their home in eastern Montana, his grandfather used to visit the wheel every summer solstice. He came to pray, pay respect, and keep his soul right with the universe. He always came a day before the solstice so that he might spend the entire night watching the star-shadows arc across the wheel and merge as one with the sunrise's magical dance of spokes, cairns, stars, and sun. According to his grandfather, there was no better spiritual place on the planet. "My grandfather is now too old and frail to spend solstice nights at the wheel. As for me, I'm not about to spend days and nights camped up here on this cold mountain—just staring at a bunch of rocks. That's his thing, not mine."

The grandson admitted he didn't believe the wheel held any special spiritual power and he didn't follow his tribe's traditional customs. Out of boredom, he shared with Sid the little of what he knew about the cultural significance of the site. "But you have to understand," the grandson said, "my grandfather tried to teach these things to me my whole life, but I never paid any attention. I only cared for girls, cars, sleeping in, and having fun. Sleeping on hard and cold ground so I can throw tobacco at a bunch of rocks—that's not my idea of fun."

As his grandfather continued his silent clockwise prayers, the grandson did his best to explain what the old man was doing—and why. He also gave Sid a lesson in their people's history. As the young man explained, hundreds of years ago, bands of Athapascans moved south from Canada to form what is now the modern Navajo and Apache peoples. During their journey, they encountered the wheel while passing through the Northern Great Plains. The people living near the wheel had an intimate knowledge and connection with the wheel and the original builders. "Some of the stories filtered back to my people—the Athapascans that remained up north—but most of the understanding of the wheel continued south with the people that became the Navajo," the grandson said—as Sid listened attentively.

"Are you saying the Navajos know the wheel's original story?" asked Sid.

"Well, the tribal elders do…well, that's what my grandfather believes. My ancestors back in Canada, all they knew of the wheel was that it held powerful medicine, and that power must be respected and honored. My people may deeply respect and revere the wheel, but they know no more about its original purpose and meaning than I do. For that, I guess you'd have to talk with Navajo elders. For me, I have no interest in such things. It's just sheep manure as far as I'm concerned. I'm only helping my grandfather carry out his silly old rituals."

Shortly after exhausting the young man's knowledge on the wheel, the old man motioned to his grandson of his readiness to head back. After they both disappeared beyond the horizon, once again, Sid had the Bigfoot Medicine Wheel to himself.

Before he headed down, Sid wandered around the scarp, just beyond the sight distance of the wheel. As he wandered, he began noticing more rock cairns. Lots of them. He followed the cairns, hoping to see if they formed a pattern or hinted at a meaning.

The afternoon cooling provoked upwelling mountain winds that grew stronger as the sun's warmth sank below the horizon. Just then, as Sid passed through a small evergreen clump, he saw in the distance another old man gently tossing something on the ground. From the looks of it, he appeared to be spreading tobacco or sweetgrass. *If so, why here?* Sid thought. *This is not the wheel.* Sid remained motionless in the evergreen clump as he studied the old man's movements.

After a long time at the same spot, the old man turned and headed into another tree clump and then disappeared. Intrigued, Sid crept closer while keeping his eyes on the precise but nondescript spot that had fascinated the old man. As Sid approached, he saw a small and darkened hole—a cave entrance. The smell of tobacco and sage still lingered in the air. The old man must have provided a spiritual offering to the cave. Questions flooded Sid's mind as he stared into the darkened interior. Why this cave? And where did the old man go?

While at the cave entrance, Sid scanned the far treeless slopes looking for signs of a scurrying old man. The search only brought a chill to Sid's bones. Out from a backpack, he pulled out his favorite sweatshirt—the worn-out orange one with a faded Nike emblem blazoned across the chest. Despite the sweatshirt, Sid still shivered under the growing coldness. After more scanning and shivering, he figured the old man had already left. Taking one last look around to make sure no one watched, Sid grabbed a flashlight, which he also dug from the backpack, and scrambled into the tight hole.

Beyond the throat, loose rocks were everywhere—above, below, and all surrounding. He became acutely aware that if the loose rock he stood upon gave way, he would be in a world of hurt. The whole setting gave the impression of an imminent implosion. Sid continued into the loose rock zone, but with the same careful speed that a tree sends down roots. The throat proved smaller and tighter than it looked. He wondered if it had shrunk.

Root-like, Sid lowered his feet and hips through the opening. With light taps of his feet, he eventually found a secure foothold. With this, he lowered the rest of his body through the entrance. Sid found himself suddenly immersed in the cave's darkened danger zone. The old man hadn't gone this far into the cave, Sid concluded. Just then, Sid's shoulders became stuck in a tight constriction lined with sharp crystals. Although the Velcro-like crystals were tiny, they held Sid tight to the cave wall. A less-than-light tug did nothing to unfreeze the grip. A more forceful effort sent loose a cascade of unstable rocks—one that fell on his head and drew blood. More rocks rattled into unknown depths just as his shoulders scraped past.

Once free of the trap, Sid stopped to consider his options. The flashlight's glare off smooth white walls temporarily blinded him and made it challenging to see the passage ahead. The urge to continue surged strong in his veins. Some force wanted, compelled, Sid to probe deeper. He obeyed. He inched his way forward. After another ten feet, he suddenly stopped cold.

Like the comings of a mountain storm, an unknown and previously unexperienced wave swept over Sid. Instantly, the cave walls narrowed, and deadly loose slabs appeared out of thin air. As Sid's nape hairs stood in rigid concentration, he suddenly realized his compromising position. Poised loose slabs risked entrapment above, below, and to the sides. Dreaded fear welled within him that if he moved in any direction, even slightly, a collapse would instantly bury him. Panic had suddenly taken control over all senses. "No one even knows I'm here," he muttered as visions of dying on the edge of Medicine Mountain swept over him as he grew faint.

Determined not to have the cave serve as his sarcophagus, Sid focused his remaining energy on one final lunge—toward the cave entrance and out of his burial chamber. It worked—he cleared the obstruction. He was nearly back at the entrance when, again, he stopped cold. Someone, or something, had grabbed his foot. He frantically pulled to set it free, but nothing broke the hold. He was stuck.

Sid tried to logically think his way out of his predicament. *It didn't feel like a loose slab had wedged against my boot,* he thought. Instead, it had the feel and sensation of skin, muscle, and tissue—he kicked and lashed out upon the thought, but the something held tight. It didn't feel human. His kicking did nothing to loosen its grip. With his flagging logical reasoning, Sid regained temporary control over his burgeoning senses. As the sensation of muscle against muscle, flesh against flesh, grew in intensity and overwhelmed his futile logical reasoning, Sid's yanks become desperate and frantic. In one of his many frenzied pulls, Sid accomplished nothing other than ripping his orange sweatshirt and putting a gash across his forehead. Redness moistened the cave walls—still, he remained stuck in the thing's grip. The will to survive is strong in most people, so just as Sid readied himself for his next big yank, suddenly, the grip on his boot vanished.

Sid needed no further motivation or logical pondering. He forged ahead as fast as his failing energy and worn body could endure. As he slid past the tight chamber, a nubbin caught his torn sweatshirt and its tattered remnants fell deeper into the frightening cave. Ignoring the sweatshirt, Sid lunged for the entrance and the star-filled safety of the world above. Glistening with sweat and gasping for breath, Sid collapsed on the ground next to a small cairn. A faint smell of sage and tobacco filled Sid's lungs as he lay motionless on the escarpment edge—where he wondered what had just happened.

After his breathing and heart rate returned to normal, he looked up and found himself staring at the same five pillars that he had seen earlier, but this time, filtering through the starlight, they stared back.

"What just happened?" he asked the five watchers. "Was it only fear and panic?" He continued his ruminations and communications with the five onlookers as the evaporating sweat returned a chill to his bones. Rationally, he thought it had to have been only a loose rock that pinched his boot. However, he had a distinct memory of hearing a voice—an inhuman voice.

Such thoughts demanded him to ruminate on things he had never previously taken seriously. After a few moments, he forced his mind back on a logical track. He began ticking off the pros and cons of each potential explanation.

One of the wildest thoughts he considered was the legend of little people he read about years ago. Sid remembered that the Apsáalooke's little people stories went further back than legend or memory. Modern-day Apsáalooke, at least the ones still following traditional beliefs, still routinely make ceremonial offerings to little people. The gifts serve multiple purposes, ranging from a sign of respect, to payment for consultation services, to pay-offs so they wouldn't spread their evil ways any further. The hand that grabbed his boot felt like it had evil intent.

Little did Sid know that in the mid-1930s, less than two hundred miles from there, miners found in a cave what looked like a mummified infant not much more than one foot tall. That mummy sat on display for several years before a curious visitor sent it to the lab for analysis. The tests came back that it was a mature adult in the later years of his life. The freakish specimen became known as the Pedro Mountain Man. The Crow were not surprised. They knew what the find represented. They were also not surprised when people began finding more fully grown infant bodies in other nearby caves—some not far from Sid's ordeal.

Realizing that his panic attack and wild speculations weren't getting him anywhere, least of all out of the cold, Sid packed up and headed down the trail. Since he had lost his flashlight in the cave, Sid descended to his SUV using only starlight to point and guide his way.

As Sid continued walking back, he noticed fluttering shadows in the starlight. Migrating painted lady butterflies filled the sky. He long heard of such high-altitude mass butterfly migrations. Witnessing such a magical experience prompted Sid's mind to again wander to distant shores. To endure and sustain global migrations, butterflies must have a clearly defined destination and purpose encoded deep within their DNA, he thought. "Maybe there's a clear purpose and meaning for my life too," he mused. "Maybe the world contains mysteries even more magical than globetrotting butterflies—maybe, Medicine Wheel Mountain spoke to me."

Sid wondered where he fit into the Earth's connections. On that star-filled walk off Medicine Mountain, Sid realized that he would search for these answers down in the red-rocked canyon country—by talking with the Navajo elders. Within a couple of days, Sid Emerson turned his Jeep Cherokee south for the next phase of his life.

CHAPTER 10

There's a stillness and weight to Mojave Desert summer air at the cusp between night and pre-dawn. It is the stillness that makes the radio's cackling even more dramatic. With an instinctual perfection that comes from groggy practice, Sheriff John Smithers blindly reached for the mic sitting on the nightstand next to his old video game console and last night's beer cans, which were emptied just hours earlier.

The southeastern California interagency dispatcher's alertness contrasted sharply with John's condition, prompting a grunt. The dispatcher matter-of-factly alerted John to a reported airplane crash. The Cessna likely went down unnoticed weeks ago, but hikers had just found it and begun rummaging through the debris. *The hikers were probably looking for cash or drugs*, John thought as he fell out of bed. *I will never understand people's fascination with seeing burned and mangled bodies*, John grimaced. *I've seen enough to last a lifetime.*

As John rummaged through his fridge to see what food he could snatch, he silently spoke to his cold and ever-dependable icebox. *What were they doing in the Owlshead Mountains?* This wasn't as much of a question, and certainly not for his fridge. Anyone who had been with John as long as his Frigidaire had would have also known that he wasn't referring to the airplane. Based on experience, the plane probably carried narcotics—one of the many secret flights to meet drug dealers on the Owl Lake playa. To John, unregistered middle-of-the-night airplane traffic around Owl Lake required little investigation or inquiry. He had experience with middle-of-the-night, call-to-duty annoying dispatchers and early-hour refrigerator raids. The only odd part: *What were hikers doing in the Owlshead Mountains?*

The dispatch office only had vague location details. She said only the Owlshead Mountains. While dressing, he thought if everything goes right, the crash will be out of his jurisdiction, over on the San Bernardino County side of the mountains. *Why does everything need to happen in my county?* he said to himself while strapping on the Motorola. With a sigh, he relented to the inevitable. Besides, even if on the San Bernardino side, John knew it made more sense for his office to respond.

John requested from dispatch to have two deputies from the Tecopa office respond to the southern Owlsheads by driving along the wash-boarded road skirting Fort Irwin and Death Valley National Park. John told dispatch he planned to have Ed fly him from Shoshone and then make concentric circles attempting to spot the wreckage from the air. As he left for the airstrip, he muttered to himself, "Fools will get themselves killed looking for death and looking for treasure."

John liked flying with Ed—no chatter. He only talked when needed. *I'm not in the mood for chatting.* Despite the brightness of the mid-morning sun beaming into the airplane's vibrating plexiglass, John still hadn't fully woken. Ed and the Cessna's arcing over the Ibex Hills suddenly woke him from his thoughts of yesterday's troubles and the hard night he tried hard to shake. The dark and denuded manganese-rich rocks around the old New Deal mine brought back even darker memories. Despite not being active for years, the mine looked freshly visited and worked. However, mines on the San Bernardino side of the line concerned him not the least. He also had little concern for plane crashes, drugs, or foolish people who made his job even harder. He was now fully awake.

From the New Deal Mine, Ed's sharp banking removed the last shred of John's sleepiness. By then, they headed straight toward Owl Lake. John knew most activity in the Owlsheads centered on Owl

Lake's playa. This large, smooth, and remote dry lakebed offered a perfect landing site for midnight drug smuggling and large-volume exchanges. Most unidentified plane crashes in the area are low-flying planes attempting a drug run. It didn't take much for a low-flying plane in the depths of the night and the depths of the Owlsheads to experience a down-draft that plunges them into rocks, spewing cash, drugs, and body parts across slopes and ravines. As soon as planes go down, drug owners, troublemakers, and treasure seekers begin combing the ridges looking for whatever they can snatch before wind or wildlife scatters them for good. John has never liked the Owlsheads.

After circling for an hour, Ed called John over the headphones. He spotted a body. Dark clothing and tattered remains on the playa's shimmering whiteness were hard to miss. John not so silently cursed, "The body *is* in my county." John liked nice and neat bows with no complications, and this corpse presented no neat bow. He ordered Ed to circle the body as John radioed central dispatch.

Before he ordered ground crews to respond, John needed to figure out a couple of details—so that they might conduct a proper investigation. *Where did this guy come from? Where was he going? Where is his rig? Where is the reported crashed plane?*

Despite no trees, John knew this seemingly barren landscape held many secrets. Despite John's county being nearly the size of the state of Hawaii, the land's rugged emptiness wouldn't reveal its stories without a struggle. He knew the millions of draws, washes, banks, arroyos, scarps, entrenchments, boulders, and crags held more than mere mysteries and sunbaked rocks—they also held crazies, troublemakers, and complications.

As John, Ed, and the plane made increasingly wider arcs, circles, and figure-eights in search of cars, clues, and crashes, John began getting sleepy again. His drowsy mind wandered to his first plane crash investigation, not far from nearby Windgate Pass. That plane also smuggled drugs, but to the Lost Lake playa. Low-lying planes needed to fly especially low in this region to avoid alerting Fort Irwin or the China Lake Naval Weapons Center. The military doesn't take kindly to unregistered planes flying into restricted airspace. To both clear the mountains *and* avoid military detection required planes to fly low and close to Windgate Pass. Sometimes, too close.

The isolated travel corridor into Death Valley, through Wingate Wash and Windgate Pass, had been the route used by the famous Twenty Mule Teams used to take hauling borax out of Death Valley and into waiting southern California markets. Muleskinners named Windgate Pass after the erratic winds that commonly howl through its narrow constriction. While mule teams may have found the route convenient, low-lying aircraft do not. An erratic wind gust in this namesake pass sent *that* Cessna down.

John's mind remained on reminiscing on his first airplane crash investigation. Even though that Cessna flew at low speeds and the pilot was likely aware of the dangers, the pilot likely thought the plane had cleared the pass, since strewn fragments of the plane, pilot, and passengers littered the balding crags immediately below the divide. At the time, rookie John had the unenviable task of bagging and carrying body parts.

Just like at the Windgate Pass crash, there doesn't appear to be any signs of drugs or money, John thought as he contemplated his new Owl Lake mystery. *Maybe pilferers already picked the site clean*, John pondered. *It seems as if they always arrive at crashes before my deputies. How do they always get there so fast?* John must have asked this question out loud because Ed shouted back to John that he didn't hear the question.

"Never mind," John shouted back to Ed, as the plane banked once again.

On John's first crash investigation, a business long believed to be a shell company for a drug cartel owned the plane that went down. John had insufficient evidence to make any arrests. Back in those days, it bothered cadet Smithers that drug smugglers often got away and eluded arrest or conviction. However, John cared more about such things in those days. If he was being honest, John could not truthfully say that he no longer cared; he just didn't care for complications. Too many years, shady characters, unexplained things, and too much craziness had dulled his senses and ability to care. *Caring takes time and money*, he often rationalized. *Caring creates stress and caring causes complications. I don't have the time or money to deal with all that goes on in my county*, he kept telling himself.

Ed's voice in the headphones jarred John from his reminiscing. He had found the wreckage. While John daydreamed, Ed had done all the work. John said to himself, *I like flying with Ed*. John only needed to transfer Ed's information to dispatch. He realized the plane had crashed in San Bernardino County. *It won't be my investigation after all*. Likely, his office would only assist.

About the same time that John, his deputies, Fort Irwin, China Lakes, the San Bernardino County's sheriff's office, and the Federal Aviation Administration began coordinating their investigation of the Owl Lake body and the plane crash, Paddy roamed the high country only a few miles away. Based on a tip, Paddy searched the rugged terrain north of Windgate Pass, not far from Barker Ranch— the place where John Smithers' predecessor found and arrested the craziest of crazies, Charles Manson.

John needed no introduction or reminder of Charles Manson. Despite the number of years since his arrest, it seemed not a week went by without some aspect of the Manson drama rearing its ugly head and forcing John to retell the story to the public, the press, or folks too young to remember. Charles Manson and his devoted crazies remained one of John Smithers' most complicated headaches—the kind that never, never went away.

The sheriff always felt that most of his troubles stemmed from Charles Manson, even though it had been decades since the Tate and LaBianca murders and Manson's arrest at Barker Ranch. John often mumbled to himself, *Why couldn't Manson have squatted on a ranch in San Bernardino County?* The fact that he hadn't forced the sheriff to tell and retell Manson's story many times over, since from that point forward, the psychopath and the Panamints became intertwined.

Charles Manson, once described by a psychologist as aggressively antisocial, formed a commune-cult and a group of nut-case cult followers. He convinced himself that the world would descend into a race war, and this would in turn be the beginning of the rapture. Manson talked his followers into murdering several people in Los Angeles.

To lay low after the grisly murders, Manson and his cult hid in the Myers and Barker ranches, deep in the southern Panamints, not far from Windgate Pass. The ranch owners hadn't been there in years. The Panamints have always been a good place for strange people to drop off the face of the earth. *Just like Sid Emerson*, the sheriff said to himself.

John needed a distraction to get the Manson story out of his head, for it had become like an earworm, an annoying song that you can never shake. The media's attention on Manson's arrest brought notoriety to both Barker Ranch and the Panamint Range. This sealed their reputation for being *the* place for the wanted and unwanted to hide and escape. This also led John Smithers to have to constantly deal with a long string of modern-day Manson followers, those escaping the law, and the many crazies attempting to escape their own self-imposed insanity. The way John figured it, other like-minded crazies were the only thing that anyone found when they escape into the Panamints.

The Barker Ranch drew so many crazies that Sheriff Smithers often wondered why a business didn't set up a commercial tour—it would be the perfect commercial vortex, where crazy, unexplained things happened all the time. *It would make a fortune.* John shivered with the thought. *That's all I need*, John sputtered while looking out the window during Ed's return flight.

Despite being decades since Manson's arrest, every few weeks, unknown and unseen crazies still placed new Manson decorations, memorials, and offerings at the Barker Ranch. John had no explanation why so many people honored Manson and kept his mythical image alive. John never discovered how the Manson followers came and went without being seen. Far fewer offerings occurred after 2009 when a fire destroyed Barker Ranch. *I'm sure the Barker Ranch owners are glad to finally rid themselves of the grisly memories that haunted the place.* Burning the ranch slowed the nutcase offerings, but they didn't stop. Hardly a week went by without some new Manson tribute suddenly appearing on the charred remains of the infamous ranch.

To add to the sheriff's headaches, Manson tributes and celebrations extended well beyond the Barker Ranch ruins. Just a few weeks earlier, Mandi Mitchem and "No-name Maddox" staged a sit-in and demonstration in Ridgecrest. They hoped to spread their hate and sign up new recruits to further Manson's demented cause. Fortunately, for John, they held that demonstration in San Bernardino County. However, Mandi and No-name had held similar demonstrations in *his* county in the past. They were slowly building new recruits and followers. The way John saw it, this became further sign of their troubled times.

As soon as John snapped out of his deep thoughts, the Cessna's wheels touched ground on Shoshone's airstrip. There were so many reasons that John liked Ed—he took care of everything. He silently muttered, *I wish Ed could take care of the Manson crazies and my Owl Lake investigation.*

CHAPTER 11

Some stories are lost to time and memory, relegated to the mysterious depths of the cosmic ether. Others are as bold and vivid as today's lunch still dripping from the chin. Rare it is to be both. Such was the case with the initial outing of the Los Angeles Lizard People. The currents that led poor George Shufelt to his unfortunate fate began a long, long, long time ago, but his immersion began during the heights of the Great Depression. From that point on, he began his slow drift down the river of no return.

George Warren Shufelt had the misfortune of birth into the Lost Generation—people like Jake Barnes, Harvey Stone, and many of the other male characters in Hemingway's *The Sun Also Rises* who faced both the senselessness of World War I *and* its aftermath. The scale and horrors of the "War to End All Wars" were unlike all others. Humans seemed incapable of such atrocities. To George and the rest of the lost, all they knew and all they believed in before the war had suddenly seemed hollow or trivial. It shook core principles, faith, and value systems. Ten years after these traumatic events, society nearly crumbled in the depths of the Great Depression. Widespread disillusionment and societal fracturing, and all they once held dear, became too much for any one generation to shoulder or endure. The generation lost millions of lives during the senseless war and many of those that survived lost hope of a brighter future.

Those who came home lost purpose and direction. J.R.R. Tolkien once famously said, in his book *Fellowship of the Ring*, "Not all those who wander are lost." But for the Lost Generation, many that wandered were indeed lost. This may have been the case for

George Shufelt since throughout his life he too wandered in search of a purpose. He felt he had a destiny to fulfill—he just didn't know how far or deep the quest and hauntings would take him. Little did he know, mysterious forces called him into realms far beyond his Midwest upbringing.

Like many of the Lost Generation, George Shufelt wandered the country in body and wandered the universe in mind. First, he loitered in old Texas, then he drifted into the promising new lands and opportunities of a young and maturing Los Angeles. After all, Los Angeles shone as the city of hope—the City of Angels.

Like many of the Great Depression's lost and unemployed, George took to the hills in search of gold, silver, and glittery riches. Like Bud Torgerson generations later, George Shufelt had faith that there *had* to be a better life. Perhaps striking it rich would help him find it? However, like all others poring over the San Gabriels, he found only more hopelessness, sorrow, and a weakening back.

Oftentimes, inspiration springs from desperation. During one fruitful moment, it occurred to him that if his age and bad back prevented him from prospecting, he would find his Shangri-La in a less physical manner. His new quest gave birth to hope once again. Determined to make a mark on society and a name for himself, George began building a gold-finding machine. However, this quest demanded a prerequisite invention and a compelling and markable background complete with credentials. A simple wandering high school graduate would never do. Therefore, without any additional schooling or training, he instantaneously became an "engineer." He worked hard to mold the image of a man of science, education, and intellect. While an engineer title opened doors, it would take a treasure-finding invention to seal his fate and reputation.

After developing a compelling pedigree and grandiose vision, George found the invention of a gold-finding machine more elusive. Undaunted, over time and through perseverance, he came up with a prototype. To further shore up his reputation, George billed his new treasure-finding machine as the epitome of science. George Shufelt became a master of blurring the distinction between science, faith, and religious zealotry.

Whenever any person even casually wandered into George's eyesight, he struck up a conversation. Before long, he showed his wandering guest every intricacy of his invention. "Hear those clicks?" he often shouted as his machine beeped, gurgled, and hissed. "That there is the sound of a deep labyrinth of tunnels lying under *your* city," he beamed to all gatherings, regardless of the crowd size or its participants' level of interest.

Typically, such demonstrations elicited a few questions, such as "How do you know those beeping sounds are tunnels, and not just a bunch of beeps?"

"I'm glad you asked," George would say as he ratcheted up both his volume and speed. "See, if I move the machine a few feet over here," he would say, as the whole crowd shuffled along with him and leaned in to hear more beeps. "See, no beeps and no tunnel signals over here, but there were over there," as he pointed to his previous machine location. "I calibrated the machine to neutral, meaning no beeps, while on solid ground. Since my machine is not beeping here, it means it's normal solid ground—here. But over there," again, pointing to the earlier machine location, "the ground is less solid. So, I ask you, why would the ground be less solid over there and not over here?"

"Tunnels?" someone from the crowd would interject.

"Exactly! Tunnels. My machine detects underground tunnels. Isn't she a beauty?"

Usually, after such public spectacles, the crowd's interest perked up as they moved in closer for a detailed look at George's special machine—and "history in the making."

George's invention consisted of an elaborate tripod-mounted box holding a metal wire suspended in a glass tube. Think of a vertical divining rod. Think of a dangling single wire. With this contraption,

George claimed he could detect and map gold, silver, and other precious minerals.

For the lost, good stories are more convincing than data. Who needs proof when you can have George? Since George had keen marketing and promotional skills, his machine and boasts caught the public's attention. Fortunately for George, he lived in an era of high public interest in science and technological ingenuity. It was also an era of scientific naivety. Few worldly things could attract more attention during the height of the Great Depression than a mysterious guru, and leading science authority, claiming he invented a machine that could easily find gold.

George's antics attracted the attention of attorney Rex Irving McCreedy. At the time, he actively looked to invest in the next great thing—not unlike the investors in the Leadville mining hoax three generations earlier in Death Valley. Rex and George began a collaboration to take the gold-finding machine to the next level. To add to George Shufelt's colorful quest, Ray Martinez stepped out of the shadows to claim he owned an old map showing the Spanish had buried gold somewhere on Los Angeles' Fort Moore Hill. To locate the specific site, Ray needed help. For the next few years, George, Rex, and Ray formed a unique and colorful partnership. The three of them, armed with faith in Ray's map and George's machine, determined to find buried Spanish gold.

The three entrepreneurs convinced the Los Angeles Board of Supervisors to grant them a digging permit. George gave a compelling argument. The county granted them a permit but limited the depth of excavations to fifty feet. Armed with a pick, shovels, a treasure map, and George's wonder machine, they began digging.

Word quickly spread of George's magic machine and their gold diggings. Crowds gathered and anxiously watched the spectacle—free entertainment in the heights of the Great Depression. Undeterred after each failed hole, George recalibrated his machine and dug elsewhere. Soon, the grounds became pockmarked with failed attempts. After too many new attempts, new holes, and new recalibrations, the public quickly lost interest and the novelty wore off. George, Rex, and Ray also ran out of time—their permit expired.

About this time, they chanced upon stories promoted by a well-known psychic. The psychic claimed to be a Hopi chief who went by the name Little Chief Greenleaf, told her a story of an alien race of reptilians living in catacombs deep under Los Angeles. According to the legend, the lost city was one of three such dwellings built by a race of shapeshifting Lizard People. Lizard People had been apparently living undetected under what is now Los Angeles for five millennia. The psychic told George Shufelt that Lizard People, being shapeshifters, could take many forms, including human.

George took the psychic's warnings to heart. Fear welled up in George that alien Lizard People might be masquerading as humans and living as his next-door neighbors. George overcame fear by combining it with the much stronger force of greed and an equal measure of marketing acumen. George hurried home to fine-tune and recalibrate his remote sensing equipment. Hope once again rekindled, this became the missing piece that connected all the dots that George so desperately wanted connected.

Many philosophers claim humans desire order out of chaos. This may be the reason some people see patterns and order out of a series of random dots on a map. Faithful believers may see some dots form along a line. Far fewer people may begin to envision these imaginary lines holding special meaning. In the case of Ray's map, the dots not only had no meaning, but they also didn't connect, and they didn't point to Spanish gold.

Undeterred, and unwavering in faith, George came to his ultimate solution—it made perfect sense. In George's mind, the gold-filled catacombs that his machine discovered did not come from the Spanish; they came from alien Lizard People. Hope's light burned even brighter—he hadn't found the gold yet because Lizard People dig deep tunnels. He had only been looking at the Spanish

Conquistador depth, George convinced himself.

Who knows what goes on in the depths and catacombs of a person's mind? He or she may not even know themselves. Was it a fundamental need that compelled George to connect dots in ways that formed patterns while other people saw only random noise? He had such unwavering faith in his invention that he desperately grasped at any explanation that kept his dream and hope alive. Therefore, the existence of a secret society of alien shapeshifting reptiles that were hoarding gold under the city became a more rational explanation that the consideration that his precious machine didn't work.

Almost instantly, George's lines between dots stood out in vivid detail. Determined to find this mysterious hideout and the buried gold he *knew* had to be there, he returned to the county commissioners to renew his digging permit. He laid it all out: the alien Lizard People legend, their hidden gold, and his renewed faith that his machine would unlock the mystery. He expected many questions but received only a few.

"Why should we grant you a new digging permit when the last time you came up empty-handed?" One commissioner asked.

"Because, I have new and better information this time," George beamed. "Everything is aligned and collaborated, ranging from a world-famous psychic, an elder Hopi chief, Navajo legends passed from one generation to the next, and an ancient treasure map—"

The commissioner interrupted by saying, "Indian legends, treasure maps, and psychics are all well and good enough, Mr. Shufield, but where is the science?"

"I'm glad you asked that," George answered in a pitch that became especially piercing. "I was just going to add that all the pieces of collaborating evidence that I just presented perfectly align with my impeccable calculations and scientific workings of my science-based machine. You see," George said with a booming crescendo that everyone hung onto until George unleashed his culminating release, "in our time, and within this age of reason and scientific enlightenment, you can't doubt science, and my machine is pure science—at its best."

"You said your machine is based on science?" the commissioner responded.

"Yes, it is pure science," George affirmed.

With that assurance, the commissioners issued George a new digging permit. The permit authorized him to dig under Los Angeles to depths up to one thousand feet.

It's hard to image commissioners of any major city today granting permission for a fake scientist to dig a thousand-foot-deep pit in a dense urban center to search for gold-hoarding alien Lizard People, based on a copper-wire-dangling machine, psychic predictions, and the visions of a paranormal mystic claiming to be an Indian chief that no one had ever heard of before. Apparently, the commissioners wanted to believe too. Perhaps they had other things on their mind and didn't care one way or the other. Regardless, they granted the permit on one condition: If George finds any treasure, the county gets a one-half cut.

With fresh permit in hand, and a renewed public interest, George and crew began their new pit. This time, he deployed mechanized equipment. No longer limited to picks and shovels, George drilled a 250-foot-deep shaft along North Hill Street, in the middle of Los Angeles, not far from the present-day Ramón C. Cortines School of Visual and Performing Arts and not far from where Charles Manson's faithful followers committed their infamous murders. To some, there are some lines that are too obvious to ignore.

Determined to expose the Lizard People and their sinister plots, but more importantly, prove to the world his invention worked, George toiled and toiled away. He busied himself to an even higher degree. Even more than before, he whipped people up, but this time, the frenzy just as quickly vanished. Soon people went back to their everyday lives and practical concerns. Adulations and hero-worshiping soon turned to public taunts and ridicule. Media attention ended abruptly—as had George's funding. The drilling rig fell silent. George had plumbed the depth of his once glorious hope. He eventually faded from the public's eye having never exposed the Lizard People or becoming rich by stealing their golden treasures. George Warren Shufelt suffered a lonely death in 1957.

Later, in the university library in Flagstaff, Sid Emerson pored through Navajo and Hopi archives and other original sources for collaborating reports of the identity of Little Chief Greenleaf. There were none. There never had been a Little Chief Greenleaf—in either the Hopi villages or the Navajo Reservation. *Is this all just an elaborate hoax?* he asked himself. Had this become just another Leadville?"

As Sid well knew, a hoax can live longer than the truth. Sid also uncovered that the quest for the lost city, its treasures, and the shapeshifting Lizard People did not die with Shufelt—it was too compelling of a Western legend. Years after Shufelt passed away, rumors circulated throughout southern California that miners had found a deep tunnel that connected with an underground expanse hidden below the Panamint Range near Death Valley. Area residents speculated that this had to be Shufelt's lost city. Sid determined to check out the Panamints, but first, he needed to follow up leads from the Navajo's redrock country.

Chapter 12

During Sid's drive to the Navajo Reservation, he pondered the George Shufelt story and its connection with mystery spots, ley lines, medicine wheels, and Lizard People. About a year before his niece, Katherine, would begin her search for him in the Panamint Range, Sid began his search for alien Lizard People legends within the Navajo Nation.

Sid would have loved to interview George since he had always been fascinated with the hopelessly lost, and few were as lost as George. However, George died when Sid was only six years old. However, Sid hoped to interview a Navajo or Pueblo elder who had at least met George Shufelt. Sid also wanted to meet a Navajo elder willing to tell him original stories of when their ancestors passed through the Northern Great Plains and first encountered medicine wheels. Someone on the Navajo Reservation had to know this story as it passed down from generation to generation, Sid convinced himself.

Sid wandered around the reservation and took up residence in Toadlena, Teec Nos Pos, Staale, and wherever else his whims took him. Despite his efforts, all leads turned out to be dead ends. Sid found no George Shufelt memories, medicine wheel stories, or Lizard People evidence.

While lonely Navajo outposts led him no closer to his goals, living off the grid grew on him. He began dreaming of an alternative life, one immersed in ancient customs and deep spirituality. For Sid, a crass commercialism and pampered life increasingly appeared hollow, shallow, and artificial. During his reservation wanderings,

Sid reflected upon life, happiness, and the truly important. For Sid, life in the Navajo hamlets seemed less lonely than being surrounded by thousands of city strangers. Sid had found that life in crowds became a never-ending attempt to avoid contact—at least deep contact. Within city enclaves, walls surrounded houses, fences closed in yards, and there were even barriers between seats in public places. With so many people, to maintain privacy, sanity, and awkward encounters, Sid had become accustomed to moving around others and their own personal spaces, or ignoring their presence—but most of all, avoiding any contact at all. Sid found life in the reservation refreshing. He may not have been a shapeshifter, but he felt he had done his share of shapeshifting to accommodate crowds and people's expectations. With the Navajo, he had none of these concerns. He felt liberated. He felt free.

Navajo towns aren't really "towns;" they are small communities were everyone knows everyone. It would be hard to hide a Lizard People here without everyone knowing it. Therefore, on a whim, he left the Navajo reservation to check out the Hopi pueblos. Besides, Chief Little Green had been a Hopi. On his way, Sid stopped to get gas in Chinle.

While driving along Chinle's clay and greasewood-lined highway, Sid scanned the surroundings. Chinle gave Sid the impression of being an anachronism—too modern to evoke the Navajo culture or rich history, but its squalor gave no sense of hope for the future. While scanning the town, Sid saw only rutted half-measures leading one halfway to nowhere. Chinle would make an interesting research topic, Sid ruminated, an interesting sociological research project in of by itself, he thought as he pulled off the road at the first and only gas station.

While filling his Jeep with gas, Sid spotted a lone man sitting on a sandstone boulder next to the gas station's restrooms—whiling away his time by watching people that happened to cross his field of vision. At the present, Sid was the only person in his view, so the old man turned and called out, "You headed up to Canyon de Chelly, or only passing through?"

Before answering, Sid scanned the slight wisp of a man. He looked as if a stiff breeze could topple him and crush his wide-brimmed white cowboy hat. "No, I'm not here to sightsee or pass through. I'm here looking for answers, but now I'm heading to the Pueblos."

"Answers to what? Maybe I can help you. I used to be a Navajo guide."

"Maybe you *can* help. Do you have time to talk?"

"Do I look like I don't have time? Well, I don't have a lot of time, but that's because I'm old. I may drop dead any moment now, but until that happens, I have plenty of time. What do you want to know?"

"First of all, I am Sid. I am originally from Michigan, but I've spent the last couple of months within the Navajo Reservation."

"I'm Chauncey. Except for a little time away in college and a little time fighting in your war, I'm from here and I'll die here. This is my home."

"You said you fought in a war? I served in Vietnam."

"I fought in your World War II. I served as a Navajo code talker. Do you know about code talkers?"

"Sure, I've heard about them, but I never met one before. Nice to meet you, and thanks for your service."

"So, you have questions? Chauncey asked while Sid just stood and stared.

The thought he was talking to an actual Navajo code talker caused Sid to not notice the gas pump had long since shut off. As Sid paid for the gas, a change of plans popped into his head. The Hopi and the pueblos can wait, Sid decided. "May I pull up a spot on your boulder?" he said to his newfound friend, a real-life code talker.

"Sure," Chauncey said. "There's plenty of space."

Sid sat down on the sandstone slab's far edge and began a long series of questions. The two of them talked about everything under the sun—and beyond.

Sid's stomach grumbling alerted him that the two of them had been talking for two hours. For two hours Sid had become a kid again. Chauncey had experienced so many things that Sid didn't know where to start—or end. In a short two hours, Sid learned that after serving as a code talker during the war, Chauncey went to college to become an archeologist. Sid wanted to ask follow-up questions about Chauncey's archeological work under the Southwest's leading archeologists, but he forced himself to remain focused. Instead, Sid probed the elder Navajo on Chauncey's past, reservation life, and his general reflections on life. Only after he felt they had developed enough of a rapport did Sid ask about Lizard People.

"Do you want to meet one?" Chauncey interrupted.

"Who?" Sid asked.

"A Lizard People," Chauncey said with a slight hint of a grin.

Hesitantly, Sid answered, "Sure, I guess."

"You're sitting on one right now," Chauncey said as he burst out in laughter. "They're shapeshifters, and this one took the form of a rock."

"Yeah, yeah," Sid said to Chauncey as his laughter showed no signs of stopping.

"No, I'm serious," Sid countered. "Do you know anything about the Navajo's Lizard People legend?"

As his laughter subsided, Chauncey squinted his eyes and pursed his lips, as if willing himself to get serious. When talking resumed, his words became slow and deliberate. "In my long life, I've seen many things that can't be explained, at least by me. I can't say I believe Lizard People exist but from other things that I've seen, I guess I can't dismiss them either."

"Thank you for answering me," Sid offered. "Do you know anyone that fully believes?"

"My people tend not to think too much of such things, or talk about them, to *bilagaána* like you, but I know an elder that may talk with you about such matters—if he's willing and in the right mood."

Toward the end of their gas station talk, Sid took up Chauncey's offer to introduce them.

Early the following morning found Sid helping Chauncey into his Cherokee at the same gas station. It didn't take Sid's Jeep long to leave the pavement and start up a rutted two-track through a thick pinyon forest surrounded by slickrock outcroppings. The red clay "Chinle mud" roadbed would be impassible if it were wet. Reservation rain turns clay roads snot-slick, but fortunately, on this day, the clay was brick-hard and dry. However, the hardened ruts made for a bouncy ride. They seemed to be making good time, but Sid had no idea where they were going. He had never been to this part of the reservation before. Eventually, Sid and Chauncey broke out of the pinyon-juniper forest and arrived at a hogan that had suddenly come into view.

Long before Sid's Cherokee rolled to a complete stop next to the hogan, three young Navajos walked out of a thick juniper clump to greet the suspicious strangers. With a twisted face, the eldest barked, "Who are you and why you're here?"

Chauncey spoke first. The animated conversation, all in Navajo, lasted two minutes. During their whole conversation, they both pointed and looked at Sid. All Sid could do was squirm in his seat, trying not to look out of place. Eventually, Chauncey called for Sid to introduce himself.

"*Yah-ta-hey*. My name is Sid Emerson. Chauncey said the Navajo elder living here may be able to answer my questions on ancient Navajo legends. I am a researcher. Would this be okay?"

"Why you here?" the young woman, not much more than a kid, asked.

In as few words as possible, Sid summarized his earlier conversation with Chauncey, all the while repeatedly glancing around. Chauncey remained still as if attempting to fade into the pinyon-juniper backdrop. It was clear to Sid that acceptance to speak with the still unseen tribal elder rested with him alone.

The woman whom Sid had been talking to so far served as her grandfather's initial screener.

"Is this a cruel trick Chauncey's playing on me"? Sid said to himself as he continued repeating his introductions to the Navajo teenager. Without a sign that they understood, Sid had no idea what to do other than repeat himself, only slower. As he began the third attempt, an old man, much older and frailer than Chauncey, stepped out of the hogan. As soon as he arrived, all other conversations and noise stopped cold. The youngsters looked at the old man, Sid looked at the old man, and the old man looked at Chauncey, who in turn stared at Sid. The silence was broken only by an old hound that came out and sniffed at Sid's feet. Just then, the old man stared at Sid and called out, "Come," as he shuffled his way back into the hogan.

The old man, Tsio Yazzie, motioned to Sid and Chauncey to sit. There weren't any chairs or floor mats, so Sid sat cross-legged against the hogan's wall on the far side facing the door. While Tsio fretted about, picking things off the floor in an obvious sign of nervousness and hesitation, Sid slowly scanned the hogan. For a person who had so many experiences as Tsio likely had, Sid wondered why there were so few things displayed to show his years.

On the wall closest to Sid's left were numerous scattered and disheveled boxes, chests, and trunks. One well-worn, drab, olive-green trunk looked old, and military issued. Sid silently wondered, *Is he a code talker too?* If so, Sid wondered if the chest contained artifacts from the war. Sid would have loved to interview both Chauncey and Tsio about their war history, but that too would have to wait until another day.

Continuing his scan, Sid noticed several old Navajo rugs along the walls. They were probably worth a lot of money, he thought. A few had fallen, crumpled on the floor among half-opened boxes. Letting such cultural treasures lay crumpled on the floor seemed to Sid unusual from what he knew of Navajos. Navajos usually treat such things with utmost respect.

Tsio stopped his pacing and sat down next to the door, as far away from Sid as he could sit without stepping outside. After a long and awkward pause, Tsio spoke in a soft and hesitant voice, "Chauncey says you want to know stories about the Lizard People. Why do you want to hear such foolishness?"

"I know some people believe, and others do not. I'm not here to judge, only to learn and listen. If you have old stories about the Lizard People, even legends you don't believe in yourself, I would love to hear them."

"The story of alien Lizard People is nothing other than a trick old people play on naïve youngsters," he said as Chauncey let out a snicker, remembering his shapeshifting rock joke he'd said earlier. "So, why do you want to hear kids' stories?" Tsio asked.

"I would love to hear any story that you may have heard—that's all. Even if they seem foolish."

Tsio must have warmed to Sid, because after more small talk he grinned and winked at Chauncey, as if Tsio had played his own practical joke on Sid. Sid knew that Navajos were famous for this type of humor. Whether Tsio was serious or not, Sid could do nothing but play along.

Tsio interrupted Sid's thoughts with a blunt question of his own. "How much is it worth to you?"

"Are you asking for money—money to talk?" exclaimed Sid.

"You want to know, don't you?" the old man said. "My time is valuable because I don't have much left. I'll tell you about the Lizard People, but it'll cost you a hundred bucks."

After Sid paid the old man, Tsio winked once more to Chauncey and then cautiously launched into a story. "Mind you, this is the only version that I can remember. This is all I can do." Tsio refused Sid's request to record the story. It may have been because traditional Navajos thought the separation of a person's body, voice, and soul could lead to bad things happening. Equally plausible, Sid thought, this could all be Tsio's idea of a joke. Regardless, Sid honored the request by only taking notes.

"One reason my people respect and pray to the sky is that it's full of Sky People. Sky People guide and show us the right way. We rarely talk about such things with *bilagaána*. For us, our relationship with the Sky and Star People is deeply personal."

Sid interrupted Tsio. "Sorry, and I apologize for my ignorance, but who again are Sky and Star People?" Sid asked for clarity.

Turning to face Chauncey, Tsio's conversation reverted to Navajo. After much concern and finger-pointing, eventually, Chauncey nodded to Tsio, which prompted him to continue his story, although he didn't answer Sid's question.

"The Great Star reminds me I had filled my earlier life with foolishness, just like you. I should've spent more time gaining wisdom, but fools don't listen. With old age comes happiness," Tsio said with a chuckle, "but then again, I'm old." Tsio trailed off in soft murmurs, as if remembering something amusing.

"Thousands of years ago, long before our current North Star found its way north, an alien race of Lizard People, known as Archons, came to Earth. They came from a distant planet orbiting the star we now call Thuban."

"Yes, I've heard of Thuban," Sid answered. "It's in the constellation Draco."

"Yes, Draco—the serpent," Tsio added. "There were several races of Archons." Sid listened with a straight face. "Most were taller than humans—if they stood on their hind feet. Although the reptilians could talk through a complex system of clicks, hisses, and guttural sounds, they mostly communicated by reading thoughts."

Just then, Chauncey laughed and asked Sid, "Are you really believing this stuff? You do know he's just playing with you."

"As I said, I'm only listening, but with all due respect, it's not that much more fanciful than Spider Woman dragging bad little girls and boys up Spider Rock and devouring them," Sid countered.

"Oh, that's just a tall tale we tell little kids to learn right from wrong and to respect their elders."

Tsio interjected, "Do you want to hear about Archons or Spider Woman—which is it?"

Chauncey shifted in his seat and bowed his head.

"Sorry. Please go on with the Archons," Sid said to Tsio.

Tsio continued as if there had been no interruption. "Due to the heat and radiation from nearby Thuban, they had a barren and uninhabitable planet surface. Because of the harsh conditions, Archons lived underground in caves. As their population increased, they ran out of livable cavern space, so the Archon culture broke up and drifted apart. Over time, they eventually became different races—"

"How many races were there?" Sid interrupted.

"Don't get ahead of yourself. You kids are all alike—no patience. I'll get to it in my own due time."

Just then, Chauncey jumped in, turning to Tsio, "I remember this part—may I?"

"Please go ahead," Tsio nodded.

With that assurance, Chauncey grinned and began telling his favorite part of the story. "Apparently, the different Archon races hated each other and held each other in deep suspicion, just like you *bilagáana* don't like us Navajo. The Archon races constantly fought, not by any divisive or all-out war, but a slow and incremental eruption of violence that plagued, hung on, and cursed people for generations—just like your people are doing to the Navajo."

Tsio nodded, but added, "Being shapeshifters made the Archons even more suspicious of each other."

Chauncey's snickering caused the story to pause, as both Tsio and Sid stared at him.

With a glare that hinted displeasure with being interrupted, Tsio continued. "Due to shapeshifting, Archons could no longer tell who were friends or who were enemies. Everyone became suspicious of each other, even within the same clan and family."

Sid frantically tried to both pay attention to what Tsio said *and* focus on his notetaking. Sid worried that he was not doing either justice, despite having already filled one small notebook. Sid reached into his backpack and pulled out a new notepad. Tsio continued, unmoved by Sid's degree of readiness.

"The surface of their home planet had become too harsh, so the Archons couldn't live there anymore, even in the deeper caves. Besides, the Archon races kept killing each other out of hate and suspicion. They all knew they needed a change, but no one wanted to be the first."

With a chuckle, Chauncey added, "Maybe when they were kids, they needed Spider Woman to keep them in line."

Ignoring the comment, Sid turned to Tsio. "Is that when they came to Earth?"

"Yes, but they didn't come all at once. They came in a series of waves, much like your ancestors that came across the Bering Land Bridge. Each wave and each race came separately and settled in different places around the world."

Tsio stopped to stretch his legs, get a drink of water, and let the dog in. Once sufficiently ready, he slowly sat back on the floor, crossed his frail legs, and prepared for the rest of the story. Chauncey hadn't said much, other than an occasional scoff at the naïve and foolish notions of *bilagaána*. However, he seemed to be enjoying Tsio's entertaining story.

In Tsio's soft but determined voice, he continued where he'd left off. "Since the Archons were familiar with caves, having lived in them for long periods back on their home planet, they moved into earthen caverns—caves just felt right."

"Did all the waves that came here live in caves?" Sid asked.

"No. Not all—only some. The ones that remained on the surface faced many challenges. Humans hated the Archons even more than the Archons hated humans—or hated the other Archon races. Humans, being more numerous, kept raiding Archon villages. Humans wiped out Archon communities and even entire races. Those that didn't flee underground resorted to shapeshifting to look like humans."

"Are any of the Archons with us today?" asked Sid. "Is this where the Navajo Skin-walker legend came from—from Archons?"

Defiantly, Chauncey spat out, "No. They're different. Skin-walkers are not Archon aliens."

Tsio softly countered, "Well, most Skin-walkers aren't Archons, but as the story goes, a few Skin-walkers were indeed remnants from the original Archon races—if you believe that or not is another matter."

As if trying to convince Sid on something he wasn't sure of himself, Tsio hesitantly said, "A few elders knowledgeable about the old ways say they can tell the difference between a real human and a Lizard Person shifted into human form."

Sid's pencil paused with Tsio's abrupt sudden stop. After a long silence, Tsio turned to Sid and said, "Well, that's the story of the Archons, at least the part that I can remember or care to share."

Chauncey chuckled and thanked Tsio for the afternoon entertainment. Turning to Sid, he said, "This had been so much better than more sandstone slab sitting at the gas station. Thank you."

The conversation between Tsio, Chauncey, and Sid shifted into small talk. Sensing the interview was over, Sid put down his notepad and pencil and thanked Tsio for his storytelling and the intrusion into his day. Chauncey and Tsio shared a few words in Navajo, and before long, Sid sped down the two-track through the thick pinyon-juniper forests on his way to drop Chauncey back at the Chinle gas station.

To Sid, the Lizard People legend was a dream come true—a worthy topic of research. Once again, he packed his few belongings and left his welcoming home with the Navajo, pointed his rig west toward Death Valley and the Panamint Range—and never looked back.

CHAPTER 13

Like most Panamint miners, Stade and Bud's father knew only of hard work and broken dreams. Mining never entered Stade's heart or thoughts, but since it became the family's obsession, he relented to the fact that mining would be his sad destiny as well. Above all else, he wanted two things: *not* turning into his father and to escape the crushing poverty and lonely desperation of a life as a hardrock miner. On the first chance he had, Stade enlisted in the Vietnam War and turned his back on the Panamints and the future he clearly saw waiting for him if he stayed. After the war, Stade moved east and enrolled in college and law school. He never became rich, but more importantly, he never became a Panamint hardrock miner. He lived comfortably in his world apart.

Stade had escaped their father's contagion, but his younger brother wasn't as lucky. Bud's infection set in while Stade served in Vietnam; there wasn't anything Stade could do about Bud's condition, even if he had known. As such, increasingly, their father shared more and more with young Bud, most notably, toiling in hopeless mines and keeping alive hopeless dreams. Bud and his father also shared a complex relationship, although they were never close. When he thought about it, Bud never liked his father all that much, and Bud never knew if the feeling was mutual. However, the contagion didn't care; it still transmitted, willingly or not. Some claim it may have been genetic. Other things they shared included broken backs, broken wallets, broken relationships, and an unwavering faith that they would someday hit the mother lode—someday.

Their father died during Stade's last year in Vietnam. No one knew for sure what ailment caught up with him, whether it was cyanide, lead, mercury, asbestosis, or just a broken body. No one that has spent any time around hardrock mining thought of looking any deeper for a contributing cause. They all understood. But not Bud. He knew differently. He blamed his brother for their father's premature death. Bud convinced himself that their father would not have had such a hard life if only Stade stayed put and helped in the mines, rather than running off to Vietnam like a spoiled brat. There was only so much mine work that one or two people can do. Their father tried the best he could to shoulder the load single-handedly.

Bud never forgave Stade. Stade and Bud had the same argument, over and over, so Stade chose never to return. Not even for a visit. This made Bud even madder. Stade never met his nephew, Billy. Never met his sister-in-law, Bonnie. It was as if Bud and Stade were no longer brothers.

Therefore, Stade surprised everyone by offering to take in Bonnie and Billy after Bud died. Bonnie graciously accepted. She also appreciated that Stade lived in Pennsylvania, far removed from the Panamints and painful memories. Stade even paid for Bonnie and Billy's plane tickets and to move their stuff from Los Angeles to Philadelphia.

Bonnie felt a little guilty for enjoying her new life in such a spacious home. She enjoyed it more than she thought she had the proper right to—considering her lot in life. Every day she thanked Stade for rescuing Billy from the life of a miner. *Billy can grow up in peace, comfort, and stability*, she thought and prayed every night.

Poor Bud Torgerson never found *his* peace, and the deputies never found his body. Later, when the miners who found Bud's body came back with the deputies, they became lost and confused. Eventually, they stumbled upon the right spot; however, they found only a few personal items and Bud's rodent-gnawed wallet—there was no longer any body to recover. The deputies figured coyotes had scattered his bones.

Bonnie grieved that even in death, her poor Bud couldn't escape Panamint mines. "He will never know peace," she sobbed. She thanked Stade again for rescuing Billy from such a fate.

Bonnie settled into her new Philadelphia life faster than she'd expected. She especially liked normal dinnertime conversations. Stade, Bonnie, and Billy talked. Bud never talked—he was never around. The times he dropped in, Bud spoke few words, and only about mines, striking it rich someday, and other half-baked schemes to pay the mortgage and buy food. She left that lonely turmoil behind.

As time went on, Bonnie blocked out any thoughts of her former life and existence. As for Billy, he studied hard and became a good student, but Philadelphia life for him wasn't as warm and comfortable, especially in his teenage years. While he loved his mother and uncle, he didn't like living in Philadelphia. It was too settled, too citified, and too normal. He missed the West and felt an urge to tromp in Death Valley mountains. After all, Bud Torgerson's blood still ran in Billy's veins.

Bonnie didn't understand, appreciate, or recognize her son's Torgerson blood leanings. She saw only motherly pride. Most disturbingly for her, as Billy grew older and taller, his head sprouted tight, spindly, Art Garfunkel-like blond curls—not unlike Bud Torgerson had when he and Bonnie first met.

As Billy grew older, he also grew restless and wanted to know his father better, and not just from faded childhood memories or motherly warnings. He wanted to visit their old home. He especially wanted to see his father's mine workings. He had these yearnings ever since he turned sixteen, but he kept his longings secret. He knew she wouldn't let him go and his uncle wouldn't understand. So, quietly at night, Billy read about his father. He studied Death Valley mountains, mining, and the few scraps and notes left from his father's life and death. There wasn't much, but Billy read it all—and he wanted more.

His dreams of moving back West clashed with his mother's plans for his future and career—but he didn't tell anyone when they asked. His mother always asked. A typical conversation went, "Billy, have you decided what college to go to, what degree, and what law school?"

"No. I don't want to go to law school. I haven't even decided if I want to go to college."

"What do you mean, you don't want to go to college? How can you become a lawyer and take over your Uncle Stade's Philadelphia law practice if you don't go to law school?"

"I dunno."

"Have you applied to any scholarships yet?"

"Not really."

"What do you mean, 'not really,' Billy? You are much too aimless in life. Do you want to be a nobody in life? Do you want to end up like your father? So, it's settled, you are going to apply yourself in school and choose your college and law school—right?"

"Yes, Mother."

Billy had no interest in being a lawyer, and if there were any footstep-following, it would have been his father's. With every passing year, Billy grew closer and closer to the father he barely knew, and by his eighteenth birthday Billy had become totally captivated by Death Valley mountains and Panamint mines. However, Bonnie and Stade knew nothing of Billy's interests and passions. So, on his eighteenth birthday, Bonnie and Stade doubled down on their pressure for Billy to enter law school and follow Stade's footsteps.

By his eighteenth birthday, Billy had enough of their Philadelphia life. He blew up to his mother, "Enough already about being an attorney. No offense to Uncle Stade—he's been very kind—but I don't want to go to law school. I don't know what I want to do, but I don't want to make a mistake by deciding before I'm ready."

Bonnie stood silent, trying to process the bombshell she had just heard. Through sobs, "I never knew you didn't want to be a lawyer. You planned it your whole life—what happened?"

"No, I didn't. That was your plan, and Uncle Stade's. I don't know what I want to do, so right now, I want to take a break, travel, and think things over. I want an extended vacation along the Canadian eastern seaboard to gather my thoughts."

"Canada? What about college and your future?"

"I promise I'll return no later than six months. If I don't decide anything different, I'll return and buckle down and focus my energy on college and a career, but right now, I need to think things over. Please, respect my wishes."

Reluctantly, Bonnie relented. It didn't seem that she had much of a choice. It was not as if she could force him to go to college. The next morning, Bonnie gave Billy a big hug, and while doing her best to hold back tears and full sobbing, she mustered only, "Be safe, and return."

"I promise," Billy said. With that, they parted ways.

As Billy headed out of town, he felt guilty for not telling his mother the whole truth. He indeed wanted to travel and planned to return as he'd said. However, he hadn't said he planned to go to Death Valley and his father's old prospects, instead of Canada. Billy figured deep down she may have known.

Before he left, Billy searched his uncle's attic for an old chest that he remembered once overhearing his mother and Uncle Stade arguing over. She and Stade rarely argued, so to Billy, this stood out. During the argument, Billy overheard his mother wanting Stade to destroy his chest. Stade refused. As a compromise, Stade promised to store his chest in the attic and keep its existence hidden from Billy. This chest, and its contents, had long occupied Billy's mind. He could not leave for Death Valley without finding the forbidden chest and whatever secrets it held.

It took only a few minutes of attic rummaging for Billy to find a heavily scraped and gouged cedar chest. This must be Stade's chest,

Billy mused. It sat in the corner under an old sheet and covered with Halloween decorations, old school memorabilia, and the type of discarded junk one usually finds in garage sales that no one ever buys. Billy paused momentarily to look over his shoulder before reaching down to open the chest. It was locked.

Upon closer inspection, he found the metal latches were broken and the hinges rusted loose. Before damaging the fragile hinges by opening it, he first inspected all sides—looking for what, he had no idea. The only markings were faint and heavily gouged. They appeared to be initials. At first, Billy assumed it read "S.T.," for Stade Torgerson, but after bringing a bright light to it, the chest clearly read "B.T." Billy whispered to himself, "This must be Dad's chest, not Uncle Stade's." Billy wondered, "Why would they want to keep Dad's stuff hidden from me?" Billy couldn't resist finding out. The decrepit hinges groaned as Billy opened the dusty lid as he peered inside.

Bonnie always found Stade's house warm and inviting, but after Billy left, it only seemed cold, lonely, and empty. Its loneliness was even more acute since Stade left for a few weeks on a business trip. Since Billy took off for Canada, Stade had often been away on business trips. This was the first time she felt alone since moving in with Stade. In some ways, it reminded her of her life with Bud. However, back then, she had her Billy. Now she had no one. She mumbling to herself, *At least Stade provided stability for Billy when he needed it most.* In more ways than one, Stade had been more of a father to Billy than Bud ever was, she mused.

To wile away time and get her mind off her loneliness, Bonnie began cleaning the mess that had accumulated in the house recently. The kitchen had become a mess, and the attic hadn't been deep-cleaned in years. She took on these projects to get her mind off things—to get her mind off her worries over Billy.

She gathered loose boxes containing old holiday decorations that didn't belong in a musty attic. She grabbed an armload and dragged them downstairs. As she began putting the stuff away, memories flooded her thoughts. After two hours of attic cleaning, she came upon the old cedar chest—the one that held Bud's mining notes and life's mementos.

The old chest's dust cover looked out-of-place. It was too neat and orderly. As she approached, she noticed the broken latches lying loose on the attic floor. She rushed to the chest, flung off the sheet, lifted the lid, and nearly doubled over when she found the chest empty. She instantly knew what had happened. Billy took Bud's things. She also realized he was probably *not* touring the East Coast as he had promised; Billy went to Death Valley. "My Billy is gone!" she screamed.

Over the next few weeks, Bonnie's Philadelphia friends kept reassuring her by telling her that Billy probably just wanted to connect with his father in the only way he thought he could. For the sake of her caring friends, she nodded in agreement, but she knew differently. She sensed that the same forces that pulled upon Bud's tortured soul had their grip on her dear Billy. "Can't the damned Grapevines and Panamints leave us Torgersons alone and in peace?" she sobbed every time she thought about it.

Little did Bonnie or Billy know, but the many business trips that had taken Stade away from home the last year weren't business trips. Stade hadn't been honest with her. It seemed that Bud was not the only Torgerson inflicted and obsessed with silver. Maybe Bonnie had been right. "It's the Torgerson curse," she often said. Instead of lawyer-related business trips, depositions, and court dates, as he said, Stade had been sneaking off to the Panamints to find and claim his brother's silver—riches that he thought were rightfully his. It became an all-consuming passion.

All the time Stade searched the hills for clues and traces of his brother, he never let on his identity. Few around Death Valley ever saw this mystery person or caught his name. He easily blended into the mind-your-business crowd and don't-ask-questions culture that permeated the entire Death Valley mountains and mining scene. However, what he failed to anticipate was soon, both he and his nephew Billy would be in the same place and at the same time.

CHAPTER 14

Months before Katherine came into Death Valley looking for her uncle, Sid Emerson rolled into the park looking for something else entirely. Both introductions were through Shoshone—one of the park's lesser-visited paved entrances. For Sid's introduction, his multi-year odyssey began in the Northern Great Plains, then took him through the red rock Navajo country, and eventually deposited him gap-mouthed at the foot of the Panamints and the sand- and salt-encrusted dead-end finality of the Amargosa River.

After passing the flood-scarred lowlands of the Amargosa Valley, Sid's fully loaded Jeep Cherokee made the gentle climb to Salsberry Pass, passing the upper Greenwater Valley along the way. The Greenwater Valley is one of several parallel valleys within the region—Death Valley being the most famous. Separating each valley are rugged mountain ranges with enticing names such as Funeral, Grapevine, Saline, Cottonwood, and Last Chance. Sid's neck strain became intense as he passed under the imposing ramparts of the Panamint Range—the highest of the Death Valley ranges.

The Death Valley thermometer read over a hundred degrees, but snow still lingered on the highest Panamint peaks. For a region known for valleys, it is the mountains that dominate the landscape. In such rugged, trailless, and inhospitable land, remoteness and inaccessibility are everywhere—these are mountains in which someone could easily get lost in.

Immediately upon entering Death Valley, the road split into a choice—gravel or paved. While there are hundreds of miles of gravel roads in the park, most are impassable without a 4x4. The main paved road is an elongated black snake that hugs the valley's eastside leading into the salt-encrusted Badwater Basin and then into Furnace Creek—the economic, social, and visitor hub of Death Valley. While Sid wanted to see firsthand the glistening white salt pan of North America's lowest point, and taste its bitterness, he turned onto gravel heading north along the bottom of the Panamint scarp.

He didn't come into Death Valley for the Badwater Basin. Instead, Sid came for two *known* reasons—to learn more about the Lizard People legend and to discover why so many eccentrics are drawn to Death Valley's formidable and inhospitable wilderness. Little did Sid know, but unknown forces pulled him in too. Not unlike Bud Torgerson, and countless forgotten people before them, Sid had no idea what he was getting himself into. He also had little appreciation that his path followed the Amargosa River along its one-way trajectory into Death Valley. Evaporation is the river's only escape from Death Valley's grip. For Bud Torgerson, death was his only escape. No one knew what the Panamints had in store for Sid.

As Sid and his Cherokee sailed along the empty road, more mountains filled the skyline. Death Valley thoughts churned through his head at full speed. What is it about the place that drives so many people to the margins of obsession and conspiracy?

The Panamints, unlike any other mountains Sid had encountered, had no simple or elegant ridges rising singularly to an individual apex. The mountains here formed a convoluted series of twisted walls, bleak ramparts, and multi-colored headwalls, all heaped one on top of another. Sid found it impossible to discern one heap from the next, one summit from the next, or even pick out individual valleys that the map clearly shows slice through the range. While scanning the mighty Panamint barrier, he mused, "If the Panamints can easily swallow entire valleys, a race of intelligent Lizard People would have no problem staying out of sight of prying eyes."

Having passed the turn-off to Warm Spring Canyon over ten miles ago, Johnson Canyon should be coming into view soon.

While he couldn't see any break or weakness in the rampart walls, he knew the canyon must be there…somewhere. Sid stopped for several minutes while he considered a side trip up Johnson Canyon to visit Hungry Bill's Ranch—the deserted homestead lying below and east of the historic mining town Panamint City. According to Sid's information, there was no easy way to reach Panamint City anymore. Most people hiked up from the west side, near Ballarat, the historic ghost town. Sid chose to continue past more history-filled canyons until his dust-coated Cherokee once again merged with the lonely black snake—a short distance south of Furnace Creek.

Long before arriving at Furnace Creek, Sid balked at the glaringly out-of-place patch of greenness beyond. The greenery did not come from the exotic tamarisk shrub. Nor had it come from mesquite trees long nurtured by the Native Timbisha Tribe. The green scar came from a privately owned golf course fed by millions of gallons of precious water—water that should have been feeding the regional aquifer, native mesquite, indigenous peoples, and local wildlife. Instead, to Sid's disgust, it fed golf course turf so park visitors could marvel at playing golf in a private verdant oasis in the middle of Death Valley. The water fed a grotesque unnatural being—certainly more alien and out of place than any Lizard People, thought Sid as he rolled by without stopping.

His Cherokee passed by many Death Valley miles, complete with alluvial fans, searing heat, salt-encrusted waysides, and imposing Panamint horizons. Sid hadn't seen another vehicle or person since leaving Shoshone. The Jeep strained to climb the steep grade, as the relentless heat followed Sid and his SUV up the lonely mountain pass nearly a mile in elevation. As the Cherokee neared the pass, the rising heatwaves distorted the remnant image of Death Valley still visible in Sid's rearview mirror, but far below in another world. Sid noticed as he approached the pass that shrubs and a few scattered trees began sprouting out of nowhere. He stopped at the summit pass to take it all in—and to gaze upon both western and eastern Panamint slopes.

In total silence, except the wind's mournful howl, Sid remained at the divide for at least fifteen minutes. *It's such an enchanting place*, Sid thought as he took in the sights and breathed in the juniper-scented air coming from the stiff wind. He breathed deep a vigor he hadn't known in years. He felt alive.

As Sid coasted down the long grade without the aid of gas, he noticed a deep blue Ford Expedition in his rearview mirror. *Such an irritant people can sometimes be*, he thought. *Here's this guy ruining my entire experience.* Sid silently cursed his alien intrusion. He stepped on the gas to once again be alone with his thoughts. Despite the new speed, the same one-mile gap persisted between the two vehicles. The Expedition had sped up too, matching the Jeep's speed, pace for pace. Sid spoke to his rearview mirror, "Are you following me?"

Not much farther down the long grade, Sid turned onto the Panamint Valley Road, heading south for Ballarat. Sid sighed in relief when he saw that the deep blue Expedition hadn't followed. His attention turned to Ballarat, the ghost town lying on the opposite side of the mountain from Hungry Bill's Ranch—that place he had contemplated visiting just a few hours earlier. As the sun began setting, Sid pulled off the main road and followed a two-track up a deserted draw behind orange lichen-spattered rock outcrops. This is the perfect place to spend the night, he said to himself as he parked and turned off the overworked Cherokee.

Just as Sid started his dinner, consisting of a can of sun-warmed pork and beans, a beat-up GMC Yukon turned the corner of Sid's two-track and nearly hit the Cherokee blocking the remnant road. The deserted draw that Sid pulled into was not as deserted as he thought. The GMC driver got out and walked up to Sid. "Hello, excuse me; do you mind moving your Jeep so I may get by?"

Glancing around, Sid responded, "There's no place to turn around. Does this two-track go anywhere?"

"It's not really a road, at least not anymore. It used to be. It used to be the access to an old mine that lies just a quarter mile beyond."

"Are you working the mine?"

"No, I'm monitoring bats that live in the mine."

"So, you're a biologist?"

"No, I'm just interested in bats."

Sid Emerson and Nick Rauchoulbe continued their back-and-forth talk, forgetful of bats, mines, and partially eaten sun-warmed pork and beans. Nick recently retired as a supervisor for an international mining conglomerate. Although mines had been his livelihood, bats occupied his heart and mind.

Nick had lived in the area for years, and few knew the area mines as well as he did. Neither Sid nor Nick had anything more important to do, so Sid picked Nick's brains on the area, the mines, the bats, and its people—human, as well as the lizardly kind.

Nick happily shared his knowledge of mines and bats, but as far as Lizard People were concerned, Nick only shrugged and laughed.

"If you want to talk about Lizard People, you should meet Lizard Len. He's a hoot. He's always spouting Lizard People this, Lizard People that—everything to him is Lizard People. That's how he got his nickname. Don't know his real name, supposedly Len."

"Where can I find Lizard Len?"

Chuckling again, Nick said, "Well, if you're a Lizard People, he'll find you. If not, he lives off a distant… Well, I don't really know where he actually lives, but he often hangs out in Ballarat. He loves to talk there—to anyone that'll listen. I think he and Ballarat's only resident, Rocky, are friends. Rocky is his nickname. I don't know Rocky's real name either. Rocky's friendly enough; however, don't make the mistake of asking, 'Where's Bullwinkle?' He hates that joke."

"Noted, and thanks!"

After the conversation began slowing, Sid got up to move the Jeep farther into the greasewood thicket, so that Nick could squeeze by and be on his way. As Nick drove off, his mind returned to bats and abandoned mines. As the glow of Nick's taillights faded into the night, Sid finished his pork and beans and then drifted into

Panamint dreams—a world of mysteries, secrets, and a race of Lizard People scurrying about. Sid slept well that night.

Sid slept longer than planned. Despite racing his Cherokee along the empty roads, he didn't arrive in Ballarat until 6:45 a.m. The place was deserted. To kill time, Sid drove the short distance to the Surprise Canyon trailhead. He saw only two cars when he arrived at the small parking lot. The occupant of one had just stepped out and began milling about.

Sid felt an urge to talk with a woman as she readied her pack for an overnight hike up Surprise Canyon but decided not to disturb her focused concentration. Perhaps wondering why Sid just stood there doing nothing, the hiker smiled at Sid and called out, "Are you hiking to Panamint City too?"

"No, I'm just here waiting to talk with people back in Ballarat."

"People in Ballarat, you say? Except for Rocky, I didn't know anyone else that lived there," she said with a grin.

"Yes, I hope to speak with Rocky. Do you know him?"

"Sure, everyone knows Rocky."

"My name's Sid Emerson. I'm also going there to meet a man going by Lizard Len. Do you know him too?"

"Hello, by the way. I'm Missy Flores. I don't know any lizard guy—what did you call him?"

"He goes by Lizard Len, but I don't know his real name. Say, tell me about your hike."

"It's fantastic; you should go someday. Panamint City is nice too, and you can't beat the scenery. Surprise Canyon is one of the few streams in the area with *real* flowing water—year around. Imagine that—flowing water in Death Valley. How cool is that?"

"I'd say," Sid added.

"There're not that many," Missy offered. "But it's even greater now that the road's been closed to 4x4s for several years. The BLM used to allow trucks to tear through the streambed. Since that stopped, lush vegetation is growing back."

"So, you obviously have hiked it several times before?" Sid asked.

"I've been up Surprise Canyon and to Panamint City, but this will be my first through trip," Missy added.

"Through trip?"

"Yeah, instead of hiking back the same way, I'm going over and out the other side, down Johnson Canyon into Death Valley at Hungry Bill's Ranch."

"I've heard of the place," Sid said, "but how do you get back to your car?"

"I've made arrangements with a guy to swap car keys when we pass each other in the middle—see, he's starting at the other end. Hopefully we don't pass each other without swapping keys."

"Giving someone your car keys in Death Valley's far backcountry, I hope you know and trust this key-swapping person."

"I know what you mean. But I think I can trust Mark Levison. I don't really know him, but he's from Ridgecrest, and I've seen him up here a couple of times before. He seems okay. We've swapped keys once before on another hike through. You should hike here on a pass through someday—it's fun. Maybe we can swap keys next time."

"I may just take you up on that offer someday."

With that cue, Miss Flores shouldered her pack. Straining under the load, she began her slow plod up the old mining road that led to Panamint City and the heart of the southern Panamint Range. Seeing her disappear behind the greenery cued Sid to head back to Ballarat.

On the short drive back, Sid thought about what to ask Lizard Len. He also looked forward to talking with Rocky. *Both Lizard Len and Rocky should be great subjects for my research project,* thought Sid, as he strolled up to the thrown-together shack that served as the town's visitor contact station.

"Hello, my name is Sid Emerson," he said as he approached the old man slumped against the contact station's decrepit and bulging walls, not far from the historic sign. "I'm looking for Rocky."

The voice from behind the sign said, "You'd found 'em. What you'd want 'em fer?"

As the man stepped into the full Ballarat sun, Sid did a double-take. The man defied gravity and nature's laws—he shouldn't even be able to stand. His craggy, warped, and convoluted skin hung on his face as if he and Panamints shared the same erosional history. Sid hesitated to shake his out-thrusted hand for fear it would shatter into a cloud of dust.

Rocky was not as old or frail as he appeared. Too much time in the desert will do that to a person's skin. There's something about the place that sucks the youth out of anyone and anything—they don't call it Desert Hag Syndrome for nothing.

"I heard you know just about everything that goes on around here," Sid said.

"Maybe I do, en maybe I don't." Looking at Sid curious-like, he added, "Folks round here tend to mind their own bus'ness. Unless'n it be Ballarat or mine history they don't go asking too many questions—git you or 'em in trouble."

"I'm not here for any trouble. I just want to ask old-timers about area legends—strange things, the stranger the better. I'm fascinated by the Panamints, its colorful history, and wild stories. For instance, I just met Missy Flores, and she said you may know how to reach Lizard Len."

"You met Missy? Sweet gal. So, if'n it be Lizard Len you're after, better'n not be a Lizard People, or he'd eat you up alive, he will," Rocky said with a choking and animated laugh that sounded as if he had just expelled years of accumulated dust and cigarette smoke. "If'n you want to talk Lizard People, Lizard Len yur guy. As fur me, I don't put no stock in Lizard People. Never had! But Lizard Len sure does. He'll talk yur ears off, yes, he would—if'n you give him a chance. He's always hangin' out hern, talking 'bout this'n or that—all 'bout Lizard People. Can't git 'em to shut up."

"Do you know where I can find Lizard Len?"

"I'm not inclined to tell a stranger much 'bout another man's bus'ness, but if Missy sent you here, I reckon you'd can't be all bad. If'n you come here Tuesday. He'll be here. Always comes Tuesdays. Come Tuesday, he'll talk to you'd 'bout Lizard People, but once 'he'd begin talkin', can't get no word in edgewise."

As Sid began to leave, Rocky blurted, "Is that it? Don't yu'd wanna talk 'bout Ballarat's minin' history?"

"Maybe some other day," Sid said as he climbed into the Jeep. With several days waiting on his hands to speak with Lizard Len, Sid headed into Ridgecrest to check out the place and stock up on supplies.

The next day, Sid, loaded with enough provisions to last several days, pointed his dust- and bug-plastered grill back toward the enticing Warm Spring Canyon Road that he passed by the previous day, with the hope of making it all the way to Butte Valley and Mengel Pass—deep within the southern Panamints. It was an isolated range, but not that empty, since it was filled with old mines, prospector camps, feral burros, 4x4 day-trippers, and an occasional loner that only wanted to remain alone.

Death Valley's late afternoon's sun shone on Sid's overheating Cherokee as it climbed into Warm Spring Canyon. Despite the burden, Sid made good time along this easy, by Panamint standards, section of road. However, even the best Death Valley backcountry roads are wash-boarded and jarring. Sid's Jeep strained another three-quarters of a mile in elevation—over a span of less than ten horizontal miles. Based on local rumors, the Warm Spring Canyon Road was a "granny road," compared to the infamous Lippincott Mine Road, located in the northern Panamints.

Curiously, in a range known for the horrendously dangerous drive-at-your-own-risk 4x4 roads, the Lippincott Mine Road had a posted warning sign: "Caution, Route Ahead Not Recommended for Vehicle Travel." This reminded Sid of Dante Alighieri's famous quote in *Divine Comedy* as they enter the gates of hell: "Abandon all hope, ye who enter here."

Sid's route proceeded on the puckerless Warm Spring Canyon Road. A few washboarded hours later, he arrived in lower Butte Valley. A left turn brought him to a view of Striped Butte—the warped, twisted, and folded multi-hued peak dominating Butte Valley's expanse. The twisted and alternating white and gray bands, dappled with orange lichens and mineralization blotches, appeared to have been created by the hand of a playful deity. A short hike brought Sid to its domed summit, where he imagined he could see the edge of the earth—if it had one. Within Butte Valley, the word *expansive* takes on a new meaning—depending upon temperature, season, and the mood of playful deities.

Before turning to head down to his Cherokee, the unmistakable curling dust cloud of an approaching car appeared in the distance—maybe four miles off. Reaching into his backpack, Sid pulled out his binoculars and intensely studied the roiling plume as it got closer and closer. "Damn! It's the same blue Ford Expedition that followed me yesterday," he snorted. "I knew it was following me. Who *are* you?" Sid's question and curiosity remained unanswered since the Expedition turned away—off toward Arrastre Spring.

At Anvil Springs, Sid filled his water containers at the mineral-encrusted pipe stuck into the spring's orifice. This pipe's gushing pipe had long served as a Godsend to all thirsty throats and tired souls that happened to pass through on their way to nowhere—and anywhere.

The sight of gushing water in Death Valley's parched landscape got Sid wondering. *If Lizard People exist, don't they need water too? If so, why aren't they ever seen at springs? It's a big land, but not large enough to hide an entire race of alien Lizard People, is it?* he asked himself. Looking again at Anvil Spring's water gushing out of a crack in the bedrock, Sid could see how the ignorant or naïve may easily imagine that the ground under Death Valley was hollow. As the legend went, Lizard People lived in air-filled caverns deep below Death Valley. Water from this spring must also flow underground, not unlike in the nearby Amargosa River. Sid figured, if there were enough water and space underground to hold and sustain entire cities, then perhaps Lizard People could remain hidden for years. *That seems absurd, just thinking about it*, Sid thought.

An amusing thought came to Sid, as he filled the last of his empty water jugs. *If I were the suspicious type, I could imagine Lizard People looking up at me through the Anvil Springs water pipe.* With a smile, Sid confessed, *I'm glad I already gathered my water before any aliens detected my presence. Who knows what they would have done to me?*

Before moving on, Sid scanned the surroundings—toward the old cottonwood stump, past the willow sprouts and the green carpet of wetland plants, all the way to the old miner's cabin. From what he'd read, when caught at the right time of year, water gushes out of the spring and feeds an immense field of yellow floral enchantments. *I can see living here*, Sid said to himself.

Many people used to do just that. They held up near springs while they worked area mines. Mining may have only been an excuse to squat on cheap land as they withdrew from society's ills and confusing ways. Also, many poor people took to the hills during the Great Depression. Desperate times breed lost souls.

Sid once read the sad tale of the person who built the cabin at Anvil Springs. He and a companion came into the Butte Valley in the mid-1920s looking for gold. After much searching, they located a quartz vein containing high-quality gold-bearing ore. By the looks of it, the vein would be worth a fortune. They quickly descended for much-needed supplies. They returned three weeks later, loaded with supplies and equipment and ready to take on mining their newly discovered vein. However, the entire landscape became confusing, with each rock outcrop looking markedly similar, as did each cliff, twisted hummock, and canyon headwalls. Everything looked familiar, yet nothing was. They lost their gold vein.

Other miners worked in the Anvil Springs area over the years. Like others before them, many also built cabins to live in while they worked their mines. At least one miner lived in a nearby cave. The unnamed miner even built a masonry wall and attached a door to a cave near Anvil Springs' old stamp mill.

As Sid wandered the area, he stumbled upon a modified cave home. However, instead of finding just Great Depression relics, there were cups, clothing, tools, and a neatly rolled sleeping bag—all looking as if they had been abandoned only recently. Suddenly, a chill passed through Sid's spine. "Someone's living here," he gasped.

Shamelessly, Sid rummaged through the cave-house looking for signs of the identify of its occupant. Not finding anything, Sid pored over the other mines and chloride camps throughout the rest of the old mining district.

To get a better view, Sid climbed the slope above an old, falling-down, corrugated sheet metal shed covered with chicken wire and tarpaper. At mid-slope, he came upon a mine entrance—an adit. It looked freshly worked. Pulling a flashlight from his small, olive-green backpack, Sid peered into the mine's gloomy stank. The adit continued level for twenty feet before it came to a vertical shaft, with a horizontal adit continuing beyond. Sid scanned the shaft's steep and slick wall, looking for any way to cross. A narrow shelf that skirted the left side appeared to be the only route. To contemplate his next move, Sid shone the flashlight beam down the shaft. The void swallowed all light and revealed nothing—except for a faint outline of what looked like old timbers and broken mining debris. As Sid lifted the flashlight beam higher, something white stood out. A bright white notebook lying on the horizontal floor on the opposite side of the shaft became Sid's only focus—and fixation. "It looks new," he said. "How did a notebook get on the far side of the pit?"

Sid's curiosity got the better of him. Cinching the backpack tight to his chest, and with the flashlight held by clenched teeth, Sid began the traverse of the narrow crumbling ledge that skirted the shaft's left side. He got halfway across before his hands became so sweaty, they kept sliding off the rounded handholds. Soon, the traverse became harder, much harder, than Sid anticipated, and the ledge grew smaller and crumblier. He had no other safe choice other than to turn around or back up. However, futile attempts to back up only produced more sweat and more slippery handholds. "I can't get back," he cursed. In near panic, he figured it must be easier to move forward. So, he pushed on. How he would get back once he crossed didn't yet cross his mind.

With a total concentration that rid him of fear and thoughts of sweaty hands, he crept inch by inch along the crumbly ledge. "It's working," he grunted. With only two feet more to go, he cried out, "I'm making it! I'm almost there!" Soon after a deep exhale, Sid leaned down and, with his outstretched arm, tried to grasp the nearest edge of the adit's level floor on the pit's far side. As he shifted his weight, his foot popped off. Feeling his handholds slipping, Sid's boots clawed at the pit's vertical rock, searching for anything that could take weight off his failing arms. Eventually, his boot found a nubbin—enough to regain his footing and composure. Sid made it across to the other side. Without any delay, he scanned the notebook looking for clues.

Sid discovered it was a journal, but it listed no dates. It seemed to Sid that whoever wrote it had been searching for some dead guy's mine. The name Bud Torgerson appeared a couple of times, but Sid was unclear if he wrote the journal or if it was his mine. Sid didn't know any Bud Torgerson. Thinking it important, Sid stowed the journal in his pack and began contemplating going back across the same traverse.

The return went without a hitch. After arriving back in the sun's oppressive glare, Sid, with notebook in pack and questions on mind, headed back Death Valley's east side. He had a notion of whom to ask to find answers.

CHAPTER 15

Over the last few weeks, Paddy rethought his original condition for taking the job, that he would only work alone. *She's all right—for an Easterner*, Paddy admitted to himself. With a semblance of a smile, *I respect her gumption and willingness to get up and do.* He heard about her trip to Hunter Mountain, alone. *I can't have an Eastern lady, especially her, go into the Panamints alone. Fortunately, she only ran into Ron*, Paddy thought as he wrestled multiple concerns simultaneously.

Working alone made perfect sense to Paddy then, but upon reflection, he realized he hadn't thought of it from Katherine's perspective. *She's antsy to find her uncle.* During a moment of clarity, *It's not reasonable for her just to sit alone in a motel room while I roam around lookin' for her uncle. I need to find a way to involve Katherine. If that means letting her into my life, temporarily, so be it.* Although Paddy knew it was the right thing to do, he fully understood that his life would suddenly become much more complicated.

At the same time Paddy considered the search from Katherine's perspective, Katherine, sitting alone in her Ridgecrest motel room, also reconsidered their partnership arrangement. She had grown lonely sitting in her room, wandering around Ridgecrest, and being a stranger in a strange land. She could never envision living like Paddy, just sitting around a trailer watching the world go by. And she wasn't about to do that while Paddy was out and about looking for her uncle. While she knew Paddy kept busy doing all he could to find her Sid, she wanted more. Katherine wanted to know what Paddy knew—and as soon as he found out. She wanted to help. Mostly, she wanted company.

On the following morning, on a whim, Katherine drove to Paddy's isolated trailer to confront him with her new demands. She arrived early to catch him before he left for the day. She parked the rented Camry near Paddy's trailer just as the first ray cast an eerie shadow across the greasewood and the alluvial fan's faint undulations. She expected him to be sipping coffee on his table under the mesquite, but nothing outside stirred. A faint glow in the trailer offered the only sign of life. She was about to knock on the bent and faded door, when Paddy's booming voice called out, "Door's open, Katherine, come inside."

Paddy had been enjoying the pre-dawn morning and nursing his first cup of coffee. He noticed an approaching car through the kitchenette's smudgy window, silhouetted against the star-lit morning sky. A moment later, he recognized the Camry.

As soon as Katherine darkened the trailer's confined doorway, Paddy blurted without looking up from his coffee, "Damn, the place is getting busy these days."

"Excuse me. Shall I leave?"

"Of course not. I'm not talkin' about you. Please sit down. But the place is getting crowded, you must admit."

"I would never say this place is crowded—not in the least," she said while staring at the mouse-chewed chair that Paddy was offering.

"Just the other day," Paddy added. "While up near Mengel Pass, I saw two rigs drive by that day alone."

"My, that sounds crowded, indeed," Katherine chuckled.

"Laugh all you want to, but it is. Throughout that whole day, I saw three dust plumes off in the distance—all on the same day. The Panamints ain't the same anymore."

Paddy's continued rant lasted longer than his coffee. Once the mug went dry, Paddy bolted up and began pacing. "Sorry for the mess," he said as he frantically began picking up loose items strewn through his trailer. "I wasn't expecting company, especially a lady."

"No worries. I hope you are not picking up your squaller on my part. I would think you know me well enough by now that you can be comfortable and be yourself when I am around."

"Comfortable? That'll be the day," Paddy snorted.

After stopping his nervous cleaning, Paddy poured a second cup of coffee, and without asking, poured a cup for Katherine and placed it on a freshly scrubbed TV tray that normally served as his dining table. He figured she would appreciate coffee as they discussed whatever she came to talk about. *Why else would she be here?* he muttered to himself as he took a sip of coffee.

Dispensing with normal pleasantries, she blurted, "You are searching for Uncle Sid today, aren't you?"

"I planned to. I planned to meet up with Lizard Len and ask a few questions. About that, I'm glad you came by. I want to ask…I wanted to ask you…if you're a mind to… I wanted to ask—"

"Goodness, Paddy. Spit it out. What do you want to ask?"

"I know I said I wanted to only work alone, but I've been thinkin' about that…"

"About that," Katherine interrupted. "I know I agreed to stay behind and let you do all the searching and investigation, but I changed my mind. Would you terribly mind if I come along and help? I know it is against your original condition for taking the job, but it is important to me."

"Er…well…if it's important to you, I guess I can make an exception," Paddy said. "But if you're doing 'bout half the work, it's only right that you pay me only half the money. Ain't that fair?"

"Thank you for the kind and gracious gesture, but I am fine with our previously discussed rate. You deserve it for all you are doing. I just want to help and be busy. That is all."

"Then we have an agreement, Ms. Emerson. Would you care to accompany me on a visit to Lizard Len?"

"Yes, Mr. Darwin," as she curtsied, "I would be pleased, but why Lizard Len?"

"You said your uncle sent you a letter, or message, that mentioned Lizard Len's name. I thought that's just as good of a lead as any other."

Paddy and Katherine headed out to pack his rig with a full day's supplies, including two extra spares and plenty of water. As he loaded, the morning's first rays shone upon the trailer's flank. Paddy paused and smiled as he noticed the dawn's warming light had given his trailer's normal dull brown siding an enticing luster. *The desert is perfect for such subtle beauty*, he thought before calling out to Katherine, "Hurry up, it's time to go. We're burnin' daylight. Let's go."

As they drove off, Katherine looked behind at the morning light cast upon the ever-diminishing view of Paddy's trailer. *I have never seen light play in such ways*, she thought as her eyes scanned the entire eastern horizon. *It really is lovely, in a rustic sort of way*, she mused. Shortly after, they broke eye contact. Paddy, with exuberance in his voice that Katherine had never heard before, began telling her Lizard Len's background and history.

The truly famous require no last name. Within the rock music world, further identification beyond John, Paul, George, or Ringo is pointless. Dylan and Elvis also says it all. Similarly, around Death Valley, the name Lizard Len needs no further clarification. Does his birth name, even if he had one, really matter? Lizard Len's character and personality were unique, and clearly transcended the confines of who he once was in whatever distant, unconnected, and irrelevant past where such things mattered. From that christening point forward, he became Lizard Len.

Lizard Len did not obtain his distinction by being world famous like the mop-tops, Dylan, or Elvis. Instead, he earned it by his reptilian quirkiness and his devotion and faith in Lizard People. For Lizard Len, Lizard People were not mythical or fantastical storytelling—they became the terror that kept him awake at night and caused him to look over his shoulder from sunrise to sunset.

Rumors say that because of his deep suspicion of government and science, he may have once been an academic, a military leader, or even a government scientist. Lizard Len never talked about his past, other than hinting that a long time ago he once had a life-changing experience. That traumatic event apparently prompted his shape-and-identity-shifting—into Lizard Len.

Lizard Len claimed to have intimate knowledge of Native American cultures, specifically the Navajo. This led some to conclude he may have spent some time with the Diné. However, he made similar claims about other secrets and mysteries, ranging from medicine wheels to the Kennedy assassination, to the whereabouts of Jimmy Hoffa. Paddy explained to Katherine, "You need to understand, when it comes to Lizard Len, whatever the guy says has to be taken with a grain of salt."

"He sounds entertaining *and* informative."

"Well, I guess you can say that. Today, we'll see."

Lizard Len loved talking about Lizard People, but when asked when he first heard of the aliens, he becomes tight-lipped. Some claimed he might be the mysterious Little Chief Greenleaf who sent poor George Shufelt on his historic one-way trek down his Los Angeles catacombs.

However, Lizard Len hardly looked Hopi or Navajo. "Besides, unless he's a shapeshifter, he would have to be over 120 years old, and by all appearances, Lizard Len is only in his mid-sixties," Paddy said to Katherine as they drove down the road while preparing for their interview.

"Do the Timbisha know of Lizard Len?" Katherine asked.

"I don't think so. I'm pretty sure the Timbisha give the Lizard Len type a wide berth." After a mile or more of silence, Paddy interrupted the droning road noise. "Some say Lizard Len has always been in Death Valley—that he's a fixture predating even the Timbisha." After a moment of silence, Paddy added, "The Timbisha would likely scoff at such a notion." Paddy never took his eyes off the distant horizon.

"Drunken tavern talk has it that Lizard Len is the *real* extraterrestrial visitor." Turning his head toward Katherine, he added, "Desert newbies love to speculate on Lizard Len's former life."

Paddy would have preferred having his front teeth pulled, or to sing a "I Got You Babe" duet with Katherine while in the crowded Furnace Creek Lodge, than to talk to Lizard Len about Lizard People. However, something told him that understanding the Lizard People legend would be key to finding Sid. To get him through the interview, Paddy kept telling himself, *It can't be as bad as what I endured in Afghanistan.*

Rocky arranged the interview. Lizard Len agreed on some conditions: that Rocky also be there, he would be free to talk without restraint, and they conduct the interview at a safe place—like Ryan Camp. Lizard Len didn't trust many people, but he trusted Papa. So, his choice of Ryan made perfect sense to Paddy.

Lizard Len never trusted Paddy. Rumor has it that Paddy had a "Lizard People look about him in the eyes." When others told Paddy that rumor, Paddy scoffed at the notion of being a Lizard People. Not only because he knew the truth, but it didn't make any logical sense. Paddy replied, "If the Lizard People's goals were to spy on humans and report their findings to conspiring federal government officials, then I must be the world's worst Lizard People. I go weeks on end holed up alone in an isolated trailer, far from any human outpost, reptilian catacombs, or government official. I would suck as a Lizard People."

On the long drive to Ryan, Katherine filled the time with sharing stories of growing up in Boston and of her happy visits she had with her Uncle Sid. She thought back on the many notes her uncle had written to her, including the last one she received before he went missing.

Dear Kati,

Hello. I'm writing to let you know I'm okay, at least physically. I've interviewed a few long-term residents and conspiracy-minded people here. Their core beliefs are so off-the-wall it's quite troubling. They accept them without question—as if it were a religious cult, and they, its disciples. While their fixation is unhealthy they do have some valid points. These conversations got me questioning my core beliefs as well. One disturbing piece of information I recently discovered will require some follow-up. However, based on the information I have, and the stakes involved, I better tread lightly. Tomorrow, I'm heading into the rugged southern Panamints—to check on some leads. I'll let you know how things go. There's so much I want to share with you—more later.

Take care.
Love,
Uncle Sid

Katherine's fond memories of her uncle's letters ended abruptly as Paddy broke her train of thought and brought her back to the Mojave Desert. "Sorry about havin' no air conditioning," Paddy said as he tapped the controls. "Been broken a couple of years or more. Must be 130 degrees in here. Maybe we should've taken your Camry."

Katherine didn't answer. She had been too deep in thought to come back so soon. She kept looking out the window with an unfathomable series of Mojave scenes that flashed back and forth outside of the speeding Bronco as it careened through one shimmering heatwave after another. Suddenly, she regained her frame of mind and blurted, "I heard you were in the military and served in the Middle East. That you were involved in heavy fighting with al-Qaeda and the Taliban?"

"Who told you that?" snapped Paddy.

"I did not mean to intrude or offend—sorry. I thought Dr. Ron Telling mentioned something about that. I meant no offense."

"Ron shouldn't tell you such things. If I want to tell you or anyone about my past—I'll be the one doing it. That's how it works. Ron's supposed to be my friend."

"He told me no gossip, and we meant no intrusion," Katherine countered. "I could tell he really likes you. I think he was trying to be a good friend. Again, sorry."

A moment later, Paddy rolled down the window. The roaring of the Death Valley air whipping through the cabin overwhelmed all sounds and thoughts for the next ten miles. After the excruciating awkwardness had subsided, the Bronco began ascending the long and exposed, black-smudged rubble and alluvial fan leading into Ryan. The surrounding cliffs and ramparts dwarfed the tiny townsite and made the distance between Paddy and Katherine seem even more remote.

They walked the long path leading to Ryan's mess hall in silence. To Paddy, the walk seemed longer than he remembered. Regret had occupied Katherine's mind too much for her to notice the walk. The next thing Katherine remembered was Paddy holding open the large front door to Ryan's Mess Hall—and him smiling as she stepped inside.

Lizard Len and Rocky waited on a bench next to a massive dining table. The sound of Papa scraping paint from a nearby windowsill punctuated the air—along with the faint whiff of ancient timbers. Images of a room full of stout and weary miners eating and blowing off steam usually filled Paddy's mind when he stepped into Ryan's historic mess hall, but on this day, he only thought of Katherine. Papa must have heard them enter, since he put down the scrapper and joined the other four as they were silently staring at each other. To help Katherine, Paddy broke the silence by offering introductions. He and Katherine sat next to Rocky and opposite Lizard Len, while Papa remained standing against the door frame.

At first, Lizard Len dominated the talking—until Katherine agreed to take notes. Rocky hoped to just sit and watch. Papa wanted nothing more than to finish scraping the windows so he could later paint. Paddy didn't want to say anything, but to leave early, he wasted no time getting to the flesh, blood, and sinew of the matter, "What can you tell me about Sid Emerson and any reported connection with Lizard People?"

In hindsight, Paddy regretted not restricting his questions to only Sid. It never took much prompting to get Lizard Len talking about Lizard People, and with the opening Paddy just gave, they got an ear full.

Lizard Len began by asking, "You sure you want to hear? Most people don't wanna know the truth—they think I'm crazy."

"I wouldn't ask if I didn't want to hear. I'm not here to judge—so, please continue."

"Okay, then I'll tell you the truth, but in baby steps, because the *truth* is much bigger than just Lizard People. The truth crosses a wide swath of humanity and life on Earth."

"This is great—please continue," Katherine said, "but do you mind if besides taking notes that I also record the interview?"

"No recording," Lizard Len snarled. "Notes are fine, as long as I can review them before you leave, but no recording. I don't want the government to get their hands on it."

"Got it, notes—no recording," Katherine reassured him. "Sorry, please continue."

"Where was I? Oh yeah, humanity. Get ready, guys, for a dose of the truth. It's a truth that'll knock your socks off. It gets at the core of who we are as a species," Lizard Len explained with wild hand gyrations.

"Okay, here goes…. If you don't count government minions, there are five types of human-looking creatures on Earth: Draconians, Seekers, Protectors, Contentors, and people like me—folks that know the truth. The first three are Lizard People, and only the last two are humans."

"So, if there's only five on Earth, what am I?" asked Paddy.

"I dunno yet. You spend a suspicious amount of time supposedly by yourself. That's suspicious enough, but the fact that you're listenin' to me now is a good sign. That's the only reason that I'm sitting here and talking to you now. As far as Katherine Emerson is concerned, I haven't heard of any Lizard People coming from Boston, and I respect her for wanting to find her uncle. Humans got to stick together, you know."

"I'm pretty sure I'm not a Lizard Person," Paddy said, "and I doubt Elizabeth is as well."

"You wouldn't admit it, even if you knew," Lizard Len added.

"So, getting back to your story, there are three types of Lizard People: Draconians, Seekers, and Protectors?" asked Katherine.

"It's not a story, it's the truth" snapped Lizard Len.

"Sorry, I meant no disrespect."

Appearing not to notice the interruption, Lizard Len continued. "All Lizard People were of one kind when they first arrived five thousand years ago. Since then, the Lizard People evolved and adapted. We, the Earth's original inhabitants, forced their change. We didn't like them none at all. We knew the truth—that Lizard People were evil monsters."

Katherine stopped her notetaking. "Evil how? Maybe they did not understand each other," Katherine said while glaring at Paddy, "because sometimes a failure to communicate can lead to misunderstands and problems."

As if exasperated, Lizard Len blurted, "Evil in all evil ways. The point is, they were, and remain, evil. So, humans fought back. There weren't enough Lizard People to hold their ground, so we humans pushed back. We ended up killing most of them. The few survivors fled underground or shapeshifted into human form."

Katherine leaned forward while pointing to the Mess Hall's floor. "Where did this supposedly happen, here in Death Valley?"

"No, no, no." Lizard Len shook his head. "It happened out on the northern Great Plains somewhere. They only came here later.

Eventually, the Lizard People that shapeshifted into human form ended up keeping their human shape for thousands of years. Over time, they lost the ability to shapeshift back. They were stuck in human form."

"So, they kept their secret for thousands of years?" Katherine asked.

"Some of them. The ones that lost the ability to shapeshift forgot they were Lizard People."

"Are you saying there are Lizard People around that do not know they are aliens?" asked Katherine.

"Yes. Definitely! Although they don't *know* they are aliens, but at the same time they sense they're lost and out of place, that they don't belong. If deep down they weren't evil, I would feel sorry for them, 'cause they're lost. Nothing's worse than having lost your soul."

"Yes, I imagine that is true," Katherine chimed in while looking at Paddy.

Too animated to notice Katherine and Paddy's subtle gestures to one another, Lizard Len looked around to ensure everyone had soaked in his truth. Rocky hadn't shifted his expression since he first sat down, but he likely hadn't missed anything. He had heard this all before. Nonetheless, his eyes flirted all about so as not to miss anything.

As Papa retreated further into the door frame, Lizard Len continued without missing a beat. "So, they kept searching for answers, but they eventually even forgot why they were searching in the first place. Many turned out to be loners, drifters, malcontents, disturbed, and lost."

"Are these the Seekers? Katherine asked, while pausing her notetaking. "Is it because they lost their identity?"

"It's not just me; that's what everyone calls them. But yeah, because of their urge to seek but never finding anything."

"Sorry for interrupting," offered Katherine. "Please go on."

"The truth feels good, doesn't it?" Lizard Len said directly to Katherine. "You're asking good questions. You've been fed the government lies and conspiracies for so long, you have *no* idea how liberating the truth can be. But as I was saying, because Seekers have this nagging feeling that things aren't what they appear to be, they're extremely dangerous. No one knows when their Lizard People memories will kick in. When it does, they'll rise against us. Well," Lizard Len said while looking at Paddy, "at least us humans."

"If that is what a Seeker is, then please tell us about the Protectors," asked Katherine.

"Yeah, yeah, I'll tell you the truth about the Protectors, but first, does anyone have any beer? I'm thirsty."

"Beer, here with me now? No," Paddy said in bewilderment. "I had nothing in my hands when I came in."

With the conversation turning to beer, Papa suddenly became visible. "I have a few beers in de back room, but they'd be warm or even hot by now."

Lizard Len flicked his tongue. "A warm beer is bett'rn than no beer at all."

As Papa retrieved a Budweiser six-pack, he shifted his hands from time to time to cool fingers of canned heat. Katherine grimaced as Lizard Len popped open the Bud and began guzzling. The brew nearly scalded Lizard Len's hands and throat, but he didn't notice or care. After an especially long belch, he blurted, "Now that I had a beer, are you ready for more truth?"

After letting go with another warm belch, Lizard Len continued, "The Protectors also had taken human form for so long they lost the ability to shapeshift. However, unlike the Seekers, Protectors have no nagging sense of being out-of-place, so they don't search for the unknown. They do nothing of importance or consequence."

Perhaps it was seeing Papa running back to get the warm beer, but suddenly, Rocky began squirming on the bench. Out of nervous energy, he chimed in, "Yeah, yeah, I heard Lizard Len say it hundreds of times: these Lizard People are content with the way things are." Turning to Lizard Len, "Did I'd git that right?"

"Exactly. See, Rocky knows the truth," continued Lizard Len. "Their idea of a better life centers on how it had been in the past, long before the corruption of modern ideas and modern thought. They saw change and new ideas as alien and a threat because it disturbed their world order. In many ways, the Protectors are nearly human. Over time, they will become human sheep."

"You calling us sheep?" snapped Paddy.

"I ain't callin' you a sheep, or a human. I ain't calling you anything—yet," said Lizard Len while standing to meet Paddy's quip.

"Settle down," Paddy said dismissively. "Don't get your slats all rattled. If there're any mindless sheep, it'll be that group of yours following and hangin' on your every move."

"I didn't say all humans are clueless sheep, only some of them—most of them. Well, Contentores are content with being sheep," Lizard Len added. "And no. No one follows me, but they would be better off if'n they did."

Sensing the tension, Papa whispered to Lizard Len, "Does anyone want me to go back an' git another six-pack? How 'bout you? Still thirsty?"

Sensing a nod from Lizard Len, Papa scurried off to fetch more warm Buds. Upon his return, the tense and non-tense non-beer drinkers alike, sitting or bounding at the table, watched in silence as Lizard Len popped one open and just as quickly finished it off. As Katherine caught up with her notes, Lizard Len let go with an even bigger warm belch.

Katherine placed her completed notes onto the table and looked Lizard Len right in the eyes. "Sorry to interrupt. Lizard People stories were important to my uncle, so they are of interest to me too, but I am more interested in finding him. Tell me about the last time you saw Sid Emerson. Did he tell you where he was going?" Katherine picked up her notes again and waited for an answer. Lizard Len silently sat and watched the ensuing staring match begin—and to watch Katherine twist and wad what were once meticulously clean notes the more her waiting persisted.

Paddy's eyes darted back and forth between Katherine and Lizard Len before he turned to Katherine and interjected, "If I may interrupt. There'll be plenty of time for that—later. I think we should let Lizard Len finish his story, or should I say, truth, of the Lizard People."

"Thank you," answered Lizard Len. That was one of my conditions for this talk. Besides, if you want to look for suspicious people that may have information their hiding about your uncle, if I were you, I would talk to that supposed ant guy."

"You mean Dr. Ron Telling?" blurted Katherine. "He seems like such a nice, normal person. Surely he's not mixed up in any of this."

"What better disguise to avoid being noticed?" Lizard said matter-of-factly. "As if you really believe he's out alone in the Panamints looking at bugs—get real." Lizard Len smirked.

As Katherine bowed her reddening face to avoid eye contact with Paddy, she noticed the wadded notes. Page by page she straightened each perspiration-stained page. "Sorry," she said, "please continue." Her words barely had time to bounce off Ryan's age-cured wood paneling when Lizard Len unleashed his biggest belch yet. The belch had not fully come out before he commenced where he left off, apparently unconcerned with Katherine's question.

"Getting back to my story, no, the Contentors follow the corrupt U.S. government and the even more corrupt U.N., letting the government pull the strings and manipulate the mindless and weak. For decades, the federal government's been working and conspiring with the Draconians."

Nearly jumping out of his seat, Rocky interrupted, "This is the part I love—it's crazy, just crazy! Ain't it? Tell them about the Draconians—the Draconians."

"Sure," Lizard Len said. "I'll tell you the truth about the Draconians, just as I've been telling you the truth about all the Lizard People. The Draconians are the Lizard People that originally hid in caves. Since they didn't permanently shapeshift into human form, they never lost their shapeshifting ability, and they certainly didn't forget their Lizard People evilness. They spent hundreds and thousands of years preparing for war and world domination."

"Sorry, Lizard Len, for saying it, but I think Rocky's right—that does sound a little crazy," Paddy interjected. "How do you know all this? Lizard People probably didn't just up and tell you."

"I know this by not being a mindless sheep—that's how," Lizard Len snapped. "The Draconians have been shapeshifting into human form and spying on us long enough to learn our ways and find our weak spots. Over this amount of time, they are bound to slip up, from time to time," Lizard Len added. "It is then that we can learn the most if we keep our ears and eyes open—and our minds. The worst part of it is the federal government is helping them, and they are helping the government."

"Why would the government help aliens take over the human race since they are humans too?" asked Katherine.

"All humans have the capacity for betrayal. Did you ever hear of Judas?"

"Of course, but for what purpose?" added Katherine.

"Fear. The government fears us—people with the truth. The government is seriously outnumbered, so they fear an uprising. To pacify us, and turn us into mindless sheep, they need to feed us lies, so they turned to the Draconians. To fight back, we need to expose government corruption, expose the Draconians, and expose all Lizard People in all forms, and we need to deprogram minds back to their original human condition."

Lizard Len leaned back in his chair, stretched his legs, and then after a long pause asked Paddy, "So, are you going to help, or are you a sheep like everyone else?"

"Do I look or act like one of your Lizard People? Get serious," snorted Paddy.

"Or, worse yet," countered Lizard Len. "Did the government send you? 'Cause if they did, my life's in danger. If you're lying, you and I will have an issue—a serious issue. I'm trusting you with the truth—don't disappoint. Don't be a Judas."

"We're not here to help, hinder, or betray your cause. As I said earlier, we're just trying to find information that may lead to Sid Emerson. Is that what happened? Did you talk with Sid and did he somehow disappoint you?" Paddy demanded while pounding a finger into the mess table's thick wooden planks. "I can be trusted. I'm not in league with anyone, other than helping Katherine find her uncle. Other than that, I just live by myself in my trailer. So, tell us the truth. Do you know the whereabouts of Sid Emerson?"

"Not so fast, Paddy," Lizard Len snapped. "I'm not convinced yet that you are who you say you are. For all I know, the government is putting you up to this because *they* want to find Sid Emerson. I'm not about to play into their hands so easily. Maybe later, I'll tell you more. Maybe."

"Why in the world would the government be interested in my Uncle Sid?" Katherine pleaded. "He is a harmless person interested only in knowledge and understanding."

"Perhaps you just answered your own question," Lizard Len scoffed.

Wanting to change the conversation's dynamic, Katherine interjected, "Lizard Len, if you think Lizard People are all around us, is there anyone around, other than Paddy, that you think may be a Lizard People? Anyone we may know?"

As if proud that he knew an answer and could contribute to the conversation while letting Lizard Len cool down, Rocky jumped in. "Sure, you know some. They're everywhere. Ever hear of Richard Nixon? Lizard Person. Ever hear of Mark Zuckerberg? Lizard Person. Ever hear of Ronald Reagan? Lizard People."

In disbelief, Katherine said, "I can understand people not trusting Zuckerberg and the whole global digital world domination scene—I do not trust him. I can also understand 'Tricky Dick' being suspicious, but Ronald Reagan? Why him?"

Papa, no longer content being wallpaper, answered, "It dates to the early *Death Valley Days* radio broadcasts. I know that 'cause the radio, and then later TV broadcasts, were funded by the 20-Mule Team borax mining company, right here in Ryan."

Lizard Len nodded. "Did you ever hear of *Death Valley Days*, that old radio program that ran from the 1930s to 1945?" Lizard Len added, "And then on television from the '50s to 1970?"

Paddy nodded, and said, "That's right, Ronald Reagan used to host the show."

"The whole series centered on Death Valley. Each show tol' true Western tales," Rocky said with a grin of satisfaction.

With the conversation turning to a subject close to his passion, Papa added, "The Borax Mining Company, they'd own this very building we're sittin' in now. They'd produced the *Death Valley Days* films."

"That's right," as Lizard Len took over. "During the filming of *Death Valley Days*, powerful Lizard People saw Reagan's charm, charisma, and ability to connect with the common folk. It was then they hatched their plan."

"Yeah," Papa beamed. "Right here in Ryan."

"That's right, Papa," Lizard Len said. "Lizard People killed the real Ronald Reagan, and a shapeshifting Lizard Person took his image and identity. After that, the imposter Reagan announced his interest in politics."

"You are saying the President Reagan I saw on television as a youngster was an alien?" asked Katherine in disbelief.

"Yep. You now know the truth. The Lizard People had been waiting for such a charismatic leader. The alien Reagan molded and manipulated his way into politics and with the help of Lizard People and the corrupt government, he rose to become president. This was all to sway the American people toward their first step to world domination."

Papa calmly added, "Nixon too was Lizard Person, but he lacked the, what do yuh say…personality and charisma needed to manipulate us."

"Manipulate the masses, the sheep," Lizard Len added. "Ask Torrey Small over in Ridgecrest—he knows the truth. For a few years now, he's been inventing ways to disrupt their communication signals. He knows the truth about the government and about Ronald Reagan."

Katherine interrupted, "Is Torrey Small the crystal-making person that Paddy mentioned?"

Turning to Katherine, Paddy whispered, "Yes. Torrey's the guy that we'll be interviewing in a few days—the guy that leaves resinous globs at cave and mine entrances. Yes, it's the same guy."

"They are not 'resinous globs;' they are finely tuned radio disruptors," Lizard Len snapped. "Anyway, the Lizard People got rid of Nixon by concocting the whole Watergate debacle. If Nixon had been a human president, do you really think such a powerful person as a U.S. president would get caught with his drawers down in a nickel-and-dime robbery? Of course not! The Lizard People planned it to make room for Reagan."

As if to make sure her notes were accurate, Katherine asked, "What about Ford and Carter? They were between Nixon and Reagan."

Rocky joined in the conversation. "Carter, with all his smiles, was nuttin' but a temp'rary mistake—them ol' Lizard People never saw comin'. The public just hyped him up as a reaction to Nixon."

Lizard Len took over from Rocky. "You guys are all missing how deep the conspiracy goes. Lizard People are smart. They are in for the long haul. Yep, it all got started by Reagan on the set of *Death Valley Days*, but it goes deeper than that. Haven't you ever thought it too convenient that many of the era's famous and influential TV and Hollywood stars got their start on *Death Valley Days*, and then quickly rose to headlining magazines and newspapers around the country?"

"Hollywood stars were Lizard People too?" asked Katherine.

"You bet they were," said Lizard Len. "Many actors from *Death Valley Days* went on to star in popular shows of the day, ranging from *M*A*S*H**, *The Hulk*, *Bewitched*, *Gunsmoke*, *The Andy Griffith Show*, *Baretta*, and *All in the Family* to *Lost in Space*. That is because they were all Lizard People. The Californian Lizard People rose to prominence on *Death Valley Days*, and then almost like overnight, they infiltrated into society from the top—down."

"That's not all," interjected Rocky. "Tell 'em about *Star Trek*."

"Yeah, that's right, Lizard Len added. "Both Leonard Nimoy and DeForest Kelley, from *Star Trek*, played on *Death Valley Days*. They were Lizard People. Worst of all, where do you think *Star Trek* got the idea for phasers, tricorders, and transporters?"

"I'm guessing you are going to say Lizard People," Paddy chimed in.

"I certainly do," said Lizard Len. "Don't you think it odd *Star Trek* often showed wildly futuristic technology that only a few years later became real and commonplace?" Lizard Len replied as if it was obvious. "It's because they borrowed Lizard People technology they brought from Draco."

"So, you see, not only have the Lizard People and their government conspirators infiltrated powerful and influential into every aspect of our society, but they've also been infusing alien technology into their hands so that one day they may take over the human race," Lizard Len said with one final passionate sigh.

Everyone silently looked around the table, as if deciding who would speak next. Shuffling her pile of notes, Katherine cleared her throat and slowly began, "Well, you certainly gave us much to think about, Lizard Len—thank you. Thank you for educating us on the Lizard People," Katherine said with a soft, soothing tone. "But I fail to see how this relates to my uncle, Sid Emerson."

"Oh, sure. I'll talk about your uncle," Lizard Len said. "But first I needed to set the stage and provide context."

"Are you implying that my uncle was one of them?" Katherine probed.

"I didn't know Sid Emerson, so I can't say one way or the other if he was a Lizard People or not. He stopped by Ballarat to talk with me, but we never hooked up and we've not spoken. I know nothing of his disappearance."

Drilling down, as if wanting to make a point, Katherine asked, "When specifically had you planned to talk with my Uncle Sid?"

"I don't recall what day he stopped by, but as for me, I never had plans to talk with your uncle. Why would I? Is he a Lizard People?"

"My uncle is not a Lizard People."

"All Lizard People say the same thing. But if you want a lead, I suggest you talk with that Ron Telling guy—you know, that ant doctor. I heard your uncle and he spoke. Also, you may want to talk with Mandi Mitchem—she's quite the nutcase, you know. Go talk with her—"

Seemingly satisfied with the entire day's conversation, Lizard Len leaned back and proclaimed, "You now have enough of the truth—more than most. The question is, how much do you truly believe, and what are you going to do about it? Are you gonna let them all take over our country and our world? Are you a person, a human person, or are you a sheep?"

After a thoughtful pause, Katherine said, "You certainly gave us a lot to think about—thank you! I appreciate the information, your honesty, and hearing your perspective. Unless someone has anything else to say or ask, I think we are done here, for today. Thank you, Lizard Len. I also thank Papa for the use of the fine historic building deep in the fabulous Ryan, and Rocky who made the arrangements." Turning to Paddy, "We should probably go—is that all right?"

After Paddy and Katherine climbed back into the Bronco and began driving off, Paddy noticed in his rearview mirror Lizard Len and Papa in a deep conversation. I wonder what that is about, Paddy said to himself.

Paddy figured he and Katherine had a lot to think about as well. After many miles of silent driving, Paddy said to Katherine, "I'm sorry for snapping at you earlier. You and Ron did nothing wrong. I just don't like to talk about my past. Again, I'm sorry." As he reached over and gently put a hand on Katherine's shoulder, he said, "We have a lot to talk about."

CHAPTER 16

Sheriff John Smithers grunted as he opened the autopsy report on the Owl Lake body. *I don't need a doctor to tell me why the guy died,* John fumed. *Shriveled like a dried prune—in Death Valley! What more information does anyone need?* Despite considering the report a waste of time, he read and pondered every word. *Foolish people die all the time in Death Valley's heat.* John knew this better than anyone because he picked up dried prunes all the time. *They're all just like fleshy grapes, with such a thin and delicate skin—especially those that underestimate the dry and desiccating air.*

Temperature's fickle and relative. "But it's a dry heat," John often heard visitors say. Such ignorant pretensions only marginalize the thermometer's ill tidings because there's more to temperature than red liquid height in a glass tube. However, such parlances are for normal conditions, normal high temperatures, and normal humidity. John knew more than most—there's nothing normal about Death Valley.

John Smithers had seen what heat can do. Death Valley heat shrivels and withers away body fluids until the visitor is "raisined and bakened," at least that's how John referred to it. *Once raisined and bakened, there's not even enough water left in a human carcass to intertest a coyote, except to perhaps scatter whatever remaining bones and leathered hide.* John wished that coyotes had gotten and scattered this Owl Lake body before they found the guy and had to begin an investigation.

It occurred to John while reading the autopsy report, *Death Valley should have its own temperature scale.* Anything below 110 degrees is normal, but even that, with high winds you can feel body fluids whisk away into the air. The blue sky's voracious appetite is relentless, and its thirst never ends. When the wind increases, the sandblasting feels as if the gods are pummeling the water out from your reddened skin as if a dehydration death is not dramatic enough.

Experienced desert rats don't notice the temperature until it exceeds 116. It is in this danger zone that John knew most visitors get into trouble. Regardless of a person's experience, anything above 116, a person can feel the parasitic sky-feeding at the cellular level. Breath and chest heaves become labored, and each step is one step closer to raisined and bakened.

After John read the autopsy report, his mind wandered back to temperature. *The next critical threshold is 120. For any visitors wandering in 120-plus, it is only a matter of time before dispatch calls me for another body recovery.*

John equated living in Death Valley as living in a war zone. As such, desert rats learn a few tricks to outmaneuver the enemy—at least temporarily. For one, locals always carry water jugs in their rig, even if driving short distances. Stranded vehicles exposed on the battlefield are just asking to get hit. If your rig can't get you out, walking rarely can. Rescue before desiccation is often not a realistic option.

Desert rats carry everything under the sun to jerry-rig field repairs—to protect them from the sun. One of the more useful tricks is to carry an insulated pad. With ground temperatures exceeding 190 degrees, lying down to change a tire can easily cause first-degree burns. Even lying on the ground wearing jeans is uncomfortable at best. The withering ground temperature quickly finds your Levi metal rivets, and you end up with rivet-sized burns seared into your flesh. For the ill-prepared, Death Valley usually wins. *It certainly did for this poor fool on Owl Lake*, John said to himself as he tossed the autopsy report on his desk, thereby knocking two other police reports onto the floor.

The autopsy report identified the body as Chuck Albion from San Bernardino. John muttered inaudibly something about *San*

Bernardino County, as he looked up Chuck Albion. He had no priors. John learned through an internet search that Chuck Albion was a well-known adventure-seeker with a huge social media following. John laughed at Chuck's self-appointed job title. "Influencer is not a job," John sputtered, as he began speculating how Chuck Albion heard about a plane carrying drugs and cash going down. *Somehow, he found out. He must have been going in to make a video of the crash site to post on social media.* However, he apparently didn't know that dying from heat in Death Valley rarely creates media attention anymore. "Why haven't my deputies shown up to work yet?" he sputtered. "This ain't normal."

What was normal, at least for the sheriff, was that none of his deputies had yet found any of the plane's cargo, including its money or drugs. *Chuck Albion didn't have any on him, and coyotes never scatter money or drugs*, John mused. *Did someone beat Chuck to the money and drugs? Maybe another "influencer" got there first.* John considered asking a deputy to keep an eye out for social media postings. *That is if they ever report to work. Where are they?*

As if they heard his question, dispatch called with an answer. The dispatcher relayed a report of a dead body in the Funeral Mountains near Chloride City. All deputies were on other calls, so John agreed to check it out by himself. *Probably a foolish visitor*, John thought. There was nothing left of the historic Chloride City, but according to the dispatched report, there was still some of the body left. *This should make the identification easy.* Still, John thought, *It will be a long evening.*

Like many of the other early towns in the hills, Chloride City began with a small strike that didn't amount to much. But everyone thought *this* would be it. Miners laid train tracks and ran mules back and forth the 180 miles between San Bernardino, 360 miles round trip. The silver boom in the first couple of years seemed promising, but by year six, all were abandoned. Fanciful dreams never stay dead for long, because twenty-four years later, the nearby Bullfrog mine discovery brought new life to Chloride City. The town lived long enough for the hopeful construction of new homes, storage sheds, adits, and cyanide stamping mills. But, in less than ten years, residents abandoned Chloride City once again—this time for good. Now, there was nothing left other than fallen-down shacks, a few half-standing tin sheds, broken ground, broken backs, and all too real broken dreams.

Having a dead body near Chloride City didn't surprise John Smithers, since it was a popular tourist stop. As John drove to Chloride City, he muttered, "Damn tourists, got lost or something." John initially planned to drive to the scene as fast as he could, but upon a second call from dispatch, he took his time. Dispatch reported that a couple deputies had finished their earlier calls and were already headed to Chloride City to investigate.

By the time Sheriff Smithers arrived, his deputies had secured the scene and had begun the investigation. However, this was no ordinary tourist. The driver's license on the body belonged to Billy Torgerson, Bud Torgerson's son. Day-hikers, going where they shouldn't have gone, found the body lying at the bottom of an abandoned mine shaft at the base of a forty-foot hole in an otherwise horizontal mine tunnel. Deputies found inside the wallet Billy's driver's license, credit cards, and six hundred dollars cash. "Billy Torgerson is dead," John muttered. "Go figure." John hadn't seen Billy since just a boy—when he and his mother left Death Valley for good. "What's Billy doing back?"

His body lay in a hole near the mine's entrance, at the twilight zone, the transition place between the entrance's light and the dark interior. A mine's twilight zone is especially dangerous, since coming from the brightness of the desert sun, a person's eyes can take a few minutes to get accustomed to the darkness. It's easy for tourists to walk right into a hole in such a place—before eyes can adjust. "I can see this happening to a fool tourist, but Billy's been around mines a lot as a boy," John said under his breath. "He should've known better.

I guess that is what Eastern city-life will do to you—you lose your common sense."

Random theories bounced around the sheriff's head as he careened down the dusty and bumpy road back from Chloride City. However, he had other things weighing on his mind. He had just heard from dispatch that Bonnie Torgerson arrived back in town—looking for her missing son. John now faced the most unpleasant part of his job—to inform a mother that her young boy, at the prime of his life, had just died. Years earlier, John personally broke the news of her husband Bud's death; now he needed tell Bonnie about the death of her only child.

For too many times, John had had similar conversations. They were not getting any easier, but John knew this one would be different. John took his time driving to Trona, where dispatch had said Bonnie Torgerson had checked into a motel. *Billy should've known better, especially considering how his father died.* "Stupid kid," he cursed. Suddenly a thought came to John. *Everyone around here knows of Bud Torgerson's death and of having lost his long-sought-after silver mine. There's already a ton of people looking around for the lost Torgerson mine. Do you suppose that also brought Billy? If so, stupid, stupid kid.*

Regardless of what brought him back, John had to break the news to his mother. In many cities, the police deliver such news through a minister, clergy, or a local church leader, but that would be a luxury in his county. This time, like many times before, John went alone.

After knocking several times, John firmly called out, "Hello, Ms. Torgerson, this is Sheriff Smithers." After repeating it once more, he heard the door unlock. Appearing was a middle-aged woman who looked much too old and weary to be the Bonnie Torgerson he had once known, even if it had been a few years. She looked like she had just gotten up, even though it was early afternoon. As she waited for John to say something, she leaned into the door frame as if nodding off.

"I'm Bonnie Torgerson. Is there something the matter?" she softly mumbled.

"Bonnie Torgerson, remember me? I'm the sheriff, Sheriff John Smithers"

Standing erect, as if only then becoming fully awake, she not so softly sputtered, "What sort of trouble has Billy gotten himself into? Is he in jail?"

"May I come in and have a seat?"

Without a word, Bonnie swung the door open and turned to head back inside. Sheriff Smithers followed. Pushing her still unopened luggage aside, Bonnie pulled up a couple of chairs at the kitchen table and plopped herself down into one. John became unnerved when her blank stare appeared to look through him and onto the motel room's distant, food-stained wall.

The sheriff gathered his nerves and broke the silence. "There is no good way to give you the bad news, but yesterday, our deputies found your son Billy in the bottom of a mine in the mountains above Death Valley. I'm sorry to say, but Billy's dead."

When delivering such news, John had seen all sorts of reactions, ranging from anger, sadness, and denial to outright bawling. The hardest ones for him were the ones who didn't say anything—they just stared. John would end up fidgeting, hoping the sound of shuffling feet would drown out any meaningless platitude that he might happen to offer. It had always been easier for John when the time and nervousness could be taken up by calmly and smoothly answering the mother's probing questions. This was not turning out to be one of those.

At first, Bonnie Torgerson had no questions. She just sat there in cold and chilling stillness with no apparent emotion whatsoever. John didn't know if he should answer unasked questions, comfort her, or in any way react in her stead. He just let her absorb the news at her own pace—which meant they both sat there stone-faced and in stone-cold silence.

More for his sake than for hers, to break the tension, John softly mumbled, "Again, I'm terribly sorry for your loss, but could you answer a few questions?" After a long, awkward silence, John continued, "Do you know what Billy was doing in an abandoned mine in the Funeral Mountains?"

Suddenly, Bonnie broke her silence by blurting, "Funeral Mountains? You found my Billy in the Funerals, not the Panamints?"

"Yes. Visitors found him in the bottom of an abandoned mine near Chloride City, about ten miles south of Leadville."

"Yes, I know where Chloride City is—it's above the old Keane Wonder. What was my Billy doing there?"

"That is what I hoped you could answer."

"I assume he was looking for his father's old mine, but Bud never worked anything near the Keane Wonder. He knew this, so… why? Why…my Billy?" she said as her icy expression broke—not the normal grieving mother's tears, but a full-blown and pent-up Death Valley tempest and flash flood. "I'm all alone," Bonnie wailed. "Both my Bud and Billy are gone! All for damn mines. Mines gave us nothin' but misery and death. Billy wasn't even supposed to be here," she cried as tears began pooling up on the tabletop. "He said he wanted to travel the East before going to college… Damn mines and damned Panamints—damn you, Bud! I should have put my foot down and not let Billy go. I should have put my foot down with Bud…. Now my whole family is dead, and it's all my fault!" she screamed as she ran into the bedroom and slammed the door behind her.

John's awkwardness continued as he remained sitting at the table, looking for any movement of the door, or for a sign that he could politely leave. *Should I follow her into the bedroom and attempt to comfort her?* he wondered. *Or should I remain here until she comes out seeking help?* He knocked gently and softly spoke through the thin motel walls, "I'm terribly sorry for your loss, Bonnie. If I can do anything, please call me at the sheriff's office. I'll leave my card on the TV stand." With that, John Smithers walked out the door, headed straight home, changed into civilian clothes, and had a beer, then another, then another, and another—until the night's heat had numbed him so much that he lost count.

CHAPTER 17

Despite the heat and wind shear, Paddy rolled the Bronco's windows down somewhere along Highway 127's lonely expanse south of Tecopa. The roar and desiccating effects comforted his nerves and cleared a clogged head. *That was too much time spent with Lizard Len, too much paranoia, and too much talking,* Paddy said to himself. Uncharacteristically, Katherine welcomed the same desiccating wall. For Paddy, open roads were perfect times for quiet thought—and after the Lizard Len interview, he had much to think about. They also needed to plan their next interview, the one with Torrey Small and his crystal-worshiping crazies. Paddy didn't consider them as crazy as Lizard Len, but they were crazy enough that he wanted the window down for quite some time.

Thoughts of mad conspiracies stayed with Paddy as he hit the open highway north of Four Corners. At that point, his thoughts increasingly shifted to Katherine. He would never admit it to anyone, but Paddy liked having her around—even during tense times such as this. She exuded a comfort to Paddy that he hadn't felt in years—thoughts that he never expected to revisit. Unfortunately for Paddy, the window only opened so wide.

Paddy hoped to interview Torrey Small in the morning, but his plan ended there. He had no appointment, nor any idea of how to contact him. Paddy expected someone as eccentric as Torrey Small would stand out in any crowd. *Someone in the town of 28,000 probably could point me in the right direction*, he thought. Both Paddy and Katherine shared an unspoken concern—an interview with another eccentric conspirator was much too soon after their recent Lizard Len experience.

Over the last couple of years, Paddy heard many rumors about Torrey. They said he obsessed over Lizard People and government conspiracies even more than Lizard Len, but he had greater control over his faculties.

Even as a child growing up in Barstow, Torrey loved working with his hands. Somewhere in his teenage years, he dreamt of becoming a mechanical engineer. Despite not doing well in math and science, Torrey still set his sights on being an engineer. Therefore, after high school graduation, he enrolled in Cerro Coso Community College's Indian Wells Valley Campus. He began taking general lower-level courses: English composition, statistics, and calculus. However, only a couple of weeks into his calculus course he became hopelessly lost. Reluctantly, he withdrew and enrolled in algebra instead—to prepare for calculus next semester. For the rest of the semester, he studied and applied himself, but he ended up with only a C in algebra and a D in English composition. He failed statistics.

Torrey's college mediocracy failed to get him into engineering school, so he dropped out of college and took a series of short-term jobs just to pay the rent. He ended up working as a salesman at the local RadioShack. Torrey had no passion for sales, but he received a significant discount on electronic parts. He spent all his free time tinkering and experimenting with electronics.

Torrey lived in a quiet enclave in an already quiet back-section part of Ridgecrest. His lonely olive-drab ranchette was indistinguishable from all the others by being circled by long-dead xeriscape plantings. People driving by often saw his garage open and he inside hunched over electronic components at his workbench making Lizard People receiver globules. However, if anyone drove by recently, they would have found his garage shut tight. Wind-blown paper and plastic debris offered the only movement, except for an occasional, and equally drab, side-blotched lizard scurrying for cover.

⁕

Paddy didn't sleep well that night. To clear his mind and burn energy, he walked Ridgecrest streets and experienced Ridgecrest's predawn hours—fighting the urge to jump into his Bronco and head deep into the Panamints—alone. *I wouldn't do that to Katherine*, he admitted. The next thought brought forth a smile. *Maybe we won't find Torrey.*

Dawn sprung on Ridgecrest like it does most of the time, uneventful, lonely, and hot. Paddy knocked on Katherine's door—she immediately answered and looked fully ready to go.

"Where are we meeting Torrey Small?" she asked.

"I'll find him," whispered Paddy.

"Are you saying you don't know how to find him?"

"I'm saying I'll find him."

"What, by blindly knocking on every door? Is that your plan?"

"If need be, yes—if that'll be what it takes, 'cause I said I'll find him."

Paddy had a better plan than knocking on every door, but he wasn't in the mood to share his thoughts.

"If we are going to work together, please do not leave me in the dark," Katherine snapped.

"Fair enough. We're going to RadioShack. I heard a rumor he works there. I don't know, but it's a lead."

"Okay, thank you," said Katherine. RadioShack it is."

Upon Katherine's nod, Paddy steered the Bronco's wheels toward the north side of town, off China Lake Boulevard.

When they walked into the store, they were immediately confronted with more people than Ballarat ever sees over the span

151

of an entire holiday weekend—and over one-quarter of Shoshone's total population.

Six customers cruised the aisles. One busied himself drilling the salesman on drones. The patient salesman answered every question on even the most minute topic and detailed technical specifications imaginable. The way the salesman handled the customer impressed Paddy, especially considering his youth and likely inexperience. Paddy figured it must be a hard place to work during the Christmas season.

"Is that Torrey?" Katherine whispered to Paddy as she pointed to the salesman.

"I'm not sure," answered Paddy. "We'll find out."

"If so, I sense the kid may feel more comfortable if you spoke with him alone," she muttered to Paddy. "I think it best if I wait outside. Do you mind?"

"No, I don't mind," Paddy said. "I'm just surprised. Thought you wanted us both to talk with him."

"I want answers, I do not care as much how they are obtained," Katherine said as she walked out the door.

Paddy then waited alone for a break in the sales pitch. It didn't come until after the customer bought a medium-utility drone.

"Hello, my name is Patrick Darwin. I'm looking for Torrey Small. Do you know where I may find him?"

"Torrey won't be coming in until later this afternoon. If you're here to buy a drone, I should be able to help you. I'm Tim Nagat."

"Nah, I'm not here for no drone," said Paddy. "I want to ask him about a guy he may know."

"Does this guy have a name, and what does Torrey have to do with it," replied Tim, as his eyes darted around the store as if he was looking for potential paying customers.

"I'll be happy to explain it to Torrey, but the guy's name is Sid Emerson—and it's only a family matter."

"As I said, Torrey's not here," Tim said hesitantly, as his eyes continued flicking across the store. "He's kinda my boss," Tim offered. "So, I'm pretty busy now, so if you would excuse me—"

"If he's your boss, you likely have his number. Would you please call him for us? It's important."

"Please come back later some other day."

"No, I think I'll wait here," Paddy said.

"We are busy. If you're not a customer, you can't just loiter around," Tim said as his voice began cracking.

After seeing that Paddy wasn't going anywhere, Tim went into the corner and called Torrey—his "sort-of boss," friend, and the master crystal-maker that Tim had been studying under for the last year. After the call, Tim busied himself with customers, while Paddy browsed the model drones.

Thirty minutes later, a young red-headed man came through the door and introduced himself to Paddy. "Hello, I'm Torrey Small. Sales Associate Nagat mentioned you wanted to talk to me about some lost guy," he said while wondering what Paddy Small was doing here. "How may I help?"

Torrey's much younger than I expected, Paddy thought as he reached out to shake Torrey's outstretched hand.

After more introductions and chitchat, Torrey graciously agreed to answer Paddy's questions, but not in the store in front of customers. "How about Pita Fresh in two hours? It's a restaurant right down the street on the right—can't miss it."

As Paddy passed through the front door, Tim was ringing up another drone. Business had been good that day.

At 7 p.m. sharp, Paddy walked into the restaurant alone and chose the back corner booth. Torrey arrived two minutes later and joined him. As they waited for their kabobs, Paddy began his questions.

From their discussion, Paddy learned Torrey led a loosely organized group of conspiracists centered on the power of crystals.

Not only did they make crystals, but they deployed them in remote caves and mines throughout southern California.

They spent the entire dinner, and then some, discussing Lizard People and government conspiracies. For Paddy, the odd conversation took him back to Lizard Len's rants—just the day before. Throughout dinner, images of Katherine kept flashing across Paddy's mind. *It doesn't seem right to have dinner and discuss her uncle without her,* Paddy thought. However, most of the conversation had been about Lizard People—things he already heard from Lizard Len. Torrey evaded all direct questions about Sid, and his vagueness extended to his crystal-making operation, where he claimed copyright protection, trade secrets, and personal safety concerns. Other than having good kabobs and an equally satisfying salad, Paddy began thinking the entire interview had been a waste of time.

Maybe I can get more out of the other crystal makers—maybe Tim Nagat, Paddy thought, as he watched Torrey consume the last of the kabobs. Paddy was about to call it quits and return to Katherine when, without warning, Torrey invited Paddy to see his workshop and crystal-making equipment. *Maybe Torrey had begun to trust me,* Paddy thought. *Maybe the dinner wasn't such a waste of time after all.*

After paying for the meal, Paddy followed Torrey's Durango to his drab-olive home surrounded by dead xeriscape plants. There were no side-blotched lizards, drab or otherwise, scurrying for cover as Paddy followed Torrey through a series of padlocks leading to the crystal maker's coveted workshop.

On the garage wall hung spools of wire, multi-meters, scrap metal bins, and every conceivable hand tool imaginable. Near the door hung barrels containing powder, likely used for the globular resin. Dozens of shelves held an untold number of storage trays of unrecognizable junk. Other trays contained things Paddy had no idea what they were or their use or purpose. It was a tinkerer's dreamscape—and an ideal workshop for a mad scientist. Paddy knew Torrey was no scientist, but he began to wonder about the *mad* part.

Picking up a turd-like resinous blob, as if it were a newborn child fresh from the womb, Torrey regaled Paddy with the history of different Lizard People disruptor device designs. He caressed and fawned over each model. Torrey held a newer prototype up to the light to proudly highlight the crystal's translucence. "It's mesmerizing, isn't it?" remarked Torrey, as a glistening refraction sparkled across his broad smile.

Paddy's smile was less about the device's beauty or refined engineered design, since it was merely random metal fragments, including pieces of foil, a few nuts, screws, and a couple of nails, all held together in a roundish, amber-colored resin globule. *It looks like something a second grader would bring home to his mother from art day in school*, Paddy muttered to himself. However, Torrey cherished each of his "children."

Paddy thought he saw a tear well up in Torrey's eyes as he slowly rotated another globule in his hand and also held it up to the light. "It's my first model, Torrey proudly chirped, without looking up or taking his eyes off his beloved offspring. "Although it was the first, it really didn't work all that well, but isn't it a thing of beauty?" Torrey proudly proclaimed. "It was a huge leap forward in craftmanship and precise alignment of the internal components." Paddy nearly choked trying to hold back both a laugh and his evening's kabobs.

"The newer improvements include being able to precisely tune the receiver to specifically match frequencies the Lizard People use to communicate with secret government officials," Torrey said matter-of-factly. Torrey claimed credit for most of the work that went into his crystals, but he also credited his young proteges, Tim Nagat and Mark Levison. Torrey let his whole crystal team use the garage and lab.

According to Torrey, the crystals are the only means to interrupt radio communications between the subterranean Lizard People and the government's and military's secret facilities hidden in obscure surfaces throughout the West. He said Ridgecrest was the perfect home base to mount his counter-offensive since a high concentration of the secret communication sites were located near Death Valley.

"The government has for a long time wanted total command and control over the American population," he spouted with a passion that would have made Lizard Len proud. "They are afraid of us, because we do, after all, outnumber them—both bureaucrats and Lizard People combined."

"Although the government wants total control, their numbers and technology would always be insufficient," Torrey added. "This is why the government depends on Lizard People and their advanced technologies." He continued explaining that since their alliance, the government had been quietly and secretly hiring people, using weak justifications, such as needing more accountants or biologists, but Torrey claimed he had proof of their lies and deception.

"The government has no intention of hiring accountants or biologists. The real purpose of the hires is to slowly build an army of federal bureaucrats, with the help of the Lizard People, to take over the country—the way they took over the United Nations and the European Union," Torrey said with conviction.

Although Torrey called his devices receivers, the way he described them, they more properly functioned as signal scramblers. According to Torrey, they didn't receive communications, "at least not yet." Instead, they scrambled signals and prevented the Lizard People and the government from receiving incoming messages. Convinced of their effectiveness, Torrey and his fellow crystal crew had been quietly hiding the devices in as many cave and mine entrances as they could find.

Torrey claimed that having both the Lizard People and government traitors know of their disruptor placements proved a constant challenge. He said agents routinely sent out patrols to search for and destroy every crystal device they found. Torrey and his crew needed to constantly replace the receivers in a never-ending game of cat and mouse. This also required Torrey and his patriots to roll out a consistent supply of new scramblers. Torrey spent most weekday nights and all weekends working in his workshop making new receivers or deploying them at cave portals across the wide-open lands throughout the region.

Paddy tried once again to switch the conversation over to Sid Emerson, but this time, a little more directly. It was as if Paddy had suddenly activated one of his devices. Torrey's demeanor changed in an instant, and he clammed up. Gone was Torrey's raptured intensity and fawning over his little resinous devices. His smile evaporated faster than a Death Valley mudpuddle.

Sensing the awkwardness, Paddy diverted his conversation back to crystal devices. "How do you know what frequencies the Lizard People use?"

Torrey, in a halting and measured manner, said, "Well, you just learn to fine-tune them entirely by trial and error." They then lapsed again into silence.

Paddy, tired of humoring Torrey and his crystal-making cult, asked, "How do you fine-tune your little resinous turds, because, goddamn it, they are only a glob of resin with nuts, nails, and foil inside—gads!" Paddy regretted his choice of words as soon as his emotions blurted them out, but the conversation had reached a dead end and Torrey wasn't answering any questions about Sid anyway. Paddy just couldn't feign interest any longer.

Torrey said nothing. He only stared as if deep in thought as he quietly placed each receiver back in its original location and protective case. As soon as the last cherished model returned to its proper place, he snapped, "You got to go now—you got to go now. I mean now! You're one of them, aren't you?" he screamed.

"Sorry, I shouldn't've—"

"Never mind," Torrey interrupted. "I don't want to hear it. I don't want to hear anything more from you. Forget you saw anything. If you should come back again, you will be dealt with." As Paddy left, he repeatedly apologized for his rudeness and poor choice of words.

He climbed into the Bronco and drove off into the Ridgecrest night as Torrey stared, making sure he, in fact, left.

Paddy cursed himself as he drove to pick up Katherine. *If Katherine had been there, she would have kept me in check, but now I blew it,* he fumed. "Paddy, you damn fool. She'll be mad at me for losing control," he lamented to himself. He had learned about crystal making, *but how is that gonna help me find Sid Emerson?* "Now, it will be much harder to find her uncle," he grumbled.

As he repeated circling Ridgecrest, Paddy calmed down enough to become reflective. *It would be wonderful to be as passionate about something—anything, as Torrey is about his crystal fetishes. Passionate about something—anything.*

CHAPTER 18

If body recoveries and delivering tragic news weren't enough to keep the sheriff busy, he also contended with fringe elements. John Smithers frequently worried the fringe kept getting sucked into *his* county. "Why don't they just blow on past to San Bernardino County?" he often said to himself—and anyone else who would listen. At least John was grateful that most of the New Age crystal worshipers lived in San Bernardino County, but they wouldn't stay put. *Now, if only Lizard Len would move to San Bernardino County,* he muttered.

Why doesn't Lizard Len and the other conspiracy nuts just move on to some other obsession? It is not as if they've successfully exposed lost cities, Lizard People, or even their so-called secrete chambers. Still, they keep trying. Why?

"John, are you talking to me?" a deputy asked as he passed John's office and overheard him muttering.

"No, just thinkin' out loud," he said, as he moved to shut his office door. *Now, I can think without distractions.* After resting comfortably back behind his desk, John continued pondering his county's many crazies.

John knew all too well that when a person tried hard enough to find something, their mind conjured supporting evidence. If one stared at a random series of dots, over time, or aided by delirium or chemical substances, he or she would begin seeing patterns and connections.

If John were more of a thinking person, he would know that this explained why ancient civilizations came up with star constellations. When the ancient Greeks looked into the sky, the stars connected in ways that formed familiar shapes, ranging from hunters to scorpions and dragons. It became their way of creating a little order out of an otherwise immense, imposing, and chaotic universe.

John, a man of mostly practical beliefs, could sometimes get in deeply philosophical moods. He knew many Western cultures see life as linear. *Life has a start and an end, a birth and a death.* Other cultures, and some crazies, see the world as circles—with a birth, a death, and then a rebirth. Although John claimed not to be a thinking man, he could see the warmth and comfort of a symmetric and circular world with an infinite amount of "redoes." Imagining a stressful and chaotic life on a linear path to death, as if you were simply a leaf in a maelstrom, offers no comfort or spiritual enrichment. John shook himself to stop his philosophizing. *This is not helping me solve any cases. I need to focus and think logically.*

Then again, if John were a thinking type, he might better understand the Lizard People conspiratorialists. They too might find the world much too complex for their comfort. For them, it might be less painful to conjure alien manipulators than to take a deep, hard look inward.

John's attempt at forced mental discipline only resulted in a change in his philosophizing. "How can I use logic to understand crazies, when nothing they do, or think, is logical?" he said out loud to himself while safely behind the closed door. His mind instantly conjured the classic governmental conspiracy paradox. Many of the conspiracy-minded paint government employees as ignorant, inept, and incompetent, but at the same time they accuse them of being the architects of a masterfully complex and elaborate international and intergalactic conspiracy. *This defies common sense*, John thought. *The government can't be both inept dotards and masterful strategists.*

Another common conspiracy-minded belief also defied John's sense of logic, common sense, and order. In today's social media-dominated world, every action, move, or expressed thought that John ever had could be instantaneously transmitted throughout the world.

Surely, big secrets such as evidence of a race of aliens living among us would have leaked by now. *No large organization, even the federal government, can keep the lid on secrets as big as that.* John just didn't buy it that there was a race of shapeshifting Lizard People conspiring with the federal government for world domination. Still, many of his residents did. They believed it passionately—like Lizard Len.

John knew Lizard Len felt victimized and manipulated by powerful forces, those ranging from an evil rampant government run amuck to him—John Smithers the sheriff. John had known Lizard Len for many years. Consequently, he believed they had an understanding. This was not the case with the crystal worshipers. *Lizard Len just rants*, he thought, *and the crystal people mainly just co-opted New Age and Native American beliefs as they developed a harmless pseudo-spiritual religion, or rather cult.* However, John believed the Manson fanatics went beyond that—they were dangerous.

John's worries about the Manson fanatics may have been a case of déjà vu, since coincidently, the radio's crackling and squelching interrupted John's ponderings. Dispatch called to report an impromptu pro-Charles Manson rally happening at that very minute.

John raced out of his office as he called on the radio for every available deputy to meet him in Lone Pine. As John's cruiser rolled down the open roadway, he began talking to himself. "Well, Mandi, instead of hanging low, like you normally do, and leaving your sick little mementos at the Barker Ranch, this time you're inciting violence outside the Eastern Sierra Visitor Center. Why now? Why there?"

On this last question, John already knew the answer. Even *he* never liked the idea of the interagency office and visitor center. With so much federal government hate around here, placing two federal agencies, the Forest Service and Bureau of Land Management, together in one spot did nothing other than create a high-profile target for any anti-government conspiracy nut out there. Today, it happened to be Mandi Mitchem, No-Name Maddox, and the rest of the crazy Manson crowd.

Two deputies had already arrived by the time John rolled onto the scene. It didn't take John long to find the source of the problem. In the corner of the parking lot stood Mandi and No-Name Maddox—both spouting hate and violence against the federal government. John had always figured Mandi to be a bad apple. She believed in government conspiracies, but unlike Lizard Len or the crystal-worshiping nut-jobs, the Manson crowd sought outright violence and rebellion. John worried that was what they planned for this day in Lone Pine. The crowd shouted at Mandi as John approached her on foot. She yelled back. *Somebody's gonna get hurt*, John said to himself as he lifted the loudspeaker to his mouth.

"This is Sheriff Smithers of the sheriff's office. Everyone calm down, go home, and be on your way before I start arresting people. Go home!" John directed the loudspeaker to the crowd. "Freedom to demonstrate is well enough, but not to the point of inciting violence. If you do not stop now, I will arrest you—each and every one of you."

John and No-Name Maddox's eyes met at the exact same moment, and they both froze in their tracks. No-Name began slowly looking around as if considering his next move. The loudspeaker picked up John's sigh as No-Name quietly walked away. John's attention turned to Mandi Mitchem, still holding her ground. Mandi's defiance took John by surprise, since No-Name had the reputation for being the hot-headed one, more so than Mandi.

While looking directly at John, Mandi continued her hate and venom to the scattering crowd. "What we have here, folks, is the county police, reported to be on the side of you and me, but they are no better than the oppressive federal government," Mandi shouted. "The government is not *them*. It's us. It is about time we rose and kicked the oppressors out or force them to serve the will of the people." By then, most of the spectators had seen the writing on the wall—they had turned around and walked away.

The few remaining urchins listened carefully, but they made no sound or gave John any indication of their plans or how far they would be willing to push it. John didn't know what got into them—he knew most of them since they'd been teenagers.

By John's estimate, they were mostly good people, just easily excitable when it came to the federal government's presence—or any other easy excuse to explain their lot in life. John noticed the crowd was evenly split between Manson followers and those who would rather take care of Manson and his looney followers the Death Valley way—not under the eye of cameras, media, or scrutiny. Most probably didn't mean any harm, John thought. It must have otherwise been a slow day in Lone Pine.

Directing his amplified voice to Mandi Mitchem, John said through the megaphone, "No one has a permit or permission to demonstrate. Everyone has exactly three minutes to disperse."

Mandi shouted back, "In a democracy, people don't need no stinkin' permit from the oppressors to talk. It is *you* that need a permit from us. I give you no permission to oppress us any longer." Just then, someone threw a rock at Mandi, and it barely missed her skull. John didn't see who'd thrown it, but the crowd began to get out of control fast.

Mandi shouted back so forcibly the words were unintelligible. This gave her no satisfaction, so she too picked up a rock. This time, the projectile hit its intended target—a poor sap just trying to get a photo. As blood stained the Lone Pine parking lot, John and his deputies moved in, grabbed her by the arm, and dragged her to the police cruiser to arrest her in a less vulnerable location.

On the long drive to Shoshone, John fumed, *Why are there so many crazies in my county?* One thing that John didn't consider: There was a little crazy in everyone in his county—they just needed the right catalyst, or reason, to erupt...and to react.

CHAPTER 19

The Cessna circling overhead grated on Paddy's nerves and patience as he left Mengel Pass on his way to Barker Ranch. Planes in these parts, at least during broad daylight, usually meant someone is lost or has died. In a country as big as Death Valley, planes are common. A person can't drive everywhere, so what else are they supposed to do—walk? Seeing the plane got Paddy thinking. *I'm not getting very far findin' Sid Emerson*, Paddy confessed. *A plane can search so much faster than I can on foot…but, even if I could afford one, where'd I look?*

Paddy's smile broadened as his mind shifted to Katherine. *If she were here, I would be constantly watching her every move to make sure she remained safe.* Paddy worried for Katherine not just because of the desert's harshness, but also due to whom he hoped to meet.

If Sid sought Panamint outcasts, few were as crazy or as outcasted as modern-day Manson followers. So, of all the places and times to find Manson's maniacs, what better place than Barker Ranch on the anniversary of Manson's arrest there? Rumors had it that Mandi Mitchem and others would be there holding a vigil. While Sheriff John Smithers hadn't heard the rumors, Paddy had. Although they rarely advertised such things, at least publicly, Paddy thought it was worth a try.

Upon arriving, Paddy found no vigil, no ceremony, and no Mandi Mitchem. He only found the charred ranch remains strewn about on a wind-swept Panamint loneliness. After he got back from the charred remnants of the Barker Ranch, Paddy stopped to give Katherine an update. However, this time, Katherine provided the update. He had been alone for a long time, deep in the Panamints searching for Sid, so he hadn't heard about the Lone Pine incident and Mandi's arrest. "From the sounds of it, I missed a lot," Paddy said dejectedly.

Despite the embarrassment of not hearing about these things first, Paddy felt himself perking up upon Katherine's briefing. Although he would never admit it, he had grown fond of his time with Katherine. *For a Boston lady, she is not that bad,* he said under his breath as she finished updating him on all that he had missed.

As an aside, Katherine mentioned receiving a call earlier in the day from Nick Rauchoulbe. In the stillness of Death Valley's 108-degree late evening coolness, the news heated Paddy's blood to Death Valley noontime levels.

Despite living many years in the Death Valley region, few around knew Nick well. Up until the last two years, he worked as Tonto Minerals' mining supervisor. After he worked for Tonto Minerals for thirty years, the corporation presented Nick with a choice—move to their failing central Colorado mine operation or leave. Nick chose early retirement. He then began spending his entire free time roaming the open desert springs, draws, canyons, caves, and mines in search of bats—for they had long been his personal passion.

Back when he worked as a mine supervisor, few outside the mine saw Nick, but now, even fewer people did—all due to his nighttime ghostly wanderings. Some said he was a government spy. Others claimed he was an alien Lizard People. Paddy, being once a close friend, knew all the rumors were lies. Except for that one incident, they likely would still be friends. They never patched things up, so over time, they drifted apart. They wandered separate ways—Paddy within himself, and Nick within darkened mountains, playas, caves, and mines looking for bats.

Due to his odd nighttime wanderings, Paddy figured Nick might be a good person to ask for leads on Sid Emerson's disappearance. For the sake of Katherine, Paddy put aside old grievances and called

Nick and left a message. Nick never called Paddy back. Instead, he called and set up an interview appointment with Katherine—and left a message on her voicemail.

Katherine didn't know Paddy had already asked him for an interview. When Katherine called, Nick picked up on the first ring. "Hello, this is Katherine Emerson. Your message said you may have information on my Uncle Sid Emerson's disappearance?"

"I might. I saw Sid when he first rolled into Death Valley, and I later saw him talking to Lizard Len. May I come over to your room so that I may provide more details? Later, I can also show you around the area."

"Yes, I would like that, but could we come to you?"

"We?"

"Yes, I've employed Patrick Darwin to help find my Uncle Sid. We would both like to talk with you. Do you know Patrick Darwin?"

"Yeah, yeah, our paths may have crossed a time or two, but why can't I just talk with you? He's your uncle, isn't he?"

"Yes, of course he is, but I am from Boston, and I do not know the area well, so I hired Paddy. I would prefer having Paddy with me since what you have to say will make much more sense to him."

Nick's slight pause had not gone unnoticed to Katherine, nor had his slightly higher-pitched response. "Sure, sure, both of you come over at 9 a.m. this coming Wednesday."

As Katherine told Paddy about Nick's call, she turned to him and said, "Sorry about the change in our plans."

Paddy just sat there. Lately, it had become a ritual for Paddy and Katherine to have breakfast together at the same restaurant. He looked forward to these Wednesday breakfast conversations. *That damned Nick. I bet he knew all along. I bet he's just pushing my buttons.*

Paddy's mood had not gotten any better by the Wednesday they were to meet with Nick. Katherine couldn't help but notice Paddy had been silent ever since she mentioned Nick Rauchoulbe. *I thought*

Paddy would be happy for the help, Katherine silently fumed as she looked upon what looked like a grown man pouting.

Paddy just sat in silence as he mulled things over. *What game is Nick playing?* Paddy wondered.

Katherine and Paddy rolled up to Nick's house fifteen minutes early. He greeted Katherine warmly at the door. Turning to Paddy, Nick said, "Been a long time, hasn't it? How are you?"

"The same, but it looks as if you've changed. No?"

"As we get older, we all change." With a warm smile, he turned to Katherine. "Hello. It is lovely to meet you, Katherine Emerson. My name is Nick Rauchoulbe. I'm well known around these parts. I get out and talk with people, with friends. I don't just hole up in a lonely trailer. I'm here to help. I may have some information about your uncle. Won't you please have a seat inside so we may talk?"

With that, he gently placed his hand on her shoulder and guided Katherine into his living room and offered her the sofa. Nick sat next to her, leaving Paddy to scan the room looking for an empty chair. As Nick began talking to Katherine, Paddy grabbed a stool from the dining room and hauled it into the living room. Katherine turned toward Paddy and gave him a subtle but warm smile. The only thing Paddy saw of Nick was his back.

Nick continued his story uninterrupted. "I never formally met Sid Emerson, but I saw him around from time to time when he first came into Death Valley. No one could miss him, since he came in asking a lot of questions. Such things here get noticed."

Never turning his attention from Katherine, he paused long enough to offer her a drink. As she declined, Paddy interjected, "When did you last see Sid Emerson?"

Turning even more directly to his guest, he said, "Katherine, I last saw your uncle a few weeks back. He was in lower Johnson Canyon talking to that nut-case Ned Sipe. I didn't follow up or intrude, but it seemed like they had been together for a long time. What they were arguing about—I haven't a clue. Knowing Ned, probably about Charles Manson murders. As far as I've heard, no one saw Sid Emerson again."

Paddy asked, "What would Sid Emerson know about the Manson murders that would so interest Ned Sipe?" After getting no response, Paddy repeated a second time, and again a third.

Sensing tension between the two, Katherine repeated Paddy's question, but this time Nick answered, "I don't know. That's what Ned Sipe does, and that is who he is. Maybe it's because Sid waltzed into town and started asking too many personal questions of things that are none of his business. It puts some people off."

"Like you?" Paddy quipped.

Again, ignoring him, Nick changed the topic and asked Katherine about Boston, how long she planned to stay, and other small talk. Nick's doting on Katherine had not gone unnoticed—to both Katherine and Paddy. Paddy withdrew inward. The shifting of feet, tapping of fingers, and less subtle guttural sounds became his mantra. Suddenly, Paddy bounced to his feet, interrupting Nick's nonsense talk, and blurted to Katherine, "Are you ready to go now?"

Glancing at Nick, at Paddy, and then back at Nick, she said, "I guess it is about time we should be leaving." She answered with a scowl that only Paddy could see. "Nick, before we go," she said, "by chance, do you know where Lizard Len lives when he is not hanging out in Ballarat?"

"Regarding that, I can only offer this," he said as he scribbled on a piece of paper and handed it to Katherine before giving her a warm goodbye. As Katherine and Paddy climbed into the Bronco, she glanced at the note. It consisted of only a phone number, presumably Nick's.

The interview's awkwardness kept both Paddy and Katherine quiet during the long drive back. They each had unspoken things they wanted to say—but didn't. The silence broke only when Katherine suggested they talk with Ned Sipe—and to pay Lizard Len another visit.

"Sure. That's exactly what I'm looking forward to," Paddy said, although his facial expression told so much more.

Katherine threw Paddy a scowl. Paddy normally protected his emotions with an outer casing, much like a tin can, but on this day after their meeting with Nick Rauchoulbe, a few cracks broke the seal.

CHAPTER 20

With Mandi cooling off in the cell and the injured photographer released from the hospital, John looked for a little peace and quiet so he might solve some of his many open investigations. However, that was not to be.

Two days after the pro-Charles Manson demonstration at Lone Pine, the telephone ringing interrupted John's peaceful moment. "I'm not getting any closer with my cases…" he said as he reached for the offending contraption. "I wonder what it is this time."

The county administrator called to request the sheriff's assistance in managing another Charles Manson-related event. He wanted John to help a Charles Manson follower; however, not the typical follower, like Mandi Mitchem, but the equally crazy Ned Sipe.

The county administrator anticipated a large crowd and media circus at Barker Ranch in a few days, so he wanted John and select deputies up there in Class-A dress uniforms to keep the peace and get the county some positive media coverage for a change.

John muttered soft enough so that the county administrator couldn't hear, "Damn it, Ned, didn't I have to deal with you only a few weeks ago? Why are you back so soon?" John hung up the phone after telling his boss, "Sure, we will be there to babysit Ned Sipe."

In an empty landscape full of eccentrics, Ned Sipe stood alone. He too was a loner, but unlike many, Ned has *always* been that way. Instead of spending his youth playing outside with friends, like everyone else, Neddie camped and hid in his parents' garage. In this regard, he had a lot in common with Torrey Small, for during Ned's alone time, he built things. He had little interest in carpentry, wood, or welding metal. Like Torrey, Ned immersed his mind in a world of circuits, wires, capacitors, and electromagnetic servos.

However, their devices were worlds apart. Ned believed he could harness electrons and electromagnetic forces and use them to serve humankind. This optimism and faith in his technical prowess opened a whole world of wondrous possibilities for this once quiet, shy, misunderstood, mistreated, and persecuted little boy.

Over the years, Neddie turned into Ned. However, this little boy in a man's body still looked upon electronics as his savior and pathway to being somebody—somebody with fame, power, and respect. If he could only harness the power of the electron in a unique way, he would show the world that he was not invisible—or so he thought. First, he toiled in his parents' garage until that fateful day on his nineteenth birthday when his parents kicked him out and told him to get a job.

Ned didn't like people. They reciprocated. Therefore, he couldn't see himself as a salesman, although he felt an attraction to the prospects of receiving a generous RadioShack employee discount on all electronic supplies. Instead, Ned took a desk job processing insurance claims. He worked well with numbers, and he liked the job's penchant for solitude. Besides, he thought, it would only be a temporary job. He had faith in his experiments and that one day they'd pay off. If one of his experiments became big, he planned to quit the insurance business and his loathsome pedestrian existence.

With his first few paychecks from his insurance claims job, he set up a tiny shop in a little garage in a rented bungalow on the outskirts of Ridgecrest—not far from Torrey Small. In his little shop, day after day, month after month, and year after year, Ned toiled himself deeper and deeper into the void. On some ill-defined day, Ned Sipe crossed the critical point of no return.

A fascination in death continuously swirled in Ned's dark vortex of a mind. This was more than mere Gothicism. His commitment ran deep. Even he had no idea where his fixation came from, but he figured it had to do with electrons and electronics. Ned fancied humans are merely electronic circuits constructed with biologic parts—not unlike in the movie *The Matrix*. After all, the brain and muscles operate by electronic impulses. To Ned, death meant a breakdown of a person's electronic circuits. His theories led Ned to a variety of ideas and new experiments that he pursued in between his nine-to-five insurance commitment.

Sheriff John Smithers never thought much of Ned's ideas, and he thought even less of Ned's contraption, but if the country administrator told him to babysit Ned, then babysit Ned and his machine he would do. However, if he must waste his time babysitting, he figured he might as well have the new recruit tag along. His boss "encouraged" John to hire more female deputies, since the county had received far too many complaints of sexism and sexist attitudes coming from John's deputies. So, babysitting Ned Sipe was just as good as any job for this recruit. On the day of the event, as John passed her cubicle, he said, "Saddle up. Change into your class As and meet me at my SUV in fifteen minutes. We're heading out to Barker Ranch for the day. I'm gonna introduce you to Ned Sipe."

As John waited at his SUV for the already late recruit, he couldn't figure out how best to manage Ned—this most unusual nutcase. Originally, Ned dreamt of inventing a machine to match or duplicate the electronic impulses generated by a living body. By his estimate, it would be the ultimate machine, one that could sustain life. Maybe, it could even revive the dead, or so he dreamt. Ned had confidence that he could meet this and any other ambitious challenge.

Ned had many thoughts and ideas, but he lacked the mental capacity to carry them through. In this regard, nature had not been kind, for he never grew beyond being a little man with limited depth. No one who knew him ever accused Ned Sipe of being an intellect. Nerdy, yes, but he lacked not only knowledge, talent, and abilities but also the special spark that graced the truly successful. If he ever had talents and abilities, the void absorbed them a long time ago.

Confidence was the one trait that Ned had in abundance. This kept him toiling on his life-energy machine for years on end. He knew he would find the secret—one day. However, days turned into nights, darkness turned to dawn, summers faded into winter, and years morphed into the next.

He long ago abandoned the goal of replicating life's spark. Such sophisticated goals required the type of funding and grey matter that always eluded him. Instead, he latched onto a primordial idea that consumed his last five years. Ned believed electronic energy not only pulsed through the living but also the once-lived. Ned believed electronic signals still circulated through the dead, although with a different character than within living tissue. If true, he thought, this would not only be a good first step to his ultimate goal, but it would also have tremendous commercial appeal. Ned's faith that his machine would one day make him rich grew into a religious intensity. To Ned, it was more than mere cash; he salivated for fame and notoriety. Ned normally went to great lengths to repel people, but few can sustain such one-dimensional force indefinitely, since even a magnet has two poles that meet somewhere in the middle. Ned instinctively knew that if he was to sell his inventions to people, he needed to practice his people skills, so he began exploring this mysterious *middle*.

John was about ready to take off without the recruit when she came into sight running as fast as she could. She hand-pressed and smoothed wrinkles in her class A dress—all on the run and while carrying, and almost dropping, her tactical gear. *She's juggling things better than most rookies*, John thought, as the recruit arrived at the car out-of-breath but wrinkle-free. Without a word, they both clambered into the SUV before John pointed it in the direction of Barker Ranch.

A minute later, the recruit broke the silence. "Who is Ned Snipe, and what are we doing?"

"His name is Sipe, and we are babysitting."

"Babysitting, sir?"

"Well, that's what I call it. Ned worked the public into a frenzy about a stupid machine he invented. He's demonstrating it at Barker Ranch in front of local newspapers and TV stations. Since the media will be there, the county administrator wants us there for crowd control and to be media darlings to supposedly improve our public image. So, yes, babysitting."

"What does his machine do?"

"Ned fancies himself an inventor. As the story goes, Ned's life took a turn a few years back when he picked up a rumpled newspaper left lying about. The back of the paper had a remembrance piece on the anniversary of the infamous Charles Manson murders."

"Charles Manson," the young recruit interrupted. "Wasn't he the person that killed those Hollywood people back in the '50s?"

"Late '60s, actually. But yeah, it hit the national news for a long time. Law enforcement finally caught the creep up at Barker Ranch—at the place we're heading."

"Why is today's event held at Barker Ranch?"

"Supposedly, in the same article that Ned read a few years back, it also had a story of Charles Manson petitioning the court to let him out of prison. This article gave Ned an idea—he doesn't get many, so this one became distinct. Ned envisioned a new experiment— one that would make him rich and more famous than even Charles Manson himself."

"I still don't understand," the recruit asked, as the two sped down the empty highway leading toward Barker Ranch in the southern Panamints.

"Conspiracy-minded maniacs have long speculated the charismatic cult leader murdered more people than he admitted," John explained to the recruit. "At times, various Mansonphiles had pointed to nearly every dirt mound or sunken desert hollow as a 'sure sign' of an unrecorded Manson victim."

"That does sound crazy, sir," the recruit said.

"You don't know the half of it," John said. "Manson maniacs thrive on tasty speculation, and the media eats it up faster than a handful of pinyon nuts. This is why Ned and the media are hosting their spectacle at Barker Ranch."

"What does his machine do?"

"Nothin'," the sheriff answered, "but Ned claims it detects buried bodies."

"No fooling? He believes his machine can detect dead and buried tissue. Is he all there, sir?"

"He's a loon as far as I'm concerned, but he uses just enough techno-babble to make fools think he knows what he's talking about."

"I assume you're talking about the county administrator, sir?"

"Well, I'll let you decide for yourself on that one," John added. "Anyhow, about Ned, as he explains it, dead tissue emits a unique electronic signal. To maximize media coverage, Ned linked his dead body detecting machine to the public's sick fascination with Charles Manson. In Ned's mind, his machine has commercial applications well beyond locating new Charles Manson burials, but none with such a built-in media allure."

"I hadn't heard of Charles Manson in years," the recruit said.

"Well, around here, you'll hear his name often. That is what attracted Ned to the Manson story—a public spectacle with built-in notoriety," John explained. "He hopes to showcase his scientific acumen, novel ideas, creative inventions, on-screen presence, and self-described superior intellect.

Such hopes caused Ned to daydream and speculate that newspapers, magazines, and social media posts would feature his name. Ned dreamt that office lunchroom gossip throughout California or even the nation would be *Ned Sipe this, Ned Sipe that*. While daydreaming or not, Ned could see, taste, and feel his upcoming notoriety. Many times, late at night or early in the morning, Ned would mumble to himself, "Just you wait. Everyone will be sorry for not believing in me."

Ned knew his challenges were steep. He not only needed to invent a machine that would detect dead tissue, but it also needed to differentiate between human flesh and the wide assortment of desiccated carcasses of animals that all too frequently dropped dead from dehydration. This was, after all, Death Valley. He sketched ideas on a yellow notepad, threw them away, and sketched some more, then threw those away too. He knew an idea would eventually come to his weary head—someday.

To flesh out his ideas, Ned furiously sketched plans for a machine to detect fluorine gas, since the main source of environmental fluorine is from fluorination of urban water supplies. According to Lizard Len, fluorination of our water supply is a Lizard People and government conspiracy, but Ned Sipe knew *he* could use it as a distinct human-tracer. On one of Ned's scrawled-upon yellow notepads he noted that city-dwellers had been drinking fluoridated water for years. In a human body, excess fluorine embeds itself onto live tissue. As Ned's notes demonstrated, when a person dies, the chemical bonds holding accumulated fluorine begin degassing. Since wild animals don't drink fluoridated water, such a device would be the Eureka discovery to enable him to detect the presence of a dead human body, or so Ned thought—and dreamt.

Ned adorned his rod-shaped prototype, complete with copper-tubing coil loops duct-taped to an old lawn mower chassis. Ungainly, yes, and even by Ned's estimate, ugly; however, according to his calculations, it worked. He figured that he would refine the shape, profile, and chassis later. As Ned frequently said, even the original prototype Apple phone was not nearly as sleek as the final released version.

He began taking it to remote desert canyons to scan parched rabbitbrush and saltbush fields. As he passed the sensor over empty ground, his flesh-detecting machine emitted slow, hypnotic beeping pulses, but, according to Ned, when detecting fluoride-degassing dead bodies the machine hissed and clicked in rapid succession.

While testing his machine, he practiced storylines and speeches—things he would tell reporters, thousands of devoted and loving fans, and countless well-wishers: "As the sensor picks up trace quantities of fluorine gas, the sophisticated electronics convert the signal into the bouncing and rapidly pulsating beeps that you now hear coming from the machine's tiny speakers."

With his shiny new device in tow, Ned roamed where Manson explored, walked where Manson strode, and paused where the cultist stopped. Ned attempted a feat that few had tried, and even fewer would ever wish to have tried; he attempted to get into Manson's head.

My time will soon be at hand, Ned kept telling himself as the testing day drew near. It had been two years since he first sketched his now yellowed notes. Two years of toiling, two years of taunts, and two years of poverty and indignations. For Ned, it was the moment of truth. His faith complete—that his machine was ready to demonstrate it in front of a large audience.

For the next three weeks, Ned talked up his remarkable find to anyone who would listen and even quite a few who wouldn't. Since people like mysteries, conspiracies, and the Manson story, it didn't take long to generate enough buzz for people near and far to begin talking about Ned and his magical machine. The county administrator received many calls from enthusiastic voters asking what the government planned to do about Ned's claim. The administrator chose to appoint Ned as the keynote speaker for a formal presentation to the combined tourism and economic development departments and advisory committees. After all the years of being written off as a crackpot, Ned became elated upon receiving this news.

In his many Manson wanderings, Ned passed several likely locations for his special media event. Ned chose a site adjacent to the abandoned Barker Ranch as his best option for the greatest media exposure. *So, it is set—Barker Ranch will be the start of my glory,* he gloated. Previously, Ned discovered a suspicious-looking sunken depression, large enough to hold several bodies, in the otherwise smooth and flat desert surface, nearly a quarter mile north of Barker Ranch, not far from Mengel Pass. *Perfect*, he said to himself. *Perfect*.

Ned lugged his gangly machine all the way to Mengel Pass, complete with its fragile rotating arms, coils of copper wire, and the various sizes of metal tubing needed for fine calibration. He also hand-carried the pendulum, headphones, cassette tape recording device, and two large car-sized batteries. After several trips, he and the equipment arrived at the suspected burial site.

Although two hours early, by the time John and the new recruit arrived, a sizable crowd had already gathered. Doubters and believers alike began arriving to see what had attracted so much fuss. Reporters busily set up as other newspapers, magazines, TV news outlets, independent journalists, podcast stars, and social media influencers filtered in. No one wanted to be left out of such an audacious occasion. Some reporters claimed this would surely be the future talk around office lunch tables, akin to "Where were you for the moon landing?" Ned could see the headline printed vividly into his head: "Where were you when Ned Sipe revealed Manson's previously undisclosed murders?"

John could see a headline too. "Get Two Tylenol for the Price of One," he increasingly visualized as more people gathered to witness the spectacle.

Sheriff John Smithers whispered to the recruit, "This whole thing is stupid, but the boss wants us to put on a good show and look good for the cameras."

"Why does he care so much?" she responded.

"He doesn't want people to think their government is stopping American ingenuity and exceptionalism." After a long pause, he added, "I guess if this kook thinks he invented a dead-body-detecting machine, who are we to stand in his way?"

Ned Sipe convinced the county administrator to have the sheriff come to hint at official endorsement. Ned's successful granting of this request was not unlike George Shufelt when he convinced the Los Angeles commissioners for his second dig permit.

While waiting for Ned Sipe's big day, John impatiently paced about and muttered under his breath, "Humor him, he says. I'll humor him." Humor him he did, as the crowd size grew and began getting out of hand.

John scanned the whole ridiculous scene. The media busied themselves with their own electronic devices and prepped by recording introductions and background descriptions. Camera operators rushed about mounting devices on tripods. Among all the hubbub, freaks, and fools, only one person stood out to John's watchful eyes. Katherine had arrived, and she came alone. Katherine only came to fight off her growing fear that the burial might her uncle's.

Ned kept pacing back and forth, waiting for his moment to begin. John wondered just how much of a fool Ned would make of the good people of Inyo County if nothing panned out. He stood on the sidelines, intent on having Ned assume full ownership. When things go south, John didn't want any of the stain to land on him or his county.

However, *I'll be damned if I will let Ned get things out of hand.*

Unaware of isolation being a part of his strategy, Katherine noticed John standing by himself, so she approached to strike up a conversation.

"Hello, Katherine. Any luck finding your uncle?"

"You would be the second to know," Katherine replied.

"If you're worried that it's your uncle in Ned's grave, I wouldn't give it a second thought. Ned's a nutcase. There's no body buried there—it's all in Ned's mind. The county administrator and I are just humoring him. That's all."

"Thanks. That is what I thought, but something told me I should check it out nonetheless."

As John listened to Katherine, he also kept a close eye on the gathering crowd. As soon as she began walking away, a middle-aged man turned the corner, but when the man looked up and saw Katherine, he abruptly turned and ran off. *Who is that guy?* John asked himself as he witnessed the entire scene. Turning to Katherine, John said, "I've heard reports of a stranger lurking about asking around about Bud Torgerson and his silver. I also heard that he's also asking about you, Katherine."

"Me?" Katherine gasped. "Who would spy on me?"

"I don't know who that guy is, but he seems different than all the other Torgerson silver crazies," John said to Katherine. *I'll have to keep an eye out for him and figure out what he's up to*, John thought as Ned approached the makeshift podium.

Once the reporters completed their preparations, almost on cue, they descended on Ned all at once. Beaming, Ned talked of his genius and his ingenious machine. Whenever he described the machine, his baby, he never provided enough specifics for anyone to have a clue how it supposedly worked. But no one seemed to care. To them, any attempt to describe it would have been too *sciency*. They came for spectacle, not scientific precision or technical minutia. John doubted if even Ned had a clue how it supposedly worked. *Maybe this is all Ned's sick attempt to capture his fifteen minutes of fame*, John speculated as his eyes continued scanning the crowd looking for the mysterious stranger.

Ned spoke slowly into the microphone to ensure he didn't get feedback, to ensure all reporters heard every word, and to maximize anticipation and drama. What Ned lacked in scientific acumen he made up in knowing how to work a crowd. He welcomed everyone, introducing himself as the brilliant inventor who had built the miraculous dead-body-detecting machine.

With trembling hands, Ned connected wires, car batteries, appendages, and a tape-recording device, and plugged in his RadioShack headphones. He wired the speakers so sound came out simultaneously across the entire perimeter. Once it was humming and clicking, Ned began wheeling the bulky equipment in an as straight a line as he could, hoping to form a grid-search pattern.

Breathing paused as the crowd leaned in to be the first to hear the clatter from a dead body. However, the speakers and headphones remained as still as the morning air. After minutes of the same, almost on cue, the sounds of heads turning, murmuring, and rustling signaled growing disappointment and disillusionment.

Without them having to say a word, John instantaneously knew the reporters felt the event had been a waste of time. The only clicking noises heard were cameras turning off and the latching of stowage cases. The crowd began drifting off to their waiting vehicles parked lower in the canyon. As beads of sweat formed on Ned's temples and began to run across his stone-cold expression, he lunged at the microphone. "Please, everyone, please be patient," he insisted. "I just realized I hadn't properly calibrated the machine. I'll do that ASAP and I will begin the search again in a few minutes. Again, thank you for your patience."

As Ned fumbled with his machine, a couple of reporters stepped in closer. One shouted, "Can you explain why your machine failed?"

Snapping his head up from feigned calibrations, Ned spat, "It didn't fail!" In an especially shrill tone, he groveled, "My machine works. As I said, it just needs calibration. I calibrated it to the soils near my home—these soils are different!"

"It sounds like it failed to me," the reporter replied.

"Many people called Einstein and Edison failures," Ned explained, as he wiped the sweat upon his sleeve, "but Edison himself once said he never had a failure, that he successfully proved a thousand times that certain experiments didn't work."

"So, did you just prove that your machine doesn't work?" the reporter countered.

"No, no, not at all. Edison had thousands of attempts; this was only my first try. My machine *does* work. Please wait for the calibration."

After Ned tightened and loosened the same screws over and over, and placed fresh duct tape on the hatch's cover, he approached the microphone again. "Everyone, please gather around. Thank you for your patience. I just finished the calibration. I am now ready to begin the *real* grid search."

With fewer people remaining, Ned turned his machine back on, and began rolling it over the depression. As soon as it tumbled into the spot, pulsating audible clicks erupted from the speakers. However, no matter how fast the chatter, it was no match for Ned's racing heartbeat. With a pronounced smile, Ned muttered, *Thank God.*

Turning to the thinning crowd, as they were leaning in to hear history in the making, Ned interpreted the results. "Those sounds you just heard are the clear sounds of a previously unknown human burial." A few gasps came from the crowd, as two reporters thrust their microphones even closer toward Ned and his mesmerizing machine. "Given the location, at Charles Manson's last camp, it clearly indicates the burial that *my* machine just discovered *must* be connected with the Manson murders."

Ned, having regained his media-conscious composure, grabbed a shovel and began digging into the depression to uncover the body and provide further proof of his machine's success. John rushed in. Speaking softly so no reporters could hear, John told Ned, "You can't dig. If it's a body, it's against the law to dig up a grave without a permit. Also, if it is a body, it's a law enforcement matter, not a circus freak show."

The crowd and reporters began looking about, wondering what was going on. Sensing a PR-related catastrophe and being chewed out by the county administrator, John seized Ned's microphone and addressed the crowd. "Hello. I am the county sheriff. Everyone please be calm and let me explain. If there is a body here, it may be a crime scene. If so, then it's a criminal investigation." All John could hear were groans and more clicking from closing camera cases. Ned crouched as if readied to pounce upon the sheriff's jugular or seize control of the microphone—or both.

John managed to maintain control, and then spoke again into the microphone. "If it is an older burial, it may be Native American. If so, I need to consult with the Timbisha Tribe and archeologists need to be present for any digging. I am sorry you all came out all this way for nothing, but there will be no digging here today. Sorry. Please stay safe as you leave."

As the remaining crowd began to pack up and head home, Ned approached John and through his puffy red face sternly admonished, "The county administrator will hear about this. This is not over—not by a long shot."

Ned snapped the microphone away from John and spoke to the reporters still within earshot. "Thank you, everyone, for coming. I *will* get the permits and return as soon as I can. Please come back so you may witness firsthand part two of this enfolding Charles Manson saga. And remember, I accept donations. Please visit my website for details." After his concluding remarks, Ned steamed off to collect his composure.

Ned slowly and defiantly began gathering equipment and loading carts. To haul all his stuff down to his truck in lower Goler Wash took several trips. As Ned packed his stuff, John's deputies, including the new recruit, packed all their traffic cones, temporary check-in points, first-aid stations, barricades, and the assortment of other equipment deployed for the debacle. For Sheriff John Smithers, it had been a busy day. He headed home to get some much-needed rest.

CHAPTER 21

Torrey Small's nerves kept him up all night. The Pan America Illuminati conference that he had been waiting for years had just started. The scuttlebutt was that it would be even better than the last symposium, the one held in Victorville three years previously. Not only did that experience help Torrey better understand the Lizard People truth, but it was the catalyst for his deep emersion into the Lizard People communications specialty. Torrey had too many aggressive plans to sleep the night before the Pomona's PAI conference. Besides attending as many sessions as he could, he hoped to network with the search committee members—to lobby them to support him to host the next conference. He also planned to announce his forming a Ridgecrest PAI chapter, since most of this year's early registrations had come from the expansive Mojave region between Ridgecrest and Death Valley. Torrey believed the growing prominence of true believers within the Death Valley area created fertile grounds for a new face to rise within the Pan American Illuminati ranks—a situation that Torrey feverishly planned to exploit.

The convention's first sessions went better than he could have hoped. He learned so much, made good contacts, and put feelers out to gauge the level of support for a new chapter. "This is the best conference—ever," chirped Torrey to his proteges, Tim Nagat and Mark Levison.

At Katherine's prompting, even Paddy showed up. She prodded his attendance to learn more about the Lizard People and hopefully Sid Emerson's disappearance. However, since Torrey Small still thought Paddy was in league with the Lizard People, he wouldn't likely divulge any information to Paddy. This is where Katherine came in. Both she and Paddy agreed that she would pump Torrey for information, since Katherine's unrecognized face would allow her greater opportunities to listen in on conversations without any preconceived barriers and baggage.

During the lunch hour of the convention's first day, Torrey staffed an exhibit booth alone. He sold his "Patriot Signal Disruptor" devices, the new name given to his resin globules. Torrey believed he set the new PSD's frequency at the precise kilohertz needed to disrupt the newer and more sophisticated communication signals used by both federal agencies and alien invaders. Torrey knew they would sell well at the convention. By the time Katherine approached, he had already sold out all pre-made devices. Using a few demonstration models, he began taking backorders. Katherine walked up to the booth, picked up a brochure, and feigned interest in one of the resin globules prominently displayed.

"This looks interesting—tell me about it," Katherine said while fondling the ugly resin blob.

"What you have in your hand is the world's best PSD device, specifically crafted and designed for use in the Mojave Desert," Torrey beamed. "It took me years to perfect the design. All my products are one hundred percent guaranteed. Would you like to know more?"

"Yes, please," Katherine said.

"I currently have six models, each tuned to specific frequencies. While all work in this region, that specific model is fine-tuned and optimized for Fort Irwin frequencies."

"Seems impressive, but for me, I need basic information. I'm new here. For instance, what exactly is a PSD?"

"PSD stands for Patriot Signal Disruptor. They go by different trade names, but none are as good as my models."

"Did you make this?" exclaimed Katherine.

"Yes, that is my PSD design. I'm Torrey Small. These are my personal design."

While Torrey began droning away on his PSD devices, Katherine's mind wandered elsewhere. *I do not think he recognizes me. This is great, I just need to avoid acting suspicious*, Katherine thought as Torrey continued uninterrupted.

"There're well-known facts that the federal government and the military-industrial complex have run amuck, are spying on U.S. citizens, and collecting personal data on all of us," Torrey added. "The question for you is, are *you* content with just sitting by while they manipulate our lives? True patriots use PSDs to scramble and disrupt the network of their spying and corruption so we can live in freedom as the Founding Fathers envisioned," Torrey beamed.

"My, all that from this little contraption? Your PSD? I take it you are not the only one that makes them?" Katherine asked coyly.

"I wish. But no. Many people make PSDs—mine just happens to be the best. Also, I have the only ones specifically tuned for special applications."

"Like this Fort Irving one?"

"Fort Irwin. It's Fort Irwin. But yes—exactly."

"Why Fort Irwin?"

"You're new here, aren't you? Well, it all goes back to the early twentieth century, to old Goldstone, now one of the many ghost towns spread throughout the Mojave Desert, but it once had been a thriving town."

Without stopping for breath, Torrey reached down and handed Katherine a photocopy of an article on the Goldstone incident. "Goldstone miners drilled and sunk mines and wells beginning in 1910. Some nearly three hundred feet deep," Torrey explained as Katherine began thumbing through the Goldstone paper. "Other shafts reached rich gold veins and the town and economy boomed. Six years later, there were 150 miners, shopkeepers, saloon owners, and other businessmen—"

"Is Goldstone near here?" Katherine interrupted.

"I'm getting to that," Torrey said. "Things were looking good as they explored each new shaft. Then, just as things began taking off, every mine stopped, and all the miners and townsfolk left or entirely disappeared."

"Oh, my! That sounds fascinating. Is this story in this handout? May I keep it?"

"Yes, sure, it's all free. I provide this and other information to spread the truth."

"Why did the miners leave?" asked Katherine.

"No one knew, but recent research uncovered the truth. It wasn't easy. The government purged all newspaper archives from this period. They didn't want the truth getting out."

"What happened?"

"With all the drilling and tunneling in the area, the Goldstone miners intercepted a catacomb containing a race of aliens that kept their whereabouts secret. So, the aliens killed all the Goldstone miners and townspeople."

"I take it Goldstone is near Fort Irwin?"

"Yes, the Goldstone site sat empty until the 1980s when Fort Irwin began their electromagnetic experiments. The experiments uncovered aliens living below the base. You see, the aliens communicated through electromagnetic signals. However, rather than the aliens killing the army personnel, like they did the miners, and rather than the military killing the aliens, they both saw it as an opportunity to conspire and collaborate."

As a young couple approached the booth and Torrey's in-depth truth-telling, Torrey said to Katherine, "Excuse me for one moment—please wait right here. I'd love to continue telling you the Goldstone story."

Katherine didn't have to wait long, since the young couple didn't stay. "I guess they aren't interested in the truth," whispered Torrey. Once alone again with Katherine, Torrey asked where he left off.

"Why would the Army and the aliens want to conspire? For what purpose?"

"You need to read that article I gave you because the truth is all there."

After a brief pause to greet and hand out a brochure to someone walking past, Torrey continued his Fort Irwin story. "It took the government and aliens years to construct and put into operation Fort Irwin's R-2502 Special Use Airspace Complex. Who knows what secret projects they hatched in this undisclosed military base? Soon after, the government, with alien assistance, built Fort Irwin's Goldstone Deep Space Communications Complex. With this sophisticated secret communication facility and its mega-power generation capability, few things could stop the Lizard People's final takeover. Until my PSD came along."

"This little device?"

"Yes, that one. And it is only eighty-five dollars. Small price for our freedom, don't you think?"

"Will only one do? I would think it would take more than one," Katherine asked.

"Yes, of course. While each PSD is powerful, the real power comes from an entire network of PSDs working in tandem."

"May I buy one?" Katherine asked.

"Sure, but I have a little problem here. I've sold so many that lately I have only been taking orders. However, you've been really great, so I'm gonna cut you a deal. I'll let you have one of my demonstration models for only fifty dollars—cash. How's that?"

"That would be great. Thank you."

As Katherine counted out fifty dollars, Torrey asked, "May I ask your name and where you're from?"

After a second or two of hesitation, Katherine answered, "Elizabeth. My name is Elizabeth, and I'm from Texas."

After pocketing the cash, Torrey continued his sales job. "We always need to stay one step in front of them. I would like to increase my PSD production capacity, but none of it's automated," Torrey said. "We build and tune them by hand. I need funding to ramp up production and automate the process. Would you be willing to get in the ground floor of this investment? This is not just an economic investment; it's an investment in keeping your freedom."

"Well, I would have to think about it more, but thank you for the opportunity, and thanks for the information. But, speaking about PSDs, you said you have different models based on different frequencies. What are the other models—other than Fort Irwin?"

"I have an all-purpose, universal model. One tuned to China Lake Naval Weapons Center. One to Edwards Air Force Base. One tuned to the Marine Corps Logistics Base in Barstow. One tuned to a combined Nevada Test Site and Area 51, and, of course, the Fort Irwin model that's in your hand. The universal is the most popular model."

"Again, thank you for your time. I enjoyed our chat."

After her long stay at the booths, Katherine wandered off to attend a presentation, but there were many to choose from. The program indicated that "Pipelines: Pathway to Prosperity or a Paean to Purgatory" would be starting soon. She also wanted to go to the one on the Tule Springs paleontological site near Las Vegas. The program stated that government scientists had uncovered fossil evidence of an ancient race of human-sized reptilians. While that one sounded entertaining, Katherine doubted it could help find her uncle. Instead, Katherine strolled over to concurrent session B, "Lizard People, the Central Fire, and the End of Humanity."

While waiting for the speaker to arrive, Katherine began reading the material Torrey had handed her. According to the fliers, the Lizard People had been busy. They involved themselves in a proposed Canadian pipeline intended to carry natural gas from the tar sands, but, it was only a means to siphon off U.S. oil and energy resources if war with the Lizard People should ever break out.

Another flier suspected the Chinese government had been slowly buying up American loans to help the Lizard People take over global financial markets and manipulate U.S. markets and the national economy.

Within still another brochure, Katherine read that even our allies were not free from suspicion. Supposedly, an alien partnership linked Swedish technological know-how and German manufacturing capability and created a secret boring device that had been covertly tunneling under the White House and the Pentagon. Once completed, the Lizard People planned to kidnap the president and Joint Chiefs of Staff to get their clutches on the launch codes and the U.S. nuclear arsenal.

Still another brochure stated that, besides manipulating U.S. elections, Russia placed moles directly in the White House. Their sole mission is to turn the various factions and government branches against each other. With an already self-inflicted fractionalized society, it would likely not take much to tip the scale. According to a pamphlet, Charles Manson had the right idea back in the 1960s; however, instead of race being the coming apocalypse, it will instead be class and political party affiliation—all manipulated and controlled by Lizard People.

Katherine had to put the brochures away, not only because the next speaker had started, but because the thought of her dear uncle being mixed up with such people became too disturbing. She turned in her seat, looking to see if Paddy had arrived yet. No sign of him yet. *He said he would show up. He must be in another session,* she thought.

Turning her attention back to the speaker, who by then had begun an impressive fire-and-brimstone oration that had captured everyone's attention, except one. Still, there were snippets that even Katherine found intriguing. However, much of it Katherine had already heard from others.

While Katherine didn't believe in the legend, she couldn't help but be impressed with the passion displayed by not only the speaker but the entire engaged audience. *They are true believers,* she guessed. It also reminded her of something Paddy once said. *People will often believe anything, as long as someone gives them what they yearn for the most—something to believe in. With that, a little faith will take them far.*

After the presentation, she searched for Paddy throughout the hallways, the poster session set-up room, and the commercial vendor aisle. No Paddy. While she waited and searched, she bumped into Lizard Len—the conference's keynote speaker. *Maybe there is some truth to him once being an academic,* she thought as she tried to imagine him being anything but Lizard Len.

During the keynote talk, Katherine watched Lizard Len pace back and forth, a true master in how to work the crowd. She had planned to leave to look for Paddy, but the prospects of listening to Lizard Len compelled her to stay.

Toward the end of Lizard Len's keynote talk, he cautioned the audience to "keep a wary eye out for the government, so-called scientists that have been spying on us, and the biggest spy of them all—a guy that lives in a run-down trailer and claims not to interact with humans."

Paddy, a spy? Katherine smiled upon the thought. *How amusing.*

Katherine saw no difference between Lizard Len's entire one-hour talk and her and Paddy's interview with him—just two weeks ago. Having already heard it freed her to simply watch the crowd and the reactions of the most faithful. It reminded her of the chilling 1960 *Twilight Zone* episode "The Monsters Are Due on Maple Street." Viewers of that classic show sat gap-jawed upon the disturbing notion that society's most destructive forces may not be bombs or invading troops, but instead may come from within. The episode made it believable that paranoia, suspicion, and mistrust can make otherwise friendly neighbors turn on one another with only a sprinkling of seeds of doubts planted in their inflicted and damaged minds.

After Lizard Len's session, Katherine renewed her search for Paddy. When she walked out to her car, she picked up a note left on her windshield. It read, "Sorry, Katherine. I couldn't take it any longer. I hitched home. See you later—Paddy."

Katherine later learned that Paddy had made all attempts to sit in on the presentation—but he just couldn't. The language was too foreign and the subject matter too academic for Paddy's taste. He began listening to the session "Astrometric Proof of Alien Life." *Despite the science-like setting, this guy's no scientist*, Paddy thought. *Ron Telling would never be caught dead in such a place.* Paddy dismissed him as merely an amateur theologian—a zealot. According to Paddy, the man spoke with so much impassioned enthusiasm, it rose to such exalted crescendos, that it reminded him of back when his mother used to force him to go to church. Despite no longer being a child, Paddy still remembered the fieriest passages. "Four angels will appear issuing brimstone from their mouths, accompanied by locusts to usher in the end of the world," the preacher shouted from his heavenly lit pulpit.

In Patrick's mind, the conference speaker was not speaking from a podium; instead he arose from a pulpit, as he waved his arms, gyrated, and shouted. "Breastplated, fire-breathing dragon stories told to us as youth sound remarkably similar to what we now know as Lizard People," the speaker orated to his raptured audience. "This cannot be a coincidence," he added. "What the ancients took for dragons were in fact reptilian Lizard People sent by Satan himself."

Paddy had too many flashbacks. A preacher prancing about, trying to leap directly into the soul of a squirming little boy who wanted nothing more than to run away and never return. Paddy, now fully grown, had even fewer inhibitions to not run away. Before the speaker began his next passage, Paddy darkened the doorway for only a split second before fading into the Pomona pavement. With thumbs up, he headed home.

CHAPTER 22

The loner John spotted slinking away from Barker Ranch had been spending much of his time remaining unnoticed, attempting to disappear in the mountains—alone. In his search for gold and silver, he crept in the shadows. To live off the land in the desert ranges requires movement. The Timbisha knew this secret—as they survived in this country for eons. Historically, Timbisha bands moved their camps to correspond with wildlife movement, plant ripening cycles, and weather patterns. Summer heat in Death Valley's lowlands pushed them out of the valley's mesquite bosques and into the cooler Panamints during the important pinyon nut gathering season. When that season waned, they moved to their next cyclic seasonal encampment. This way, they found enough food, water, and resources to continue living in the unforgiving landscape longer than even oral tradition can recall. Modern-day people living off the grid could learn plenty from the Timbisha. The slinking loner had—for he vowed never to spend a long time in any one spot.

Isolated camps in modern times are increasingly difficult to maintain without being noticed or ransacked. More people roam the Death Valley hills than ever before. However, they usually travel to predictable places. The loner was anything but predictable. He rarely stayed in one place long: a mine here, an alcove there, or even in abandoned buildings. He stayed no more than two or three weeks in any one spot.

For pure isolation, the loner preferred the Saline Range, but only the western margins hold dependable water. Lately, he had been hiding in an alcove on the eastern flank of Sugarloaf Peak. It had all the makings of a good hiding spot, other than he had to hand-carry water all the way from Five Mile, Anvil, or Lost Springs.

On his next water-gathering day, the loner traveled to Lost Spring in the heat of a burning summer day—the least likely time to run into other people. He stopped dipping water when he saw a glare in the distance—the type of reflection that a pair of binoculars makes. It may have been nothing, but he silently slipped away to collect water from Five Mile Spring instead. *Besides, Lost Spring had always been a bit salty anyhow*, he thought. Walking to this other watering hole was no simple task since the two springs were several miles apart. However, being fit, he made the trip in record time.

As he drew water from Five Mile Spring, the loner once again saw movement and reflection in the distance. Someone followed. Someone watched. This time, *He's close*, the loner fretted. He stashed the water jugs among boulders and dashed off to find a place to hide and remain motionless.

After nearly an hour in the same spot, he slowly crept out. He barely cleared the overhang before hearing the rattling of a stone. *Maybe a coyote*, he told himself—if nothing more, as an attempt to calm his throbbing nerves. *I have few options*, he told himself as his eyes jumped left, right, and then back left. He hunkered down behind a boulder and breathed slowly and controlled. Over the sound of his beating heart, he sensed the guy getting closer with each passing heartbeat. Suddenly, it spoke.

"Bud, is that you? This is your brother Stade. I'm not here to hurt you, take you back, or interfere in any way. I just want to talk. Is that okay? Again, I'm your brother."

The loner remained crouched—lower than playa salt. Inwardly, *This can't be real. What's Stade doing here—of all places?* The loner made no sound.

"I know it's you. I've been watching you for some time. I don't know how it happened, but clearly, you're not dead."

In response, Stade received only silence. "Why aren't you… dead, I mean? Why aren't you dead? I'm glad you're not," Stade said to the silence. "Bonnie and Billy will be so happy. Please come out and let's talk."

Bud remained crystallized in his depression.

Sensing his brother was not going to budge, Stade cautiously approached. Inch by inch Stade crept closer to his long-estranged brother. When Stade got to within sixty feet, he called out again. "Sorry, money got between us, and sorry for not being there for Dad. Sorry for being young and stupid, but the past is in the past—it has been so very long ago. Please come out and let's talk, Bud, and I'll make proper amends."

Stade continued talking, apologizing, and creeping closer. For comfort, he gently reached down and felt the metal on his model 66 Smith & Wesson .357 Magnum tucked in his waistband. Despite being a hot day, the stainless steel felt cold as Stade brought it up to a ready position.

Bud couldn't see Stade, let alone the revolver, but he knew not to trust either. Bud also knew his brother had forced him into this cold decision. *I cannot let Stade tell anyone I'm alive.*

Once again, Stade called out, "Bonnie will be so happy to—"

Bud lunged. Sensing motion, out of instinct, fear, and everything else that welled up, Stade turned the revolver—but too far to the left. As Bud closed in fast, Stade pivoted, but not fast enough. Bud made contact—and hit him hard—and then a flash appeared. In slow motion, both crashed onto the Panamint rubble-strewn ground, as they squirmed, kicked, and gouged. Brother against brother, blood against blood. They both clawed for the revolver. Stade's hand arrived first, but Bud's greater strength had the upper hand. The Torgerson brothers fought like they never had before—each driven by desperation.

Despite fighting for his life, Bud began seeing the scene play out in slow motion—not unlike an out-of-body experience. Bud saw the future. He sensed his greater strength would prevail. In their youthful fights, Bud always won—and he had confidence this fight would turn out the same. After all, Stade was only a desk-jockey, a Philadelphia lawyer, while Bud lived the life of a hard rock miner. For the longest time, neither brother gave up any ground and neither gained control over the Smith & Wesson. In the heat of the fight, instead of prying the gun from Bud's stronger grip, Stade took a desperate chance—he let go and leaped for a chunk of ore lying nearby. With both hands and all the force his desk-jockey shoulders could muster, Stade drove the rock directly into Bud's sweat-smeared temple.

The rock's long arc gave Bud time to reposition his hand on the revolver, lift, and fire. But due to the heat, passion, and sweat, Bud's frantic aim missed. The bullet ricochet off rocks far to the left at the instance the rock landed red-centered on Bud's blood-smeared forehead. Bud Torgerson crumpled on a pile of waste rock discarded earlier from an abandoned mine.

Realizing what he had just done, Stade dropped the rock and collapsed next to his brother's still body. Driven by heaving lungs and throbbing pain, Stade sobbed. "I never wanted to hurt you. I'm sorry, Bud. I had to. You forced it on me. I'm sorry."

Stade laid motionless for several minutes, trying to absorb what had just happened. The desert air's stillness seemed absolute. Stade suddenly jumped at the broken silence by a sound—of Bud whispering. "Bud, you're alive!" Stade muttered. Crawling over to his gut-shot brother, Stade looked Bud directly into his eyes. "Please, you got to tell me. I got to know. Where's your silver mine? You know, the one you discovered right before your death…well, you know what I mean. I got to know."

Bud only gurgled blood upon the darkly stained rubble.

"It's not for me, honest," Stade added. "It's for Billy. Please, Bud, I got to know."

In a bout of fitful sputtering, Bud whispered, "There is no silver. Never was, damn it. I made it all up," as he coughed up more blood.

"What? You made it all up? I don't believe you. Why?"

In a weak voice growing feebler by the second, Bud managed a few sentences. "People called me a loser, 'cause I searched for so long and given up so much…and what did I have to show for it? Nothing," Bud spewed. "I found nothing. My poor Bonnie. Poor Billy. They deserve better," Bud said as he coughed up so much blood that small rivulets began dribbling down his chin onto the dust next to the mine tailings and waste rock.

The parched dust quickly absorbed the once pooled blood, leaving not even a stain on the darkened ore fragments. With a voice that faded fast, Bud pleaded, "I didn't want my son to think his father was a loser. I wanted the Torgerson name to mean something, something to look up to."

"It still can," Stade pleaded. "If you tell me where I can find our silver."

"Don't be a fool. There is no silver, but the Torgerson name can live on with Billy. I want something better for him than this—" Bud said as his words trailed off to more coughing and more blood. "My life had been a waste. I didn't want Billy's life to be wasted like this. I knew if I faked my death, Bonnie would take Billy away and start a new life—a better life than I could ever give."

"I don't believe you. You're keeping secrets from me, aren't you? You're lying," Stade screamed to his fading brother.

Bud's breathing grew shallower, and he coughed up more blood. With labored effort, he choked, "I swear, there's no silver—at least not yet. With Bonnie and Billy away living a better life, I continued looking… I know it's here—somewhere."

"Bud, don't die on me," Stade pleaded. "Stay with me a little longer."

Bud turned his glazed-over eyes to Stade. "You're my baby brother. How come you tried to kill me? Help me. I'm bleeding bad. Please, help. When I find the silver, you can have half—just help me."

Stade looked down at his big brother and whispered in his ear, "I don't believe you, you son of a bitch." Before turning away, Stade stood up, carefully re-aimed—and fired.

Stade dragged Bud's body to an unknown, nondescript abandoned mine in the nameless canyon next to Five Mile Spring. He set the corpse up in a way that made it look like Bud had died in a mine collapse. However, back at the murder scene, during the entire heat of passion, throughout the fight, death, and Torgerson ordeal, neither Stade nor Bud had the time or inclination to take a close look at the blood-stained rock that Stade drove into his brother's temple and forehead. The thick coating of now coagulated blood smears obscured the dull shine of high-quality silver ore—and there were plenty of others sloughing from the nearby mineral vein.

CHAPTER 23

On the long, open highway running between widely spaced mountain ranges, Katherine and Paddy had a lot of alone time together. Sometimes they talked, but mostly Paddy remained silent within his thoughts, closed off and separate—like the cracked salt basin rolling away from his rearview mirror.

For as long as I live, Katherine pondered, *I will never figure out men. Men in my life…* She paused to reflect on that last thought. *Yes, I would have to say, Paddy is now a man in my life.* It had been some time…and even then, none that hadn't just kept rolling along. That suited Katherine fine. *None of them turned out to be any good*, she thought as she turned to watch Paddy do all he could to avoid talking. *Communication.* The thought came to her. *Communication is the key.* However warm the thought, on this ride, Katherine had been just as closed-lipped as Paddy. A wall of silence separated them as wide as the bone-dry mountains that sped by the Bronco's open window.

Paddy, like most men, think they are direct, but they are not, she thought. *They are all elusive—including Dad. Why is it all the men in my life are elusive?* Turning again to the stoic driver, *I must admit, Paddy is different. For one, he's likeable.*

Katherine Emerson's parents were well-off. As long as "Kati" could remember, they had money. She had all the comforts in life expected of upper-bracketed families. She also had clothes, music lessons, horses, and everything else little girls wanted—except love and attention. Her parents were never cruel or cold, just distant. She supposed that they did the best they could. They hired nannies, tutors, and caregivers. They just never hired love-givers.

Kati's father worked as a bank manager in downtown Boston, but he and his family lived in a large house in a well-manicured estate in the Back Bay-Beacon Hill neighborhood. Although life at home became dreadfully boring, little Kati knew nothing different. However, for as long as she can remember, she felt as if there had to be more. Only after her Uncle Sid's visits did she know the depth of her emptiness. Unknowingly, Sid taught her that there could be more to life than Back Bay-Beacon Hill picket fences. Uncle Sid treated little Kati as a person—one with dreams and aspirations. He gave her a broader view of life. But most of all, through Sid Emerson, Kati discovered the freedom and beauty of unconditioned love. Every year, Sid stayed with Kati and her parents for three or four weeks. In hindsight, these were the best weeks of her life.

As Katherine reminisced about her uncle, she increasingly kept glancing at Paddy. Each time, he seemed only one-half focused on driving. *What goes on in his head?* She wondered. *He has not moved or twitched in the last hour. How long can he keep this up?* Katherine silently fumed. *Just look at him. If he had his way, he would not say a single word on the whole trip.* Suddenly, Katherine noticed a trickle of sweat form on Paddy's cheek. "Do you mind rolling your window up so that I may turn on the air conditioner? Katherine asked.

"Sure. I'm sorry. Are you hot?" Paddy asked as he wiped the sweat as it began dripping from his cheek. "The air conditioner barely works." After Paddy rolled the window up and turned on the air conditioning, the fan blades groaned and sputtered a bit, and then fell silent. "That dang thing never works when you need it. I guess I'll have to roll the window down again. Sorry."

⚬⊸⊷⚬

Until Katherine gave Paddy the welcome relief of the air conditioner talk, his mind had been on his past—hard times during the war, and the even harder times when he returned—and on his family. He missed them dearly. No matter how much he enjoyed spending time with Katherine, even during the many quiet moments, it brought back a flood of pain and regret. Many silent moments after their air conditioner talk, he turned to look at Katherine. He saw a person deep in her own musings. Instinctually, Paddy did something that he hadn't done in quite some time—he smiled. However, as what happens to all things weathered, it faded as quickly as it came—before Katherine had a chance to notice. The two of them escaped other lost opportunities too, since they were both moving through the dry and weather-hardened landscape that extended well beyond Death Valley.

❦

In the heat of the Bronco's cab, with a broken air conditioner, Katherine's mind drifted back to her uncle. *Uncle Sid was much more of a father to me than Dad ever was.* During the weeks that Sid visited, he and Kati took daily walks. They walked to the nearby Charles River, walked to the frog pond in the beautiful gardens of the Commons, and walked down the Bulfinch-designed narrow streets of Beacon Hill or the wider lanes of Back Bay.

Kati had no idea what her Uncle Sid did for a living beyond those wonderful weeks. At the time, she also didn't know he had served in the Vietnam War as a Marine Corps staff sergeant. Katherine has since regretted not getting to know her uncle beyond those few weeks a year in Back Bay-Beacon Hill. *I was too self-absorbed,* she admitted. *Perhaps, all children are,* she thought, as Paddy and his Bronco continued silently rolling down the open highway.

If she hadn't been such a normal, self-absorbed child, Kati may have noticed Sid's metals and military decorations. They came from a particularly hard-fought battle on the slopes of one of the country's countless unnamed hills. Hueys dropped his platoon behind a hill with orders to push the Viet Cong off and claim the worthless piece of jungle for their own. However, no one knew how many Viet Cong were bunkered on the hill or how many would soon arrive as backup.

As far as Staff Sergeant Emerson knew, the entire operation may have only been for show. Regardless, the Viet Cong pinned Sid and his men down for two days before the Americans could sneak off to a place where Hueys could extract them from the long-forgotten hill. The Marine Corps awarded Sid Emerson with both a Purple Heart and a Silver Star. Kati knew nothing of this part of Sid Emerson until long after she became Katherine. Kati knew only that Sid Emerson had become the best father an uncle could ever provide—even for only a few weeks a year.

Despite having driven thousands of miles through many deserts, on this road trip, the landscape appeared to Paddy to stand still. His gaze into the empty road that snaked toward a lonely gap between distant mountains brought Paddy's mind back to Katherine. To shake such thoughts, Paddy forced himself to concentrate on Sid Emerson.

To Paddy, it increasingly looked like Sid had disappeared against his will. *Few of my interviews so far had narrowed the search any*, he admitted. *There are so many conflicting stories and rumors that need straightenin' out*, he thought. No silver bullets or evil fingers pointed to any one individual, although Paddy had hunches. As he looked out the open window at the many low shrubs passing by, he silently muttered, *He's quite the odd creature. I just don't trust him or his ridiculous machine.* Paddy suspected, somewhere out there beyond the alluvial fans, sunflowers, desert holly, and creosote, Ned Sipe was probably digging up an ancient grave claiming it to be yet another Manson murder. *The guy's nuts.*

He must have been muttering to himself louder than he thought, because Katherine replied, "Did you say something? With your window down and all the wind and dust whistling through, I did not make it out."

"Nothin'. I was only thinking to myself." With that, they both fell back into their private thoughts.

Speakin' of trust, Paddy thought, quieter this time, *somehow, Nick is probably involved, or at least knows more than he's admitting…and what's up with him and Katherine? Is he just trying to push my buttons?"* Paddy stopped himself short, and instinctually reached down to crank the window open, but it was already open. *I know Katherine doesn't trust Lizard Len—the guy's certifiable, but I don't see him doing anything to Sid Emerson*, Paddy considered after fumbling with the window. *However, it is often the fools that are the most dangerous.*

Focusing on Sid Emerson was not helping to get his thoughts off Katherine. *I don't even know that much about her. But I do have a good sense of people. I probably should tell her about Jen and Rachel…but I just can't. Not yet.* People who knew him would bet good money on Paddy never bringing up Jen or Rachel to Katherine. Deep down, Paddy knew he wouldn't either.

⚬⚭⚬

While Paddy's in-truck thoughts were his way of avoiding difficult conversations, Katherine, sitting right next to him, had not done any better. She regretted not being there for Sid when he needed someone, and now believed she was doing the same thing with Paddy. She sensed something from his past troubled him, but she didn't want to pry.

Katherine tried to get Paddy to open up while driving to Ryan for the Lizard Len interview, but that didn't go well. Little did she realize how much he regretted how he handled that entire conversation. I know she was only trying to help, Paddy kept telling himself; he just wouldn't say it out loud. With neither one of them talking, the few remaining miles of creosote, desert holly, mesquite, and the ever-present gravel expanse passed by slowly.

It is taking me longer to find Uncle Sid than I ever imagined. I was naïve. I thought it would only take a couple of weeks—tops. But now it has been over two months. I hope he is okay, Katherine fretted. *So far, Paddy had done most the work.*

At the time, Katherine never fully understood how much she, as a child, had helped her uncle. During Katherine's younger years back in Boston, Sid needed Kati as much as Kati needed her Uncle Sid. However, Kati eventually became Katherine and went off to college for a degree in financial management. After college, she lost track of her uncle. Since then, they only occasionally communicated—until his retirement. Since his explorations began, he wrote Katherine nearly every day—until they suddenly stopped after he came to Death Valley.

Annoyed with how everything was going, Katherine shattered the Bronco's tranquility by blurting, "Why is it taking so long to find my uncle?"

"Where did that come from?" Paddy said, looking confused.

"I was just thinking out loud."

"I'm looking for him, and makin' progress, but sorry it's takin' so long. It's just this is a big land with lots of places where a person can get lost."

"It is not you. I know you are working hard to find Uncle Sid. I am just frustrated with myself. That is all."

"We'll find him," Paddy said, trying to reassure her.

"Sorry for my outburst and impatience. I am worried that he needs help—now, not later."

Katherine also worried about Paddy. *I know so little of even his friends and family. I am not sure if he intended to or not, but he once blurted out the names Jen and Rachel. Who are Jen and Rachel?* She may have guessed as much, but even the people around Death Valley with some familiarity with Paddy's past, such as John Smithers and Ron Telling, avoided bringing up his past. She wondered, *Is this out of respect? A code? Or just the easy way out?*

Paddy and Ron are an unlikely pair, Katherine thought. *I will have to ask Paddy—when the time seems right.* Papa tended to think the reason John and Paddy could relate to one another was because they both had witnessed the horrors of war. Ron Telling didn't serve, but he too seemed haunted by his past. In their own way, each had become accomplished in keeping their past in the past. In a land as vast as the Death Valley wilderness, all three craved space.

Some friendships are as hard to imagine as a cool Death Valley rain. By all appearances to those who had lived in the area long, Paddy and the ant man were best friends. *It's an odd pairing. Ron with his Ph.D…and Paddy, he's anything but an intellectual,* Katherine thought. However, the two shared common inflictions. For one, the lonely desert had grown on both men. Perhaps what they liked about each other were their differences—and their willingness to not let things like questions or comments stand in their way of enjoying the day, one day at a time. They related to each other at face value—not what others expected or what they had been in the past. When they were together, Ron wasn't a scientist, and Paddy wasn't a hopeless loner with a broken past.

Paddy and Katherine's silent road trip through Death Valley's open expanse ended upon their arrival at their destination. They simultaneously broke the silence by saying goodbye and other pleasantries. With a few passing words, they planned to meet again in a couple of days for their next trip.

On this same day, over in Los Angeles, Dr. Ron Telling had just arrived home from one of his many extended expeditions to the South American rainforest studying competition between ant species and communities. He planned to remain home for several days before moving to his next project, but he found life in Los Angeles boring. He needed to escape his empty and cold home. At the spur of the moment, he packed two weeks' worth of food and his ant collecting kit, and on a whim, got into his F-150 and pointed its nose toward the Panamints. After three decades of looking at Death Valley ants, the area still held mysteries and secrets. Before heading to the Hunter Mountain plateau, also on a whim, he pulled into Barstow—and up the long, dusty road leading to Paddy's trailer.

As Ron pulled up to the trailer, he found Paddy outside sipping a beer with a chilled one on the table—waiting for Ron.

"Is that mine?"

"Who else? For a scientist, you certainly ask a lot of dumb questions."

"How'd you know the dust was mine?"

"The smell. Besides, who else would come up this dead-end valley?"

"From what I've heard, you've had a few visitors up here, and you're making visits yourself. I guess you've gotten to the point where you don't even like *your* company either?"

"Oh, you've heard about that. About Katherine?"

"Oh, it's Katherine, is it? Not Ms. Emerson? Are you going normal on us?"

"Says the man whose only friends are bugs."

"True, but they never offer me beer."

After a long pause as Paddy scanned the horizon while Ron stared into his beer, Ron broke the silence. "A while back, I met Katherine while biologizing up on Hunter Mountain. Seems a nice gal. It sounds like you're helping her track down Sid Emerson. Find anything yet?"

"Only suspicions. I don't think this is the normal Death Valley stuff. I think somethin' truly happened to him, but so far, I don't know who or what. Maybe I'm not cut out for detective work."

"Who's cut out for anything? Initially, I didn't think I would be up to a career in the sciences, but it all worked out. I'm also guessing you didn't think you were cut out for rescuing al-Qaeda and Taliban hostages, but from what I heard, you were damn good at it."

"Go to hell!"

"Sorry. What did you put in this beer?"

After another long pause of horizon and beer staring, Paddy blurted, "What do you know of Ned Sipe and his crazy dead body detectin' machine? You're a scientist; is there much to his claim? Can his machine work?"

"I'm just an ant man, but from my perspective, he's full of it, a simple attention-grabbing huckster. An idiot. Why? Is he a suspect?"

"Not anything close to a suspect. Not yet. I don't have any proof, only suspicions. The guy is starvin' for attention and to prove to a gullible public that he's a brilliant inventor. I think he's getting desperate to prove he's more than just a con man. If he killed Sid, buried the body, and then used his machine to 'find' the body, wouldn't that create quite the story?"

"You may have something there," Ron mused.

"The media would paint him to be a great hero and genius. I think you have it right—he's a huckster and an idiot."

"But if he's good at manipulating people and the press…"

Paddy paused, as if mulling things over in his head. "I'm also keepin' an eye on Nick. We used to be friends, but no longer. I just don't trust the guy."

"From what I've heard, it couldn't be that he's sweet on Katherine. Are you getting a little jealous?"

"Now, who's the idiot?… So, when are you going to finish that damn beer?"

In short order, Ron finished his beer, made a comment or two about the weather, said goodbye to his old friend, got in his truck, and drove off.

On the long drive to Hunter Mountain, besides kicking up a ton of dust and further damaging his truck's suspension by taking the thousands of washboards at too high speed, Ron had plenty of time to think about ants, the rainforest, and Patrick Darwin. *He seems different*, Ron thought as he continued taking the washboards and ruts at full speed. *She's changed him. After all he went through in Afghanistan, all the pointless death and misery, the grizzly fighting, and being shot down with an RPG-7, now, his biggest fight is with his own demons—ever since holing up in that damn trailer of his*, Ron thought.

Perhaps Katherine Emerson came at the right time. Before Katherine came around, Ron thought Paddy had become the poster child of the new Lost Generation.

This prompted Ron to think of the famous J.R.R. Tolkien quote from his book *Fellowship of the Ring*: "Not all those who wander are lost." Ron chuckled to himself since he thought this could apply equally well to nearly everyone in the Death Valley region. It certainly applied to the many broken miners who had scurried throughout the ranges only to die as poor as had Bud Torgerson. Ron turned his head into the open truck window, and then as if speaking to the billowing dust, said softly, "Not all who mine seek riches." *Nothing around Death Valley is ever quite the way it seems.*

CHAPTER 24

Paddy had time on his hands, and time on his knees, although he long ago had lost track of such silly notions as time. He had become accustomed to talking to himself. *What is time anyway, and why worry about such meaningless dribble? I don't have time for that. In the end, what did it get me?* Paddy's mind remained fixed on his current predicament, although he wondered what his life had gotten him—*other than trapped in this shithole of a mine.*

No one will find me, 'cause no one knows where I'm at, Paddy fretted. *Even if they did, who would care? Well, maybe Katherine. Maybe she wouldn't? I've been pretty cold to her lately. Well, that just means I'll need to find my own way out.*

Lucky for Paddy, he had on a large pack when he fell—as it cushioned his fall. Although the pack's contents were still with him, most had been smashed. Pulling out a knife, Paddy palmed it with determination. *This can come in handy.*

Looking up at the shaft he had fallen, Paddy got an idea. Not the rational or sane type that occupied normal people's brains, but nonetheless the type that brought a smile to Paddy's bruised face, causing him to wince.

With a speed borne from survival mode, but not yet the point of desperation, Paddy broke apart the wooden debris that littered the mine's floor. *This might just work.*

After nearly an hour or more, perhaps minutes, surely not a day, he broke apart enough old two-by-fours to form a small pile that he carefully stacked at his feet. He counted twenty-five, each about sixteen inches long. *This may just do. I may get out of here yet.*

With the knife he had since childhood, the knife his father gave to him, Paddy sharpened one end of each wood stake. He then found a stout three-foot-long two-by-four not as weathered and brittle as the rest. Swinging the two-by-four felt good. Paddy imagined he bludgeoned each of his many demons. *Well, Paddy, wishin' and thinkin' will get me nowhere.*

He took a close look at the many cracks running up the mine wall. He hadn't noticed them earlier. Paddy knew desperate minds often only focus on things of immediate importance, and up until this new idea, the cracks hadn't been important. Now, they were his means of escape.

Paddy placed the flashlight on the floor, leaning it against an old timber in such a way that the light shone on the cracked wall. *That'll do just fine.* Picking up the first sharpened stake, Paddy drove it as forcibly as he could into the lowest crack using only his hands, arm, and shoulder. A few stout blows with a two-by-four drove the stake further into the crack. The sound of each blow caused the stake's vibrations to increase in pitch. To Paddy, the sound represented soundness, integrity, and escape.

Standing and balancing on that stake, while leaning against the wall, Paddy managed to drive in another stake in the same crack, only three feet higher. He selected the best-sized stake to match each successive crack-stake combination, as Paddy inched up the near-vertical mine wall. Used to hard work, Paddy's arms didn't start to tire until several stakes snaked up the wall. His mind focused on nothing else, not even Katherine. *I must keep at it—no matter what,* he told himself. *There are only three possible outcomes: reach the end of the climb, reach the end of the cracks, or reach the end of my nerve.*

Climbing the stakes brought back childhood memories of struggling on the pegboard in the school gymnasium. He didn't enjoy it then either, but at least climbing cracks in the mine wall had a purpose and offered a glimmer of hope. "If this doesn't work," he mused, "I'm a goner."

Things went well, at least for the first half. Then the climb got dicey. The cracks were either too small or too big for his stakes. "All my stakes are the same damned size," he screamed. "You idiot!" *There's nothin' I can do about it now*, he figured, *other than to nest two or three together to form one united large-diameter stake. Most of all, calm down, you fool.*

Double wedging them against each other works in theory, but when he attempted it with one hand while precariously balancing on lower stakes, each nested combination shifted and wobbled too much for Paddy to trust. *If only I had a real hammer, I could smash the stacked pieces in soundly, but no: I only have a splintered two-by-four as a hammer.* Fully aware that he had little choice, Paddy exhaled, as if draining his lungs of air would reduce the strain on his wobbly stakes. After each exhale, he gingerly stepped and shifted his weight onto the next pair. This worked for a time, but without warning, the stake he stood on rotated and exploded. The next moment he lay on the bottom of the shaft, next to broken stakes, his shredded backpack, and his still flickering flashlight.

When Paddy came to, it took his eyes minutes to focus and even longer to communicate with his brain. He lost all sense of time, but he had the clarity of mind to realize that this time, time had meaning. Still lying and still in pain, Paddy groped for the flashlight and turned it off to save batteries. Somehow cradling a darkened flashlight gave him a sense of warmth. With it, Paddy curled in a fetal position and fell back to sleep.

He woke up cold, hungry, and in just as much pain. Turning the flashlight back on, Paddy conducted a self-exam to check for injuries. As if on autopilot, he jumped to the type of self-exam that he routinely performed in Afghanistan after being shot or having rolled over an IED. His injuries now weren't as severe as they were in Afghanistan, but, over there, he wasn't alone or trapped in a mine.

Paddy, you old fool, he cursed. *You're lucky you didn't crack your skull again*, he pondered, as if a blow to the head and a quick death wouldn't have been better than the fate that awaited him now with a broken and throbbing leg. "Paddy, how are you gittin' yourself out of this one?" he said to the darkness.

While trying to figure out his next steps, Paddy sat back against the wall and slowly turned the flashlight on and off, on and off. This gave him time to notice the repetitive drips from the ceiling—somewhere in the noise-filled distance. They were in a cycle of three—one primary, and two intermittent ones. *Why are drips so loud?* he wondered as he flicked the light on and then back off again. *Where is the water coming from? The surface is a desert—as dry as a bone.* Thoughts of the desert surface were only a painful reminder of Paddy's thirst and hunger.

With a little jockeying, and a lot of pain, Paddy positioned himself under the one steady primary drip. Lying on his back with his mouth open, he got one out of every ten drops into his cottony mouth. Most bounced off his forehead, cheek, chin, or nose. His cursing progressively became louder and louder. "Damn it, stop moving! I just want a few drops of water—is that too much to ask?"

Once his mind freed itself to mastering the perfect head position to collect the drips, his undisciplined brain kept drifting to far-away thoughts. *I have so much I should have told her*, he thought as he worried himself nearly back to sleep.

He hadn't had such thoughts since he lost his family. He spent far too much time trying to keep it that way, as if isolating himself in a trailer made his grief easier. *There's something about Katherine that makes it seem I've known her for years*, Paddy's left brain said to the right. Paddy, with a discipline and determination borne from military training and years of avoidance practice, willed such thoughts to the recesses of his subconscious mind. Disturbed by where his thoughts took him, Paddy shook them off by trading one pain for another. Once again, his stubbornness had paid off.

Out of boredom, he flicked the light on and off again, each time cursing himself for his lack of self-control. After watering his chin for who knows how many minutes, hours, or days, Paddy suddenly bolted up—he heard something. Just when he imagined it to be brain damage, he heard it again. As loud and passionately as he could muster, he called out and frantically flashed his light toward the top of the shaft. Paddy's flashlight beam joined forces with someone's light up higher. "I'm down here!" he shouted.

Suddenly Paddy's mind filled with questions. *Who would possibly be here—of all places? Is it the same person that caused me to fall? Is he the driver of that deep blue Ford Expedition that's been following me? If so, do I ignore him?* Rational thoughts slowly returned to Paddy's clearing head, because after all, *What choice do I have? Wait for a better or more dependable offer?* he quipped. "Hello up there," Paddy yelled.

Before long, a crackling, raspy, smoker-type voice called from above, "Who's down there? Are you okay?"

"I'm Paddy. I fell down the shaft. Can you help?"

"Hold on, I'll be right back." After this savior from above left, the silence returned, and then the drips—this time louder than ever. For the first time since this ordeal, Paddy felt alone. *Is he comin' back? I shouldn't have used my name.*

After seemingly twenty minutes of silence and loneliness dragged by, the same raspy and comforting voice returned. "Hello! I got a rope. I'm lowering it to yuh. Holler when you got it."

By dimmed flashlight, Paddy watched the end of the rope flick back and forth in slow, jerking motions. It occurred to Paddy that the raspy-voiced man hadn't identified himself yet. *There's something about this that doesn't smell right,* thought Paddy, as he called for more rope. After three more flicks, "That's it, tie her off," Paddy yelled.

"She's tied off, come up if you will."

Climbing a rope hand-over-hand up a vertical wall is hard enough in the best of situations, but Paddy wondered if he could make it with a broken leg and being busted up from the fall. Knowing no other way, Paddy gave it a try. He propped the flashlight against the same broken timber, walked up to the same cracked wall with the same broken and splintered wooden spikes, grabbed the same rope, and began the climb. Stabs of pain ran through him upon the slightest movement of his left foot, but he managed to use it—at least a little. Wrapping the rope around his arms, he climbed hand-over-hand while using his right leg to stand on as many of the remaining stakes, wide cracks, and any other foothold—anything that took the strain off his draining arms and lessened his stabbing pain.

Miraculously, he found he made progress. Soon, he looked down on his previous high point. However, the climb grew harder once he no longer had stakes to stand on. Using a burst of fast-fading energy, Paddy lurched to the top and flung himself onto the floor.

"You okay?" said his raspy-voice savior. "My name is Hector. Let's get you out into the sunlight."

"Thanks. You saved my life."

After getting out into the searing heat and dryness, Paddy sat against a boulder and soaked in the Panamint sights and smells and all the water Hector gave him. As Paddy finished off the last of the water, Hector retrieved the rope. The mine still claimed Paddy's flashlight, but no one went back down to retrieve it, and no one offered.

What Hector did offer was raw, homemade pemmican. Paddy hated pemmican—he thought it tasted nasty—but he accepted and treasured every bite. "The pemmican's great, isn't it?" asked Hector. "It'll fix you up and get you moving in no time."

"I'm not about ready to move, not quite yet," moaned Paddy, "even with the pemmican." Hector consoled him by saying, "I'm not scootin' you off, not quite yet. I mean fer you to rest up in my place. Don't worry, it weren't far."

Hector helped Paddy hobble to the same cave home Paddy had rummaged through earlier. Paddy hung his head and didn't say a thing, hoping Hector wouldn't figure it out. Likely, Hector had noticed but he didn't say a thing. He simply handed Paddy a tin can full of first-aid supplies.

Once fully cleaned and bandaged, Paddy took Hector up on his offer to take a much-needed nap. As he slowly drifted off, Paddy scanned the cave walls in a different light than when he had earlier. Hector's make-due place looked comfortable—in a primitive sort of way. Paddy muttered under his breath, *It certainly beats the bottom of the mine.* As he began to nod off, he thought, *I could see living here.*

CHAPTER 25

At the time of Paddy's mine ordeal, Katherine knew nothing of his whereabouts or troubles. *I should have gone with him*, she fretted, while pacing across the breadth of her tiny motel room. *I got to do something.* On a whim, she drove to the Timbisha Village to ask a few questions. *At least I will be busy doing something.* During the long drive, she began realizing how much she relied upon Paddy. *I need to be more self-sufficient*, she muttered. *Without cell phone reception, I cannot call. Besides, who would come? The sheriff? He would not help search for Uncle Sid, so why would he help search for Paddy? Papa? Rocky? Nick?* Katherine suddenly realized that without Paddy, she would be alone.

For some reason, Paddy did not want to talk with the Timbisha. It makes no sense to me, thought Katherine. A gut-level feeling gnawed at her that the Timbisha might be able to point her in the right direction—to Sid Emerson. *We will see*, she thought, as she pulled her Camry up to the tribal headquarters in Lone Pine. Luckily for her, Chairman Jimmy Two Claw had some idle time. He greeted Katherine warmly and invited her into his office.

As Jimmy Two Claw pinned Katherine to her chair with an overabundance of talk, she no longer wondered why Paddy had been hesitant. She guessed Paddy would not like Jimmy Two Claw. For over thirty minutes he wouldn't let her say a word—she was stuck to the hot vinyl chair as Jimmy filled up the spacious office with words and consumed all available oxygen. *He talks and talks, without really saying anything*, she marveled. *He likely has no idea of what happened to Uncle Sid but is too much of a politician to not say anything*, she speculated as Jimmy droned away.

After another thirty minutes, she learned nothing useful. Instead, Jimmy Two Claw informed Katherine of his ambitious plans to build a casino on a small patch of tribal land near Death Valley Junction. It seemed the tribe needed money and Jimmy Two Claw needed both recognition and the fulfillment of his child-like dreams. She could imagine there were few economically viable options for the patch of scrub and salt crust. However, Jimmy talked of the Death Valley Junction parcel as if were prime real estate—at the only intersection between Death Valley's Furnace Creek, Shoshone, Beatty, and Pahrump. Katherine chuckled upon thinking of Pahrump. It's Vegas' modest bedroom community located just a mere one hour away, over a small pass, from the vice-ridden metropolis—as the locals say, "Over the hump to Pahrump."

The Las Vegas mindset had clearly bitten Jimmy Two Claw— not the vice part, Katherine sensed, but the flowing money part. "If Vegas can never have enough casinos, as all around here say," Jimmy informed Katherine, "why can't the Timbisha get in on the action?" He must not have been wanting an answer since he quickly changed the subject to another money-making idea.

As Jimmy Two Claw droned away, Katherine amused herself by imagining that Jimmy Two Claw wanted a casino as badly as Bud Torgerson wanted silver, or George Shufeld wanted Lizard People catacombs. Katherine expected more from a tribal leader. *He seemed no different than many others around Death Valley—driven by a fixation. Driven to grow a casino empire. Lizard Len's driven to expose the truth about Lizard People. And the crystal makers, Ned Sipe, and the Manson followers all have their fixations.* Upon reflection, Katherine considered if she was just as driven to find her uncle. *What is Paddy's obsession—other than hiding from his past?* Upon further thought, Katherine guessed that Jimmy Two Claw's casino fixation was the most normal. Katherine imagined that they only thing holding Jimmy Two Claw back from his goal was internal in-fighting with the Timbisha.

Jimmy talked of strong resistance to his plans from other Timbisha members. *Why does the Tribe spend so much time and effort on internal fighting?* Katherine wondered. From what Katherine heard, the Timbisha had nearly insurmountable social and economic challenges. *The last thing I think they would need is internal in-fighting and political intrigue*, Katherine pondered.

Katherine got from Jimmy Two Claw's pontifications a hint that the tribe's internal problems started two years earlier—exactly the time Jimmy Two Claw rose to power. From Katherine's perspective Jimmy Two Claw had abundant energy and ambition but lacked public support of tribal members. Katherine had no way of knowing that the tribe struggled not only about whether to build a casino or not, but also for the heart and soul of the entire Timbisha culture and way of life.

Within this war among themselves, Jimmy Two Claw and the official tribal officers formed one camp, and the Timbisha living in the Furnace Creek Village became the other camp—as well as their alter ego. There was much more than the entire breadth of Death and Saline Valleys and the intervening Panamint and Cottonwood Ranges separating the tribal office from the Furnace Creek Village Timbisha. This was especially true for the outspoken tribal elder, Paula Estevo. To the slight, ancient, and diminutive, but anything but frail, Paula, the thought of a tribal casino disrespected centuries-old traditions and formed the wrong impression of the Timbisha to outsiders. Her people needed money and hope, but according to Paula, their salvation did not lie in a Las Vegas-style casino. "A casino has nothing to do with Timbisha history, culture, beliefs, and values," she often argued. "Nothing, at all," she spat back in such a way that left little doubt what her thoughts were on the matter. Paula was anything but subtle.

If someone wanted to witness firsthand Paula's lack of subtleness, all they needed to do was ask her opinion on the name *Death Valley*. The Timbisha had lived in these valleys and mountains for as long as the land itself. To Paula, her people's land was not death; it was life—it was hers and her ancestor's home.

In many ways, Paula served as the unofficial Timbisha spiritual leader and public icon, although she held no title other than one of several tribal elders. Jimmy Two Claw stripped her of any official position in tribal affairs, hoping to diminish her sway and influence. It didn't work. Timbisha, old and young alike, gravitated to Paula. The media loved her too. However, her natural-born leadership skills also came with an outspoken, snarky, and unpredictable personality. Jimmy Two Claw did not like her gravitas and style, for she had the kind of power and influence that Jimmy could only dream of. Equally clear to the Timbisha were Paula's opinions of Jimmy Two Claw.

Paula not only unofficially represented the Timbisha's Furnace Creek Village, but she also represented the proud traditions of a people and culture that had lived in the greater Death Valley area for a millennium—or more. The Timbisha and the closely related Western Shoshone tribes were the Great Basin's oldest inhabitants. As European cultures came to North America, eastern tribes moved to the Ohio Valley, Ohio Valley tribes moved to the Great Lakes region, Great Lakes tribes moved into the prairies, and on and on— it became one traumatic migration and dislocation after another. With all this shifting going on, very few dislocated tribes wanted to go into the arid and mysterious Great Basin. Therefore, the native Basin tribes experienced fewer disruptions than any other tribes on the continent. They continued residing in the same place they had for eons—perhaps stretching nearly back to when their ancestors first populated the North American continent. As such, Katherine thought that if there had been any alien Lizard People infiltration into the land, the Timbisha would know.

The Timbisha have a long history of not being treated well by the U.S. government. Paula saw and experienced this in her younger years. As such, she approached her discussions with non-Timbisha with a nomadic temperament and approach. If things did not appear to be going well, she would move on, adapt, and return later during a better time, season, year, or millennium. The Timbisha had time. However, Paula had fewer years herself, so she had long since lost patience for such matters. She had seen and heard it all, felt too many disappointments, and heard far too many broken promises. Now, in her old age, Paula suffered no fools and no empty platitudes. To keep her eyes fixed on the long-term, Paula tended to view non-Timbisha's antics with either humor or derision—or both.

To Paula, all non-Timbisha were crazy and confusing. She also didn't understand the crystal people, Manson followers, Ned Sipe, Lizard Len, or the alien conspiracies. She also didn't get miners—past or present. She had seen so many strange people move in, stay for a short time, and then move on. However, the Timbisha landscape had not been any better as a result.

After listening to Jimmy Two Claw, Katherine became desperate to meet with and talk to the iconic Paula. After she said her thanks and goodbyes to Jimmy Two Claw, Katherine turned her Camry toward Furnace Creek and the Timbisha Village.

Katherine had no means to contact Paula or make an appointment. Finding her would be a challenge, but not nearly as much as getting Paula to agree to a sit-down interview about Sid Emerson and the Lizard People conspiracy. Luck shined bright on Katherine that day, since not only did she find Paula, but she agreed to talk.

Paula would talk only in the village's Tribal Community Center, located just a short walk away from her home. The tribe had recently built the community center using funds made available from a federal grant. The center served as the focal point for visitors to learn about the Timbisha culture. Paula believed this educational center would better serve the Timbisha culture more than a casino.

Katherine and Paula arrived at the community center at the same time. In the extended time it took Paula to bend over and have a seat,

Katherine sized up Paula as not wanting any small talk or normal social pleasantries. Katherine got quickly to the point.

"I am here to find my Uncle Sid, Sid Emerson. He went missing many weeks ago somewhere in the Death Valley mountains. I am hoping you have some information that would be helpful for me to find him. Did he come by and speak with any Timbisha?"

Paula paused for a long time, shifted in her chair, and twisted her well-weathered face, before eventually blurting, "Why? Do you think we killed and ate him?"

"Of course not, I—"

"Relax. Relax. You people are so…the words trailed off in guttural laughter. "Yes, yes, I met Sid Emerson and answered his silly questions about Lizard People and other nonsense. He came here and sat on the same bench as you now sit."

"You mean to say you spoke with my Uncle Sid? I had not heard that before. It does not surprise me, but when and where was that?"

"I don't know—I don't keep a calendar. I wanted as little to do with him as I want with you now, but yes, we spoke. He sat right there and asked a lot of questions about things that I had little interest in."

"What were some of his questions, and why did he stop by?"

"You'll have to ask him or his Lizard People. Do I look like his secretary? I didn't take notes—or even pay that much attention."

"He must have said something you can remember?"

"He asked about Lizard People as if I know anything about your people's crazy stories. I told him he was a fool to believe in such nonsense."

"What did you tell him?"

"I just said, I told him he was a fool to believe in such nonsense."

"Besides that, anything else?"

"He asked about aliens. I told him the only aliens around here are you White people, and I don't know or care where you live, above ground or below ground, as long as it isn't around here. I then told him maybe if you people lived underground in the Lizard

People's catacombs, then maybe you wouldn't bother us Timbisha so much."

"Do you know anything about the Lizard People's stories and legends?"

"I don't bother with White people stories. If there were Lizard People, my people would know it—we were here first and have seen it all."

"Is this what you told my Uncle Sid?"

"I told him, but he didn't listen. I told him we know about this land and what happens here since this is our home and we're connected to it—and it's connected to us. I pay little attention to what others do, other than when they disrespect the land or our people."

"Did my uncle, Sid Emerson, say anything to you about being in danger or if he suspected someone may want to hurt him?"

"Sorry, sweetie. We didn't talk that much, or maybe I don't remember," Paula said with finality. "I'm old, you know."

Sensing any more probing would go nowhere, Katherine wrapped up her questions. "Thank you, Paula, for our wonderful conversation. I have enjoyed it. I have one last question. Before leaving, did my uncle say anything about where he planned on going next?"

"Again, do I look like his secretary?"

"Please—he's my family and the only link to *my* past."

Katherine noticed a slight relaxation of Paula's otherwise upright and rigid shoulders, as she softly answered, "Family is important. I'll give you that. On his way out, he said something about going to Anvil Springs."

"Is that it? Is that all he said?"

"Well, he said something about before heading up to Anvil Springs, based on some crazy story Lizard Len told him."

"Lizard Len?"

"Yes, that is what you people call him, do you not? Lizard Len."

"Lizard Len?" again Katherine asked.

"Yes, Lizard Len. I'm hard of hearing, but that's because I'm old. What's your excuse?"

"I am sorry, I am just surprised. Lizard Len said he had not met or spoken with my uncle. I wonder why he would have said that."

"I wonder what all you White people say and do. Honestly, I really don't pay much attention to disrespectful people."

"Are you saying he was disrespectful? That does not sound like my Uncle Sid."

"Well, not you uncle, but White people in general. They dishonor the land. The miners didn't come here to honor and respect the land. Manson didn't either. The crystal people leave those stupid trinkets all over—this is pure disrespectful. Your uncle came here seeking Lizard People and legends that fit *his* curiosity and *his* stories; they are not *our* stories. After he, the miners, and all the crystal crazies take what they want, they too will be gone, leaving us Timbisha to pick up after your mess."

Long after Katherine left the community center, Paula remained behind thinking of Sid and Katherine Emerson, Lizard Len, the crystal crazies, and Lizard People. All the aliens meant nothing to her. They were but dust grains blowing across the playa. A dust speck is only noticed if it gets in your eye or ground as grit between your teeth. Eventually, the irritant comes out and the wind simply carries it away. To Paula, the Timbisha had been here for thousands of years. They'd seen a lot of dust blow in and then blow out. From Paula's perspective, lately, it seemed as if the dust had piled up especially high and remained longer than normal.

Paula stepped out of the community center to stand alone. With blurry eyes, she scanned the wide arc of the Furnace Creek mesquite bosque. To her, she saw only beauty and grace as she reflected on nature's traditional cycles and rhythms. To Paula, all alien intruders acted like they were homeless and lacked a grounding center. They were people out of sync with nature. They were people seeking things that couldn't be found in Timbisha land. She wished they would all just pack up and head home. With that, Paula grunted and walked the remaining distance through the mesquite bosque to her adobe home on the far side of the village.

Katherine had a long drive back to the Ridgecrest motel. It provided her with time to think about her uncle, the Timbisha, and Paddy. *Why would Lizard Len lie? If he didn't outright lie, at least he evaded our questions.* Katherine also wondered what Paddy would think about the news. This thought brought her back to worrying about Paddy. It also got her thinking. *I know so little about the man. What is it about his past that drove him to escape into a run-down trailer at the far end of nowhere-land?*

On the long drive, she also wondered about what happened between Paddy and Nick. "What is it about everyone's past around here that haunts them?" she blurted out louder than the clanging sounds coming from the Camry's air conditioner running at full throttle. Besides not knowing much of Paddy's past, she happened to be stumbling into, unaware, another concern growing between Paddy and Nick, but this one happening in the present. She had much to discuss with Paddy, but that would have to wait until morning.

CHAPTER 26

On the morning following her meeting with the Timbisha, Katherine found Paddy's mesquite-shaded table empty as she pulled her Camry up to his last berm. Three knocks on the trailer generated no stirring or callouts. Finding the door unlocked, Katherine stepped inside and looked around and found no note to ease her growing worry. *Paddy has always been here for our agreed-upon meetings,* she fretted. She could not tell from his rumpled or unwashed Navajo-style blanket how long since he had last slept there. An hour of idle waiting combined with doing dishes and picking up the place did nothing to quell her suspicions. During the entire time, no one walked through the door and no dust cloud shone on the horizon.

Two hours of cleaning brought her no closer to figuring out what to do to help. Even if her phone worked from Paddy's trailer, who would she call? She knew what Sheriff John Smithers would say. *If not the sheriff, then who else would help?* Given the situation, and knowing the way men tend to be, she figured calling Nick would be a bad idea.

By noon, Katherine's hunger told her to give up waiting. Momentarily, she considered finding food in Paddy's trailer, but that didn't seem right. Besides, his refrigerator and cabinets were empty. *What does he eat?* she wondered as she sorted through moldy and long-expired food tucked behind refrigerator trays brimming with beer. *How does he live this way?*

She climbed into the Camry to drive into Barstow. At least there, she could be within cell phone range. Sure enough, on the high spot before approaching town, a delayed message from Paddy caused her phone to jump. With no explanation, the message said, "Katherine, this is Paddy. Sorry for not being there this morning. Something came up and I'll have to go deep into the Panamints. I'll explain later. I'll be home this evening—tops."

Did he find a lead? Katherine asked herself as the Camry kicked up a billowing cloud into the afternoon thermals. *I will have to head back this evening to find out the latest scoop.* Katherine headed the rest of the way into Barstow to grab a bite to eat and kill a few hours.

Later that afternoon, Katherine wound up counting paces within the confines of a not very large trailer. The sun had set, yet still no sign of Paddy. She searched and found a light. She also found that Paddy's trailer seemed even smaller by candlelight. She could take only two more hours before exhaustion and a worried mind put her to sleep. She awoke on the dusty couch with most of the morning already gone. Still no Paddy.

Katherine drove to her Ridgecrest motel and found no message on her phone or in her motel room. There was nothing left for her to do other than wait, worry, and wait. That afternoon, she called the sheriff's office and spoke with one of the deputies. They told her just what she'd expected. She waited a few more hours in Ridgecrest before driving back to Paddy's place and waiting for him there. Katherine spent another night alone in his trailer.

The following morning, she brewed a pot of Earl Grey tea that she had brought from Ridgecrest, then sat outside at his table to watch the Mojave sunrise. This was Paddy's favorite place to watch the world go by. Katherine began to appreciate what the table meant to Paddy as she watched the parade of oranges, yellows, and magentas filtered through the scraggly screwbean mesquite's bare branches. Long after she started sipping the Earl Grey, but before it grew cold, she saw a dust plume on the far horizon above the mesquite. *Paddy's right,* she reflected. *No one can sneak up on a person here since the dust always gives them away.*

As the plume got closer, a Bronco's lines began to take shape. *Is that Paddy?* It pulled up to the berm, leaving dust to continue its path and begin settling on the surround mesquite and greasewood. Leaving the tea on the table, Katherine ran up and gave Paddy a big hug. "Where have you been?" Katherine scolded. "I have been worried sick. For all I knew, you died in a mine shaft, or someone mistook you for a Lizard People."

"I'm all right. I had a bit of a scrape, but I'm no worse for wear," Paddy answered with a grin wider than Paddy had grinned in a long time. "No need to worry. This stuff happens all the time, but thanks!"

"What happened?"

This and the rest of Katherine's questions remained unanswered. Paddy clearly wanted to avoid talking about whatever had happened in the Panamints, or wherever else he went.

Katherine's anger grew softer when she noticed Paddy limping. He also winced as he climbed the steps into the trailer. Once inside, he barked, "What did you do to my trailer? You ruined it—it's clean and picked up."

"I waited for you for two days. I had to do something to take my mind off thoughts of you lying dead somewhere out there," she vented. "And yet, I get no explanation."

"I'm fine, but my leg hurts a bit. You didn't need to mess with my things. Everything had a reason for being where they were..." Paddy paused as if reflecting on something. "Let me start over— thanks, Katherine." Next, he paused to scan the extent of his clean and unrecognizable trailer. "I'm all right. I just need a couple days of rest, then I'll be fine to go. Please have a seat and we'll talk about our next trip."

Paddy and Katherine threw out a few plans and ideas to each other, but mostly they talked. They talked for over two hours, up until Paddy said he needed to get some rest. They agreed to meet again at Paddy's trailer two days from then. She left without knowing anything that had happened to him, but nonetheless content that things were good.

As planned, two days later, Paddy and Katherine headed out together. The trip began like many of their other rides, with each being within their own heads. Only a few miles down the road, Katherine looked over at Paddy at the exact same moment that he looked at her. Instantly, and in unison, they averted their eyes—Katherine's eyes dropped to inspect her hands, while Paddy's reached for the window crank to hide his growing blush. Soon, the handle's creak, and Paddy's sighs, filled the air—both competing with the dust for supremacy. Much to Katherine's surprise, less than a mile later, Paddy rolled his window back up and broke the silence. Katherine didn't know what to make of Paddy wanting to drive and talk at the same time. Like they had in his trailer a couple of days earlier, they talked—nothing overly personal or uncomfortable, but talked nonetheless.

Katherine knew enough now not to push too far and expect him to share too much or too fast, so she switched the subject and asked about his latest progress in finding her uncle. Paddy shared nothing new on that end, nor did he give any explanation as to why he had gone missing for two days. Instead, Katherine took the opportunity to fill Paddy in on her discussion with the Timbisha. Her strategy appeared to work since Paddy and she kept talking.

"What do you make of what Paula said about Lizard Len?" Paddy added.

"If true, that she spoke with my uncle, then it means Lizard Len lied to us. We should have another talk with Lizard Len—don't you think?"

"I never trusted him," Paddy added, "and that whole alien conspiracy crap, especially the idea of Lizard People. But I trust him more than I trust Ned and his stupid dead-body-detecting machine. Ned's worse than the Manson maniacs. He's a media-seeking showman, charlatan, and fake. I wouldn't put it past him if he's behind the whole thing—everything."

"I do not know; I think he is just a vain and lonely man desperately wanting not to be a nobody."

"Desperate enough to kill?" After a pause, Paddy continued, "Sorry, I didn't mean it that way. I know your uncle is still alive. We'll find him." After another long pause, Paddy added, "I also don't fully trust the Timbisha. They're always lurking about."

"That's pretty rude! Paula and the other Timbisha treated me wonderfully. You know they have been here for hundreds, if not thousands, of years, so they are not 'lurking about.' They live there."

"I really didn't mean it that way. They're all right, I guess. I don't have anything against them *per se*. I guess it's a sign that I'm talking too much—when I do, I start talking nonsense."

Katherine interjected, "I hope he is alive. I think he got himself into trouble. Maybe he stumbled across the wrong person at the wrong time. The sheriff said there were a lot of drug runners and secret plane landings in isolated areas. Maybe he saw something he wasn't supposed to see."

As they were rolling down the washed-boarded and rutted dirt road, they spotted a beat-up GMC Yukon parked at a spring near Hidden Valley. Katherine spouted, nearly coming out of her seatbelt, "It's Nick's truck, isn't it?"

"What's *he* doing up here?" Paddy sputtered.

"What do you have against Nick? He seems like a nice man—nicer than you are being right now."

"I just don't trust the guy, that's all."

"You don't trust a lot of people. Patrick Darwin, if you keep that up, you will always be alone."

"At least being alone I can be in peace."

With that, Paddy fell into momentary silence, until Katherine chided, "You *are* turning around to see if Nick needs help? Aren't you?" Since they had just rolled past.

With a grunt, Paddy spun around, sending a billowing dust cloud into the shimmering heat. Paddy's Bronco came to a screeching stop alongside Nick's GMC. Paddy and Katherine both got out of the dust-covered rig and stepped into the little patch of greenery surrounding the spring. Katherine, alone, called for Nick.

Out of nowhere, Nick appeared, walked right past Paddy, and went straight toward Katherine. "Hello, Katherine, it's great to meet you again. You look quite lovely today."

"We're here to ask questions about Sid Emerson," Paddy blurted. "When did you say you last saw him?"

"Goodness, Paddy, we only stopped to see if Nick needed help. You do not need to be so abrupt. It is not like Nick is a suspect or anything."

"He's not?"

Turning to Nick, "Sorry for Paddy's surely mood," Katherine offered. "What Paddy meant to say is we are here to see if everything is okay. Do you need help?"

Nick stepped in between his new arrivals and began talking to Katherine directly. All Paddy could muster, other than a scowl, was a roll of his eyes at Nick's chitchat, the type that bored him and normally would send him back to the trailer. But this time he tolerated it—barely.

Eventually, Paddy couldn't stand it any longer, "What are you doing, Nick?"

Nick didn't answer. Paddy repeated his question, but this time even louder.

"You mean what am I doing here, at this spring?" Nick snapped back.

"You know what I mean—what are you doing?"

Nick could tell from the tone that Paddy was asking about Nick's intentions regarding Katherine, but Nick's stubbornness nearly matched that of Paddy's. Sensing Paddy would continue escalating the tension if Nick didn't answer, Nick sighed and added, "I'm setting up my bat nets at the spring—I'm netting bats this evening. Katherine, do you care to join me and watch some beautiful bats on this beautiful evening?"

"Thanks for the offer, but considering you don't need help, Paddy and I should be on our way."

Back in the confines of the Bronco, Paddy and Katherine sat in silence next to a window as firmly open as their conversation closed.

CHAPTER 27

As it had with George Shufelt, boisterous claims of mystery machines cannot go unnoticed for long—even within the Panamints' quirky, eccentric, and conspiratorial realm. Word of Ned Sipe's dead-body-detecting machine had even reached Stade Torgerson.

Stade, while undercover on one of his secret "business trips," never strayed far from Five Mile Spring—momentarily pausing his search for his brother's lost silver mine. *That damn Ned Sipe and his ridiculous machine*, Stade fumed. *He's leading a gaggle of reporters, misfits, and eccentrics right to where I buried Bud.* While Stade had a low opinion of Ned's mental capacity, he didn't doubt his persistence and determination.

If Ned stumbled upon Bud's grave, he would exhume the body thinking it to be another Manson victim—and he'd find a Torgerson instead. *If so, I'll never get my silver.* Stade blurted out, "I can't let that happen."

Stade knew Ned's type well enough that he wouldn't listen to just anyone telling him to stop searching that area. Besides, Stade couldn't tell anyone anything while in hiding, at least not directly. Therefore, Stade planned an indirect approach—subterfuge. *What better way to manipulate a conspiracy-minded person than with an even greater conspiracy?* This idea led Stade to think of Lizard Len. Stade had never met Lizard Len, but he'd heard rumors of his colorful suspicions.

To find Lizard Len, Stade first found a nice shady spot far from Ballarat that he could hole up in and watch the town's comings and goings. He didn't want to look suspicious by hanging out for days in a town of one. *I can't be too careful.*

Lizard Len never showed up on the first day, or the second. Stade grew impatient. *With Ned Sipe getting closer and closer to finding Bud's body, there have already been too many annoying delays.* Stade's nerves eased a bit early on the third day after spotting Lizard Len. He stopped by at the visitor center information booth on his customary Tuesday chat time with Rocky. Stade walked slowly up to the booth pretending to be a visitor.

"Hello. Do you work here?"

"Naw, I don't work here. I don't rightly work anywhere. What are you looking fur?"

"For information. I'm new here—I just came from Lone Pine where I chatted with a man that just came back from Death Valley. This guy told me people were flocking to the spot where Charles Manson buried one of his victims—"

"You heard what?" Lizard Len said in bewilderment. "I've not heard of no such thing."

"Yeah, crazy isn't it? Stade said. "The burial is not far from a place called Bill Hunger Ranch. Can you point me to Bill Hunger Ranch?"

"You must mean Hungry Bill's Ranch," Lizard Len said while scratching his head. "I've not heard of any Manson burial near Hungry Bill's place."

"It's breaking news—it just happened. Supposedly, a prisoner that spent time with Charles Manson overheard him talk about murders that had so far been undetected."

That made sense to Lizard Len, but he couldn't quite figure out how this out-of-place visitor would have heard such a rumor before he had.

The visitor continued, "The guy over at Lone Pine said several media crews will be coming to follow up this big new lead. So, I came to see what's up with all this hubbub. So, where is this Hungry Bill's Ranch?"

"Oh, that media crew," Lizard Len said to cover his embarrassment. "I know all about *that*. I know everything that goes on around here. That's why they call me Lizard Len, cuz the only one scurrying over the hills more than me is lizards—and I'm not real sure about them neither."

"Nice to meet you, Lizard Len."

"Anyway, there ain't nothing to *that* story. That's as old as the hills and has been checked over more than ticks on a tick-dog. I'd not waste my time with that."

"Okay, thanks. I'm just asking. The Lone Pine guy was probably just joking. Thanks for setting me straight."

"Sure. Yeah, the guy was pullin' your leg, more than likely."

With that, the undercover Stade got in his car, drove away, and began waiting for the rumor to spread to Ned Sipe. *It shouldn't take long*, he thought.

As soon as Stade drove out of sight, Lizard Len rushed to tell Ned Sipe about the news. He'd love to hear it. Besides, as Lizard Len figured it, Ned would likely even pay for this information.

After Lizard Len gave Ned Sipe the news, for a small finder's fee, Ned Sipe chirped, "No big city newspapers or TV crew are going to find any secret Manson burial without me leading it. This is *my* story and *my* expertise." However indignant Ned became over the thought that anyone would investigate such a thing without him, he salivated over the prospect of highlighting his machine in front of national news. *I'll be famous*, he thought. With this newer development, Ned abandoned his current search near Five Mile Spring and began his redeployment to Hungry Bill's Ranch.

The way Ned figured it, Hungry Bill's Ranch made perfect sense. It wasn't that far from Panamint City, and Manson spent time there and likely knew the area well. Ned paid Lizard Len to help him move his machine, batteries, wires, carts, and all other needed supplies over to Hungry Bill's Ranch. Stade's diversion worked beautifully. With his brother's gravesite safe, Stade eased his mind and went back to his search for the Torgerson silver.

Earlier, Stade heard rumors that Bud often prospected on Gold Hill near upper Galena Canyon, so Stade headed that way to check it out. With determination, two flat tires, and three quarts of oil, Stade finally made it to the road's end. He had no idea where to start. *Should I head south toward the Queen of Sheba Mine?* Stade pondered. *No, I don't think so. There's no point in retreading picked-over ground.* Instead, Stade headed northwest. He figured going up Six Spring Canyon, over to Middle Park, down to Arrastre Spring, up and around Gold Hill, then back down Galena Canyon would take a week—tops.

Stade left his rented Jeep in Galena Canyon and struck out on foot. The temperature, by his guess, was over 105 degrees. He slowed down to conserve water and prevent overheating. Besides, he knew when people hurried, they make mistakes. *The mountains here, and in this heat, are too unforgiving for stupidity.*

It took Stade several hours to traverse over to Six Spring Canyon, checking out the many adits and mine portals along the way. All the ravines took time too, as he had to climb up one side, and then find a way back down the other, only to ascend again on the far side. The up and downs and over and arounds through the labyrinth took time. The rough going burned more energy and used more water than Stade anticipated. *If the route didn't ease up, I'll have to come back another day.*

On day three, Stade hadn't left middle Six Spring Canyon and he only had one quart of water left. He knew if he continued as planned, he'd be in a world of hurt, so he changed plans. Above all, he needed water. Rather than traveling all the way up Six Spring Canyon to Middle Park, then down and over to Arrastre Spring, he headed directly to the springs—the only water he knew of in the area.

A day later, and nearly to Arrastre Spring, he estimated he has just climbed up and back down a total of ten thousand vertical feet— the land was *that* brutal. Nearly spent and almost completely out of water, Stade needed to get to the spring soon. Shortly before arriving at the spring, he came upon a cliffy area that blocked the straight-line route that he had been traveling. Scanning up and down the canyon, he figured he could reach the spring by skirting the cliff band after climbing up and over another one or two thousand feet. However, Stade estimated it would take too long and take more water than he had left.

Instead, he opted to climb directly down the cliff band. *It must be passable*, he thought. *I'm a good climber and in decent shape. If I head straight down, I may be able to reach the spring in a couple hours.* Down the cliff he crept, one step and one loose rock at a time. Stade found the going steep, but passable. If not for the loose rocks, it wouldn't be that bad, he thought.

Stade made it to the last cliffy section—not far from the spring. Fortunately, with the steeper angle, there were fewer loose rocks to navigate. Standing on a nubbin, he contemplated his next move. To the left appeared easier but it was covered with loose grit and ball-bearing-like shards. To the right looked harder, but cleaner. Stade chose the harder but safer option. As he shifted his weight to make the first move, the nubbin exploded. Stade plunged through the air and bounced from ledge to ledge until he came to a full stop at the cliff's bottom—less than a quarter mile from Arrastre Spring.

Darkness enveloped him when Stade came to. He had no idea how long he had been out. Miraculously, he felt no pain. Fear overwhelmed him upon the realization that he couldn't feel, or move, his legs. He had enough rational mind left to know that both were bad signs. He could move his arms, but with great pain. *It's dark and I'm stuck deep in a ravine—I gotta move.* Stade decided to wait until daybreak. Sometime before the Milky Way's first glow above the eastern horizon, Stade passed out.

When he awoke, the sun and heat had already drained him of energy, despite being in a shaded ravine. Flies were lapping the still oozing blood on his legs, his hip, and the back of his head. Stade knew he was in bad shape. He also knew that no matter how bad his injuries were, his situation would be much worse without water. He needed to make it to Arrastre Spring.

With as much concentration he could muster, Stade blocked out the stabbing, throbbing, dull, and sharp pains, and inch by inch, he crawled by pulling with his arms and dragging his useless body and legs over the mostly horizontal slope. After seemingly hours, and having passed out numerous times, he arrived at the tussled grasses and sedges that marked the remnants of the spring. The sight should have brought on the type of dread that would have overwhelmed all thoughts of pain, bloodied flesh, and cut and bruised fly-desecrated skin—but he accepted it with macabre humor. Arrastre Spring was as dry as a bone.

Bleeding fingers dug into the moistened sand and soil crust. Knowing even dry springs often held water somewhere deeper, sometimes only a few inches down, he scooped, dug, and carved a sandy hole two feet deep. Stade waited patiently for groundwater to seep into the hole. Stade waited, waited, and waited. Still, only bone-dry sand. He dug deeper and found only more sand. Knowing what *that* meant, Stade gave out a weakened sigh that morphed into a blood-spewing laugh.

An hour passed as he reflected on the path that led him there. Afterwards, Stade used the last of his strength, skin, and blood to sit upright. In his time of resignation, the first notion that came to mind was the beauty that lay before him. He fondly looked down on Warm Spring Canyon Road in the near distance. Further out, beyond the Panamint scarp, his crusted eyes lovingly scanned past a sliver of the Owlshead Mountains. Above, in the sky, he saw the richness of the ever-present sun. However, instead of welcoming him on his journey, it glared and mocked him. *It makes no difference*, he said to himself, *they're one-and-the-same*. He imagined the landscape trying to speak—directly to him. Not so much in words, but in thoughts and understandings—all mental. Sun and man, rock and flesh, and predator and prey all became as one, and this combined mass conversed at great length with itself on a range of topics, including Stade's once obsessive quest to claim his brother's nonexistent silver.

I killed my own brother over this futile obsession, he reflected. *I planned to kill Billy. How did I ever get to this point? No amount of silver is worth this cost.* The sun no longer agreed nor disagreed; it only mocked. Stade had learned too late that the sun always did what it wanted as it ruled over the harsh land and all weakened souls that happened to intrude or get in the way. It clearly ruled over Stade Torgerson. In a gambling hall, the house always has the advantage, but in the land of death, the sun holds *all* cards. He had gambled and lost. Stade continued this one-way conversation and reflection until all had faded over his last and final horizon.

CHAPTER 28

Katherine had no idea where they were at until they pulled into Shoshone—the small town she had heard much about, but she had only been there twice. Her first impression did little to move her, nor did this one. *Still*, she thought, *living here would beat Paddy's lonely outpost and decrepit trailer*. Katherine finally broke the long silence. "Shoshone, what are we doing here?"

"I want to talk with John Smithers," Paddy said. "He's expectin' us—me. Come, let's go!"

The morning's heat hung still over the valley. *It'll be a hot day*, Paddy thought. That alone should keep people off the streets. As they parked, Paddy remarked, "There're more people out and about than normal for Shoshone."

"—for Shoshone," Katherine interjected. "What are we talking about, a total population of thirty?"

"Something like that," Paddy said as he glanced up and down the street. "Ever since Rosy left for Ridgecrest—the town is still smarting from that loss."

As Paddy gazed at the crowd milling in the street, he still couldn't wrap his head around why all the people. *Nothing ever happens in Shoshone*, he thought. Regardless, Paddy and Katherine jockeyed through the crowd until they reached the sheriff's office's front door. After a long wait at the outside intercom button, Sheriff John Smithers opened the door and invited Paddy and Katherine into his office.

"So, Paddy, what can I do for you?" Turning to Katherine, "Have you found out anything about your uncle?"

Paddy interjected, "That is what I, we, want to talk to you about."

"Let's hear it."

"While we have no evidence yet," Paddy said, "we have recollections from several people that strongly imply Sid Emerson had not willingly wandered off as you seem to believe."

"You don't say," John said with a smirk.

"We wish you will reconsider looking into it yourself," Katherine interjected.

"From whom, crazy Lizard Len, Ned and his ridiculous dead-body-sniffing machine, or the old coot Rocky?" John chuckled, as his smirk turned into full laughter. "Tell me you have more leads and evidence than a bunch of crazies or attention-grabbing nutcases?"

"We would, if you helped out more than just sit there on your ass and mock our efforts while we try to do your job," Paddy said as he bolted from his chair.

"Please calm down, both of you," Katherine scolded. "Would it help if I fill out a formal missing person report?"

"Excuse me, ma'am, but you're not hearing me, and it doesn't matter what damn form you fill out unless you have solid evidence indicating otherwise, I conclude Sid Emerson had just wandered off and is acting weird like everyone else around here."

As Paddy contemplated how to respond, a deputy burst into the office, causing John to turn and bark, "Damn it, what the hell are you doing? Can't you see I'm busy here?"

"Sorry sir, but you got to come outside now quick."

"Stay put," John barked to Paddy and Katherine, as he ran out the door as fast as such a heavyset person can run in such situations.

At first, Katherine heeded his order, but Paddy had no intention of following anyone's orders. After Paddy stepped outside, Katherine soon followed. Once upon the street, Paddy and Katherine stepped into a crowded chaos unheard of and rarely seen in Shoshone. Demonstrators, including Mandi Mitchem and No-Name Maddox, were shouting pro-Manson slogans and carried Manson signs. John's eyes scanned up and down the street, assessing the scene before acting. "A full-fledged Charles Manson demonstration—right here in Shoshone," John muttered to whoever listened. "Of all places!"

The demonstrators held most of the left side of the street, while an anti-Manson crowd on the opposite side shouted back. Pushing and shoving got folks in the center street riled up. John spotted a deputy doing her best to separate the two factions and ratchet down the escalating drama. Suddenly, a shot rang out from nowhere and everyone dove for what little cover Shoshone streets offered in broad daylight.

While most of the crowd scrambled for safety or squirmed behind inadequate cover, only Paddy and John remained calm as they scanned the surroundings for any signs of where the shot came from.

Mandi hid behind the small roadside rock that Katherine had already found and occupied. It wasn't large enough for even one person. Mandi's more aggressive squirms pushed Katherine more and more into the open. Just then, Paddy and John saw movement on the hill overlooking the west side of town—just as another shot rang out. The round hit the rock that barely shielded Mandi and Katherine. Paddy motioned to John that he would circle the hill's left flank if John took the right.

This last shot left little doubt for Katherine or Mandi that one of them had been the intended target. Without a word, Mandi grabbed Katherine and pushed her out from behind the rock. Katherine fought back with a sharp blow to Mandi's head, but her refined Boston breeding proved no match for Mandi's Panamint strength and determination. Paddy hadn't yet noticed that Mandi put Katherine in danger, so he continued circling up the hill.

Paddy nor John got far up the hill before another shot came from the same hilltop. Paddy nor John noticed the round had hit immediately next to Katherine, and neither noticed the rock splinters that tore into Katherine's abdomen, or her blood that spilled into the street.

As soon as Mandi saw blood oozing into Katherine's shirt, she ran to find better cover, leaving Katherine alone to bleed in the dust.

A few seconds later, John topped the hill and found only empty rifle shells. *Where's Paddy?* he wondered. *He should have been here already,* John thought as he scanned the hilltop, alert for any movement. John hadn't known that Paddy, after seeing Katherine lying on the ground, had already raced down the hill to help. "Katherine, Katherine, are you okay?" Paddy screamed as he tore down the hill, oblivious to the shooter—or anything else.

"Paddy, the shooter's not up here," John shouted, unaware that Paddy was already halfway down the slope rushing to Katherine. "Keep an eye out!" the sheriff warned, but Paddy hadn't heard.

To reach Katherine faster, Paddy pushed his lungs, legs, and muscles far beyond convulsions. "Katherine, I'm coming."

Paddy ran as fast as he could, but he wasn't fast enough. Katherine had bled for much too long. When he arrived, her chest and lungs were motionless. Upon closer inspection, Paddy heard a faint but raspy gurgling noise. "Katherine, you're alive!" Paddy said as he gently turned her over to get a better look at the wound and to see how much life she had in her cheeks.

As Paddy held his hand gently behind her back, she turned her head and moaned, "It probably doesn't look as bad as it feels." After a brief pause, she added, "But it got you talking, didn't it?"

"It doesn't look that bad," Paddy assured her. "You look fine to me—just hang in there. I'll get you to the doctor ASAP."

Lifting her head closer to Paddy, with a thready voice that faded with every word, Katherine moaned, "How is Mandi? I think the bullet was intended for her."

"She's fine. You just need to worry about yourself. The medics will be here soon."

By this time John had arrived back. His deputies continued the search and guarded the place to ensure the shooter didn't come back and finish the job.

While Shoshone only had a population of thirty, it had its own doctor and health clinic. The doctor, with Paddy and John's help, strapped Katherine to a stretcher and carried her into the clinic. The wound was bloody, but not life-threatening. Instead of an airlift, the doctor called for an ambulance to come from Pahrump, Nevada. Sensing Paddy needed calming, the doctor said to Paddy, "The ambulance should be here in only a few minutes."

As the doctor continued his assessment, he narrated his findings to both John and Paddy, who waited with Katherine—eager for any news. "The bullet missed her," the doctor reported. "But an inch-long rock fragment tore into her stomach." The doctor did all he could do to stabilize Katherine, but she needed an operation. The doctor said the most dangerous part is when the surgeon can't find all the rock fragments. Even small bits left can cause serious problems and complications down the road.

After the ambulance came to take Katherine and Paddy to the Pahrump Medical Center, a deputy admitted that the shooter had gotten away and left no evidence other than a few empty rifle cartridges. Sheriff John Smither's job just got a lot more complicated. He surely would not be spending any time looking for Sid Emerson.

After everyone left, the streets of Shoshone returned to their normal desertedness. After all else within earshot had left, the deputy turned to John Smithers and admitted what she'd found on the hilltop. She didn't want to say anything in front of civilians. While she hadn't seen anyone on the hill, in the distance, she'd seen a vehicle speeding away, heading west toward Jubilee Pass. It was a deep blue Ford Expedition.

CHAPTER 29

With an efficiency borne of experience and routine, Nick Rauchoulbe took no time placing and anchoring his two base poles in a perfect site deep within Butte Valley. He had never trapped bats in Butte Valley before. He hadn't spread the spidery web-like mist net between the poles yet, because birds and other day-flying critters would entangle in it and likely rip the fragile and delicate netting. Mist nets are designed for one-tenth-ounce bats, not hawks with slicing talons. He contemplated he had just enough daylight to drive to Willow Spring to see if it would serve as a good site for next week's netting.

Willow Springs had everything he looked for in a good bat netting site, but he didn't stay there long, because he needed to get back to Butte Valley before sunset. At Butte Valley, he would likely document pallid bats and pipistrelles, and if luck would have it, maybe western small-footed bats. The site had just the right combination of cliffs, open water, buggy riparian vegetation, and most of all, clear air lanes for bats to maneuver. *Bats don't want to work any harder than people do for their food.*

The sun had just dipped below the horizon when Nick returned to his still intact poles. Careful not to let cactus or anything sharp rip the net, or let it drag on the ground, he took several minutes to mount the net onto the poles. First, he attached one end of the net to one pole, then he step by step unfolded the net while backing toward the other pole—all the while not letting the net touch the ground. Once at the far pole, Nick applied just the right amount of tension to the strings to keep the net's support structure taut while letting the individual netting curls hang in upright loose coils. After finishing, he jotted down the date, time, location, and weather conditions just as he glimpsed the fluttering of the night's first bat. Nick loved moonless nights in Death Valley. The night sky had the least light pollution of anywhere he had ever seen. The broad arc of the Milky Way would soon shine in all its Death Valley brilliance. The sky, weather, and vibe were all perfect—and with only light wind. *This will be a perfect evening.*

Against a stary backdrop, Nick watched slow-flying small bats fly just out of reach of the net. By their slow flight and small size, he guessed they were pipistrelles. With his attention transfixed on the lovely flight of small bats high in the sky, he at first didn't notice a large bat flopping in the net, getting more entangled the more it struggled. After gingerly entangling the pallid bat from the net, Nick measured it and took notes.

Pallids were Nick's favorite. This large and aggressive specimen did her best to fight back and flash her teeth, attempting to look fierce. To Nick, he saw only cuteness. Nick hurried because he noticed the bat had recently been feeding pups. He didn't want to stress her or her pups any more than needed. After a few more seconds of notetaking, Nick lifted high the pallid as if it were a delicate flower and watched as she launched herself into the starry night—somewhere between Draco and the Big Dipper.

That bat took Nick two minutes to clear from the net, weigh, take notes, and release, but by that time, two other bats had entangled in the net—one fought his tormentor, and the other lay motionless. Knowing healthy bats usually don't hang limp in the net like that, Nick turned first to this hapless bat. Mist nets don't usually hurt bats, but sometimes inexperienced people handling them do, but Nick was as careful as they came.

As he slowly unsnarled the net, one gossamer layer after the next, Nick suddenly stopped all motion and held any further breathing. The large ears and striking black and white body were unmistakable. *A spotted bat*, he beamed—the rarest bat of all. He dashed off to the other bat, a western small-footed, and frantically released it, then he ran to each pole to slacken the net to lessen the chance of netting any more bats—the spotted bat would take Nick's entire time and concentration.

As Nick became fond of reminding people, the fact that the spotted bat was not listed as a federally threatened or endangered species had more to do with politics than with any true and credible threat assessment. Few spotted bats have ever been caught. Consequently, biologists know little about them. So, Nick planned to take careful measurements of this beautiful female—and plenty of photographs. She too had been feeding pups recently.

Rummaging through his field bag, Nick pulled out his rarely used radio telemetry equipment. He carefully placed a few drops of special adhesive between her shoulder blades, and then into this soft goo, embedded a small radio transmitter. To Nick's trained eyes, it seemed to be a good glue job. *I hope it holds for a few days before falling off*, he thought.

Nick wanted to hold and watch it longer since this was his first, and likely last, spotted bat he would ever see. Regretfully, he cut his visit short by lifting her high in the air. While Nick spoke to it softly, the spotted bat left Nick's caring hands and flew into the darkness toward Striped Butte.

Nick packed all his gear and belongings and began driving to the Geologist Cabin, the researcher's field shack, where he planned to stay for the remainder of the night. As Nick drove along the rutted 4x4 road, a shooting star swept across the heavenly inkiness next to Striped Butte's silhouette. Nick thought, *This is a good omen*.

The next morning, Nick left the Geologist Cabin early, with enough water, food, energy, and fitful passion for an anticipated long day. He had no money for an airplane to track the spotted bat's radio signal, so he hoped the bat hadn't traveled far. He planned to drive around on 4x4 roads with a radio receiver, hoping to pick up a signal from the spotted bat's transmitter. If he couldn't get a signal from a road, Nick planned to search by foot, rope, or any other means necessary to locate the bat's maternity roost.

Nick drove up and down Butte Valley, from Mengel Pass over to Willow Spring, and then down to Warm Spring Canyon. Still, no signal and no bat. *I can't lose my spotted bat*, he silently cursed. The tiny transmitter's signal could only travel up to one mile, so Nick needed to get close. *I wish I had a plane, or at least field assistants*, he thought. Still no bat signal. Although tired and exhausted, Nick didn't want to give up for the day, but there were only a few spur roads still left to try, and without at least a weak signal, blindly searching across Death Valley's expanse would be a fool's errand. Therefore, Nick tried each road, no matter how obscure. The road at the head of Redlands Canyon—no signal. The same for Russell Camp. On his way out, just as the road made its big turn at the end of the spur southwest of Gold Hill, Nick heard a faint but distinct signal. And then it fell silent.

As fast as he could park and grab the receiver, food, water, rope, and other survival gear, Nick jumped out of the Jeep and began making quarter-mile-radius circles around the last and only signal spot. About halfway around the arc, he picked up the signal again. His pace and heart rate quickened to match the clicks emanating from the handheld receiver's speaker. The more he pushed, the stronger the signal became. *I'm getting close, old Nick. This will be the first time anyone has ever found a spotted bat maternity roost.* He kept up the relentless push.

Nick climbed higher. Higher. The view into Warm Spring Canyon reminded him of why he loved this landscape—the ruggedness and wildness. Adrenaline wouldn't allow him time to enjoy the desert sublimity. He kept after the signal. Suddenly, he could go no further. The signal came from a crumbling cliff. Eyeing it, Nick figured it would be too dangerous to climb the cliff—too filled with loose rocks—even with copious quantities of adrenaline surging through his veins. Nick's passion for bats often pushed him on into dangerous terrain, but never to the point of foolishness. He cursed himself for not also attaching a luminescent strip that could be visually tracked at night. Nonetheless, Nick smiled in a way he hadn't caught himself doing in a long time.

Below his not-to-be bat roost cliff, Nick sat on a flat boulder and let his mind wander to spotted bats, Death Valley, and his old mining days, but mostly about the austere land that extended toward the horizon and beyond. Despite beginning to cool down, Nick could still see shimmering heat waves radiating into the late afternoon cobalt sky. *How I love this place*, Nick thought as he let loose with a deep sigh.

With the calm satisfaction that only comes from deep joy, Nick pulled out his well-worn binoculars and began scanning the land inch-by-inch, gully-by-gully, and greasewood-by-greasewood—not for bats or any practical reason, but just to soak in the experience. With his eyes on alluvial fans, his mind shifted toward Katherine Emerson. Through portals other than binoculars, he began seeing his life had been far too lonely.

Nick knew Katherine had come only to find her uncle. *If by chance, she turned her eyes on me, would she stay? Probably not*, he concluded. *She'll likely go back to Boston when it's over.* His next thought ended even more abruptly. He stopped his slow binocular scan to retrace his last few seconds. He saw something. A slow pan across Arrastre Spring caught his attention. There appeared to be a body below the spring. To check it out, it would take Nick the rest of the afternoon.

Nick's descent to Arrastre Spring took less time than he'd anticipated. It helped having his mind occupied. Upon arriving, he walked up to the corpse leaning against a boulder. Nick knew enough about finding dead bodies that he made sure to take notes of what he observed, so that he could report it to the sheriff. *I'm surprised a coyote or mountain lion hasn't scattered the bones by now.* The identify of the few dead bodies that Nick had stumbled upon in the past had always been a mystery. *It's hard to get much information from a dead body when most of the flesh has been stripped off,* he mused. On this one, ripped clothes hung from its torso, while the rest of the person's clothing had been scattered about. Near the body, Nick found a faded wallet. "Ah, the best source of information a corpse can provide," Nick said out loud as he peeled the wallet open. From the wallet's dried leather, he pulled out a Pennsylvania driver's license. Nick had to spit and rub on it to read the faded name. It belonged to Stade Torgerson. Nick didn't know Stade Torgerson, but figured the guy had to be related to Bud.

Days later, Sheriff John Smithers found nothing at the scene or on the body that indicated Stade Torgerson's death wasn't anything other than heat and the environment—just like so many other deaths John had seen in his county. However, the sheriff's conviction and conclusions did little to settle the rabble that soon erupted. Word spread fast of the Torgerson mystery and further Torgerson drama. To some people, this only meant the government had covered something up. For most people, this provided further proof that Bud Torgerson's silver strike had to be real and ripe for the taking.

CHAPTER 30

John wanted to visit Katherine in the hospital, but he had far too many cases, crises, conflicts, and crazies to chase. He couldn't afford personal pleasantries. While he wouldn't admit it, deep down John Smithers liked Katherine Emerson. She had admirable traits, but in hard times such as these, that's a trait he could ill-afford himself.

No matter. From what John heard, Katherine had not been lonely. Her many visitors included Ron, Papa, Lizard Len, Rocky, and, of all people—Paddy. He hated hospitals and doctors. John would have loved to catch Paddy sheepishly slinking into the hospital trying not to be seen. That would have been quite a sight, John mused.

Katherine must be growing on Paddy. At least someone around here is happy, John thought as his mind wandered to his old friend. *Paddy could use the company, and it's good he's not holed up by himself all the time.* From what John had heard, Katherine had also been visited by Nick. John didn't even know they knew each other. *For being new to Death Valley, she sure has grown on people and made an impression,* reflected John.

Katherine did not take hospital confinement well—it was too much time spent in her head, she mused. However, moving around the hospital room allowed her sufficient time to shake off her past, regrets, and failings. It also kept her mind off Paddy since she had much to consider. What would she do after she found her uncle? This was only one question that plagued Katherine's mind during idle hospital times. After her Death Valley experiences, her mundane life back in Boston appeared as appetizing as hospital food—but so did remaining in Death Valley. Even more worrying were her thoughts: What if she never found her uncle?

One thing her dreadful hospital confinement taught her was that for far too long now, she had been living as a passive bystander, preferring someone, anyone, to lead and show her the way and to direct her fortunes or misfortunes. The more she thought about such things, the angrier she became. She realized that it was her way of avoiding pain and avoiding failure. She vowed to take control of her life—that is, once she discovered what she wanted. *But letting others decide everything for me is a sure way to avoid happiness. From now on, I will take more charge in my life.* But first, she needed out of the hospital.

To help her get out of her head, she switched on the television. On the first station her channel-surfing landed on was an interview of Ned Sipe. He claimed to the entire TV audience that his newest model of the dead-body-detecting machine had recently found definitive proof of more Charles Manson murders. Katherine jumped out of bed and switched the television off.

When not in the hospital visiting Katherine, Paddy pushed even harder to come up with more leads on what had happened to Sid. Some good news on her uncle would do a world of good for her, Paddy thought, as he followed up one lead after another. His hard work began to pan out. People from all stripes had been coming out of the background and sharing with Paddy potential leads on Sid Emerson's whereabouts and reported sightings. Paddy assumed most would likely go nowhere, but having this quantity of fresh leads marked good progress for a change.

Days tended to blur into one another for John Smithers and his unrelenting caseload. He still hadn't solved who shot Katherine. He had no more leads than he had on the day of the shooting. It appeared this might become just another unsolved cold case file. However, John still had follow-up questions for Katherine.

Normally, the sheriff would send a deputy into the hospital for this type of questioning, but John needed to get out of the office and clear his head. As soon as he arrived at the Pahrump Medical Center, John discovered the hospital had released Katherine just a few minutes earlier. According to a nurse, Paddy took Katherine back to her Ridgecrest motel. The nurse said for her entire hospital stay, Paddy had doted over her and her every need. *This is not the Paddy Darwin that I know*, thought John, as he contemplated their friendship over the last several years. *Katherine is changing him for the better.*

Since John had other cases he needed to attend to back at the office, he sent a deputy to Ridgecrest to question Katherine. He still hadn't wrapped his head around the entire Torgerson mysteries. *What was Stade Torgerson doing in Death Valley, and why had he been sneaking around undercover?*

John could see clearly that Stade had died of heat and exposure. He needed no autopsy for that determination. *Stade may have been a greedy son-of-a-bitch, mysterious creeper, and not a good uncle to Billy or brother-in-law to Bonnie, but what laws did he break?* John asked himself. *It's not as if I can arrest him for being a lowlife. If so, I'd have to arrest everyone around here.* John's mind increasingly turned to the younger Torgerson. *What happened to poor Billy?*

Billy's case kept John up at night more than even normal. There were odd things about the death that still didn't make sense. It's not unusual to fall while in a mine's twilight zone, since eyes had not yet grown accustomed to low light levels, but the fact that he is a Torgerson gave John fitful nights. *It's just too fishy*, John kept thinking in the pre-dawn hours as he shifted and shifted again in bed. *With Bud's lost silver mine and Stade's mysterious lurking about, it's just too coincidental that the one person that happens to fall to his death is another Torgerson.* From John's experience, nagging suspicions usually mean something. *It means I have another smelly fish on my hands. If not, there must really be a curse on the Torgersons.*

To learn more about Billy's death, John pored over Stade Torgerson's multi-volume journal. The end of Stade's journal number four ended in mid-sentence, as if it continued into another, yet, missing volume. According to his journal, ever since Bud's death, all those years ago, Stade coveted his brother's silver discovery—wherever it was.

Through the journal writings, it seemed clear that Stade suspected that Bud had told Billy the location of the silver mine. Since Billy hadn't shared this information with his mother or uncle, Stade wanted to keep the silver to himself. "That greedy bastard," Stade wrote in the journal. "After all I did for him."

From scrawls in the journal, John pieced together that Stade suspected Billy had planned to legally claim the silver once he turned eighteen and no longer a minor living under Stade's roof. Stade also believed Billy kept Bud's secret from his own mother since she would never have approved of Billy getting into the mining business. John needed no journal to tell him that. *Bonnie would have done anything to keep Billy away from Death Valley mines.*

According to his journal, Stade originally invited Bonnie and Billy to live with him after his brother Bud's death only to stay close to Billy and the secret of the Torgerson silver mine. Stade hoped to legally adopt Billy or marry Bonnie—whatever it took to claim the inheritance for himself.

John had been around and dealt with all kinds of people. Despite his exposure to the raw human condition, a chill ran down John's spine after reading Stade's journals. He had rarely experienced someone as cold. Stade's journal entrees referred to Billy, his nephew, as only a means to an end or as competition, since he alone, as the eldest Torgerson, was the rightful heir to the Torgerson silver mine.

John wondered if Billy knew how his uncle felt. *If so, that must have been hard on poor Billy.* John kept studying the journal for clues. From what John could tell, Billy was a good kid, and he and Bonnie were the only Torgersons who did not have gold or silver lust coursing through their veins.

On the surface, Billy's death looked like an accident, but something deep down kept John thinking otherwise. His deputies found a brand new Cloudbuster signal disruptor located not far from Billy's body—*just like the local crystal wackos make*, John told himself. Because of this, John pulled Torrey Small in for questioning. He seemed evasive. Surprised, yes, but still evasive.

Torrey claimed the Cloudbuster but denied placing it there. "I have no records of deploying Cloudbusters anywhere near that mine," Torrey said.

John believed him. *I have always had a sense when someone is lying or hiding things*, John thought as he continued questioning Torrey. *He may not be lying about this*, John thought as he watched Torrey squirm in the interrogation chair. *But that doesn't mean he's innocent.* John fumed. *I just need some proof that he did something illegal*, John concluded. *He must be put away and forever out of my hair.* John mulled over these thoughts as Torrey droned on about something unrelated. *Torrey's Cloudbuster next to Billy's body proves nothing in the court of law*, John reflected. *That's just circumstantial evidence and it wouldn't convince anyone of Torrey's guilt or explain Billy's death.* "Torrey needs watching," John wrote in his notes. With a deep sigh, John silently cursed, *Torrey may end up getting away with it. Not if I can help it*, he spat. John just needed a new lead and more evidence. *I will just have to chew on this a bit more.*

Besides the Torgerson cases, John still hadn't finalized the Owlshead death investigation, the miner's fight at Skidoo, the Russel Camp medivac evacuation, Nick's death threat from Lizard Len, or the bomb scare at the Timbisha Community Center. *If this weren't enough, Ned Sipe and the media are continuously harassing me over his supposed new Manson murder find. These 'finds' all seem to occur when the media comes into my county.*

From John's perspective, the Russel Camp fiasco was a real sticky widget. The fight ended with five arrests, but it got started when a guy from Tonopah accused someone from Grand Junction of following him, hoping to be led to Bud's mine. The Tonopah guy would have nothing of it. A nasty fight ensued, and others came out of the salt brush and joined in. The deputies arrested five, but four others wound up in the hospital, one so badly hurt the deputy had to call China Lake for a medivac.

That's the only good thing that came out of Katherine being wounded, John contemplated. *Her being laid up in the hospital and then her motel room, and Paddy tending her every need, keeps them from getting caught up with the crazies out there. If not, someone would likely hurt them, claim they're Lizard People, or were hiding secret mines. There is just no self-control anymore in the Panamints. I hope Paddy and Katherine do not contract the Torgerson curse—*

"You weren't listening to me, were you?" Torrey asked John. "You know as well as I do, I'm innocent."

"I know of no such thing, Torrey. That is why I'm investigating."

"Am I free to go?" asked Torrey.

"Yes, yes. Just do not take any long trips. We may still need a few answers."

Trying to purge his mind of his heavy caseload, John's thoughts wandered back to Paddy and Katherine. *Now that he's moved into a motel room next to Katherine, so he could be there for her and help her out—how's he paying for it all?* John wondered. *Paddy never has any money. Katherine must be paying him well. One thing is for sure, he certainly is not the Paddy I used to know.*

CHAPTER 31

Bonnie took the news of Stade's death hard. She had lost her husband, son, and now brother-in-law. She asked as many questions of John as expected—but no more. Sheriff Smithers had questions of his own, but it didn't seem the right time, so he waited. John wanted to probe into what Stade was doing here and why he'd been sneaking around the Panamints as a mysterious stranger. *Questions can come later*, John figured. *She's been through a lot.* While leaving, he said, "Again, sorry for your loss. If I may intrude, will you be around tomorrow morning for follow-up questions?"

"Yes. Thank you, Sheriff. You've been kind," she said.

The news and speculations of Stade's death went viral on social media. Rumor had it Stade knew the location of his brother's lost mine and he had been secretly mining Torgerson silver. A few wannabe miners speculated that Stade had been murdered because someone had discovered his identity and wouldn't give up his secrets.

The Torgerson mystery piqued the public's interest more than anything in years. Lizard Len, Torrey Small, and the rest of the crystal crowd convinced themselves that Lizard People had killed Stade after he accidentally stumbled onto their catacombs. They also believed the sheriff and the entire federal government tried to cover it up.

Every new speculation fueled additional, even wilder leaps of logic. The suspicious-minded connected imaginary lines between Bud, Stade, and young Billy—and new lines formed daily. They spun a spidery web of suspicion over the entire Death Valley region.

In the morning of the following day, John knocked on Bonnie's motel door to ask his follow-up questions. No one answered the door. The manager reported that Ms. Torgerson had checked out the previous night. John never saw Bonnie Torgerson again. Years later, rumors had it that she moved east. Some claim Bonnie had a mental breakdown, while others claim the Lizard People caught up with her again. The only known fact is that no one from the Death Valley region ever heard from Bonnie Torgerson again.

❦

Back in the Panamints, Torgerson speculation fueled an even greater swarm of wannabe prospectors throughout the range, including get-rich hucksters, charlatans, treasure seekers, conmen, and those seeking a deeper immersion into the void. Once kicked, the ant nest colony worked themselves into quite a frenzy. Some came for gold, while others came for crystal enlightenment. Still others came to witness history in the making. More than a few came for first contact with an alien species.

In equal proportion, the contact contingent divided themselves into those wanting to kill Lizard People, join them, or be Earth's self-bestowed intergalactic ambassador. Regardless of the reason they came, there were far too many lost souls than Death Valley's primitive wilderness would ever allow or accommodate. "She'll chew them up and spit them out," John lamented to his deputies. "Before the week is out, there'll be three more dead—mark my words." On one day alone, Rocky at his once-lonely Ballarat post had met newly arrived immigrants from Winnemucca, Grand Junction, Moab, Thermopolis, Libby, Pocatello, Klamath Falls, Ephrata, Modesto, Spearfish, Amarillo, Show Lo, and Alamogordo, let alone a bevy from Ridgecrest, Pahrump, Beatty, and Barstow.

Even Lizard Len, Torrey Small, Rodney Horrovick, Mark Levison, No-Name Maddox, and Jimmy Two Claw joined the fray—well, not Jimmy himself, but rather paid representatives willing to get dirty. Dirty they got, in more ways than one.

The silver-fever desperate seemed not to have considered that most areas they searched, crossed, and double-crossed had all been in the national park. Even if someone found silver, the National Park Service wouldn't let anyone mine it. John assumed the only way it made sense to them would be if they conducted late-night or otherwise subversive prospecting. This would have to include in-and-out incursions while hoping not to get caught after digging or blasting holes. They figured, if drug smugglers can get away with illegal plane flights onto Owl Lake, they could get away with a little late-night silver mining within the remote backcountry. Mostly, John figured no one had given such nuanced, logical, or practical thoughts to the matter. Gold fever and rational thought do not go hand-in-hand.

Once infected with gold fever, no thoughtful reflection could exorcise or purge wild ideas or even wilder demons—not even Torrey's radio inhibitors could work their magic on breaking greed and desperation's powerful hold. Nothing had worked for Bud Torgerson, and certainly, nothing would quell this new Panamint mob. "It's crazy in the Panamints. Everyone's turning on one another," Rocky lamented.

Beatty and Tonopah folks forged an alliance to push back incursions from the Texans. Similarly, the bedraggled Grand Junction, Moab, Thermopolis, and Libby ruffians formed an impenetrable alliance all their own. Most of the remainder wandered alone, ransacking mining camps, historic cabins, and any hikers they randomly and suspiciously came across. No one saw what happened to the hapless Ephrata old man after he wandered alone, for some ungodly reason, into the Owlsheads—and disappeared without a trace.

John's phone rang nonstop. On one call, dispatch notified him of four separate but simultaneous demonstrations—with everyone screaming at each other and threatening serious retaliation for whatever their latest perceived slight. There were demonstrations against the government, a demonstration against the National Park Service at

Furnace Creek, a crowd gathering in Shoshone pleading with the unaffiliated to help overthrow the government, and several activists that seized the opportunity during the unrest to incite violence to push for a new state spanning rural southeastern California.

Lizard Len couldn't just sit idle during such transformative times. He took it upon himself to rally against the military-industrial complex. Alone, he stormed the China Lake Naval Air Station border crossing intending to take over the entire base to save America from the Lizard People. Fully human naval security officers promptly arrested him.

Ned Sipe had been in the news the last couple of nights claiming he and his machine could find both bodies and gold, and that he had proof that all recent commotions were linked to Charles Manson. Ned claimed he would reveal these linkages once he recovered Manson's additional victims. "They are still out there. I just need a little more time and a little more money." With full confidence in his machine, he pitched a proposal to the county board of supervisors. Like children enamored by shiny new bobbles, the supervisors would have issued Ned a permit to dig a 250-foot pit under the Shoshone Airport as had Los Angeles granted Shufelt on his wild claim. However, Ned Sipe only requested a modest permit. He lacked George Shufelt's vision, personality, and gravitas for anything more grandiose.

Even Mandi Mitchem, after being released from jail, came out of nowhere to whip people into a race-hating frenzy. She claimed, "We are now entering humanity's final race war—the one Manson originally had in mind." Hate and suspicion spread like wildfire throughout the county. If things didn't quiet soon, John would need to swallow his pride and ask San Bernardino County for assistance.

John feared the heat might turn into a self-sustaining wellhead fire. *Once ignited, wellhead fires are the hardest to extinguish*, John reminded himself. There would be nothing left for John to do other than call for a state of emergency and have the governor send in the National Guard. However, this act alone would surely be the catalyst for an even greater conflagration. John vowed, *I need to get ahead of this. Things can't continue this way indefinitely.*

As John knew all too well, with this many desperate souls pouring and pouring over the hills, someone would surely conjure additional conspiracies as fanatical crowd gatherings spiraled out of control. John ordered all-hands-on-deck for all his deputies, and then addressed his deputies. "I've heard rumors that Ned Sipe planned to hold his next media circus not far from Hungry Bill Camp. I've also heard that a wild-eye group from Gallup are in the area looking for both lost silver and lost burials. From what I've heard, they're probably too drunk to tell the difference. So please, be careful."

A crowd from Gallup set up camp near Hungry Bill Camp, determined to prove John right. They came not for silver bobbles. They heard rumors of a suspected burial of an unidentified new Manson victim. Ned already had his machine stowed near Hungry Bill Camp. He planned to have a media extravaganza, but he needed more equipment and supplies.

By the time Ned's supplies arrived by cart, the Gallupese were long gone, but their pockmarks and desecrations were everywhere. Shaking his head in disbelief, Ned muttered, "Amateurs!" He vowed not to make such a mess. In Ned's mind, planning made a world's difference. Based on his unwavering faith in his mind and machine, Ned expected to find a new Manson-murder victim. While he had abundant faith, he knew the rest of the world operated on evidence. As such, Ned would have done anything for conclusive proof. "I will just have to unleash my brilliance on the unsuspecting media and general public," he said out loud to himself. "That would surely draw all the attention from Bud's silver to me and my machine."

While Ned planned his next media event near Hungry Bill Ranch, the recently departed Gallup contingent had moved their search for silver to the Five Mile Spring area. Only two hours later, one wannabe miner stumbled, quite accidentally, across what looked like a carefully concealed grave. This miner needed no magical machine to detect a coffin-sized pile of stone. With a frenzy borne only of greed and desperation, the man pried rocks from the grave, hand-over-hand and muscle-over-muscle, as he heaved and grubbed, smiled, and giggled. He unearthed a human skull. More digging uncovered a torso, leg bones, and the leftover pieces of what the Gallupese believed to be a previously undiscovered Manson murder victim. He needed no fancy machine to notice a wadded piece of paper buried next to the skeletonized remains. As soon as the Gallup man opened the fragile document, his hopes bled away as fast as desert spit. "You aren't a Manson murder victim after all," the man said to the skull. "You're Bud Torgerson."

Word spread quickly of Bud's newfound latest death. "If Bud didn't die in the mine as reported, who lied, and why?" The entire reading public in southeastern California asked.

John asked this question as well. For a crowd already whipped into a frenzy over the speculation of Bud Torgerson's lost silver, Billy's and then Stade's deaths, Stade's lurking about mystery, and now Bud's body being found twice, this all just cranked up the heat—that's all he needed.

On this same day, John heard from dispatch that a group of Nick followers clashed with No-Name Maddox. Over what, John hadn't figured out yet. However, it had something to do with the belief that recent events would soon spring forth by Charles Manson's Second Coming.

The frenzy affected more than mere fringe elements. Nick fostered his own devoted following. Rumor had it he had been working the secret Torgerson mine. Since Nick had been a miner, people found it easier to believe that he had caught the Torgerson silver fever than for him to be wandering the desert looking for bats. "What's up with that?" more than one person was overheard asking and speculating.

Rumors also circulated that Nick knew nothing of the whereabouts of Torgerson's silver. Instead, Nick must be a Lizard

People operative, or maybe a Lizard Person himself. "This would logically explain his late-night supposed bat wanderings," they kept repeating.

Rocky and Papa screamed at the press on nearly a daily basis, accusing the Timbisha of murdering Stade Torgerson. Torrey Small's riled up folks by claiming the sheriff had been working to subvert our democracy—all at the hands of Lizard People and their government conspirators. Even reasonable and calm people had become vocal and suspicious.

Paddy had been uncharacteristically vocal about his suspicions of Nick. He kept showing up at the sheriff's office, saying, "Look, John, I think Nick is hiding something. I think he may know more about Sid Emerson's disappearance. After all, he lied on more than one occasion."

"No, you look—Paddy. I have enough on my hands without you bothering me too. The only reason you suspect Nick is 'cause he's sweet on Katherine. It's pure jealousy. Get over it, man! Katherine has the same information as you do, but do you see her here complaining about Nick? Just go home, back to your trailer, back to your Ridgecrest motel, or go back to Boston with Katherine, but get out of my office!"

Even Katherine couldn't shake the rash of speculations and accusations sweeping the land. She became convinced that her uncle had stumbled across a drug deal, and that this led to his disappearance. When John heard of this, he muttered, "Has the entire county gone crazy? These types of things don't happen in San Bernardino County."

Pushed beyond his furthest threshold, John knew he needed help. The governor sent in National Guard troops to quell the fever, violence, destruction, and desecration of what was once a rich mining cultural legacy.

Despite the China Lake jail cell walls separating him from the rest of the world, word of the Panamint chaos eventually reached Lizard Len. Unlike before, he didn't view the recent events sweeping throughout the land as the coming Lizard Apocalypse. The Naval Command took note of Lizard Len's new outlook, so they released him from prison, since they needed the jail space for worse offenders.

After being released from jail, Lizard Len felt like a new man. While in prison, he saw the light. From this revelation on forward, he no longer sought the untold Lizard People truth—he freed himself from, as he claimed, "Conspiracies and society's ill ways."

No matter how enlightened Lizard Len believed himself to be, this did not mean that he had not joined the search for Torgerson silver. During his prison epiphany, he discovered how much he liked the finer things in life. Fine things require money, he repeatedly told himself.

However, his lust for silver did not fully quell Lizard Len's conspiratorial mind—it only tempered it. His newfound self viewed the Lizard People-government conspiracy not as a physical or mental control of humans, but instead, control of national and international financial markets. To Lizard Len, it was just another means for the Lizard People to reach their ultimate goal: *to divide us and have us turn on ourselves.*

According to Lizard Len's new faith, investing in silver—the only currency safe from the Lizard People's influence—became the only logical and effective means to counter the invasion. This meant he, Lizard Len, needed to beat the Lizard People to Torgerson's silver.

How Lizard Len could square his silver lust with his claim that society's evils were rooted in being too materialistic was anyone's guess. However, if logic had any influence, Lizard Len would not have been involved, and there wouldn't be so many people desperate to find Torgerson's silver.

CHAPTER 32

S aving people who cannot help themselves grew to be Missy Flores' main passion in life. She would have loved to grow the world into one united community but realized that must remain a long-term goal. Changing society's norms and sensitivities cannot happen overnight. She thought a few months, a year at most, would be plenty of time to bring the world's factions together. "It's in everyone's self-interest," she often said.

Missy's father loved her greatly but thought Matilda (she allowed only her father to use her given name) too impatient and naïve. Still, he figured, if she wanted to make the world a better place, "I must have done *something* right."

Her passion to help others led Missy to Pitzer College. Last year, she graduated with honors with a degree in behavioral sciences. Once out of school, she couldn't decide how best to serve humanity. Private sector jobs seemed too commercial, and government jobs too restrictive and inflexible. She leaned toward private nonprofits, but until she decided, she wandered—sometimes far and wide. If someone wanted to wander far and wide, there was no better place than in Death Valley.

However, she spent most of her spare time hiking and skiing in the San Gabriel Mountains just north of Clairmont. Cucamonga Peak, one of the highest in the "San Gabs," had always been her favorite. From its lofty summit, Missy pondered the nature of humanity and the best way to help global populations in need. She intuitively knew helping people was easiest at the personal one-on-one level; but she feared if she got too caught up with individuals, she might lose sight of broader societal realities that often drive social dynamics in the long term. She held firm in her conviction that some issues were best dealt with at the non-personal scale. Therein lay Missy's confliction. This also partly explains many of her San Gabs and Cucamonga Peak adventures—she needed time to think. Mountains provided her counsel and perspective. For Missy, nothing opened a person's mind as much as expansive summit views.

As an alternative viewpoint, perspective, and counsel, Missy occasionally skirted the San Gabs on the east, headed north on Highway 395 to Ridgecrest, then drove along 178 to the foot of the Death Valley wilderness. Missy could think of no better place to contemplate life, seek perspective, and bring peace to inner conflict. Increasingly, she sought solace in Death Valley's mountains, especially, the Panamint Range.

She made many trips to Goler Canyon and Pleasant Canyon and up Surprise Canyon to Panamint City, but on this trip, she wanted something different, something off the beaten track—by even Panamint standards. So, this time she rolled into Ballarat to get suggestions from Rocky. She'd chatted with Rocky many times. He had many faults, and at times he was quite unpleasant, but he had always been kind and friendly to Missy. Many locals think too kind, that perhaps he had taken a shine on Missy despite being old enough to be her grandfather. Missy was not naïve in the effect she had on men, but neither was she bothered or intimidated by advances—after all, she had majored in behavioral sciences. Other than Lizard Len, who better to study for behavior science than Rocky?

She found Rocky where she thought he'd be—in the small visitor information booth that he'd built as the self-appointed Panamint historian and Ballarat public information visitor's bureau. "Hey-all, Rocky, how have you been since the last time I rolled by?"

"Wha'll, Missy, you know'd my world's incomplete without you, so I've done nuttin' but mark my days pinin' for our return. Where'd you headin' to this time?"

"That's what I'm here to ask. I'm looking for a lonesome place, where people don't typically go. There are just too many people around here since the Torgerson news broke. Say, I've not heard much about Big Horn Canyon. What can you tell me about it?"

"You can say that a-gin—even Lizard Len out lookin' fur gold—fool's gold, I say. Nuttin' but trouble. See what it got Bud and the other Torgersons. But to yur other question, if'n you want a lonesome place, you'd can't go no furthen' than my heart. As for Big Horn, I would say great place, but if'n you want lonesome, I'd suggest the Slate Range west of Wingate Pass or over'n to Sugar Loaf Peak in the southern Panamints."

"Why, what is up with Big Horn Canyon?"

"That's whad I wanna know, but my back n' bones aren't what they wer'n when I was seventy-eight. I can't git up there no more. But I'm curious as a cat in heat to know'd what's goin' on up there. Sometimes I see people slinkin' up there late at night, before sunrise, and what not. Not a lot, but mor'n used to be—that'll be fur certain. I'm curious to know'd meself. But that seems the only place the fool's gold crowd ain't goin'.'"

After a long pause, which they both looked out upon the expansive Panamint skyline, only in different directions, "Rocky" quietly said, "So, you'd headin' o'er to Slate Range?"

"Maybe, I'll let you know."

"You'd make sure you do, hun, since there's a hole in me until you'd do. Take care!"

"Bye, Rocky."

As Missy drove off, she steered her Jeep Cherokee south. On a whim, she had a notion to park somewhere beyond Goler Canyon to see if she could find her way west into Copper Queen Canyon. As her Cherokee approached Goler, she quickly pulled a U-turn on the once empty and desolate washboarded gravel road. She had never experienced such things at Death Valley before, but to make her turn, she had to wait a few seconds for the cluster of out-of-state plates to pass by. Once past the traffic congestion, she pointed the Jeep's nose back toward Big Horn Canyon. Rocky's comments got her thinking.

Once on foot, she slowly wound her way up outwash gravels, broken alluvial fans, and elevated terraces. As the heat became oppressive in the low-elevation gullies, she pondered how reflective simple gravel could be. One would never know such things until they spent much time hiking through gravel-lined bowls in Death Valley's mid-summer glory.

As soon as she passed the gullies, she entered a thick field of salt brush and a faint trail—recently used. *There is not supposed to be a trail here*, from what she heard. There are few trails within the Panamints, let alone up Big Horn Canyon, or so she thought. *Where could it possibly be going?* she wondered, as the trail increasingly veered away from the canyon and more into the unknown. By this time, well beyond looking for solace and peace, Missy became fully immersed in seeking answers to her growing curiosity.

As Missy climbed higher, the views opened into the incognito lands of the China Lake Naval Weapons Center. *I would love exploring those playas, peaks, and springs*, she thought, but the military closed all public access—and they enforced the closure. Missy's eyes rose beyond China Lake and Argus Range restricted area and rested upon the Sierra's snowy crest.

Not far beyond where she snacked at the Sierra Nevada backdrop, Missy caught the first glimpse of an old miner's cabin. The faint trail she'd been following led directly to this lonely outpost. At first, she hadn't planned to approach since there were mining relics all over the Death Valley mountains. However, as Missy began to pass, she did a double take. She felt an odd sense about this one. This cabin seemed different, but she couldn't quite place it. Then it dawned on her. It looked lived-in, at least recently.

Nerves tickled Missy's neck as they never had in the San Gabs. She turned her head left, right, and behind, hesitant to move forward or back. *Is this a squatter*, she asked herself, *or worse?* The heat shot shivers into her marrow and synapses upon the speculation of alternative explanations. Missy had a sudden urge to turn around and find the sheriff, but something else compelled her to creep to a well-concealed low spot. From the cover, she shouted, "Hello! Anyone home?"

Missy inwardly cursed as she slunk away to escape the feeling that she was getting herself in over her head. Before reaching the safety of a creosote bush, she heard behind her the muzzled but unmistakable sound of someone calling. More muffled sounds stopped her just shy of the relative safety of a large bush. Pressing her face deeply into the thick creosote, she waited for another sound. None came. Just as the smell of sweat and smoky creosote became intense, Missy involuntarily shouted, "Is anyone in the cabin? Are you hurt? If so, I can help. I won't just abandon you."

The cabin remained as still as a winter's frost. Missy crept closer. When she could almost touch the padlocked door, the pitiful sounds started again. Instead of retreating to the brush, Missy held her ground. The sounds came from under the cabin. Miner's cabins, especially primitive shacks such as this one, don't have basements. Still, the muffled sound grows stronger—it was a person. *Why under the cabin?* she asked herself, as the smells turned from sweat and smoky creosote to sweat and fear.

"Are you hurt?" Missy called out. That question generated furious clanging, metal against metal. "Are you trapped in a mine under the cabin?" Missy shouted as she frantically searched for a digging tool. Behind the cabin, she found an old pry bar. The feel of hot and hefty steel felt good in her hands. With renewed confidence, Missy placed the bar firmly behind the padlock's hasp, and with her entire 110-pound body behind it, the hasp gave way from the decrepit doorframe as Missy fell into a heap on the creaking wooden floor. She got up, held the pry bar poised for a blow, and cautiously scanned inside.

Her eyes, ears, and nose took in the stank scene. The rumbled sleeping bag in the far corner and empty cans and food containers throughout nearly blended in with the darkness. As her eyes grew accustomed to the light, notepads and dozens of holy hand grenade-style crystals sprang from the shadows. *The crystal-making guys use these devices*, Missy speculated, based on the rumors she'd heard. *They supposedly use them to disrupt government-to-Lizard People communications.* The memory came to her as she picked up the closest device and peered into the amber-colored resin and saw what looked like nuts, screws, and bolts. She had seen photos of these devices before, but she had never held one in her hand. *They're lumpier than I imagined*, she thought as she put the device back precisely in its original position. *Perhaps the squatter found them nearby and started a collection. They are much too ugly for me to ever want as a souvenir.*

Again, Missy called out, "Who are you, and where are you? I can help."

She heard frantic pounding and shouting coming through the littered floorboards. Missy's eyes darted about, searching for the muffled voice. After pushing the large footlocker aside, Missy discovered a small, padlocked door set in the floor. She ran outside to get the pry bar. The padlock's cheap shank easily gave way upon the combined force of Missy and her hefty steel bar. Flushing like a frightened grouse, someone or something flushed from below—knocking Missy onto the floor. Before she could figure out what happened, the unknown thing fled, and the cabin fell back into silence.

After Sid Emerson escaped his captors, primal instincts took over. He sought refuge in the mountains, high above the cabin. *Think, think, Sid, think!* he squealed like a mouse caught in a trap. Sid hid under a large creosote bush far removed from the cabin. He needed time and space to think. *Think, Sid, think! Who held me captive? Why? Where is he now? Who let me out? What do I do next? Everything's a blur.* Sid didn't know how long it had been, or even how he had escaped. Did the whole ordeal really happen?

He recalled being locked in a room for weeks. Months? Years? *It seemed like days or weeks since someone even last brought food and water. Think, Sid, think,* he kept telling himself. *I remember someone calling out, and I remember not wanting to answer back. But how could it have gotten worse?* he asked and answered himself as his memory began coming into focus. *I remember no longer caring. I yelled and made as much noise as I could. When the door swung open, I ran for it. I remember seeing a woman—it was just a glance. That's all I remember—until... here. How did I get here? Where's here?* Sid decided he could piece these pieces together later. As he looked out from the creosote bush to the scene below, his lungs heaved in and out the fresh, juniper-scented air. With his exhale came a deep and exalted, "I'm free."

After seemingly an eternity, Sid's instincts once again took over. He needed to move. For over a day he ran. He ran until his legs were jelly. Long past where he saw distant prospectors milling about. Suspicious of all, Sid Emerson ran past without stopping. Out of pure instinct and suspicion, he avoided all people. Throughout all his running, he had not gained his bearing. Parts looked like the southern Panamints, but he couldn't be sure. If so, the Owlsheads should have come into view by now. He stopped only for water. *The fact I found water so quickly is a sure sign this is not the Owlsheads,* he thought. *Maybe I'm in the Black Mountains.* Regardless of his location, Sid felt safe.

During Sid Emerson's mad wanderings, his mind slowly came back into partial focus, although with blurry order. He remembered interviewing people, but that is where it stopped. He remembered going on a hike up Surprise Canyon to Panamint City. *Thinking back, that young woman I talked with now seems vaguely familiar. Had we met? My mind's a fog.*

Sid forced himself to recall details of his kidnapping. A few more fragmented memories returned, but slowly. *I remember checking out the Mengel Pass area and an old mine near Willow Spring. I had not gone far from Willow Spring when I came upon a young man in the middle of nowhere. I remember talking with the guy, and before I knew it, he jumped me. That's all I remember. When I came to, I had a gag and blindfold—with my hands tied to a rock.*

To sort things out, Sid went over details one after another, again and again, hoping to jog any subconscious memories. *I remember someone untying the rope and leading me away. I must have stumbled dozens of times. Someone stuffed me into a trunk.* His memory began fading after the trunk ordeal. He remembered bouncing over so many washboards that it bruised his hips. *When he let me out, pain shot throughout my lower back. I fell so many times on the long walk up a hill, a mountain—I must have fallen hundreds of times.* He lost all memory of how he got locked in the cabin's basement.

Over the next two days, Sid held up at his little spring site, keeping out of sight and trying to piece his memories together. He recalled the first time someone came to check on him in the locked basement. *It was the same young man that I met on the trail and kidnapped me.*

On that first visit, the young kidnapper asked Sid dozens of questions: "What do you people eat?... When did we arrive on Earth?... When will we leave?" From his questions, Sid figured the kidnapper suspected that he was a Lizard Person. The kidnapper drilled, probed, and drilled to learn more of the Lizard People ways. He demanded Sid give up the names of his Lizard People colleagues and shapeshifters, and name those that infiltrated the government.

Nothing Sid said or did could convince the young man otherwise. *How can anyone prove they're not a shapeshifting alien?* Sid asked himself daily. Any attempt to prove otherwise only enraged his captor even more.

Later, another captor began showing up, but never at the same time. They apparently took turns bringing Sid food and water. They both asked him Lizard People questions. Sid saw no way out of the vicious cycle—not until the day when Missy accidentally freed him. The main thing Sid remembers of his captors was they had a connection with crystal receivers—as a line of defense against Lizard People and a rumored coming judgment day.

CHAPTER 33

Missy didn't get a good look at the man who fled from the basement, but something about him seemed familiar. The man's blow knocked her face-first into the dust- and mouse-dropping-covered floor. "What was that?" she blurted as she picked herself up and checked for damages.

Despite having banged her head badly, Missy rushed outside to see if she could see where the man went. After seeing no one in sight, Missy peered mouse-like around all sides of the cabin—again, nothing. She gathered her things, dusted herself off, took a sip of water, and hiked out.

Although her head was as splitting as the San Andreas Fault, Missy made good time on the hike to the parking lot. It didn't take her long to get back to Ballarat, locate Rocky, and ask him to call the sheriff. Rocky hesitated a moment because folks in these parts tended to mind their own business, but he reckoned if Missy wanted him to call, call he would.

It took the deputies over twenty-four hours to come since they were dealing with demonstrations, miners blasting open new mines, fights, National Guard coordination, media interviews, calls to the governor, and, yes—phone calls requesting assistance from the San Bernardino County Sheriff's Office. John had little time for a mysterious person, long since gone, sighted in a backcountry cabin by a visiting student. Besides, he and his deputies had to wrap up a body recovery on the far side of the county.

The county's two senior deputies responded. This team had the distinction of racking up the most complaints, especially from young women. Since all complaints shuffle their way up to the county administrators, John tended to keep this team away from assignments involving human interaction, but this time, he had no choice. Missy Flores agreed to meet them in Ballarat.

Missy tried to explain what she saw, but the one with the white mustache kept interrupting her. "Sure, Cookie, it warn't juz your boyfriend or drunk college buddies messing with you?"

"My name is not Cookie. It is Missy, and yes, I am sure I don't know him."

"Just settle down, Cookie, or should I say missy. Don't get so emotional on me. To make our…what we call a report, we need to ask a few questions," the white-mustached officer said.

"Sure. What do you need to know?"

"Now if'n there was a guy, as you say, he was prob'ly just a squatter and you prob'ly just scared the bugger off."

The big belt-buckled officer, who had been silent, stepped in to finish the thought. "Folks around here tend to mind their own business. They don't cotton to young granola-eating girls messing around in other people's business."

Missy took the deputy's condensation in stride since she had dealt with his type her whole life. "I heard voices coming from below the—"

"I think what you actually heard was the wind," the white-mustached officer suggested. "Wind around here makes strange noises. It's easy for city girls to let their imagination run wild."

Rocky, who had been silent throughout the whole ordeal, said to the officers, "Missy had done many trips 'round here. She's not a troubley kind—or city-folk, as you say. If'n she sez she saw sometin', then by God she saw sometin'." After a brief pause, during which the big belt-buckled officer winked at Missy, Rocky continued. "Besides, there is sometin' going up Big Horn Canyon ways. Sometin' fishy, I say…"

Turning to his partner, the big belt-buckled officer chimed in, "I think what she means—"

"Thank you, Rocky, but I know what wind sounds like, Officer," Missy interrupted to face off against the white-mustached officer. "And he wasn't 'jez a squat'r," Missy snapped, while both mocking and mimicking the deputies' insults and mansplaining. "Someone had purposely locked him in a basement with a padlock on the outside—how stupid do you think I am?"

"Now, now, little missy," the white-mustached officer scolded. "Don't get your panties all twisted in a knot," the white-mustached officer scolded. "I dunno what you saw, or think you saw, that's what we're here to find out."

"I *do* think the man was held captive; I know it. Common sense knows it."

"Emotional outburst from you ain't helping your story. Besides, the word 'captive' is strong words. Are you an expert in hostage negotiations?"

To quell her rising anger, Missy turned away from the officer with the white mustache and toward the big belt-buckled officer. After scribbling a few notes in his shirt-pocket notebook, he looked down on Missy, and said, "We won't be able to verify anything you said until we take a look-see at this here cabin you say you saw up Big Horn Canyon and try to find your squatter friend. You see, ma'am, we need to conduct what we call an in-ves-ti-ga-tion," the belt-buckled officer said slowly to ensure Missy could understand.

Sensing the futility of any more attempts at providing a basic report, Missy said to both officers, "Do you have any more questions for me? If not, I will go now."

"Sure, you may go," the white mustached officer said. "If we have any more questions, little missy, we know how to find you."

Sensing Missy readied herself to say something to the officers that may turn out to be counterproductive, Rocky darted in as fast as an eighty-year-old could possibly dart, and said, "Come, Missy, you must be hungry. Let me buy you a cup of coffee." That effectively ended Missy's failed conversation with the deputies. The deputies left to check out the Big Horn Canyon cabin. Missy climbed into her Jeep and drove back to Clairmont—yelling, cursing, and speeding the whole way.

It took the deputies two hours to find the trail Missy had described. Shortly later, they entered the cabin and found a room under the cabin, just as Missy had described. It had no lock or latch, nor any sign of a broken padlock or chain. They found no sleeping bag or crystals lying about. The officers found no trash or other evidence that could identify the squatter. The deputies speculated that Missy Flores may have exaggerated or made up the whole story.

"It may be a social media stunt," said the belt-buckled officer to his more senior white-mustached partner. "Even if what she said was true, why hadn't this so-called mystery person come in and report the crime and identify his captor?"

"Exactly," the officer with the mustache said. "If he had his reasons not to report the crime, what can we do to find a guy that disappeared and don't wanna be found?" The officer's report submitted to the sheriff read: "Reported kidnapping, but no evidence to indicate a crime took place. Likely just a squatter."

Word of Missy's hysterics spread faster than a desert canyon in flood. As soon as Paddy heard the story, he and Katherine drove to Ballarat to interview Rocky. Normally, Rocky would say nothing about what Missy told him, or he would claim ignorance. Rocky gained his reputation by minding his own business and not betraying anyone's trust, especially someone as sweet as his Missy. But Rocky knew Paddy and he had already met Katherine. He had, in fact, been the person who got Paddy and Katherine together in the first place. So, Rocky made an exception and told Missy's whole story to both Paddy and Katherine.

While Paddy talked with Rocky, Katherine just sat gap-mouthed and at full attention. She looked at Paddy, back to Rocky, then back to Paddy, before finally blurting out, "This must be my Uncle Sid!"

"If'n so, ma'am, what's yur uncle doin' locked up in a cabin fur?" asked Rocky with a puzzled look. "Why would someone do that fur?"

"Maybe it is your uncle," interjected Paddy, "but maybe not. This could be anyone, even one of Manson's crazies, an outcast, or even one of the many clueless people searching for Bud Torgerson's treasure. We simply just don't know. I would hate for you to get your hopes up."

Rocky answered all of Paddy's and Katherine's questions. After getting all the information they could from Rocky, Paddy drove to Big Horn Canyon to check out Missy's cabin, while Katherine drove to Shoshone to talk directly with Sheriff John Smithers.

It didn't take Paddy long to find screw holes on the side of the basement door that had clearly been ripped out. Paddy's fingers ran along the splintered edges where there had been a latch and hinges. Paddy also found dented wood—the kind a prybar would make. *How could the deputies miss such obvious signs?* Paddy wondered. Meanwhile, Katherine found the sheriff much too busy to see or speak with her.

Later, Sheriff John Smithers read his deputy's report. From his read, he guessed something suspicious and illegal probably had happened at that old cabin, but "What can I do?" John asked the report, as if it could hear such a wimpy question. With all the crazies around, including Manson followers, tourists attempting to go native in 125-degree heat, people shooting at each other, drug runners making low-altitude midnight drug flights through narrows canyons, and now hundreds of clueless fortune-hunters looking for imaginary silver and blowing up the hillsides, John believed he had no time to chase after an unidentified mystery person. Besides, John added, where would he look?

Upon further reflection, John regretted sending those two to interview Miss Torres. He worried that if his officers pushed the investigation, Missy Torres would probably file a grievance against his officers. "What will I do with them?" John asked while shaking his head at the "Piece of shit report they sent me." John figured that it would probably be best just to drop the investigation and let the whole thing just blow over.

CHAPTER 34

Sid's lungs choked and convulsed on the last few steps to the ridgeline hoping from the high point that he would recognize where he was at. Nothing—as also with the next ridge, and the one over. No matter which summit he peered from, or which canyon descended, nothing was familiar. Throughout this entire ordeal, in the distance, he kept seeing strangers—people and four-by-fours pouring over the land like a cleansing flood. *This can't be the Death Valley area*, he surmised. *There're too many people. I must be deeper into the Mojave Desert than I thought.* The same confliction boiled up with each distant encounter. *Should I approach? Can they be trusted?*

Everyone he sighted appeared to be searching for something. *Are they looking for me?* He wondered each time, since he didn't know how many people had kidnapped him. *What are they looking for? They look like prospectors, but they can't be, not here. This is a national park. Are they looking for me?* Sid's confusion and suspicion grew with each passing encounter. Frantically rushing about hadn't gotten him anywhere, Sid concluded. Instead, he stayed put where he could remain safely hidden and watch people come and go. After finding a perfect twisted and gnarled juniper, Sid crawled underneath and waited. *My first order of business is to find out what the people are looking for. Next, can I trust them?* Vowing not to be held captive again, Sid waited until things calmed down and he could figure things out.

When no one came around worth watching, Sid searched his surroundings for potential food and water. Food became easier to find than anticipated. The strangers roving the hills left food and other valuables in packs, crates, trucks, and laying about while they explored deep into abandoned mines or over nearby ridges. *What idiots*, Sid thought, as he gathered whatever food left lying about unattended. *Who keeps food where coyotes and rodents can so easily reach?*

During his wanderings, Sid happened upon a quiet, out-of-the-way seep with a nearby cave shelter where someone had obviously once lived. With his food, shelter, and safety secured, Sid watched in earnest—and searched for answers.

Sid found watching people's going-ons more challenging than anticipated, due to sparse vegetation and few places to hide. However, he learned a little. Their searches were much too random, chaotic, and frantic for any reasonable search pattern. *If they aren't looking for me, what are they looking for?*

Sid's watching also provided him with plenty of time for reflection. He began feeling his mental faculties slowly returning. He knew he couldn't stay in the wilds forever—well, some people can, but not him. *Can my life ever return to normal?* became his biggest worry. *How does one go about leading a normal life?* Sid spent many cave-hours reflecting upon this and other weighty matters.

Back in the normal world, the only person I care for is Katherine, my dear Katherine, he pondered as he snuck up to a fool that had just left his Jeep unattended. Lately, thoughts of his niece flooded his mind and sent a wave of intense emotions and memories surging down his spine. As Sid gathered all the food from the Jeep that he could carry, suddenly he arrived at a point of clarity. He needed to get out and get back—anywhere other than here—anything other than being alone.

The following day, a lone, harmless-looking elderly man got out of his pickup and wandered into a nearby adit. Sid cautiously waited behind a large boulder for his return. As soon as the old man shuffled out, Sid stepped from behind the boulder and called out, "Hello, my name is Henry. I'm a little turned around," Sid said to the stranger. "Do you mind giving me a ride down lower so I can arrange to fix my broken-down rig?" Sid said, while looking for anything suspicious.

The old man's eyes darted about. With a shaky and hesitant voice, he called back, "You can have anything on me—but I don't own nothin' of value. I just arrived. So far, I've found nothin' but dust and despair. I haven't anything you'd want."

"It's okay, I don't want anything other than a ride—nothing more. You don't want to strand me out here on foot, do you?"

"I don't care one way or the other—you mean nothing to me," the old man said.

"I just need a ride. This is rough country to be stranded and all alone. Please, won't you give me a ride?"

"Well, I guess. If it is just a ride. The old man threw into his truck the few items he had lying about, and then said, "Hop in but shut up—I don't want no talkin'."

As promised, Sid said nothing to the old man, and the old man said even less back. About twenty minutes of jostling at a too-fast speed over a deeply rutted and washboard road brought them to a place Sid recognized. *Searles Lakebed* popped into his mind. A couple miles beyond Trona, Sid broke the silence by asking to be let out. Without a word, the old man pulled off on C Street and into the little town of Argus. After stepping out, Sid came face-to-face with the New Hope of Searles Valley Foursquare Church sign. The sign drew him in closer.

The middle-aged woman repairing the signs outside of the Foursquare Church seemed safe enough, so Sid approached. As he stepped in close, he called out, "Hello, my name is Henry. I'm curious what you are working on."

"Hello, Henry. Nice to meet you. I'm Sarah, one of the pastors here. I don't think I've seen you here before. Are you a member?"

"No, I'm no member. I'm only passing through."

"Aren't we all? As for what I'm doing, I'm repairing this damaged sign. A poor soul chose to alter our 'Healer' sign." Clearly, Sid could see that someone had attempted to paint over the "Healer" sign to read "Dealer" instead.

Sid remarked, "I guess there're cretins everywhere."

"I would not put it so harshly. When people are lost, they need kindness and understanding to find their way back. In one form or the other, we are all lost and could use a little guidance and kindness. That is, after all, what we call a 'Fruit of the Spirit,' isn't it, Henry?"

"I wouldn't know anything about fruit or spirits, but I've known a little about being lost."

This conversation got Sid thinking of his first few trips into the Panamints, Death Valley mountains, the higher elevation forests and scrublands, the canyons and arroyos, and even the brutal heat. *The land grows on a person*, he thought as a flood of memories washed over him. *I remember once thinking I could see myself living here…but that had been so long ago…*

"Thinking about things, Henry?" Sarah asked, sensing him drifting off. "I hope it's about sorting things out. Don't worry, we *all* have things to sort through. That's a sign of a healthy mind and spirit," Sarah said while brushing dirt off her hands.

"I don't know about that either," Sid said while the pastor continued her sign repairs. The pastor's questions and welcoming comments kept Sid from finishing his wandering thoughts. During Sid's daydream, Sarah said something more about being lost…but his mind was too foggy to recall.

Sensing he had lost focus and didn't hear what she'd last asked him, the pastor repeated, "Henry, would you like to know more about the Fruit of the Spirit? If so, we will have a guest pastor speaking on that topic tonight. Would you like to come?"

"I wouldn't know anything about fruit or spirits. I do know a little about the lost part, but no, I don't think it would be a good idea. No, thanks."

"You sure?" the paster offered. "Are you tired? Do you need a rest?"

Not wanting to share too many details, Henry tried to change the subject back to sign repair.

Sensing a troubled soul, the pastor didn't allow Henry to change the topic. "As I said before, we have all been lost a time or two. It's only natural. The hard parts are to find your way back and remain vigilant, since it's so easy to backslide. What do you think about that, Henry? Are you sure you don't want to stay for the guest pastor's conversation?" she explained as Sid just stood over her, not knowing if he should stay, run, or hide.

"As I said, you're welcome to come, Henry. We all fall from time to time. We just need to get up and continue on. That's just life and human nature. But remember, Henry, no matter how far we fall, we can always dust ourselves off and return. That's the beauty of life and the beauty of truth."

"You make it sound so simple,"

"The truth *can* be simple. It can be quite liberating too. Speaking of truth, if you are not interested in coming to tonight's conversation, this being Tuesday, tomorrow evening we will have our weekly Bible study. If you would like to come, it's from 6 to 7:30 p.m. You're welcome this Tuesday or any Sunday service for that matter."

"No thank you. While I do have some things to work out, I'm pretty sure a formal Bible study is not my scene."

After Sid helped Sarah remount the repaired "Healer" and "Soon Coming King" signs, he said his goodbyes. As Sid walked away, he stopped to scan his surrounding—at nothing or no one. He just stood and scanned. Without any indication of what circulated through his head, Sid turned and walked back to the pastor and the Foursquare Church. Sarah, still fussing with signs, at first didn't see Henry return until Sid called out, "Sarah, Henry here. If that offer is still good for attending this evening's guest talk, I'm thinking I may go after all—if that's okay?"

"Sure, you're welcome anytime. You can come back later, or, if you want, you can wait in the church."

"I'll wait in the church, if you don't mind, because I need to clean up a bit. I must be quite a sight—and smell."

"Well, I've seen and smelled worse, but sure, you may clean up and wait inside," Sarah said as she stood and brushed dirt from her hands. "In fact, follow me. I think I have some clean clothes that you may change into. Come now, I'll get you set up."

Sarah handed Henry clothes that she'd pulled out of a buffet drawer located in the church's basement. They were well-worn but clean. Sid thanked her and then stepped into the church's bathroom. The place looked alien to him. It had been some time since Sid used a proper bathroom. As peeling off layer after vile layer, he contemplated, *Maybe I should just throw all my old clothes away? They're that disgusting.*

For the longest time, Sid stared at the bathroom mirror, wondering if he recognized the reflection looking back. He received no clarity on this or the other question, but he decided if he was to attend the service, he had to get moving.

The guest pastor began a conversation on healing. Being too much to take in, Sid regretted coming. *I need clarity of thought, not a sermon*, he thought.

Sarah came up later and asked Henry what he thought about the conversation. Sid, not knowing how to answer, just stood there.

"Henry, it looks as if you may need some time to sort things out. You'll need time. And it's getting pretty late now so why don't you stay tonight? There's an extra cot in the church basement. You're welcome to stay there tonight. Maybe, by morning, you will be fresh to know what your next step should be."

"Thank you, Pastor, you are too kind."

"Please, call me Sarah. Besides, that's why we are here."

As Sid settled into the fresh sheets Sarah had brought him and felt the warm comfort of the cot, his mind wandered, not so much where he had been, but more where he wanted to go from here.

Sid had no way of knowing, but while he began to settle in on the cot, Paddy had already talked to the old man who had given Sid a ride into Argus.

After dropping Sid off along C Street, the old man had a thought or two of his own. He wasn't as ignorant of his surrounds or new to the Death Valley area as he'd led Sid to believe. Before heading into the mountains, the old man overhead two guys talking at the gas station. The two men spoke about a guy named Paddy and an East Coast lady who were looking for someone that had gone missing in the Panamints months earlier.

As the old man drove the "Henry" into Argus, he wondered if his mysterious passenger was the missing guy that those men at the gas station had talked about. So, after dropping Henry off in Argus, the old man wrestled with what to do next. He normally kept to himself and minded his own business, but he'd heard about the potential reward—and he thought he could certainly use reward money. In the end, fondness for cash won out over any sense of moral or ethical consideration or social norms. For all he knew, the old man pondered, Henry might be a deadbeat lowlife who didn't deserve any honor, privacy, or the keeping of secrets.

After dropping Henry off at Argus, the old man pulled over at a gas station in Ridgecrest and asked if anyone knew of a Paddy or an East Coast lady who had been looking for a missing person. The kid behind the gas station counter said he knew nothing about such matters, but the customer eyeing oil cans and wiper fluids overheard the conversation and piped in, "You're talking about Paddy. His name is Paddy Darwin. He's the one that's helping the Boston lady find her uncle."

"Where can I find this Paddy?" the old man asked.

"Why do you want to know?"

"I don't want to bother the guy, or anything. I may have some information that he'd be interested in about the missing person, that's all."

"I guess it sounds all right. From what I understand, he lives by himself in an old trailer, out beyond Barstow. I think I know where it is. I could point you in the right direction—if you want."

CHAPTER 35

Sid woke early feeling fresh and full of energy. The cot in the church basement gave him the best night's sleep he had in a long time. He stopped by to say goodbye to Sarah, and to thank her for her kindness. "I should be going now." She tried to convince him to check into the local church-sponsored mission, but Sid just smiled. With that, Sid walked out of the church, down the road, and into the streets of the little town of Trona. There were many people milling about, considering the size of the town. He approached a small gathering at a nondescript intersection. There must have been over a dozen people there—all deeply engaged in a robust conversation. Sid sat on a nearby curbside bench to watch and listen. When the main guy doing most of the talking turned around, Sid looked him straight in the eye. *Hey, that's Lizard Len*, he said to himself—startled that he had finally recognized someone.

Trona and Argus residents rarely got an opportunity for entertainment as engaging as stories from Lizard Len, even if they were about Lizard People and government corruption. Most everyone hung on his every word, even though some only came to hear of potential clues to the location of the hidden Torgerson silver mine. Still not keen on being recognized, Sid listened from a safe distance.

While still sitting on the bench under a palm shadow, Sid noticed a guy in the Lizard Len crowd that kept staring back at him. Sid's eyes flicked up and down the street as he wondered about which direction to point his feet. *I'd be obvious to everyone if I ran.* Before deciding, the staring man began walking toward Sid. *Was he one of the kidnappers?* Sid's eyes once again darted up and down the street. *I can't risk running—maybe he'll just walk on pass. He does look familiar. Where do I know this guy from?* As the staring man came closer, his name came to Sid's racing mind. *Well, that'll be okay—I guess. As far as I know, he had nothing to do with the kidnapping.* After reaching the bench, the staring man silently sat down next to Sid.

Both men sat together in awkward silence, likely each hoping the other spoke first. Silence is often awkward for some people, but not for these two, and not this time. They both knew that eventually someone would speak first, but neither one of them wanted to be that person. After many minutes of patient waiting, Paddy took the initiative "Are you Sid Emerson?"

"Sid Emerson, you say. I knew the guy a long time ago, but from what I hear, he's gone. He no longer exists. I'm Henry. You're Patrick Darwin, aren't you?"

Without answering, Paddy interjected, "If Sid Emerson were here today, I would say that he has someone waiting for him—a gal that cares for him dearly. And from her viewpoint, Sid Emerson exists and is with her in spirit every day. I can tell from her eyes. Eyes don't lie—well, not hers. That someone would go to the end of the world—*has* gone to the end of the world—to find Sid Emerson, or whoever the man has turned into. For her, I don't think it matters."

"It sounds as if your Sid Emerson is quite the lucky guy. He must be a different Sid Emerson than the one I knew."

"Maybe so, but I would say Sid Emerson is quite lucky to have the devotion of such a wonderful person as his niece. She's quite the lady."

"You must be talking about Katherine Emerson? I knew her once—nice kid. The Sid I knew cared deeply for his niece, but those times are past. No one, not even your Sid Emerson, can turn back the clock. If she knew what was best for her, she would just walk on by and get on with her life. Having a lost person hanging on would only drag her down."

"She's the type of person that can't get on with a happy life knowin' her uncle needs help. I believe she wants to take her Sid Emerson home and help. She's been here for quite some time lookin' for him."

"Kati! Katherine—here? Now? She's just a kid."

"She's no longer a kid—and then some. She's spent a long time searchin' for answers, searchin' for her uncle."

"Katherine, here—searching for her uncle. Well, I never…"

"Yep, she's here. She'd love to meet up with her uncle. She's been searchin' for a long time."

Paddy looked down at his ragged shoes, as if reflecting upon something buried deep inside. "I guess we all search for one thing or the other; that's the nature of life; the nature of the game. You know, I think Sid just got tired. Tired of searching, and just plain tired. If I were you, I would tell this Katherine Emerson that she would be better off without Sid Emerson. Tell her to stop searching, to get on with her life."

"Why don't you tell her yourself?"

"This here talk is the most talk I had, except with myself, that I've known in months. I don't need any more talk. When you've been through what I've been through, talking is hard."

"Ain't that the truth. But as far as Katherine is concerned, she doesn't have anyone anymore. Sid is the only family she's ever had. Family is important to her. It's the one thing that remains after we're dead and our bones have blown away. I don't have any family left— they're all dead. But Sid Emerson has a niece that is alive and well."

Turning toward Paddy, but with his eyes still at his shoes, Sid said, "You know some church folks, including one in which I recently chatted with, believe we all have evil, sinful, and dark sides, that is just the way we are. That we have the personal choice to face the darkness, move ahead, remain the same, or backslide—it's one hundred percent our individual choice. What do you think of such thoughts?" Sid asked.

"Katherine never said Sid Emerson was a religious or spiritual man."

"Oh, he wasn't—isn't. But during these last few months I've had a lot of time alone and I've had time to think—pondering such matters. So, how about you, Paddy Darwin, what do you think? You seem to be someone that's experienced pain and suffering. Do you think we're salvageable? In the end, do we ever heal? Have you ever thought of such things?"

Turning his eyes toward Sid's shoes, Paddy, in a rare reflective mood, mumbled, "I never talk of such things, but sure. Yeah, I think about it—often,"

"I don't know what it is, but something about this place just sucks a person in. It's like a vortex. It sucks you in," Sid said, "and never let's go—people like you and me—it doesn't let go. Doesn't it?"

"It's the space. There's a lot of space here. Distance really—that doesn't help. But I can't think of any other place I'd rather be. The place grows on you—and yeah, it sucks you in and never let's go."

"You may be right. I can't explain it, even though I've tried."

"You know Katherine has come a long way to find you. She's persistent. I know she won't let up and she'll never leave without you. If you don't come back, that'll mean she won't be gettin' on with her life," Paddy said with his voice trailing off. "This damn place will claim another one."

"I suppose you're right. Maybe I'll stop by and introduce myself. Do you know where she's staying? Maybe she'll tell me stories of this uncle of hers."

"She'll like that." Paddy gave Sid directions to Katherine's motel room. The rest of the conversation consisted of weather, water, mines, and Death Valley places and people. After that bench conversation, with Lizard Len still droning away in the background, Sid walked off to find his way into Ridgecrest, while Paddy left in a trail of dust heading toward the Panamint Range.

On his journey to Ridgecrest, Sid reflected long and hard on what had happened these last few months. He had no idea what his future would bring, but he realized it was time for him to come home and face his reality. He also decided he needed to stop at the sheriff's office soon and tell his story. Before he had taken off, Paddy said Sheriff John Smithers could be trusted. Sid figured that was as good of an endorsement that he'd likely get. However, before he met with the sheriff, Sid knew he had one stop to make first. After the woman that he hitched a ride into Ridgecrest had dropped him off, Sid crept up the stairway to the motel's second floor—looking for Room 231.

Before Katherine heard the knocking, she heard the faint creaking of footfalls in the hall—she knew someone was approaching, as surely as Paddy could tell he was to have visitors by their dust plumes. She hadn't expected anyone today, and since it was early afternoon, it couldn't be Paddy, but who else could it be? She had been sipping tea, while thinking of the various leads and suspects that she and Paddy had collected over the last couple of months. *It must be him*, she thought. Katherine raced to the door and flung it open to tell Paddy something that she had long wanted to say; however, as the door crashed into the doorstop, Katherine nearly dropped her tea. There in front of her stood her uncle, Sid Emerson.

She had waited a long time for this moment, but now, words escaped her. No one spoke. They both just looked into each other's eyes, each not knowing what to say or who should speak first. Katherine's eyes looked past the frail and withered old man that stood in the doorway as her mind went deeper and saw her Uncle Sid of years past. *Eyes don't lie*, she thought as she gave her uncle a big hug. "After all these months we found you," she said as she looked up and down the motel's hallway.

"We?" Sid asked. "Who's we? There's no one here except me. Were you expecting someone?"

Yes, someone that I planned to share this moment with, she thought, but the words that passed her lips were, "No, I was just hoping it was you." With a sad and deep sigh, Katherine invited Sid inside. With one more look down the empty hall, Katherine shut the door behind her.

CHAPTER 36

John Smithers fretted over the Billy Torgerson case as he paced back and forth in his Shoshone office. He needed to wrap up the investigation and finalize the report; however, nothing made sense. He suspected Torrey Small and his crystal loonies, but he couldn't prove it. *I hate the idea of Torrey walking free, taunting law and order, but I just don't have the evidence for an arrest*, John lamented to himself while alone in his office. *I can't go any further with the investigation if there aren't any leads or evidence.*

John also hadn't figured out if Billy's death had any relation to the other Torgerson deaths—Bud or Stade's. There was evidence Stade had killed Bud and Death Valley had killed Stade. Since both were dead, there was no one to arrest and nowhere else for the investigation to lead.

If I don't solve this soon, it'll fuel more Torgerson silver fever, conspiracies, and even more people will be poring over the wilderness getting themselves killed, John fretted while going over the case file once again. *Hopefully, the case can be put to rest without anything pointing to lost silver or conspiracies.* John figured he would take another look later, with a fresh mind.

Still immersed in his Torgerson conundrum, John didn't notice the two people that walked up to his desk. Katherine had driven her uncle to Shoshone, and after a deputy let them in, they walked right up to Sheriff John Smithers—so deep in thought he hadn't noticed them standing there. When she first spoke, John jumped out of his seat, knocking his keyboard and the Billy Torgerson file to the floor. "Hello, Sheriff. May we have a moment of your time?" Katherine said with a grin. "I would like you to meet my uncle, Sid Emerson."

Leaving the fallen files and computer parts where they lay, John held out his hand. "So, you're Sid Emerson? Your niece told me so many things about you." Turning to Katherine, "I knew he would show up eventually."

"Yes, I am Sid Emerson. I guess I need to file a report."

"We'll talk about that later. First, I'm glad to meet you. I'm John Smithers, the sheriff in this county." After looking around, John said to Katherine, "Where's Paddy?"

"He's not here at the moment."

"Well, I guess he'll show up later then." Turning again to Katherine, "See, the two of you found him, and you didn't need any sheriff investigation or missing person report."

Sid, looked sheepishly down at his feet as he interrupted the sheriff's growing smile, said, "I have something to tell you, but what I'm going to say requires your trust. When Paddy talked me into coming back, he assured me that you could be trusted."

"Paddy said that of me, did he? Of course, I can be trusted—I'm the sheriff and I grew up here in the county. People know and trust me. What do you have to say?"

Normally under such circumstances, John would assign a deputy to take a statement and interview Sid, ask him where he'd been and why he had remained hidden for so long. But this time, despite his busy schedule and all the outstanding investigations weighing heavily on John's shoulders, he chose to conduct the interview himself. "Please, take a seat. I have many questions to ask you."

John pushed aside the piles of police reports and stale cookie crumbs that had taken over the interrogation table. Immediately upon sitting, Sid began telling John the entire story, as best as he could remember. He told him of his kidnapping, captivity, escape, and recent wanderings. Sid did most of the talking. Later, John had many follow-up questions, but at this phase, he just sat quietly and took notes.

Sid had never learned his captors' name's or if there were more than just two. He only knew his kidnappers were young and crystal makers. With that, John said to himself, *Torrey—I knew it!* "Does the name Torrey Small mean anything to you?"

"He's a crystal maker from Ridgecrest. Before my kidnapping, I interviewed Torrey. It wasn't Torrey—at least he never came by and showed himself," Sid said.

"If it wasn't Torrey, it must have been Tim Nagat. Torrey probably put him up to it."

"I hadn't seen Torrey Small since I interviewed him."

"Please, describe the kidnappers."

Sid patiently and methodically recalled all the details he could remember. "Young, medium build, brown hair, and generally average-looking." Upon hearing the description, Sid realized how vague they sounded—his descriptions could fit most people. *Given how many times they came by bringing food or probing me for information on Lizard People, I would think I could come up with a better description than "average."*

"Maybe seeing a photograph will jog your memory," John said, while looking down at this watch.

As Sid's mind focused on his ordeal, trying to think of any helpful observation, John continued with his nonstop questions. Sid found himself nodding to whatever the sheriff said or asked him. *With so many things I need to sort out and remember, why does the guy keep talking?*

In the height of Sid's recollection and John's droning, Katherine interrupted. "Whoever did this, my uncle doesn't want to press charges. Do you?" she asked her uncle. "Don't you want a normal life and to put this whole mess behind you?"

"What do you mean, you don't want to press charges?" John asked. *Why did I have Katherine sit in on the interview?* John kept asking himself, since this was not normal practice. "Don't you want to punish Torrey Small for what he did to your uncle?"

Sid turned to Katherine. "Why wouldn't I press charges?"

"You clearly have had a hard time of it—before, during, and after your ordeal," Katherine implored. "Pressing charges and going through a trial, with all its media attention, is just going to prolong your ordeal and have you deal with it over and over again. You don't need that. You need for your life to get back to normal. You need a new beginning."

"What is this?" John spewed as he threw his pen onto his desk, as it rolled onto the floor next to the Billy Torgerson case file. "You're just going to let him get away with kidnapping? Besides, technically, I don't need your permission, and I don't need for you or anyone to press charges," John snapped. "A prosecutor decides if someone is to be charged, even second-degree kidnapping, not the victim."

While Katherine and Sid argued over the matter, John tried to imagine what the prosecutor would say in this case. *It's only second-degree kidnapping. The crystal-makers didn't harm Sid, and it may be hard to prove they had any criminal intent at all. In Torrey's mind, he may have been trying to save the world from Lizard People. He didn't demand a ransom or anything. Besides,* John thought, *with everything else going on now, with the whole county going up in flames, my office and the courts have other priorities.*

After Sid and Katherine's discussion about pressing charges subsided into awkward silence, Sid turned to John. "It seems as if my mind is made up. I guess I'm not pressing charges."

"Well...I'll have to get back with you on the matter," John said as he picked up the Torgerson case file off the floor. "I may need to interview you again. Before you go, where are you staying?"

As Katherine gently guided Sid out by the shoulder, without looking back, she said, "My Uncle Sid and I will be staying at the Ridgecrest Motel."

Sheriff John Smithers began straightening the Billy Torgerson file, which had become a total mess. Before finishing, the sheriff paused. As he snapped the folder shut, he grinned and said out loud, "Well, that's an idea. John old boy, that may just work."

CHAPTER 37

RadioShack had been busy, uncharacteristically busy, even for a Saturday. Everyone from Ridgecrest appeared to be stopping to ask about two-way radios, drones, and surveillance equipment. A heavy-set miner, claiming he was "gonna find Bud Torgerson's lost mine," just bought the last drone. Ever since get-rich wannabes began poring over the Panamints looking for lost silver, Torrey couldn't keep drones on the shelves. The frantic search for Torgerson's silver had been good business. Between ringing up sales and answering drone questions, Torrey kept prodding his friend and colleague Tim Nagat if he felt well. Tim's mind seemed off, but with so many customers, Torrey had no time to help his friend or probe deeper.

Tim had many things on his mind. He recently heard that Sid Emerson had shown up and talked with the sheriff. Tim remembered all too well the day Torrey shared his suspicion of Sid Emerson. At the time, Torrey said, "That guy is surely a Lizard Person or one of their government conspirators." *Torrey said that*, Tim recalled. *I took his words to heart.* On that fateful day, Tim went over each and every word Torrey had said about Sid Emerson. He mulled those words over and over in his head. Torrey never knew it, but that brief conversation set off a chain of events that soon got Tim in well over his head and with no way out.

Tim desperately wanted to tell Torrey the whole story, but customers kept coming through the door. *Enough already with the drones*, he cursed under his breath. *It's not like drones will find any Torgerson silver.* Tim believed everything Torrey said; and Torrey told, on more than one occasion, the story of where the Lizard People stole Bud's silver and hid it deep in their catacombs.

Tim felt like screaming at a customer, *If the Lizard People and the government have all the gold and silver locked up, drones won't help!* Just then, a customer woke Tim up from his daydream: "Do you have any drones left?"

Although nearly the same age, Tim looked up to Torrey as a big brother, someone larger than life and the person he most wanted to emulate. Tim would do anything for Torrey—anything to ingratiate the master, his mentor. Above all else, Tim wanted Torrey to accept him as an equal.

"Big problems demand bold action," Torrey always said. Unbeknownst to anyone else, to gain favor with Torrey, Tim took it upon himself to kidnap Sid. Tim thought if he, and he alone, could extract all the Lizard People secrets from a real Lizard People, then *he* would be held up as a true American hero. *I would be famous, and most of all, Torrey would think of me as an equal.*

Once again, Torrey jolted Tim out of his RadioShack trance when he asked for help at the second cash register. Customers balked at the long lines. *Tim is no help today*, Torrey fretted. *I might as well work by myself. I can't figure out what has gotten into him lately.*

Stomping over to the second register, Tim barked at customers to move into the new line. On autopilot, Tim began checking customers out, but his mind remained on Sid and the sheriff. Ignoring his twitching customers, Tim mumbled to Torrey, "Torrey, after we close, I have something I need to tell you."

For the next few minutes, Tim stared at the cash register. His mind mulled over all that had happened over the last few months. Once he kidnapped Sid, he had no idea what to do next. Once he committed this impulsive act, he began realizing how much he depended on Torrey—for everything. The kidnapping was the first time Tim acted alone. This reminded him of what his father used to always say: "Tim, you're too naïve and stupid."

As Tim continued his cash register trance, he figured Sid Emerson had already turned him in to the police. *I don't want to go to jail. I especially don't want to let Torrey down—and admit that I'm naïve and stupid. What do I know after all of extracting secrets from shapeshifting Lizard People?*

Tim imagined the sheriff, the Emersons, and Torrey were shouting at him for his stupidity, but it turned out to be only a customer. "Are you going to ring up my order or not?"

Tim rang up the customer's surveillance equipment and then drifted back into his fear and insecurities. *I'm in way over my head. How am I going to tell Torrey?*

"What's that? I didn't catch that," the confused customer said. "Is this register open?"

"Sorry. Thank you for shopping at RadioShack."

"But I haven't paid for it yet. Are you okay?"

Just then, Torrey walked over and whispered in Tim's ear, "Snap out of it and pull yourself together. Work the register and pay attention!"

"Sorry, Torrey."

As soon as the customer stepped out the door and Torrey returned to his register, Tim's mind wandered back to the whole Sid Emerson mess. *After kidnapping Sid, I couldn't just let the alien go free, but I couldn't very well take it home with me or take it to work. I needed an isolated place to hold it for a day or two—just enough time to extract valuable Lizard People information.* Tim thought of the abandoned cabin and its root cellar that he recently came across in Big Horn Canyon. No one had ever mentioned this cabin. Tim figured not even Rocky knew of the place. *I thought the cabin would work. I only needed a couple of days.*

Since Torrey once said Lizard People were strong, Tim made sure to tie the knots tight. As he tied Sid's hands, other worries crossed Tim's mind. *Why can't it just shapeshift into another form and slither out of the ropes? Those are the details that Torrey's good at—not me.* However, Torrey wasn't there, so Tim had to make things up as he went.

Police shows on TV formed the basis and extent of Tim's interrogation knowledge. In real life, Tim found he could neither play good cop nor bad cop.

Tim kept repeating, "How long have you taken human form, and what have you done with the real Sid Emerson?" *I thought repeating this a few times would break and force him into spilling all Lizard People secrets. It didn't work.*

Each time Tim asked, Sid responded, "I'm not a Lizard Person. What will it take to prove it to you?"

And each time, with a higher pitch voice than normal, Tim countered, "You're cunning. Of course you won't admit being a Lizard People."

"Let's reason this out. What should I call you?" Sid asked.

"Ti… Oh, you *are* cunning. You almost had me. You can call me human or master, nothing else."

"Let's reason this out, since you seem to be a smart and intelligent young man—or should I say, master. Clearly, if I admit to being a Lizard Person, it will reinforce your belief that I *am* a Lizard Person. However, by your logic, if I say that I'm not, then this would also indicate to you that I am a Lizard Person since a true Lizard Person wouldn't admit their alien identity?" Sid kept at his logical approach. "As the intelligent master as you are, can't you see that there may be another possibility—that you have the wrong man, that I am *not* a Lizard People? If you kidnapped the wrong guy, what could I possibly say that would convince you otherwise?"

Tim jumped up and began pointing his finger in Sid's face. "See what I told you? Lizard People are smart and cunning, but I'm not going to fall for your trickery, so answer my question."

"I am not, nor have I ever been, a Lizard Person," Sid said.

"You lie. Where is your secret underground base? Who are your government contacts?"

A similar scenario played out each time Tim visited the locked basement. Eventually, Tim saw how futile the interrogations had become, so he came less and less often.

I don't have a cruel bone in my body, Tim thought. *Maybe the police will take that into account. I always left it food and water—at least enough for a human. I don't know how much food and water a Lizard People needs, but I took care of the creature.* Besides, Tim thought his plan would only take a few days—instead, it lasted months.

Tim said not a single word as dozens of angry customers formed behind his silent register. Tim's silence didn't mean his customers had nothing to say. He didn't even notice customers speaking right in front of his face. Tim's once lengthy line began breaking up. Some customers shifted into Torrey's line, while others left the store. Torrey could take it no longer—he sent Tim home to get some rest and not come back until he got his mind together. With everything inside in turmoil, Tim sped the entire way home.

Tim sorely wished he had thought things through better. Tim's initial plan only took twenty minutes to draw up. *If I had only asked Torrey for suggestions, it probably would've worked out much better. The reptilian resisted more than I ever imagined.*

Rarely idle during his whole ordeal, Sid fell into a normal routine to stave off boredom. Every morning he began his day by systematically rechecking weak spots and potential means of escape. Once Sid mentally checked off that futile task, he ate food the kidnapper left. His routine included multiple exercises to remain fit and strong. Exercising calmed Sid's mind. During his exercise routine, Sid went over each and every clue of his kidnappers' identities, and what he could do differently to convince them of his humanity.

Over time, Sid stopped denying the existence of Lizard People. It only made his kidnapper more suspicious. Instead, Sid probed his captor's mind. Sid learned his kidnapper built crystal devices. As time went on, neither of them learned anything new about each other. Sid lost all track of how long it had been. It had to have been over a month or two, he thought.

For Tim and his restless uncertainty, days turned to weeks and then into months. The reptilian gave no more useful information than it had the first day. Around this time, Tim began taking more time off from work and getting irritable around others—including Torrey. He stopped coming to the cabin every day because it would create too much suspicion. Instead, Tim left the creature enough food and water to last days at a time.

Tim desperately wanted Torrey's help and guidance, but to do so would have admitted his plan had failed. Instead, Tim asked Mark Levison for help. Mark, being another one of Torrey's young proteges, also wanted Torrey's acceptance. Mark gleefully accepted to help fight to free humanity and ingratiate himself to Torrey.

On a rotating schedule, Mark and Tim took turns dropping off food and water. Over time, they rarely bothered even asking Sid questions anymore. Besides, avoiding direct questions helped quell their growing dread. Tim just wanted the problem to go away. It finally did—the day Missy Flores happened upon the cabin's secret basement.

During Tim's flashbacks on his drive home, deputies from the San Bernardino sheriff's office burst into RadioShack looking for Tim.

"What do you want with Tim?" snarled Torrey. "He hasn't done anything."

Ignoring the question, a deputy repeated, "Where's Tim Nagat?"

"He's not here."

The deputies radioed dispatch to send a patrol car over to Torrey's workshop, in case Tim showed up. One deputy remained at RadioShack, while the other two went to Tim's home. Tim hadn't been home for thirty minutes before he saw the flashing blue strobe in front of his driveway. On foot, Tim ran for the road, but never left sight of his driveway before the deputies seized him and threw him to the ground. As they pried his arms into a position to get the handcuffs on his wrists, they ground Tim's face into Torrey's Ridgecrest xeriscape. Once he was handcuffed, the deputies hauled him to the patrol car and read him his rights. "Tim Nagat, you are being arrested for the murder of Billy Torgerson."

"What? I didn't murder Billy! I had nothing to do with Billy or any of the Torgersons. I'm innocent."

"Tell it to the jury."

Tim pleaded with the officers during the entire ride to the police station, "I had nothing to do with Billy's death—you got the wrong guy!" The deputies didn't listen. Tim wept during the remaining trip into the police station. As the deputies transferred him from the patrol car to the station, Tim shouted, "I need to speak with Torrey. Get Torrey for me!" The deputies remained silent as they escorted Tim Nagat to the holding pen.

The next day, other deputies transported Tim from San Bernardino County to John Smithers' jurisdiction. Later that same day, Sheriff John Smithers came to personally interrogate Tim. However, it didn't take long. During the interrogation, John asked typical questions: where Tim had been in the last few months, if he had any alibis, and why he'd killed Bill Torgerson. John's questions were merely a fishing expedition, trying to concoct a plausible motive. John knew for the charge to stick in a court of law, there had to be something more concrete than hearsay or the belief in alien Lizard People.

Suddenly, Tim had an epiphany—a point of clarity with less naivety. From that moment on, Tim saw John's questions as a trumped-up sham. Tim said as much to the sheriff. "You know I didn't do it. I am just a convenient scapegoat to you, aren't I? Regardless, I still want to talk to Torrey. Don't I get my one phone call? I want to call Torrey!"

The sheriff concluded the interrogation and shut off the recording. Moments before getting up to go, John leaned toward

Tim and whispered in his ear, "Even if you didn't do it, who will believe you? You've spent the last couple of years ranting about alien Lizard People and government conspiracies with the delusional belief that a few metal scraps held in a resin blob can disrupt the entire U.S. military's sophisticated communication system. *That*, compared with my testimony and the sobs of a grieving mother—who do you think a jury will believe?"

I am never getting out of this, Tim kept mumbling to himself throughout his entire walk back to his cell. As Sid used to say to him during his Lizard People questioning, *What evidence do I have that can prove my innocence? How can a person prove something to a person who holds deep convictions to the contrary?* His thoughts and worries reminded him of earlier conversations with Sid Emerson. *I didn't believe him either. The only difference is, I truly believed it, while the sheriff's only doing this out of convenience.* Tim's panic attack grew to a new level upon the metallic click of the cell door latching.

The next day, Torrey paid Tim a visit. The conversation started calm enough, but soon Tim broke down in tears as he cleared his guilty conscience. With deep pouring sobs, Tim admitted to his friend, his mentor, that he had kidnapped Sid Emerson. He admitted to all his failures and in involving Mark Levison. "I'm terribly sorry, Torrey. I've made a complete mess of things." After the next wave of sobs, "But I didn't kill Billy Torgerson. I've never even seen the guy—honest, Torrey. You've got to believe me."

As Torrey listened to Tim's outpouring, throbbing waves pounded in his head and horror, pity, and regret welled in his eyes upon the realization of being responsible for getting Tim into this mess. *Dammit, Tim, I made only a casual comment, months ago. I meant nothing by it*, Torrey confessed to himself as he sat watching his dear friend weep in the jail cell. *Poor, naïve Tim. I had no idea you would take it so literally. Now you are paying the price for my stupidity. Oh, God, what have I done?*

Despite Tim's *mea culpa* admission and Torrey's guilty inner-conscience, Torrey couldn't find the strength to come clean to Tim that deep down, he never honestly thought Sid Emerson was Lizard People—he had only spouted off. For the rest of Tim's outpouring, Torrey remained transfixed with the thought that his own words would likely bring down his young, impressionable friend.

After regaining composure and clearing his mind, Torrey spoke to his dear friend. "I know it looks bad, Tim. I'm not gonna fool you. Sorry I wasn't there when you needed me. I won't let you down again."

"No, Torrey. You've done nothing wrong. I'm at fault, not you."

"Don't worry, Tim. The sheriff has no evidence linking you with Billy Torgerson's murder. At least none that will stand up in court—even courts around here."

"Do you really think so?" Tim said with the last of his sobs.

"Yeah, I do, Tim. But I don't know how we can explain your innocence in the murder without increasing your risk in a kidnapping conviction."

"Well, Torrey, isn't murder a bigger deal than kidnapping? Isn't it, Torrey?" Tim asked with the naïve earnestness that almost brought Torrey to tears.

Once more, Torrey told Tim not to worry, keep calm, and most importantly of all, "Do *not* say anything—*nothing* at all. Got it, Tim—nothing!"

"Sure, Torrey. I'll do as you say. I'll tell them nothing."

Waves of panic coursed through Torrey's mind as he left the holding facility. *I just promised Tim not to worry, that I have everything under control, but what can I do to help? I know he didn't murder anyone, but in a court of law, this means squat,* Torrey contemplated as he walked back to his car. *I don't have any proof. What will I say, he's innocent because 'he's my friend and I believe him'?* Tim was in deep trouble and Torrey knew it. *Just like in any Las Vegas casino, where the house has the advantage, this is John Smithers' county. Here, the house advantage lies entirely with the sheriff—this is his house.* Torrey knew

John Smithers had both the resources and the unchecked power to throw any charge against the powerless, and Tim and Torrey could do nothing about it.

On the drive home, Torrey came upon a thought. *It would make more sense if John Smithers was a Lizard People. However, even if true, we can't use that defense in Tim's trial.* At the moment, Torrey saw no way out of Tim's mess. *Speaking of messes, whatever happened to Mark? I haven't seen him in days.*

After a couple of days pondering the matter, Torrey, with a stern look of conviction, burst into the sheriff's office demanding to see John Smithers. While still holding his morning cup of coffee, John strolled up to Torrey. "What's all the fuss? What can I do for you, Torrey?"

"Tim Nagat had nothing to do with Billy Torgerson's murder. This is nothing but a trumped-up charge—and you know it."

"I don't speak about ongoing investigations, but if you have any information on the case, come sit down and make a formal statement."

"You know he's innocent."

"I know nothing of the sort, and besides, what makes you think so?"

"I know because I killed Billy Torgerson. It was an accident. Tim had nothing to do with it. He wasn't even there. Arrest me and let Tim go." With that, both Tim and Torrey began sharing adjacent cells in the Independence jailhouse.

CHAPTER 38

Ron had been crawling for hours under sparse pinyon and juniper clumps throughout Hunter Mountain's northern slope. A heavy sigh drifted through the air as he found not ants, but only dust after dust. "This ain't good—not good at all," he said to any ant that may be within listening range. *It's been too hot and dry this year, hasn't it? Not good at all.* "Everything about the place is different now." *If it wasn't so dreary back in L.A., I would just head home*, he thought as he reflected upon the changes occurring on Hunter Mountain. *I don't know what I'm looking for anyhow, but whatever it is, I'm not finding it.*

While grubbing under the same dusty sky-patch, he heard a non-ant noise. Softly, so as not to scatter any wayward ant, he murmured, "It sounds like a car door—someone's at the cabin."

Normally he was uninterested in the comings and goings of people, especially when he was biologizing, but Ron's old bones and stiff muscles had been complaining about being in one spot for too long. He pulled himself upright to investigate. He didn't get far before hearing someone calling for him. "Doctor Ron Telling, this is Nick Rauchoulbe. I'm a friend of Paddy. I want to have a chat with you if you don't mind."

Ron caught up with Nick halfway between the cabin and Ron's antless pondering spot. "I'm Ron Telling. I've heard Paddy talk of you, but I don't think we ever met."

"No, we never met, but I've heard many stories."

"How did you know I was here?"

"Rocky told me. How he knew—I haven't a clue. He often knows what's going on around here, even before it happens. Normally, he keeps information to himself, but this time, he freely shared. He heard you pulled into Saline Valley yesterday heading for Hunter Mountain. I thought I would take a chance to find you near the cabin."

"What do you want?

"It's been some time since Paddy took off. I wanted to know if you've seen him or heard from him. Even Rocky doesn't know. Since you two were friends, I thought I would ask. I'm worried about him."

"If I had seen him, I don't suppose I would tell you…but, no—I've not seen him or heard a peep. My gut tells me I won't. Too many changes for him—and too soon. He needed time to process."

As Nick turned his gaze toward Death Valley, he muttered, more to himself than to Ron, "There's been a lot of changes here lately—everything is unraveling."

"Yeah, I heard the stories," Ron said. "I heard Lizard Len is running for an open spot on the county board of supervisors."

"That'll be something if he wins the election, Nick said. "If so, I would love to see the look on Sheriff John Smither's face. He may just quit if that happens."

"While we're talking, I heard a rumor that crazy Ned Sipe filed a notice to run for county sheriff? Ron asked. "Is that true?"

"Yeah, but the county rejected it because applicants are required by law to have a law enforcement background," Nick added. "Apparently, asking deputies to watch over him as he shows his ridiculous dead-body-detecting machine to the media doesn't count. So, he ups and files an application to be on the ballot in Nye County, Nevada instead."

"I hadn't heard that," Ron said with a grin. "Doesn't Nevada require their sheriffs to be in law enforcement?"

"Not to apply," Nick said, "but if elected, he has one year to get a certificate from the academy. From what I heard, he has no intention of getting certified or trained. He hopes that he and his machine will find more Manson victims, and that notoriety will be enough to let him remain as sheriff despite no experience or training."

"The guy's delusional," said Ron.

"Well, it is the Death Valley way."

"Is that what you call it?" asked Ron. It seems like a convenient way of dismissing all sorts of stuff, normal stuff—the Death Valley way."

"Don't I know it," Nick said while shaking his head. "Don't I know it."

"Regarding Paddy. Has he reached out to Katherine?"

"Katherine…Katherine… No, I don't think he has…," Nick said as he looked to the ground and kicked up a pile of dust. After a long pause, he looked toward Death Valley's lowlands. "No…none of us has… But now that I think about it, I think I'll swing by Shoshone and see if John's heard anything."

"I don't suppose I'll ever see Paddy again. I sure do miss him. The place is just not the same without him. Without interesting ants and without Paddy, there's no real reason for me to come around anymore. I don't know why I still do."

"As I said, It's the Death Valley way. It just pulls you in and never lets go."

"So I've heard—and seen." After another long pause, Ron raised his voice as he turned to Nick. "Well, I got a bit more searching for ants to do, and then it's back on the road to L.A. Good luck with your talk with the sheriff. If you hear anything about Paddy, let me know. In the meanwhile, I may see you around, here, there, or over yonder." With that, Ron headed back to his ants, while Nick led a billowing cloud that drifted toward Shoshone.

As Nick sped down the empty and lonely highway leading to Shoshone, his mind and thoughts were anything but empty or lonely. Thoughts of good times drifted into mind, as he fussed with the air conditioning. *Damn air conditioning always seems to go out just when you need it the most*, he cursed. That was the least of his worries, he figured. *Besides, it's probably only 117 degrees. That'll be my guess*, as his dust cloud faded into the Panamint horizon.

Further down the road, Nick's thoughts turned to Sheriff John Smithers. Nick had also known John for several years, but they were never close. Nick considered John to be a straight-up sheriff, *at least compared with the doozies we've had in the past. But, this time, there is something about how he's handling the crystal people's arrests and investigation. Something seems off,* Nick mused. *Even by Death Valley standards, the investigation is moving slowly, What's John up to, after all?*

Nick held out no hope that Sheriff Smithers knew of Paddy's whereabouts or would tell him even if he knew. *But it doesn't hurt asking,* Nick figured.

⁂

As Nick walked into the sheriff's office, he saw the sheriff pushing a teetering stack of papers aside and drawing in another from below his hunched shoulders and flittering eyes. Without looking up, John called out, "What brings you in, Nick? Is this about your vandalized bat gate? I don't have any information I haven't already told you."

"Naw. I'm not here for that, but thanks for the update. I came in asking about Paddy. Heard from him at all, or is anyone talking? Any rumors?"

"Say, Nick! Did you hear the Timbisha finally received their casino permit?" John asked, as if he hadn't heard Nick's question. "It looks as if your home turf will just get busier after all. I bet most of their customers will be all the crazies that have been roaming the Panamints with Torgerson fever. They'll probably blow their youth and their life savings in the casinos. I bet the income the Timbisha rake in will be the only treasure anyone around will ever see—at least that's my bet."

As John shuffled more reports, Nick replied, "Yes, yes, the Timbisha casino permit that'll drive the desperate and disadvantaged into deep poverty, but that is not what I asked about. You're either deflecting or hiding something. I asked about Paddy."

As Nick's endless talking faded into nothingness, the sweat on John's forehead began coalescing into little beads. *If I wipe it, it'll be even more noticeable,* stressed John. "No, I'm not hiding anything. With all I must do, do you think I have time to search for Paddy? Do you see all these reports on my desk?"

"I didn't say you were hiding anything—I asked why you avoided my question." As Nick stared at John, he saw minute rivulets forming weary paths across his sun-cracked and wrinkled forehead. *It's not that hot in here. My guess is John's in over his head, and he knows it. Come to think of it.* "So, if you've not heard from Paddy, how about Katherine? Hear from her?"

"No, it's been quite some time since I've heard from Katherine. Nice person that Katherine. Why? Nick, are you sweet on her? Is that why you're asking?"

Ignoring his leading question and deflection, Nick changed the topic. "So, Sheriff, how's Tim and Torrey's investigation going?"

"You know I can't talk about an open investigation. I will only say that it's a rock-solid case. I expect it'll wrap up sooner rather than later," John said as he straightened the same pile of papers that he already straightened—three times. *Damn it, Nick. Don't you think I know how long this is taking? It's killing me,* John thought as his leg began shaking. *I thought it would have been a slam-dunk, the "Death Valley way," but no, the public and media have latched onto this like no other.*

"Hello, Sheriff, are you okay? You look peaked. Should I call someone?"

The more time it's taking, the more the defense and the D.A. will find irregularities. This is really turning into a high-profile investigation, John privately admitted. *God, my goose is gonna be cooked…*

❦

Tim and Torrey are two messed up kids, Nick thought as he watched the rivulets on John's forehead flow with greater force, *but I don't see either one of them murdering Billy Torgerson. Of course, it didn't help when Tim and Torrey chose to represent themselves in the initial hearing. I think John just got caught off-guard, and now, everyone's in over their heads on this one.*

❦

This is not the Death Valley way, John cursed to himself. He had become increasingly agitated at the media attention the case had been receiving. *Investigations, even murder, do not get the type of outside scrutiny this one's getting. I want a vacation. I need a vacation.*

As Nick prepared to leave, John chimed in, "About Paddy, as I've said countless times, I didn't have time to search for Sid, but he eventually came back. I have even less time now to search for Paddy. He'll be fine. If he wants to come back, he will. If not, he won't. Anyway, it's not my concern. I suggest you just get back to your bats and let me handle my job. Good day!"

Just then, dispatch over the crackling radio broke whatever thought John had. Two reports came, back-to-back. Dispatched reported a downed plane in the Owlsheads. A witness said he saw three dead bodies and piles of cash blowing across the blanched playa. Dispatch also reported a fight had just erupted near Hunter Cabin. It began when members of two factions crossed paths. They each became suspicious of the other, and neither wanted to give up the cabin as a home base to search for secret mines. No one knows who lit the first match up at Hunter Cabin. Any of the remaining ants were likely scurrying for cover as the flames leaped into the pinyon-scented sky. As Sheriff John Smithers prepared to leave, he turned to Nick. "As you just heard, it looks as if it'll be another long day. I gotta go. Nick, please leave so I can lock up."

John sped off, leaving Nick alone on Shoshone's empty streets. Many conflicting thoughts ran through his head as he started his drive home. Everything had changed. Besides Paddy disappearing and John doing who knows what, everything else was different too. Nick stressed on these thoughts as he made another failed attempt at getting his air conditioning to work. "At least some things remain the same," he cursed at his sputtering A/C. *Since Torrey and Tim's arrests, Mark Levison looks like he took over the crystal making business. And if the rumors are true, he's making tons of profit selling nationally, and even a little internationally.* "Go figure," Nick cursed. *Torrey and Tim's trial will be quite the big deal. I don't usually go to such things, but on this one, I'll make an exception.* Nick grinned at the thought. *The trial may never bring justice, but, as everyone seems to concur, it'll surely bring loads of entertainment.*

CHAPTER 39

After Sid and Katherine were united, he didn't move back to her Boston home for another two months. In those anxious moments, they lived in Paddy's abandoned trailer. Sid wanted to leave right away. It was too hard to start a new life while still immersed in the same landscapes and among the same demons that haunted his past. The desiccating Barstow summer winds seemed to draw from his spirit more than mere fluids. He needed a change of scenery. Sid did not fully grasp the extent of Katherine's hesitation in moving. He shrugged such thoughts off because he figured there were many things he didn't know about his niece—she was no longer the little girl he once knew. *If she needs space and time, then space and time is what she'll get.*

Without warning, one day she announced to her uncle, "It's time. Let's move into my house in Boston. We leave tomorrow." This sudden, but welcomed news, came as a shock to Sid, since she hadn't spoken a word of it to him in quite some time. *Whatever demons that held her back must have resolved themselves,* Sid thought as he began packing his few remaining life-possessions.

Ever since Katherine moved to Boston, she wouldn't let Sid leave her sight. They spent most of their time together, reintroducing themselves and getting reacquainted. They talked excessively. Except for a few guarded topics, they talked about everything under the sun, moon, and stars. Since broad and cosmic bodies and forces were so much more vivid in the Panamint Range than in Boston's limp and pasty sky, Death Valley's indelible landscape often came up in conversations and deep discussions. For so long, Panamint people and places were the center of their existence, so now, even in Boston, they found it the mysterious center where all real things tend to converge and coalesce. Talking about the Panamints proved cathartic for Sid, but for Katherine, it further stirred still unquieted forces.

As for Sid and Katherine never leaving each other's sight, he figured it was his making up for lost time. He knew he could never get those lost years back, but he wanted to make the most of his remaining time—without backsliding. Katherine, too, treasured their time together, but she also used these busy moments as a distraction from unresolved longings. As such, she grew increasingly despondent with each passing night.

The whole Tim Nagat and Torrey Small affair weighed heavily on her mind, much more than Sid knew—or Katherine ever shared. She, like John, worried that the whole arrangement would someday unravel and drag her Sid back into the fray. She wanted him to have a normal life. Just recently, without Sid knowing, Katherine called Sheriff John Smithers. "Thank you for keeping quiet about the kidnapping," she gushed. "There's been no problems on your end? Is everything still as we agreed upon back in your Shoshone office?"

John got up to close his office door, before answering back, "The less we talk about this the better, but their trial hasn't happened yet—"

"Why? I thought you said this will blow over quickly and die out the 'Death Valley way'?"

"Yeah, yeah. Nothing is happening the way I expected—like they used to. It'll be best if we both just keep quiet about it and just get on like everything is normal. If not, it could all blow up in my face."

"What about for my Uncle Sid?!" Katherine snapped.

"Hey, get things straight—I have more skin in this than you or your uncle, but if I fall, you fall too. So, as I said, just calm down and shut up."

"Okay, but clarify, if you charge Tim with murder instead of kidnapping, wouldn't the kidnapping story come out during the investigation? The entire reason I agreed to this is was to ensure my uncle wouldn't be dragged through the media. He's in a fragile state right now—I won't have it. But I still don't see how this can be accomplished by charging Tim with murder. I don't think Tim murdered anyone, so why would he stay quiet on the kidnapping when it could exonerate him on the more serious murder charge?"

"I've explained it to you before, and you agreed to it—so just stick with the plan," John snapped. "Besides, the charge is manslaughter, not murder."

"The story is even in Boston's papers," Katherine anxiously added. "The article said, "As Billy Torgerson turned the corner at the mine portal, he came upon Tim Nagat as he was planting a Cloudbuster. Tim, thinking it was an alien Lizard People, lashed out at Billy and swung. The blow knocked Billy off balance and he fell into the nearby mine shaft."

"Yes, yes, I know the story. It is, after all, my investigation."

"You're not concerned if Tim talks?"

"No. Let him talk. The public and the jury will see his stories as the delusional rantings of a person that believes in a race of alien Lizard People conspiring with the U.S. government and an international consortium. No one will believe him. Sure, his story may hit the press and trend on social media for a couple of weeks, but soon there will be another sensational story to capture their attention, and Tim Nagat will disappear from the public's memories and interests faster than they did for George Shufelt."

"That's harsh."

"No, that's the Death Valley way...at least it used to be. Sid's kidnapper is held accountable for committing his crime, our county can rid itself of the crystal crazies, I get to put to rest this missing case file, and you get to keep Sid out of the circus."

"It's true I want to keep Uncle Sid out of the fray, but I still feel uncomfortable with this," Katherine fretted over the phone.

"Yes, your uncle stays out of the public's eye and the media circus," John said assuredly. "And the public and the media get their red meat. Do you think they would be satisfied with something as non-dramatic as the poor Torgerson kid just fell into a mine due to his own bungling? No, there's no nice bow in *that* story. Without someone to point their fingers to, people will turn on themselves, their neighbors, and create even greater fractures in my county. I'm giving them a clean and simple bow."

"You are the one that has always said you like a nice simple bow on things—"

"We all do," John interrupted. "Whenever a kid dies, a finger needs to point to someone or something! Otherwise, where's the justice and closure? You know that as an actuary better than perhaps most. Admit it, it's true. And, the best of all, this story doesn't perpetuate the lost Torgerson mine mystery. You know, this whole mess, everything that's been happening—all of it, began with Bud Torgerson and his rumored silver strike. This gold fever laid on top of the normal Panamint crazies and nut-jobs around here was a perfect storm for chaos. But our way, we can put some of these conspiracies to rest and let the rest, including your uncle, get back to normal. Isn't that worth it?"

Hearing John's rationalizations the second time was just as jarring as the first time, but deep down, Katherine understood there was some truth to what the sheriff said. "How about Paddy?" Katherine interjected. "Will Paddy's good name be preserved, and will he stay out of the press too? Because, as you know, Paddy had nothing to do with any of this. It was just you and me, and he had no knowledge of our Tim Nagat deal."

"Yes, yes. Paddy remains out of the story."

As Katherine and John talked, her mind wandered to Paddy and his whereabouts. She also wondered if he would approve of how they handled things. Upon further thought, she guessed he wouldn't approve at all.

"You're wondering what Paddy would think about our arrangement, aren't you?"

"I was…no. I was only—"

"Paddy would have understood the Death Valley way."

"I don't think you believe that sheriff, do you? You two used to be friends. I think you know that he would think it smells, with a deep ethical stain that'll never wash clean."

"Well, it is not up to Patrick Darwin, is it?" John said rather bluntly. "Besides, he's taken off, went off the grid. He's handling things his way and left us to handle things our way. So, for the moment, I can live with that—and sleep just fine."

"I guess so. I just want it behind us," Katherine lamented. "By the way, I meant to ask, how does Torrey play in this? Won't he collaborate Tim's story and drag my uncle into the fray, despite your efforts?"

"Haven't you heard?" John said. "Torrey's dead. After being released on bail, he somehow got mixed up with drug dealers. They found his body among plane wreckage in the Owlshead Mountains. It had all the classic signs of a drug trafficking accident. Also, since it happened across the line, in San Bernardino County, they and China Lake responded—I didn't have to be involved."

There are times, when alone and deep in thought, when Katherine would look into the night sky from her pavement-infused enclave as if searching for something. However, each time, instead of seeing a brilliant Death Valley Milky Way with all its vivid clarity, all she saw were the few smudgy points that barely penetrated Boston's waxy greyness.

She had not seen or heard from Paddy since the night before he found Sid Emerson in Trona. With a pensive smile, she reflected, *Paddy found Uncle Sid, exactly as he promised.* However, as time progressed, Katherine began to understand she wanted more out of her Panamint search—more than just finding her uncle. Her time spent in Death Valley rekindled and brought clarity to feelings that had eluded her in the past. *But now…I may never see him again.*

While she rescued one dear person, she hadn't fully appreciated the price for trading one lost soul for another. *Since I first met him, he had changed—so much*, she fondly remembered. *In the last few months, he has grown out of his shell—his isolation.* However, she also noticed that he had grown distant during their last two weeks together. She never fully understood his demons, but right when it looked like he had clawed his way back, he backslid. In the end, the demons won.

Every minute spent on helping Sid recover meant her distance from Paddy grew. *He had always been there for me when I needed him, so why can't I find the strength to be there for him now?* Katherine's questions to herself were rhetorical. Having resigned to her new reality, she left herself no means to move forward on all fronts, so she increasingly whiled away her time looking deep into the night sky.

As she stared into Boston's waxy grayness, she tried to make out the same stars and constellations that she'd vividly remembered from her Death Valley nights. When doing so, she imagined she and Paddy were looking at the same stars at that exact moment. However, while the constellations might have been the same, the stars' alignment was no longer in sync.

Whenever she felt the tug of Death Valley stars, each time she pulled back. *No, I can't. My uncle needs me*, she repeatedly told herself. *I can never again be so selfish. I can't be there for both. After all my uncle has been through, I can't abandon him.* With that, each night, she turned her back to the sky, walked inside, and shut the door.

CHAPTER 40

Blame it on the brisk wind and penetrating coldness. Perhaps the blame lies on being nearly ten thousand feet in elevation on Wyoming's Bighorn Mountain's alpine escarpment. Regardless, there were only a few dedicated souls performing ceremonies and paying respect to the Bighorn Medicine Wheel on this summer solstice.

Among those spreading tobacco and sage was the young Athapascan who had been there the previous year. It had been eleven months since he'd buried his beloved grandfather. The old man held his grandson's hand as he lost his grip on this world and began the long journey into the next. His grandfather's death had him thinking of culture, religion, spirituality, and historic traditions. The young Athapascan came to realize that keeping his grandfather's traditions alive would be the best way to pay his respect. This brought him to watching the sunrise from the cairns, ceremonial shrines, and the same five stone watchers that overlooked the holy site and its people.

This Athapascan's visit lay in stark contrast to the two White guys nearby, carrying electronic meters as they systematically narrowed in upon a small cave opening. Unbeknownst to anyone else on Medicine Mountain, these two men worked at Fort Irwin's Deep Space Communications Complex. What these two Fort Irwin military officials were doing on this alpine escarpment on this solstice pre-dawn would be anyone's guess and speculation. It would also be anyone's guess and speculation as to why they triangulated the medicine wheel and the cave portal with both Polaris and Thuban—both stars shining with a special luminance that stood out despite the brilliance of the Bighorn's celestial void.

Each star aligned just right with one of the twenty-eight spokes on the adjacent medicine wheel.

Also unbeknownst to the few conducting spiritual ceremonies, these same two Fort Irwin officials had been to this spot before. By cover of darkness, without the aid of guiding stars, they drove their deep blue Ford Expedition to the wheel's parking lot to retrieve the body of a late-middle-aged man wearing a worn orange sweatshirt with a faded Nike emblem emblazoned across the chest. These two undercover military officers took the body back to Fort Irwin.

The young Athapascan slowly circled the medicine wheel and presented tobacco and sage offerings. He noticed the two out-of-place officials leave, but gave it little thought, to better concentrate on performing his ceremony properly—and with the precision that would make his grandfather proud. After the elder performed his chant, he looked up into the warm and clear solstice night and saw Thuban shining especially bright. Otherwise, the scene was as it had been for over five thousand years.

On the following morning, when the sun rose high in the sky, its radiant light shined on migrating painted lady butterflies flying high into the thin air. Below, on the edge of the escarpment, iridescent Melissa blues and black and orange flag-like Milbert's tortoiseshells lapped flowing nectar from the nearby lupines, phlox, columbine, and stonecrop.

This enchanted scene played out for the remainder of the afternoon. As the shadows grew below the five stone watchers, it came to touch the nearby cave entrance. Upon the precise moment of touching, with the careful precision borne of experience and practice, an elderly Apsáalooke man emerged from the small and darkened hole. He removed a pouch tied to his waistband and spread its contents back into the cave. Afterward, he erected a small ceremonial cairn, and then silently disappeared down a faint trail leading to faraway places. As starlight replaced the twilight's grayness, the only sign of his passing was the faint smell of tobacco, sage, sweetgrass, and juniper lingering in the air—as it had been for thousands of years. If the young Athapascan's grandfather was there to teach him ancient customs, he may likely have said, "Your mind needs to be kept open, since there's more to the world, and this wheel, than what our limited minds and experiences can know or explain."

Back in the main office in Langley, the CIA closed and sealed *Operation Panamint*'s case file. They stored the file next to a heavily scraped and gouged cedar chest marked faintly with the letters "B.T." Over the international wire exchange, a large sum of money was transferred to multiple accounts, including Langley, Zürich, Beijing, and the Cayman Islands. All accounts were only indirectly tied to a temporary bank account registered to a casino on the outskirts of Death Valley, California.

Nature loves balance. Symmetry. Ultimately, the universal scorecard remains constant, the trading of one lost soul for another. While symmetry may reset nature and the universe, that doesn't mean it balances everyone. High in the sky, the crescent moon's soft light cast a lonely glow across the Panamints' wide, pavement-free horizon. The recent rain filled the air with pleasant juniper smells—with just a touch of creosote bush from down-valley. It also brought back deeply buried memories—both distant and recent. In this land of contrast, this stood out in bold detail. A kindred spirit's eyes cast his gaze upon the sublime Warm Spring Canyon far below with the thought, hope, and faith that he would feel contentment, but it was not so. Not at all at peace, but at least—he had returned home.

CHAPTER 41

In wilderness, one is never truly alone. Sometimes even trite and abused platitudes have merit. No one fully understands the forces that compel people toward emptiness; perhaps it is physical, a calling from above, or something deeply spiritual. In wilderness, people often seek the meaning and purpose of life, as if wild places, by their mere presence, can unlock the secrets of hidden truths. If so, the secrets must be deep within open spaces—simply being unoccupied will not do.

There is an inherent difference between open spaces in the East and the empty wilds of Death Valley. The difference is one of the gentle assurances of the old versus the vigor and energy of youth, or the friendly warmth of enduring relationships versus the passionate mysteries of new love. Forces are in action in the Death Valley wilderness. Our ancestors tamed the East, whereas the wildness of Death Valley's underbelly is beyond contention. In these wild lands, an indifferent nature is in charge; human whines are inaudible above the roar of inner turmoil and the purging of lost souls.

Abhorring a vacuum, nature fills empty spaces with storms, mysteries, darkness, suspicion, the past and present, the borderless space between life and death, Earth and sky, spirituality, and the frailty of body and the continuum of existence. For some, this may still not be enough to shield from the emptiness. The feverous pursuit of walls, money, careers, drinks, destructive relationships, and exuberances are never quite enough to numb or stem the cold. Therefore, our minds fill empty landscapes with unseen forces ranging from the sublime to the absurd.

Death Valley's rugged isolation attracts people looking for their own vision, or version, of nature's truth. This may include scientists, pseudo-scientists, philosophers, the athletic looking to test their mettle, conspiracy believers, religious deity seekers, atheists, the deeply spiritual, crackpots, social misfits, extremist groups, fringe elements, lost souls, or simply the weary that just want to be left alone. Consequently, our society has interwoven these fringe elements into the fabric of the modern Death Valley mystique.

Sometimes, the things we fill empty spaces with enrich our lives or contribute to a sense of place, while sometimes they're destructive with a want of value or substance. Perhaps this is the dark side of the force—the suspicious and destructive elements that turn us on others or conjure the frightened child's imagination that there really is a monster hiding under the bed. There is something about Death Valley that taps into, foments, and enables the dark force that dwells in all of us. There are still mysterious vortexes out there that act as black holes—places where light, energy, and matter may enter, but like the many lost souls of the Panamints, they may never again see the light of day.

ABOUT THE AUTHOR

DAVID EK held a successful and award-winning career with the National Park Service, where he led science and natural resources teams throughout the country—including Death Valley National Park (the setting for much of *Lizard People: Death Valley Underground*). His resource management work often tackled complex issues of regional and national scope. David's extensive natural resource-related writings have appeared in dozens of science and management publications—and in countless forms intended for general audiences of all ages.

On the literary side, David writes both fiction and nonfiction. Editors for literary journals have found his writing "strong" with "much to admire." His short stories and essays have appeared in *Canary, Weber: The Contemporary West*, and elsewhere. *Pedro's Pickles and the American Dream* was his debut novel. He is a member of the Virginia Writers Club and the Pacific Northwest Writers Association.

When not sciencing or writing, David has been an active rock and mountain climber, caver, and explorer of the American wilds. A native of Seattle, Washington, he currently lives with his wife, children, cat, and dogs in rural northern Virginia. To learn more about David's writings, please visit him online at https://EkDavidAuthor.com.

www.ingramcontent.com/pod-product-compliance
Lightning Source LLC
Chambersburg PA
CBHW021135310726
48971CB00002B/336